Romance lovers are falling for the Sons of Destiny

"Enchantments, amusement, eight hunks, and one bewitching woman make for a fun romantic fantasy . . . humorous and magical. A delightful charmer." —*Midwest Book Review*

"A must-read for those who enjoy fantasy and romance. I so thoroughly enjoyed this wonderful . . . novel and eagerly look forward to each of the other brothers' stories. Jean Johnson can't write them fast enough for me!"
—*The Best Reviews*

"I love this world and the heroes and heroines who reside there . . . a lively, wonderful, and oh-so-satisfying book. It is long, beautifully written, and entertaining. Light and dark magic are everywhere . . . fantasy romance at its best."
—*Romance Reviews Today*

"A complex fantasy-romance series." —*Booklist*

"A fun story. I look forward to seeing how these alpha males find their soul mates in the remaining books."
—*The Eternal Night*

"An intriguing world . . . an enjoyable hero . . . an enjoyable showcase for an inventive new author. Jean Johnson brings a welcome voice to the romance genre, and she's assured of a warm welcome." —*The Romance Reader*

"An intriguing and entertaining tale of another dimension . . . quite entertaining. It will be fun to see how the prophecy turns out for the rest of the brothers."—*Fresh Fiction*

Sons of Destiny novels by Jean Johnson

THE SWORD
THE WOLF
THE MASTER
THE SONG

The MASTER

JEAN JOHNSON

BERKLEY SENSATION, NEW YORK

THE BERKLEY PUBLISHING GROUP
Published by the Penguin Group
Penguin Group (USA) Inc.
375 Hudson Street, New York, New York 10014, USA
Penguin Group (Canada), 90 Eglinton Avenue East, Suite 700, Toronto, Ontario M4P 2Y3, Canada
(a division of Pearson Penguin Canada Inc.)
Penguin Books Ltd., 80 Strand, London WC2R 0RL, England
Penguin Group Ireland, 25 St. Stephen's Green, Dublin 2, Ireland (a division of Penguin Books Ltd.)
Penguin Group (Australia), 250 Camberwell Road, Camberwell, Victoria 3124, Australia
(a division of Pearson Australia Group Pty. Ltd.)
Penguin Books India Pvt. Ltd., 11 Community Centre, Panchsheel Park, New Delhi—110 017, India
Penguin Group (NZ), 67 Apollo Drive, Rosedale, North Shore 0632, New Zealand
(a division of Pearson New Zealand Ltd.)
Penguin Books (South Africa) (Pty.) Ltd., 24 Sturdee Avenue, Rosebank, Johannesburg 2196,
South Africa

Penguin Books Ltd., Registered Offices: 80 Strand, London WC2R 0RL, England

This is a work of fiction. Names, characters, places, and incidents either are the product of the author's imagination or are used fictitiously, and any resemblance to actual persons, living or dead, business establishments, events, or locales is entirely coincidental. The publisher does not have any control over and does not assume any responsibility for author or third-party websites or their content.

THE MASTER

A Berkley Sensation Book / published by arrangement with the author

PRINTING HISTORY
Berkley Sensation trade edition / September 2007
Berkley Sensation mass-market edition / May 2008

Copyright © 2007 by G. Jean Johnson.
Excerpt from *The Cat* by Jean Johnson copyright © 2008 by G. Jean Johnson.
Cover art by Franco Accornero.
Cover design by Annette Fiore.
Interior text design by Kristin del Rosario.

All rights reserved.
No part of this book may be reproduced, scanned, or distributed in any printed or electronic form without permission. Please do not participate in or encourage piracy of copyrighted materials in violation of the author's rights. Purchase only authorized editions.
For information, address: The Berkley Publishing Group,
a division of Penguin Group (USA) Inc.,
375 Hudson Street, New York, New York 10014.

ISBN: 978-0-425-22120-4

BERKLEY® SENSATION
Berkley Sensation Books are published by The Berkley Publishing Group,
a division of Penguin Group (USA) Inc.,
375 Hudson Street, New York, New York 10014.
BERKLEY SENSATION and the "B" design are trademarks of Penguin Group (USA) Inc.

PRINTED IN THE UNITED STATES OF AMERICA

10 9 8 7 6 5 4 3 2 1

If you purchased this book without a cover, you should be aware that this book is stolen property. It was reported as "unsold and destroyed" to the publisher, and neither the author nor the publisher has received any payment for this "stripped book."

ACKNOWLEDGMENTS

I would like to thank NotSoSaintly, Alexandra, and Stormi for their invaluable assistance in continuing to help me edit my writing; Alienor for allowing me to bounce ideas off her forehead like crumpled little wads of paper that my muse can then chase after like a cat; PiperKirby for being my cold-reader for this novel and waiting so patiently to actually get to read it; and of course the Mob of Irate Torch-Wielding Fans (this time around, it's for putting up with my insistence that fruitcake not be used as any sort of a weapon, though stale baguettes are still fair game).

A special mention also goes to: Dale, Janet, Betty, Ann, Adelaida, and Dr. Tuan, for allowing me to take over their break room at the dentist's office on a quarterly basis; Yvonne at the Infusion Center, for letting me have a chair and something to prop my laptop on so that I may continue to write during each four-hour session; my father, for putting up with my lugging around said laptop to so many of his various appointments; and my mother, for taking him to some of his appointments, too, so I don't have to deal with rush-hour traffic. Bleahhh.

If anyone is interested in joining the Mob of Irate Torch-Wielding Fans (and is eighteen years or older; sorry, but you have to be an adult to join), you can visit us at http://groups.yahoo .com/group/MoITWF. Or you can come visit my website at www .jeanjohnson.net, where all are welcome!

Hugs,

~JEAN

P.S. The teaser at the end is imperfect. Apologies!

ONE

·❧·

The Third of Sons shall meet his match:
Strong of will and strong of mind
You seek she who is your kind
Set your trap and be your fate
When Lady is the Master's mate

Time passed strangely for Dominor of Nightfall. It came and went in muzzy bursts. He had vague, fleeting recollections of the things happening around him: wooden walls that creaked, the tang of the sea ever in his nostrils, voices muttering around him, hands forcing him to get up and walk around when he was too dizzy. He recalled how the floor was too uncertain underfoot for him to readily stand when he was made to do so, and of being fed minty-flavored food and drink that instinct said he shouldn't eat, yet his captors forced upon him while he was too muddled to resist. And he had memories of eating that herbed food until the world swirled away once more.

He remembered a familiar voice, its source strangely distant yet right there in his ear, desperate to reach him. The voice comforted him with its familiarity, though he couldn't have said who even he himself was most of the time, let alone the name or the face that went with that voice. He was aware of the omnipresent chafe of chains at ankles, wrists, and throat, of a faint memory that he had once worn fine, tailored clothes, not the rough fabric rubbing against his flesh. He hadn't always smelled of sweat and worse things, of unclean things, but that was due to the fact that he wasn't allowed to bathe, nor allowed enough clarity in his wits to tend to himself.

And then it happened. They didn't come with the bitter-minty flavored food. The world rocked even more dizzily underneath Dom as he lay chained to his bed; his surroundings swayed and creaked dismally, slanting first this way, then that way at unnerving angles, while his mind slowly woke. The cloud obscuring his senses eased enough that he could hear the shouts and the snapping riggings, smell the rain and the sea, and the captive mage knew he was on board a ship on the ocean.

Dominor remembered the Mandarites and their *falomel*-laced food. He remembered the oddly dressed, arrogantly opinioned Lord and his two duplicitous sons. And he remembered that he was captive on a ship that, from the sound and feel and smell of it, was caught in a bad summer storm, one that seemed to go on and on. Long enough that the last of the mage-confusing drug wore off. As the minutes turned into hours, Dominor became increasingly, uncomfortably aware of how filthy he was, how hungry and thirsty, and most of all how *angry* he was. When Dominor realized that, when his head was clear enough to think, he tested the chains keeping him bound more or less in place on his thin-palleted bunk while the ship surged with each hill-like wave.

The chains were padlocked to thick iron staples set too firmly in the bulkhead walls for him to dislodge physically in his drug-weakened state. He tried a simple unlocking spell next, but the energy just glowed briefly for a moment, then sank into the manacles clamped at neck, hands, and feet. He tried a more complex spell, one that lit up the small cabin he was in, showing the walls, sea-damp from water seeping through the decks because of the storm. Symbols on the stout, silvered metal simply absorbed it. As they did so, the metal clamped around his wrists, ankles, and throat warmed briefly. Warningly.

He didn't know those symbols—magical languages were among the very few things that just didn't translate well without intense study, not even with the aid of the Ultra Tongue spell— but he recognized their effect. They were absorbing his energies.

If he threw all of his power at them, they might overload and break . . . and most probably burn off the flesh attached to them. Or, if they were forged with the right sort of enchantments, they could latch onto his powers and drain him to a lifeless husk.

An unpleasant thought.

Then again, so was the possibility of starving to death. Or rather, dying of thirst. That would happen first. His mouth felt like it had been scrubbed with sand, then powdered with dust. The heaving of the ship around him didn't help; it reminded him of the liquid that lay beyond the hull. It was too salty to drink, of course, but it was a form of water, and he wanted water. Preferably without any mind-and-power stealing *falomel* in it.

Odds are, they'll try to keep me drugged until we reach landfall . . . unless I can talk them out of it, Dominor offered to himself. It was a slim hope, but not an impossible one. *They're so full of themselves and their males-are-superior attitude that if I pretended to listen and pretended to convert to their ways, they'd probably decide to trust me.*

Not too quickly, of course, he reminded himself. His mind was finally clear enough to have the room for cunning, for plotting and laying out his strategies. *They'd not believe a sudden conversion. Not when they've kept me chained like an animal. They'll expect some initial rage—and I have plenty of that! But if I ask the right questions, I can steer the conversation toward the idea of converting-the-prisoner. Like the question of what could they possibly offer me as an enticement to stay, when I'm Her Majesty's Lord Chancellor.*

His mouth twisted wryly. Kelly of Doyle, the woman his eldest brother had married, had made that outrageous claim. The red-headed outworlder had proclaimed herself Queen of Nightfall, the island where he and his seven brothers had lived for three years after being exiled from their homeland, Katan. Her arrival and subsequent romance with his eldest brother, Saber, had fulfilled a prophecy spoken in verse by a woman born a thousand years before. The Seer Draganna had predicted the birth of four sets of twins, all of them mages, all of them with unique Destinies. One of those Prophetic Destinies had been the warning that some unspecified disaster would occur if the eldest ever bedded a virgin.

The Council of Mages of Katan, in their so-called wisdom, had exiled Dom and his brothers to Nightfall to prevent them from meeting any women; if they were the Sons of Destiny, then all of them had to be removed, supposedly "for the greater good of Katan."

The Council hadn't accounted for the meddling of the youngest of them, Morganen, whose predicted Destiny was to matchmake all of his siblings. He had hauled in a woman from another universe entirely to argue with, be courted by, and eventually marry the eldest of them. Even if it meant summoning the Disaster foreseen for them so very long ago.

And the Prophesied Disaster turns out to be the very same misogynistic idiots who have managed to capture me. At least, I hope my presence on this ship was the only Disaster that befell us when Saber married Kelly . . . It was an ignoble way to fulfill a prophecy, being captured and chained. Still, it only affected himself and his siblings. It wasn't a Disaster that affected all of Katan.

Dominor was glad no one could see him like this. They had taken away his finespun clothes and given him rough homespun that stunk of sweat and sea and the desperate need for a bath. His chains had enough give in them to allow him to check under the pants. No under-trousers. They'd even taken away his shoes and his socks. They had clothed him in ugly, stained, beige leggings and a matching, long-sleeved shirt. At least, he thought it was beige; the storm gray light coming through the one porthole in the room didn't really lend itself toward discerning colors.

A tentative exploration of his hair, once silky-clean, proved it was now rather greasy and tangled, especially at the back. From the growth of hair on his jaw, he judged he'd been drugged for at least a week and a half, if not longer. Dominor grimaced in distaste as he fingered his mustache and beard. He hated facial hair. The mustache, if allowed to grow long, tickled his nostrils and interfered with his food, and the beard just plain itched. Not to mention the males in his family line had never been all that hirsute, which meant that his beard would look scraggly and scrawny even when fully grown. If a man couldn't grow a decent beard, he didn't look respectable, in Dominor's opinion.

Maybe I can jump-start the "conversion" process by demanding some civilized amenities, like a shave. I could imply to them that I'd be a lot more willing to listen if they were a lot more willing to treat me well . . .

The door to his cabin opened, startling him. It banged shut

again as the ship pitched the wrong way, making someone yelp, then curse and wrestle it open again. The younger of the count's sons fell inside as the ship shifted and tilted the other way, barely hanging on to the oil lamp now lighting the chamber. A waterskin dangled off his elbow, adding to his burdens. Dominor recalled the names of his captors.

Lord Kemblin Aragol, Count . . . no, Earl of the Western Marches, that was it; representative of King Gustavo the Third. His elder son is named Kennal, and this one is called Eduor. The one who tricked me into drinking that drug-laced alcohol. He still doesn't look old enough to shave.

"Oh! You're awake."

Yes, state the obvious, you little whelp. Dominor leveled him with a firm look and spoke with the lilt of the Mandarite accent, which was how the Ultra Tongue potion he had drunk translated their language. "Yes. And I am not happy with my accommodations. Is *this* how you convince male mages from other kingdoms to work for you?"

A deliberate shift of his wrists made his chains rattle. Eduor flushed. He blinked a few times, cleared his throat, and braced himself as the ship rocked again. Looking around, he hung the oil lantern on a hook next to the door, then faced Dominor again, clutching his waterskin. "Er, well . . . here, you must be thirsty!"

"If it has *falomel* in it, I will shove that bag through your digestive system. In reverse," Dominor added not-quite-blandly, shifting to sit up on the bed. He couldn't go much farther than that, maybe enough to use the chamber pot . . . if there was one in the small cabin. He hadn't seen one, yet. But it was enough slack to lend weight to his threat.

Eduor stared at him, eyes wide. His fingers tapped on the bag clutched to his chest. "Right. I'll, ah, be back shortly!"

The door banged shut behind him. At least the idiot had left the lantern. Not that the yellowish glow of the flame lent much to the dismal décor, but it did shed enough light for him to focus on the planks lining his cramped, closet-sized prison. Unfortunately, counting knotholes was only marginally more entertaining than drifting through a minty, mindless haze.

The heaving swells tossing the ship had eased to an exaggerated rocking motion by the time he was visited again. At least he'd found a lidded chamber pot wedged under his bunk in a small cupboard. Dominor disliked traveling by ship; the facilities were primitive, the opportunity for hygiene less than adequate, and in his case, the accommodations literally stank. Disgruntled, he fixed the man who entered with a hard, unhappy glare and struck first.

"Lord Aragol, I am *deeply* displeased with the way you have treated me. Not one iota of this situation is disposing me to look *favorably* upon helping you. When we spoke at the palace, you suggested there were enticements for a mage of my abilities. Wealth. Status. Power. Prestige. Where in *any* of that does it include chaining me like a common thief, drugging me senseless, and giving me clothes only the poorest of commoners would be delighted to wear?"

Kemblin Aragol lifted his goatee-covered chin slightly. He had dispensed with the hat and the waist-length jacket, but still wore the rest of his finery, including that ridiculous codpiece-thing at his crotch. "In order to get you far enough away from your homeland that you would be forced to stay long enough to listen to us, it was necessary to keep you drugged and thus cooperative and unable to harm yourself. It really isn't our intent to let harm come to you. But with the drug we use to subdue mages, it tends to relax everything in the body, including . . . digestive muscles," Lord Aragol finished delicately. "Thus it was necessary to remove your clothing and give you something that would not matter if it were . . . stained. Though we have done our best to keep you reasonably clean.

"But, now that you are awake and aware again, we can start treating you like the honored guest you will be, once we reach the shores of our homeland."

Dominor folded his arms across his chest. "Prove it, and I'll believe it. But you have a long way to go to regain my trust," he added in warning. "Starting with *undrugged* food and drink. I am thirsty and hungry . . . and if I detect *falomel* or any other drug in any of it, you will not find my response *civilized*."

The earl unhooked a flask from his belt and tossed it at Dominor. "Water, nothing more. I'm afraid the sea is still too rough for a proper, cooked meal, but I can have some bread and cheese brought to you, and some fruit."

"That would be civilized."

Nodding, Lord Aragol stepped into the corridor, giving a command to someone beyond the door.

Taking his time, Dominor sniffed at the contents of the flask. He shook it a little, sniffed again, then ventured a small sip. Nothing more than water. Despite the pressure of his thirst, Dominor continued to take only small sips. If the water was drugged, he was not going to let it completely shut down his reactions.

The earl's eldest son, Sir Kennal, entered the cabin. In his hands was a basket with a linen bundle. His father followed him. At a nod from the elder male, the younger one stepped forward and offered the basket to Dominor. "Our apologies, Lord Mage, for any inconvenience caused by the assertive manner we used in our insistence that you visit Mandare. We wish very strongly for you to see the wonders and advantages of our land that await a powerfully gifted male mage like yourself."

"Assertive manner"? Is that the polite Mandarite version for "kidnapping"? Dominor asked silently. One of his dark brown eyebrows rose in un-quelled skepticism, but he accepted the basket without a word. It had slightly overripe grapes, a quarter-loaf of somewhat fresh bread, and a wedge of soft cheese inside the linen napkin. He wasted a small portion of the water in the flask to dampen his hands, scrubbing his fingers on the linen to clean them, since he couldn't use any spells and there wasn't a washbasin in his cabin. Breaking off a small piece of the bread, he sniffed it carefully, then took a cautious taste.

"It isn't drugged, anymore," Kennal offered with earnest sobriety. "The storm has driven us far to the south and east; we need merely turn north and we shall soon reach the shores of Mandare. Once we have sighted land and discerned our location, we will be able to put to shore long enough to take on fresh provisions.

"If we have not been driven too far east, then we should be very close to the Port of Mandellia, which is but a day's journey from our estates," he continued with rising enthusiasm, as Dominor tested one of the grapes next. "Once we have arrived there, we have a full dozen of the most beautiful slave girls who will bathe you and shave you and please you in any way you desire."

Kemblin touched his son's shoulder, taking over. "In fact, as our most honored guest, you will be pleasured as soon as you cross the threshold of our entry hall. Our slaves are well trained; they will be delighted to kneel before you and give you a most fitting welcome."

Unsure what they were talking about, Dominor eyed them warily. "What exactly is this 'most fitting welcome'?"

"Their mouths," Kennal told him and gestured at the exaggerated lump of fabric centered over his groin. "They are trained to kiss and suckle your masculinity."

For a moment, Dominor felt his groin tighten at the thought of a woman pleasuring him in that way. It had been far too long since his last encounter with a willing female . . . and that was where the heat in his loins chilled. *These men are chauvinists of the highest order. They turn their women into slaves, with no choice and no free will. Even a working wench has more dignity and decision in her chosen career than a slave "trained" to please a man.*

He carefully hid his distaste from the other two, adopting a thoughtful look. "Trained, you say? I could take any pleasure of them I'd like? And they would not say no?"

"Their purpose is to please a man in *any* way he desires," Kemblin Aragol reassured him, smiling through his goatee. "My slaves are well behaved, you have my word. None of that tedious courting is necessary, nor will any of them say 'no' when a man is in the mood for his rightful pleasure."

"And do they wear contraceptive amulets?" Dominor asked him sardonically. He couldn't allow the illusion of caving in too quickly, or they would not believe him. So he added dryly, "Or do you think to have them plowed with my seed, to hopefully reap the harvest of my magical abilities behind my back? No doubt you would have me plow a female mage, to strengthen the possible outcome."

"I will not deny that it would be a good idea for you to spread that seed as far and wide as possible," the earl admitted with a shrug. "Any Mage Lord may sow his seed upon any slave girl of a ripe enough age, whether or not he owns her. It is preferred, however, to have a male mage cast his seed into the womb of a woman without magic; otherwise, that only seems to strengthen *their* lineage, not ours. Mage-bitches wear amulets against bearing fruit for that reason, as well as enchantments and chains to bind their powers. You may rut with any woman at my estate and need not worry; only those who are worthy can be successfully bred."

"I am not inclined to beget bastards," Dominor denied instinctively. Inwardly, he winced; his vehemence against rampant procreation didn't exactly fit in with the Mandarite culture. But Lord Aragol merely nodded in reassurance.

"I can understand why, milord! No doubt you would want to have a hand in the training of any mage-born son you seeded. It is more likely for outlanders to be successful in such endeavors, which is why we seek their numbers so insistently."

"And yet we compensate them most handsomely for moving away from their former lives to live among us," Kennal added quickly. "Your rank would be at least equal to my father's, and you would have the ear of our King, as a Mage Lord!"

"You would not be missing the status you had as Lord Chancellor of Nightfall, I assure you," Kemblin told Dominor, neatening his moustache with the edge of his finger. "Indeed, your status might even be higher, depending on the strength of your magics. You yourself admitted Nightfall is but an island; Mandare spans nearly the whole western edge of a continent. You could be deeded a stretch of land larger than your former isle, with farms and craft shops, villages and villeins working to ensure your prosperity."

"And all the women you could want," Kennal stated, grinning with the enthusiasm of a young man who knew he wasn't going to be turned down. A thought which disgusted Dominor; the youth was good looking enough that he shouldn't have to coax a woman under normal circumstances, yet here he was, gloating that he didn't have to coax at all—to Dom, the prize wasn't worth it, if there wasn't any effort involved. Kennal continued, his hazel eyes bright, "You'll find a lot of your fellow noblemen will want to offer you nubile, luscious slave girls, in the hopes of currying favor with you, slaves trained in a hundred exotic arts, all of them humbled and subservient. You'll be showered with gifts of all kinds, even for the smallest of your spells."

"Or, if you like a bit of spice in your pleasures, you can visit the slave markets, buy an untamed woman and teach her where her place lies," his father finished, his hazel eyes darkening with a hint of cruelty intertwined with his sexuality. "Kneeling at your feet, worshipping you for your Gods-made superiority."

Holding his tongue, Dominor carefully did not point out that, if only the women were being born with magical powers, the Gods of both Mandare and its enemy, Natallia, clearly wanted the women to be considered superior. Of course, he knew that his attitude about magic making one superior came from having been raised in a magocracy, where the most powerful mage was made the King or Queen at each five-year turning of the throne's succession. He also knew that other lands ruled themselves in different ways. True, Aiar-that-was, to the far north, had once been a magocracy much like Katan before its sundering. But the land of the distant Threefold God of Fate was rumored to be a hereditary monarchy.

A knock on the door came as a welcome relief from the awkwardness of the conversation. Kemblin stepped outside. After a moment, his son Kennal followed, leaving Dominor alone in the cabin. With the door shut between them, the chained mage was free to relax his wary vigilance just a little.

Dominor was arrogantly proud of his powers and skills, his civility and his superiority, but he was proud of them because they were facts, not because they were opinions. There were women mages on the Council of Katan who were roughly his equal in skill and knowledge; there were noble-born sons and daughters who were of his family's rank or higher. Those few who were more powerful than him, he acknowledged their superiority and sought to better himself in strength and stamina for comparison. Those with greater knowledge, he sought to study and learn from them. Those with greater rank and civility, he bowed to when necessary.

It was just that, living on an island with only his brothers for companions and the occasional trading vessel for contact with the rest of the world, he was used to not having his superiority challenged. Morganen was more powerful than all of his older brothers, true, but Morg didn't want to lead anyone. Rydan was more powerful than Dominor, but the sixthborn of the eight of them was strange, reclusive, and disinclined to compete against his siblings. Saber was lesser-powered when it came to magic, and acknowledged that to Dominor, but he had been trained to be the next Count of Corvis before their exile; he was also the eldest and took it upon himself to keep his siblings in line as the head of their exiled family.

The rest of the brothers, Wolfer, Trevan, Koranen, and even Dominor's own twin, Evanor, didn't bother much with ranking themselves against one another. Dominor needed to compete; he was thirdborn and third-powered, and it rankled at times. It was a little irksome that Wolfer, secondborn, hadn't a very strong competitive spirit within him. For the elder male, hunting was its own purpose, not about seeing who brought back the tastier game. And while the shapechanger would still compete for sport with his next-youngest sibling, once he had learned to curb his temper and not grow angry at Dominor's taunting whenever he won a footrace or a knife-toss, Wolfer had treated Dominor with a sort of indulgent good humor that was irritating.

Not to mention Wolfer's magic was average in strength at best.

Trevan's idea of sport and contest lay in pleasuring women; Dominor had competed with the fifthborn brother to see who could better seduce a certain village girl in their past, but the red-head hadn't cared if a woman was also the prettiest in the village. Dominor liked to surround himself with luxuries, with beautiful things. He added ornamentation to the artifacts he created for the traders. Trevan did make nice things and had a knack for spell-carving wood, but he didn't go out of his way to seek recognition for his talents. The thirdborn of them craved that sort of recognition.

Koranen and his twin, Morganen, had only been twenty when they had left the mainland; moving to the Isle had been more of an adventure for the second-youngest brother than an exile. Kor's affinity with fire meant that it was dangerous for him to indulge in his passions with a woman, too, so they could not compete on that score. As the seventhborn of the four sets of twins, he wasn't even remotely interested in trying to outrank himself socially, since there were six elder brothers in the way, and his powers were indeed attuned more specifically to the element of Fire than the general usefulness of Dominor's own broader-based magic. No competition, there.

As for Dominor's own twin . . . Evanor just didn't bother to compete with his older brother.

Dom had once held ambitions to join the Council and govern Katan; Ev was content to govern a mere household. Dominor loved the feel of silk and velvet on his body; Evanor was content to wear wool and cotton. Dom wanted to have his advice acknowledged as helpful, even wise; Ev was contented when his brothers wiped the mud from their boots after he chided them. They were as different as day and night, as city and village. Dominor loved his twin dearly and certainly missed his presence deeply, stolen far from his home and his kin as he was . . . but they weren't identical twins, by any means.

Really, of all of us to have been kidnapped, I'm probably the best choice, he thought with a wry twist of humor. *Evanor is too gentle and guileless to disguise his opinion of these Mandarites and their insane opinions about one gender being superior to the other. Koranen is too . . . young, I guess one could say. Too impetuous and hot-tempered. Morganen might be all right in this situation, but he isn't enough of an actor to seem truly "convinced" by these imbeciles' rhetoric. Rydan, with the way even the most potently spell-locked doors tend to unlock and open themselves for him, would probably have escaped these chains during the storm, and then . . . I don't know . . . flown himself free? I wouldn't be surprised if he had that sort of power. Come to think of it, Morg probably knows a spell to free himself from antimagic manacles such as these.*

Annoying little twit. It irked him that Morganen knew more than he did. Somehow, he knew more than Dominor, had learned more, for all that the thirdborn son had bought the lion's share of magical tomes through the years, and was older by four more years' worth of studying as well. He loved the youngest of his brothers, but Morganen also roused most of Dom's competitiveness. Rydan didn't, but then Rydan didn't play such games anymore.

Dominor returned his thoughts to how his brothers would react.

Trevan, for all he's a self-proclaimed womanizer, would be appalled at the thought of "slave girls," and would not be able to pretend anything different. Wolfer would be snarling and snapping and growling. No dissembling there. Saber might have the mind and the cunning to dissemble and pretend to go along with his captors, having been trained by our father for the world of Katani politics . . . but he wouldn't have the magical strength to get himself back home again once he was free.

His brothers were undoubtedly seeking a means to rescue him, even as he sat there on the bunk, nibbling on some of the soft cheese he had been given. Dominor knew he could be annoying, what with his competitiveness, his high opinion of himself, and his need to prove himself better than the rest of his siblings. It was a bid for attention and respect that was as established in his nature as his birth order. But he also knew his brothers cared for him and would back him to the hilt, as surely as he would support them.

I think Evanor Sang to me, while I was delirious with falomel *poisoning,* Dom decided. *That was the distant voice I heard in my ear, I'm sure of it. But now . . . I hear nothing. He might be just sleeping, or busy with some task, but it's also possible I'm beyond his range of ability to Sing. Which means beyond the range of most scrying mirrors. It will take all of their craft and cunning to create a means of locating me. Even then, it's not guaranteed the mirror would be strong enough to turn into a Gate over such a long distance, with no paired mirror at my end to stabilize the connection. A pity the aether isn't stable enough for the great Portals to be opened, anymore.*

Which means I definitely need to work on freeing myself, so that either I can find my own way home, or a way to connect some mirror locally to their efforts, even if the link would only be strong enough to communicate, and not actually cross—

The door opened and Lord Aragol stepped back inside. He flashed Dominor a broad, quick smile that made the points of his goatee-moustache quiver. His younger son, Eduor, accompanied Kennal as they crowded into the small cabin. This time the youth carried a cut-glass goblet, into which he poured a blush wine from a bottle that his father uncorked in Dominor's presence. It looked like they were going to try to recruit him with the temptation of more of the "finer things" of Mandarite life.

Dominor braced himself to play the part of a slowly, reluctantly convinced potential ally, while the ship continued to heave and rock from the waves caused by the end of the storm.

TWO

❧

Aaaughh!"

Mikor jerked his head up from his studying. His mother, accustomed to such noises coming from down the hall, tapped him on the shoulder. "Mind your quill, Mikor. You're risking a drop of ink on the page."

"Yes, Mother," the nine-year-old murmured. He bent his head over the wood-pulp sheet and continued marking down the answers to the sheet of questions his honorary aunt had given him as a test of his knowledge of the world's history. A moment later, another outraged scream broke his concentration again, making him jump.

"Aaaaaughh!"

This time, it was accompanied by a crash. Even Mariel flinched, though normally her placid temperament withstood the often fiery outbursts from her best friend. A moment later, another crash echoed from the chamber at the end of the hall, followed by a string of oaths that made Mariel grateful for the muffling effect of the thick wooden door. Her young son would pick up such bad habits soon enough, but it would be nice to put that off for a few more years, if she could help it.

A particularly sharp smashing sound made Mikor flinch and

glance at his mother. "Um . . . shouldn't you go see what is upsetting Aunt Serina so much?"

"Oh, yes, throw *me* into the lioness' den, when she asked me to keep *anyone* from disturbing her," his mother muttered. Sighing, she stroked his dark, thumb-length curls back from his forehead. He looked like what he was, a blend of his late father, Milon, and her. His father's slightly upturned nose and dark hair, her curls and cheerful smile. She gave him that smile as she ruffled his hair. "If I die in there, you still have to finish your test, you know."

Mikor groaned but let it pass.

Leaving him to bend his head once more to his answers, Mariel left the library and headed up the corridor. Like most of the Retreat, it had been carved out of the rugged stones of the Natal mountain range. The chamber she had left had tall, thin windows that allowed plenty of light to enter for reading, carved as it was from the northern face of the Retreat's cliffs. But where she was headed was located along the southeastern face of the mountain and up one level. Technically her friend's workroom was right next to her bedchamber, but one had to go down and around and up again, through the library, to get to either.

Stopping before the thick wooden door at the end of the passage, she lifted her knuckles and rapped politely on the door. "Serina? It's Mariel. You might as well open up; better for me to ask what's wrong than to have the nuns badgering you to death."

A muffled oath came back in reply, followed by a sizzling sound. Mariel guessed it was some sort of cleaning spell, for when Serina bid her to enter, the floor was free of debris. Well, mostly free; there was a pile of pot shards near one of the chalkboards, spell-swept out of the way. There were also a couple of broken shards on top of the papers littering the large desk in the center of the chamber. Serina, her long pale hair disheveled, swept a few stray locks out of her reddened face. Mariel didn't even have to ask what was wrong as she shut the door behind her, glancing to her left at the far end of the room. After only a few moments, the cream-clad mage huffed and began her complaint without prompting.

"I've tried *every* variation imaginable . . . magic potential, magic affinity, nobility of bloodline, commoner class . . ." One of her slender hands waved dismissively at the chalk-scribbled slateboards in the frames surrounding her paper-strewn desk in the center of the room. "I've even tried to factor in *hair color*, for the Moons' sake! It cannot be done! Not with the materials on hand!"

Mariel, seeing a bit of scarlet on her friend's finger, moved forward with soothing murmurs. Catching the sorceress's hand, she crooned over it, letting her healing magic seal the scratch. "There, there. If the materials on hand won't work, then where can we find ones that will?"

Serina swept her free hand through her hair once again. "Outkingdom, I guess! Guchere . . . maybe even as far away as the Five Lands. But not the Moonlands. There's no one there I can use."

"No *one*?" Mariel asked, releasing her friend's hand in her curiosity. "You said *materials*, and yet you need a person?"

Letting out a rough sigh, Serina retreated to her desk, where she slumped onto her padded leather chair. "I told you; the cure to the Natallian problem of mage-births is not unlike the problem we had in the Moonlands, of raising the mountains over our valley and screening it from the rest of the Five Lands. We had to bind all of our mage-borns' magic into the spell to make it solid enough to keep out the other Five Lands when the old Draconan Empire was sundered. I left the Sixth Land when I was fourteen, before my powers were bound, so that I could learn and use my magic freely. I did and do go back from time to time, especially during the summers when I was released from the Academy each year. That's when I studied the old spells we used to use, including that one.

"Not that I can repeat it," the taller woman added with another sigh, slouching back in her chair, "since that was managed at the will of the Gods as well as the efforts of mere mortals. But I know *how* the spell was constructed. The spell that drains away males' magic and gives it to otherwise unGifted females here in Natallia is not that dissimilar. It *can* be unmade! But it requires a very specific ritual, and the components—for all that they are two living, thinking beings—must have very specific factors about them. Specific requirements, specific qualities . . . !"

She stopped, frustration lifting both of her hands to her hair. Her fingers only slid partway through the silk-fine strands before she grimaced and shifted. Tugging her hair out from under her hips, she made no protest as Mariel moved around her chair, gathering up the long locks so that they could be braided out of her way. For all that Mariel was only two years older than her, and Serina far more powerful as a mage, the shorter woman was too set in her ways after nine years of habit to not be motherly on occasion. Serina's own dislike for handling the mundane matters of life didn't discourage Mariel's mothering. The mage *could* handle things competently; she simply preferred to focus on her work.

"So, why don't you outline these requirements?" Mariel coaxed her friend, as she worked on plaiting the thigh-length strands in her hands. Not that the braid would last long; Serina had a bad habit of tugging on and playing with her hair whenever she was thinking. Or frustrated. It actually surprised the older woman that her friend hadn't already tugged her scalp bald.

One of the taller woman's hands gestured in a limp circle at the slateboards. "It's all there, written down. I've parsed the requirements for altering the spell onto the boards."

"I'm not an arithmancy expert. I'm a Healer," Mariel retorted, finger-combing a snarl out of her friend's pale blond hair. "Spell it out in laywoman's terms for me. The simplified version."

"The simple version? That damned spell has permeated all of Natallia, that's what's wrong. Including the lands claimed by those senseless idiots," she added with a snort, meaning the men of the Independence of Mandare. "Call it what they will, those lands are still Natallian and have been saturated with the enchantment imbued into the Font for over eight hundred years. It doesn't help that their midwives are still casting the same blessing on each newborn that was keyed into the initial spell, the same as the rest of Natallia. In fact, we can only be glad the Gucherans have their own birth customs and have resisted the Font's influence.

"The greatest reason why the rare male is born with magical power is usually because he has an outlander mother or father who does not permit the blessing to take place. Which is how I learned that the blessing has an actual influence on the transfer of magic among the local newborns." Her hand came up to rub at her brow, bracing her head. Thankfully, Mariel didn't need it upright, since she was past that point in the braiding. "Initially, I thought the spell would have to be undertaken by a pair of Natallians born under that blessing in order to undo the effects of that blessing with some new variation, but that won't work.

"For one, the blessing is too pervasive and culturally difficult to shift. For another . . . the alterations I want to make just won't work if the participants in the ritual are born-and-bred Natallians, steeped in the enchantments of the Font's magic. Because the aether is saturated, the spell is deeply set into the very bones of the locals. It would resist the change far too much. No, I need clean specimens to enter the Font and perform the ritual."

"*Enter* the Font?" Mariel choked, almost losing her grip on the strands of hair she was plaiting. "By the Gods! You cannot be serious! Only the most powerful of mages can enter the Font and emerge unscathed."

"And yet that is one of the requirements. That's why no one from my homeland will do. And I don't know if there's anyone in the Five Lands who fits the rest of the requirements," Serina agreed wearily. "The original spell needs to be followed very closely in most of its ritual, in order to keep from disrupting the aether terribly, because the spell will be crafted in the very heart of the Font. Subtle changes are necessary. The Font magnifies all magical effects exponentially.

"To that end, the couple involved in the ritual need to be very strong mages in and of their own. They also should be physically fit to withstand the stresses, which means preferably before middle age, yet still old enough to have their magics firmly under control," she listed as Mariel resumed braiding her hair. "Someone in their late twenties or early thirties would be preferable, for that reason. They also need to be single, with no commitments to another person, and willing to undergo at least some sort of mating with their ritual partner, if not a marriage outright."

"Why a mating?" Mariel asked, curious. She tried not to think of her own mating ceremony with her late husband, Milon. It had been a wonderful celebration; she could still remember the cherry blossoms filling the temple. The wedding of a Seer of his power had been turned into a nationwide celebration; Seers were rare and deeply valued by all, whatever their gender. There was no telling yet if Mikor had the Inner Eye like his father, or if he had inherited her Healing affinities, or some magic of his own, or perhaps none at all, but then he was still only nine.

"The original ritual was something of an impromptu marriage celebration. Which complicates things even further," Serina sighed wearily, one hand propping up her chin with the aid of her elbow on the armrest of her chair, the other idly touching the papers on her desk. "It wasn't *meant* to be such a binding enchantment. It was, in effect, an accident. A great, scaly cockup."

"A great, scaly cockup?" Mariel repeated the Moonlands saying, curious.

"I exhausted myself and my postcognitive spells, discovering that little fact." Her fingernail straightened one of the papers on her desk, though it didn't make an impact on the overall mess. "It wasn't during their time in the Font itself, but in what I gleaned of the hours and days before and after. Just a few carelessly gasped but heartfelt words between two lovers. Two lovers who happened to be very powerful mages, who just *happened* to think it would be *kinky* to make love in the middle of a magical wellspring!"

Her fingers snapped out, flicking their tips at the papers on her desk. They shifted a little bit at the impact, but didn't flutter to the ground.

"Idiots," she snorted. Sighing roughly once again, Serina lolled back in her seat as soon as Mariel dropped her braid, the tail end of it secured with a murmured spell. Serina tipped her head back and peered up at her friend. "You know, I wasn't sure about the opportunity your husband thrust upon me, when he claimed he Saw me as the next Guardian of the Retreat, two years ago. I thought he was insane. Even after he explained Foreseeing me finding a way to quell the war between Natallia and Mandare through some spell laid upon the Font, the way to restore a badly needed balance throughout the region. I initially thought he was talking about some more direct means of ending this stupid, pointless war."

"I know," Mariel murmured, pressing her hand to the younger woman's shoulder. "So did I. But his visions, while strong and accurate in hindsight, were never that precise."

Serina covered her friend's hand, giving it a comforting squeeze. "No Seer's predictions are ever completely clear. They're layered in meanings that we cannot fully comprehend until after their events have already unfolded. He certainly didn't know that the vision he had of riding down into the valley was a precognition of where he would be when those rocks fell. I'm sure he wouldn't have gone, if he'd known."

Mariel's mouth curved in a sad, thoughtful smile as she moved to face her friend. "I think he would've, regardless. He said a few things during our marriage-night that made me think he knew his time was going to be short. Something about me being twice as much loved with all the breath in a man's body. *A* man's body, not *his* body. Surely he wouldn't have said that if he hadn't Foreseen me eventually being widowed and thus free to find love with another. I certainly wouldn't have divorced him of my own free will, nor cheated on him; I loved him too much for that."

Rising from her chair, Serina moved around the furniture and pulled her friend into her arms, resting Mariel's cheek against her shoulder. "You're one of those lucky women who get to enjoy more than one love in the span of their lives. While some of us only get fleeting, meaningless encounters while we search for relationships with more substance."

"I think the hope of regaining love in my life is the only thing that keeps me going, some days," Mariel muttered. "Well, that and Mikor."

"Mikor is a handful. How is his test going?" Serina asked.

"Steadily . . . and don't distract me from what you're *not* telling me," Mariel scolded her friend, pulling back. The top of her light brown curls barely tickled the taller woman's nose, but she did have an intimidating mother-glare, when she cared to use it. "What other requirements await the problem at hand? There has to be something more, if you broke into your stash of throwing vases."

Serina chuckled, but it was a short, flat sound. She did have a set of shelves near her desk that were filled with cheap clay pots, perfect for throwing and breaking as a physical stress reliever. "Unfortunately, as I was saying . . . the participants have to be mages. Ones powerful enough to enter the heart of a Font and not only survive, but have enough concentration free to do . . . other things.

"And they have to be a male and a female, because one of the 'other' things they have to do . . . is conceive a child," she confessed after a wince of hesitation. Mariel's hazel eyes widened. Serina nodded. "Not only that, the female has to definitely be powerful as a mage . . . because she has to come back and give birth in the Font . . . and her husband has to give the blessing inside the Font in unison with her, to cement the alterations to the spell. Doing so will permanently weld the magics to the blessing being used all across the affected lands.

"This is *why* it is so vital for these Fonts to be guarded carefully, wherever they are found!" She tried running her hand through her hair again, only to tangle her fingertips in Mariel's efforts. Unable to dislodge her hair, Serina paced instead. "And, as it is my duty to guard *this* Font . . . I have to be the female involved. That way I can at least ensure that my half of the ritual takes place without any mistakes. If there are any mistakes on either side, I'll know exactly what went wrong, because I'll have been right there when it happened."

It took Mariel only a moment to figure out what was agitating her friend so much. *"Oh."*

"Yes. *'Oh.'* Remind me to buy more pots to throw," Serina added in a dry aside. "So not only do I have to find a male who isn't a Natallian or a Mandarite"—she paused here for a derisive snort over that latter option—"but I have to find a male who is magically strong enough to endure the Font and the ritual twice . . . I have to find one I'd be willing to marry! Even if it's only in a primitive, oath-taking, fertility-based sort of way. Which means I need a man who is not only willing to get married, beget a child, and enter the heart of the Font twice, but one who is intelligent enough to keep up with me," the mage added as she paced the half-circle of slateboards and back again. "They're not exactly as common as daisies, you know—and I haven't seen a daisy since I left the Draconan Empire!"

"Why does he have to be smart enough to keep up with you?" Mariel asked, curious. "It sounds to me like you just need a sort of temporary mate-of-convenience. So long as he goes through the first part of the ritual and is willing to show up for the second part, you technically don't need him to stick around for the rest of it. Certainly not after the child is born and the new enchantment has been successfully cast and cemented in place."

Serina stopped her pacing and stared at her short, curly-haired companion. She blinked. "Well . . . I'd always pictured myself as getting married for good. That's the whole point of marriage, isn't it?"

"The point of marriage is to provide an emotionally supportive, stable home for both parties involved, predominantly for the raising of children," Mariel corrected her. "Shared resources and responsibilities make raising a child easier than trying to do it on one's own. But you're independently wealthy, thanks to your Moonland pearls; you have or can buy all the resources you need. Including servants to help with the responsibility of raising a child, should you be husbandless at any point."

"Well . . ." Serina couldn't come up with anything to say against that idea, other than a half-mumbled, "Well, I wouldn't want to take away the father's rights."

"Not all men are interested in raising children. The act of begetting them, *yes*," Mariel sighed, then shook her head. "I think your quest to find an outlander mage strong enough to enter the Font, and biddable enough to heed your directions for the ritual, even if you have to oath-bind him into doing so, will be hard enough to complete. I admit it would be very nice for you to marry the man of your dreams—"

"—What dreams?" Serina interrupted with a snort, pulling her braid over her shoulder and fingering its plated strands as she started pacing again. Gesturing at the slateboards, she added, "Lately, all I can dream of are mathemagical formulas and arithmancy equations! And not the fun kind, either. This has been a *very* frustrating challenge for me. Not that I'm not loving it, but I've hit so many dead ends."

"Yes, well, perhaps you should just settle for someone who can give you a good bedding while you're in the Font," Mariel offered. Her pragmatic statement made Serina narrow her eyes warily. Mariel shrugged expressively. "What? I'm just being practical about it! I mean, it seems to me that, if you're the one who has to enter the Font to ensure it's guarded properly, well . . . you're mired in the local aether. The longer you stay here, the more the botched spell will seep into your bones, making it difficult for you to alter the spell."

"I *know*," the younger woman agreed glumly, flipping a hand at her chalkboards to indicate it was already factored into the equations.

"And you *are* twenty-and-seven," Mariel pointed out as Serina paced again. "You *might* have another twenty or so years of viable childbearing age, but that's only a rough estimate. Some women do become crones in their early thirties, and only the Gods know why. The sooner you get this taken care of, the better, or so it would seem to me. *I* say, as soon as you find a good candidate for the ritual, go for it. Don't necessarily wait to find the perfect man."

"You just want me to get bedded," Serina quipped, slanting her friend a wry look, "so I'll be more biddable and throw fewer vases out of frustration."

"It's been six months!" Mariel reminded her. "You're a perfectly healthy woman. You should be visiting a bed-slave in one of the Thrall Houses, if you don't have a lover or a husband. One tumble for some magical ritual is *not* taking care of your sexual needs adequately."

"It's been *eight* months," Serina corrected her. "And I'd need to practice before entering the Font with whomever it is that I'll pick. This *is* a Tantric ritual, after all. It takes skill and concentration to be able to cast magic in the midst of all that physical pleasure," she added, getting distracted by the equations again. "We'll probably have to duplicate what happened before and not improvise—thank the Gods the original couple were a bit more inventive and experimental than just 'Insert Rod A into Cog B' types! I'd be bored to tears if they were."

Mariel snorted inelegantly, choking on a suppressed laugh.

"Oh, laugh all you want," Serina chided, stopping in her pacing and braid-fingering. "I cannot calculate exactly what sort of interactions in the Font will be needed until I have the male in question in my possession, so that I can cast my diagnosis spells upon him. For all I know, hair color *will* play a part in the overall equations!"

"Well, if that's so, unless your predecessor was a platinum blonde, you'll be in serious trouble just for your own participation," Mariel quipped. That earned her a scowl for her efforts. "Lighten your mood, Serina! Look on the bright side of all this. Most healthy heterosexual males would leap at the chance to have lots of practice sex with a beautiful woman such as yourself. Male mages are no different from anyone else, in that regard. You shouldn't have any trouble convincing a likely candidate to follow your lead."

"Male mages who are strong enough to have sex in a wellspring of pure magic are usually arrogant creatures," Serina reminded her friend, pacing again. "You mentioned making him take an oath-bond to follow my lead. That might help. Of course, in order to get a male mage of sufficient power *into* a position where he'd take that oath-bond . . . He'll want something. I'll have to hear what his price will be and consider it carefully."

"Ending the inequality between the genders and the underlying cause of this damned, ongoing war is worth almost any price," Mariel returned quietly, as her friend pondered the problem. "Not any price; there are some things one shouldn't compromise over. But don't quibble too much."

"I'm very good at calculating the risks," Serina dismissed, tugging on the end of her braid. "It's what those risks will be that worries me." She glanced at the clock on the mantle over the hearth, half-hidden by one of the slateboards. "Mikor should be done with his test in another quarter-hour. I'd better tidy this up and prepare to grade his work. I want to have it done before going to supper."

"Will you be dining with the nuns this evening?" Mariel inquired, curious.

"Yes. Mother Naima wanted to discuss my accompanying another crafts shipment, this time down to the coast. Port Blueford is having its Town Faire, and she wants 'adequate protection' for the journey." She rolled her tawny brown eyes. "She keeps claiming I need to get 'into the fresh air' more often. As if I don't enjoy plenty of fresh air whenever the wind blows—which is nearly constantly, here in a mountain home!"

"I think she enjoys the prestige of being temporary Guardian while you're gone," Mariel observed. "And the wind blows no less frequently when you live next to the sea."

"But it smells nicer, to me."

"So, why are you complaining about a trip to Port Blueford, if you love the smell of the sea?" Mariel quipped.

"Because the Bay of Blueford is too far from any port frequented by foreigners, given how it cleaves the middle of the southern coastline halfway to the heart of Natallia?" Serina retorted dryly. Shaking her head, she returned to the subject at hand. "As soon as that child is born, the Mother Superior can have the whole job. She has the magic to manage it!"

Once again, she tried to run her hands through her hair, only to be thwarted by the plait confining it. Her fingers shifted to worry at the spell-bound end instead.

"Don't misunderstand me, Mariel; I've enjoyed my time here as Guardian of the Font. I've learned a lot, between reading all the tomes in the Retreat's library and researching that birth-spell. But I'm a coastal girl, not a mountain girl. I need the tang of the sea in my lungs. Fish in my diet. Sand between my toes!

"I only *have* to be here for the impregnation and the birthing, and then I can leave. That would fulfill what Milon Saw of my presence here and the impact my research and efforts will have." She gave her friend an unhappy look. "Of course, I'd hate to leave you behind. I was never as close to my own sister as I've become with you, what with her being the next Singer of the Moonlands, and all. We didn't have that much in common, and she always had more of Mother's attention."

"I've grown close to you, too," Mariel agreed. "You kept me together and going, after Milon's fall. But leaving the Retreat . . . I don't know if I'm ready for that. Not unless I knew there was a destination to go to. I'm the sort who likes to put down roots for stretches at a time. I'm not a world-wanderer like you."

"I've already traveled half the length of this continent," Serina reminded her wryly. "I'm not as enamored of journeying as I used to be. But I do know that I don't want to spend the rest of my life here. I'm a healthy, red-blooded woman. I'm not the type to turn myself into a nun if I can help it."

Mariel laughed softly. "I should hope not, if you're planning on reenacting a sex ritual." She glanced at the clock and nodded. "Time's almost up. Let's go make sure my son's not cheating and looking in the history texts while we're elsewhere."

That earned her a chuckle from Serina, who wasn't fooled as to why Mariel came into her study in the first place. "Don't you mean, let's go reassure him that his 'dear Aunty' hasn't murdered his mother in a frustrated rage with a mis-flung vase?"

"That, too."

Dominor's head ached with rhetoric. Fallacious rhetoric. To the question of why men were supposedly superior, all he received for a concrete answer was the fact that men were physically bigger and stronger, on average. Dom couldn't deny that. But the opinion that men were smarter had no solid basis in fact, as far as he could tell.

In Katan, boys and girls received the same education in reading, writing, and mathematics until the age of twelve, when they had the choice of apprenticing in a particular trade or taking additional studies. Schooling from the age of six to twelve was paid for by the government; beyond that was the realm of private tutors and apprenticeships. Though his family hadn't quibbled at purchasing the services of private, professional instructors, Dominor had noticed during his earlier schooling years that girls were just as capable as boys. Slightly more so, in fact, considering that they were more willing to settle down and pay attention to their lessons than boys tended to be.

There had been a girl, the daughter of a professional scribe, who had challenged him academically in his fifth year of schooling. Dom had beaten her in the end-of-term tests, but not by that wide of a margin. It had also taken a lot of late-night studying to do so. Women were definitely not intellectually inferior to men. The examples Kennal provided, supporting his father's claims, were easily debunked in Dominor's mind: Their "slave girls" simply weren't given the same level of education as the males of Mandare, so naturally they would seem more ignorant. The thing was, ignorance was curable by education. Stupidity, on the other hand . . . well, that led to idiotic notions that could not be easily dislodged from the feeble minds of those who clung to them.

Like the so-called superiority of males over females as a whole.

For two days now, Lord Aragol and his sons had talked themselves hoarse, extolling the virtues of the Mandarite philosophies and way of life. The more Dominor heard, the more he wanted to dig in his heels, to challenge their notions and assumptions; the more he had to endure of their spiel, the more he wanted to get off their ship. Unfortunately, to be able to gain their trust in the hopes of coaxing them into releasing his chains, he had to pretend to slowly begin to agree with their delusions. He had earned the loss of the chains binding him to the bunk and the cabin, but still bore the manacles and collar suppressing his powers. They still didn't trust him far enough for that privilege.

Men and women weren't superior to each other; they were complementary! The only superiority one could attain was in pitting oneself individually against someone else. Not in pitting one gender against the other. This Mandarite philosophy was as fallacious as believing that skin color had something to do with a person's superiority! The people of Katan came in all shades, from pale and blond along the southern coastline, to near-black in both skin and hair color along the sun-drenched northern shores, close to the region of the world known as the Sun's Belt. There was no difference in the abilities of the mages from any region that could be linked to something as silly as eye and hair color, let alone reproductive organs.

For the third time that day, a sailor knocked on the door of his cabin, interrupting Eduor's blushing but animated recital of how he'd made his first slave girl obey him, dominating her—and thankfully interrupting the way he was privately sickening his literally but not figuratively captive audience.

The man muttered in Kemblin's ear, making the expedition leader start and widen his eyes. Jaw tightening, he dismissed the sailor and cleared his throat, interrupting his younger son. "I'm afraid the rest of your tale will have to wait, Eduor. We have a pressing concern to handle. Lord Dominor, you've heard many of the advantages of life as a Mage Lord among the Mandarites," he stated smoothly, persuasively. "You've even agreed with most of the facts we've presented to you. I would rather have waited until we reached my estates to do this, but . . . it seems we are in danger from a Natallian warship. We have been trying to outrun it, but it has slowly gained on our position since it was first spotted on the horizon shortly after you roused from your, ah, slumbering.

"I'm afraid they will not hesitate to sink us, milord. This puts your own life in jeopardy, alongside ours," Kemblin continued, his tone persuasive. "Now, from what you've revealed about yourself in our conversations, you apparently have enough magic to defend this ship and assist it in escaping its pursuit. I am willing to release your enchanted shackles, *if* . . ."

"If?" Dominor inquired, arching a brow as he took the verbal bait being dangled in front of him. Somewhere nearby, something *boomed* loudly. It sounded to the captive mage like the gun-thing that the Mandarites had demonstrated back at the palace. Dom wished *he* had the type of gun-thing that Kelly had borrowed from her native universe to show the Mandarites that the people of Nightfall were advanced in all ways and therefore weren't the least bit intimidated by their visitors' nonmagical weapons.

"If you swear upon your magic that you will join and aid our cause in defeating the Natallians," the earl finished as the echo of the weapon cleared itself from their ears.

Dominor stalled for time. "For how long? Until we're free of that warship? Or a month, or a year?"

Lord Aragol smiled. "Do you really think we would want to let go of you that easily? A mage of your status? How about for a minimum of ten years? That's long enough to beget a couple of sons and see if they have any magery in their veins."

Frustrated but suppressing it, Dom opened his mouth to say he would consider it when another sailor banged on the door, yanking it open without leave.

The Mandarite gasped out his message. "Two more warships have just revealed themselves, dropping their mirage spells!

They've set us up for a stunning, and they have some sort of new shielding that sends our cannonballs astray!"

"Swear your oath, mage, and I'll set you free!" Kemblin snapped, staring at Dominor. "Rescue us, and you'll be a duke of our land!"

He couldn't do it. He could not agree to such a hellish bargain. If there was one thing Dominor disliked, it was arrogant idiocy masquerading itself as superiority . . . and this gender-thing was the most idiotic reason for anyone to go to war that he had ever heard. If there was one thing he wasn't, it was an idiot. A fool, maybe, but not a dumb idiot. Lifting his chin slightly, he gave his reply arrogantly.

"I am Lord Dominor, Chancellor to Her Majesty, Queen Kelly of Nightfall. I'll take my chances with the Natallians. Women tend to be more reasonable when it comes to honoring the sanctity of diplomats from foreign nations, in my experience."

With a growl of anger, Lord Aragol grabbed Dominor by the wrist and hauled him out of his cabin, shoving him down the short, narrow corridor, past the doors to his and his son's cabins. Thrusting the younger man out onto the midlevel of the ship's poop deck, he pointed at the two warships in view, one of them looming startlingly close. Balanced on each bowsprit, sheltered behind a blurred curtain of protective magic, two figures stood in plain view. Crackling energies played over their hands. The ships were spaced too wide apart for the Mandarite vessel to have turned in time.

"See your folly firsthand!" Kemblin shouted, shoving him almost over the railings. "They don't care who you are, only that you're a male on a Mandarite ship! By the rights of man, I hope they *castrate* you for your foolishness!"

Magic swirled and arced out between the two large warships. A sieve-like net of pastel energies crackled and connected just as the bow of the Mandarite ship crossed its territory. Sailors yelled and scrambled for cover. A few even tried to fire their pistols, but it was no good; the moment the energies swept over the men at the foredeck, they slumped insensate to the planks underfoot, weapons too poorly aimed to have done any good.

Dominor had only a heartbeat to crouch and brace himself before the stunning-spell swept over him, shocking away the world. Only the world didn't go away. The manacles at his throat, wrists, and ankles grew uncomfortably hot for a moment, then slowly cooled again. Around him, Kemblin Aragol and his two sons had dropped to the deck, rendered just as unconscious as the rest of the ship's fallen crew . . . but Dominor was unaffected.

Rigging creaked overhead, and the wind flapped in the sails. Without a man to hold the rudder steady in its attempt to turn away from the Natallian vessels' trap, the ship straightened out. Magic sparkled up over the timbers, and the ship jolted, shuddering as it slowed under the force of the spell laid upon its hull. Lines were tossed out by the nearer of the two warcraft; within a very short time, the Mandarite ship was towed up against the larger vessel, and both men and women swung down on ropes, boarding.

With little choice but to play the part assigned to him at the start of this Disaster, Dominor stood and straightened his threadbare clothes. He hadn't been given his clothing back, under the excuse that without a real bath to cleanse himself, with nothing but seawater to scrub himself, he would only stain his finery. It had been a ploy to keep him under the Mandarite's control, he knew, and it irked him that he didn't look the part he was about to play.

Still, when his movement caught the eyes of the boarding party, he composed himself and greeted the frowning, uniformed warriors. "Greetings," Dominor stated in the Mandarite tongue as a burly fellow mounted the steep stairs to the midlevel. "I am Lord Dominor of Nightfall, Chancellor to—"

"Shut up, Mandarite scum!"

Dominor narrowed his eyes. "I am Lord Chancellor to Queen Kelly of Nightfall, victim of a kidnapp—"

"I said shut up!" Swinging his meaty hand, the Natallian sailor did what the spell could not do, knocking Dominor unconscious.

THREE

❧

How does it feel, Lord Chancellor, to be treated like the lowest creature on the earth?" Kemblin hissed at Dominor. He glared at the whip-wielding man urging them into the yard of the slave market. The warship had sailed into dock too late in the day to put them up for sale, but now they could be transferred and sold in this Natallian city, Port Blueford. The former earl glared at the slaver and sneered under his breath, "Traitor to your own kind . . . !"

"Keep your tongue, Mandarite, or have it taken from you!" the sharp-eared slaver ordered, cuffing him with the coiled loops of his whip.

"You should castrate them," a woman called out from beyond the railings. There was a hard look in the woman's eyes as she added with a laugh, "Then they'd be more biddable!"

Others laughed with her. Dominor felt his entire groin region flinch and draw up tight at *that* suggestion. She was one of the buyers waiting to purchase the newest "indentured war prisoners." Slaves, in other words. The woman was clad in the local style, a sort of blue tunic-dress that reached to the ankles for women—and to the knee for men—but which was slit all the way to the hip joint on either side, unlike a true skirt. Fitted leggings showed underneath. She was a bit too plump for Dominor's taste, especially to have thighs like *that* revealed under the hem of her tunic. *And* a bit too old, bordering the gray-haired side of middle-aged. Her face, as tanned as the other Natallians he had seen so far, was seamed and lined with the beginnings of that leathery look acquired by spending too many years under the sun.

The string of prisoners he was chained to came to a halt near the sale block. He would be the last one put up for sale, with his original trio of kidnappers being auctioned directly before him as "noble war prizes." Dominor had told his newest captors over and over that he wasn't a Mandarite, that he had instead been their prisoner, and as such should surely have been set free by the Natallians, because he had no love for their enemy and definitely wouldn't do anything to help the fools. The Natallians, even less than the Mandarites, hadn't cared.

His politely restrained but very insistent complaints had eventually drawn the attention of the warship's captain in the lengthy voyage to Natallian shores. A cold-eyed woman, Mierran Falleska had informed him that no one on the ship cared about any land other than their own, that no one in all of Natallia cared, and that she'd already questioned Kemblin Aragol as to whether or not Dominor's claims were true.

According to the former earl, there was no such place as Nightfall . . . though the captain did admit she was fairly sure the Mandarite scum was lying, since there was no other reason for a Mandarite to have a precious male mage locked in chains. And then she'd had the gall to inform him that if Dominor didn't silence himself, she'd have his unruly tongue cut from his mouth.

As soon as he was free of his magic-confining bonds, Dominor had a special little spell he was going to cast on the woman. It would not matter where she was, compared to where he was at the time; the spell would fly to her and infect her. It would also be cast upon the earl, for telling the captain that Dominor was lying when he wasn't. Unfortunately, it was unlikely that he would get to see the effects of the Liar's Charm. He doubted anyone could afford both him and the earl, if the cabin boy—sold after some mildly spirited bidding for fifty gold and twelve silver as the first up on the block—was any indication.

A pity. Still, it was distractfully amusing to contemplate what subtle havoc could be wrought in the lives of a man and a woman enchanted to tell nothing but the absolute truth for a full year. The distraction was needed, too, as Dominor waited for his turn on the slave block, loathing his status as a slave.

Goddess preserve us!" Sister Amerith, head of the expedition, wrinkled her nose at the ranks of sailors being hauled past them. The nuns weren't downwind of the captive seafarers, but the stench was still a bit much. She patted the neck of her mare, who bobbed and twisted her head; even the horse seemed uncomfortable with the aroma of the prisoners. "They don't even wash them! I know they're the ones that started the war and all, but do we *have* to treat them worse than animals? Even the lowliest herd boy scrubs his pig before he brings it to market!"

"They simply stink of weeks at sea," Serina observed, shrugging.

Like the nuns, she was clad in white, but unlike them, her riding leathers were not cut in the chiton-and-trews style of Natallia; instead, she wore the fitted vest and trousers of the Moonlands. She had chosen to wear the outfit to celebrate being near the shore once more, despite the warmth of wearing leathers in a climate where it never snowed. At least, not down here at sea level. She didn't mind the craggy slopes of the mountains, but in her two years at the Retreat, the mage had discovered she needed the flat, rippling surface of an ocean to gaze upon, in order to feel content.

"Saltwater can only be used to wash with once in a while, as the salt can crust on the skin, drying it out and making it sting with a salt-rash, while freshwater is too rare a commodity to be used for casual cleaning. Thus, they stink."

"You sound as if you approve of their condition," Sister Amerith snorted.

"I merely understand how it came to be. You know that I do not approve of slavery. Nor of war." The line of prisoners was coming to an end; their entourage, with a score of nuns on horseback and a dozen more driving carts filled with amulets, talismans, holy symbols, and other crafts manufactured by the women of the Retreat, waited patiently to cross the intersection of these two streets to reach their assigned spot in the marketplace.

Her gaze slid over the last fellow, striding a little taller than the rest. His greasy dark hair hung halfway down his chest, and his clothes were the worst of the lot, stained and rough-spun. The cast of his features caught her attention; there was a subtle slant to his eyes, a minor difference in the shape of his nose, the outline of the jaw hiding under his unkempt, scruffy beard, that caught at her senses.

He looked like a foreigner, whoever he was. As he crossed in front of her, Serina noticed the extra manacles on his wrists. In specific, she noted the runes carved on them. Frowning, she squinted at the metal clamped above his bare feet. They, too, bore runes. As did the collar around his throat, a collar none of the other war slaves bore, just nonmagical versions of the other shackles.

Five bindings of magical power . . . either they've bound him in overkill, or he's very powerful indeed, Serina thought. Her mind compared that to the look of his face, and calculated what it meant. *He doesn't look Mandarite or Natallian, he doesn't look Gucheran, and he certainly isn't from the Five Lands or the Moonlands. That means he's most likely a foreign mage. A potentially powerful foreign mage . . . Brother and Sister Moon, did you drop him into my lap as a present?*

The lines of imprisoned sailors were being herded toward the slave market. Serina reminded herself that she had plenty of time to help the nuns set up their stall and ward it against theft. The best "prizes" were always auctioned last, to hold the crowd's attention long enough to ensure that most of the slaves deemed of lesser worth could find buyers, first.

It didn't take long to find the right stall, pay rent to the market representative who met them there, nor to assist in unloading the baskets and chests from the nuns' two carts. Already there was a small crowd of buyers wanting items made by the holy women, but the nuns held them back until Serina could wordlessly cast several strong but subtle antitheft spells around the stall and its contents. So long as the merchandise touched the stall, only legitimate buyers and browsers could pick it up. These thrice-yearly sales were literally the bread and butter earnings of the Retreat, though they did take time away from her studies. It was too rocky a location to grow more than a fraction of the food needed to sustain its inhabitants, mostly mountain-tolerable herbs that either seasoned their food or were turned into medicines, sachets, and pomanders with various healing, freshening, and insect-repelling properties, depending on what was made from them.

Once her tasks were done, however, she was free to go about her own business. Normally Serina would be ready to stroll through the market in search of ingredients for spells and potions, and eager to stride onto the docks. She liked to breathe in the tang of salt, fish, and seaweed while admiring the ships that ranged from one-masted fishing boats to four-masted war frigates and everything in between. Serina had grown up in a coastal town, one of the few ports that the Moonlands owned and used for discreetly invited trade; Port Blueford reminded her of her home, even if the shapes of those boats and frigates were a little foreign. But that man, the one who was quite possibly a powerful foreign mage, had to be tracked down and bought. So she hurried through the market, past fishmongers and cloth merchants, past stands of fruit—

A foul stench struck her nostrils as she passed a man opening a chest, making her stumble and gasp. She wasn't the only one. Everyone else was giving the chest and the man holding it in front of one of the fruit stands horrified looks. Serina was more startled than shocked.

"Gods Offend! Close that thing immediately!" the stall's merchant ordered. The man offering the fruits started to comply.

"Wait!" Stepping into the hastily cleared area around that chest, Serina caught the lid and peered inside. As she'd thought, the interior of the iron-bound box was filled with a very distinct, lumpy, lobed green fruit. A good thirty of them or more, if she was not mistaken.

"Please, milady!" the man with the chest said, shooing her fingers from the edges as he closed the lid. "My apologies, milord, milady; they did not smell like this when I salvaged them from an abandoned ship that had lodged on a reef. They were too hard to cut open, so I had assumed they were unripe at the time. I'll find the city midden heap—my apologies," he added again, nodding to the fruit seller.

She couldn't let him destroy those fruits. Impulse had her digging into the pouch strung at her waist, grabbing her coin purse. "Fifty gold for that chest and its contents."

"F-Fifty!" the salvager spluttered, his brown eyes wide. "You cannot be serious! Cease your jesting, woman!"

"That chest contains spell components that I can use. Fifty gold," she told him, counting out nine of the larger gold coins in her purse, four smaller ones, and ten large silver coins.

The salvager, whoever he was, narrowed his eyes shrewdly. Whatever the fruit was, he understood that she wanted it very badly and was willing to pay a seemingly ridiculously high price for it. Which meant it was valuable and rare enough to dicker. "*Eighty* gold."

Serina narrowed her eyes. "Fifty, and you leave with all your body parts still in their proper shape."

He looked down his nose at her scornfully. "And just who do you think you are?"

The fruit seller cleared his throat. "*That*, o ignorant one, is the Lady Serina, Guardian of the Nuns of Koral-tai."

Serina gave the portly stall owner a bemused look. "How did you know that, Master Merchant?"

"Brown eyes, long pale hair, foreign clothes . . . and I saw you riding with the nuns, earlier," he shrugged. "Rumor has it you're nearly as powerful as the women of the Royal Family."

Serina shrugged off the comparison; politics had never interested her. Not after her younger sister had been born with the sign of the next Singer in her eyes. That was a headache for other women in her family. She had also carefully steered clear of politics in her travels; if Seer Milon hadn't asked her to stay, intriguing her with the problem affecting the Font, she wouldn't still be in Natallia. She probably would have gone north; she might even have taken a ship across the Southern Bay to the tip of Sundara, exploring that exotic desert empire and the even stranger lands rumored to lie north of the Sun's Belt. Returning her attention to the sailor-scavenger and his chest, the mage lifted one of her pale blond brows.

"Well? I doubt you've seen this much money at one time in your entire life. I'm being more than generous, in that regard."

The thin man bit his lower lip for a long moment, then nodded, holding out his hand. "Give me the gold, and you'll get the chest and its contents . . . but I want to know what those awful things are and why they're still useful to you, even though they smell like a sun-baked privy-pit."

"They are the fruit of my homeland, and their value is highest when they smell like a sun-baked privy-pit," she explained with a tight smile, passing over the handful of coins, while he balanced the chest on the edge of the fruit seller's stall. "Because that is when their magical properties are at their most concentrated. What those properties are, however, is a secret known only to mages."

Her smile stretched, baring her teeth as she hauled the chest out of his arms. "I'd tell you what those secrets are, but then I'd have to turn you into a toad . . . and I happen to need a nice, big toad-skin for one of my current experiments. It would be wiser to not tempt me, I think."

He swallowed and wisely didn't press the point. Hauling the chest back to the nuns' stall, Serina dug a bit of chalk from her pouch and marked the chest with stasis runes, enchanting it to keep the fruit inside preserved as timelessly as possible. She wanted to open up the chest and fetch out one of the fruits for herself, dearly longed to find those two thumb-like spikes poking up from the oval rind that were just an inch apart instead of two or more like the other projections scattered over its hide. She wanted to use them like levers to pry the fruit open, exposing its succulent, creamy flesh, and the six seeds suspended at the heart in a sac of ambrosia-like liquid.

Unfortunately, there were some rather distinct properties associated with eating the *myjii*. Most immediate were the privy-stench of the unopened fruit, and the highly contrasting, heavenly aroma that would burst forth when the fruit was opened properly. But most prominent was a peculiar, weeklong iridescing of the consumer's hair, after eating the flesh or drinking the liqueur of the *myjii*, which was very hard to disguise. It only showed when sunlight struck the hair of someone who had eaten the Holy Fruit of the Moonlands, or when struck by the light from both moons, but it was unmistakable.

There was only one other object seen outside the Moonlands that held that peculiar property, picking up the rainbow-iridescent sheen of sunlight and double moonlight, and vanishing in shadow, candlelight, or the glow of only one moon . . . and it wasn't hair. True, it was an overcast morning right now, but she didn't want to risk the sun coming out at an inopportune moment and making her braid glow. Not now, and not later in the week.

Securing the chest with a few more spells to counter any possible theft—grateful the nuns were preoccupied with a crowd of customers eager for their wares—Serina hurried once more across the market. This time, dual need had her swaying toward the public refreshing rooms that were on her way to the slave market.

Ducking into one of the stalls, she used the facilities, cast a quick cleaning charm on herself, then pulled out a long, white leather thong that was looped around her neck. At the bottom of the loop, an almond-shaped nutshell hung from the ends of leather glued to its two halves. Carefully prying the shell open so that the back hinge didn't break, she gently shook out an object much larger than the nutshell itself: a gold chain strung with wire-mounted pearls of varying sizes.

Selecting a quartet of the smaller ones, she twisted them off and dropped them into her coin purse, then touched the necklace to the shell. It vanished inside, cramming itself into the small shell. This was one of the other magical properties of the Holy Fruit: Its nutshells could hold up to a thousand times their size and mass in nonliving objects, so long as the natural but delicate hinge at the back of the shell-halves remained unbroken.

The *myjii* was revered by her people; the outer smell was endured with bravery, the inner scent enjoyed with relish, the flesh and liqueur consumed with joy, and the shells hoarded carefully. Even the meat that resided in the nuts had useful, naturally magical properties; eating the seed inside the shell allowed a person to understand any spoken language for up to a week . . . and when dried and ground, it formed the rare powder *myjiin*, which was highly prized among mages around the world, as it was the basis for the extremely difficult-to-brew Ultra Tongue potion.

It was very rare to find whole, intact *myjii* outside of the Moonlands. She had no idea what had happened to the Moonlands ship to send it so far westward, or why its lost owners would have carried unripened Holy Fruit on board. Serina was just glad she had access to the fruit. There was no telling whether or not that foreign mage spoke the language shared by the Natallians and the Mandarites. Hopefully he did, but either of them could always eat a *myjii* nut so that they would be able to communicate.

The slave market was crowded with buyers. The bidding for the captured sailors was fast paced, but then it was late summer, prime harvesting time for both land and sea. Schools of fish needed to be caught, sheaves of wheat needed to be cut, bushes of berries needed to be plucked, and orchards of fruit and nuts needed to be picked. Pushing her way to the railings next to the holding area, Serina studied the rows of chained war prisoners.

The tall fellow with the long, dark hair was still there. Relieved, she settled in to wait, biting her tongue against the indignity of selling people. Even if most of them were misogynistic bastards-by-attitude, it was an uncivilized practice, in her opinion.

The clouds overhead thickened and darkened. As the sales progressed, a light rain began to fall. She and the other potential buyers were mostly sheltered by the roofs ringing the display yard and providing shelter for those who came to peruse and, it was hoped, buy, but the sailors being led one at a time to the block were left out in the open. Most of them ignored the droplets, though a handful gave the skies unhappy looks as the rainfall intensified. It was a lukewarm summer rain, but coupled with the odd, stray breeze from the docks in the distance, it would feel cold after a while. The foreign mage lifted his face to the falling drops, keeping his eyes closed as he let nature wash some of the dirt from his subtly foreign, slightly exotic features, using a manacled hand to scrub at some of the grit on his rough-bearded skin.

Her lower stomach twisted a little as Serina watched the simple but sensual act. *He really is handsome, isn't he?* she thought, studying the man waiting for his turn on the block. *Or he will be, once he's cleaned up a bit. Exotic, foreign, lean, fit, and hopefully exactly what I need. Certainly, he seems to stir a healthy amount of lust within me, even looking like this. . . . Did You send him to me, Moons? Along with the fruit I may need to communicate with him?*

Brother and Sister Moon weren't regarded as the strongest Gods in the world, but they were more omnipresent than most. Their gifts also tended to be subtler than some of the other Gods'. She'd heard of any number of blatant, Gods-wrought miracles in other lands, but the Moonlands only had one real miracle: the hiding of the Sixth Land from the rest of the Five Lands, when civil war had struck the Dragon Empire. Other divine gifts tended to be delivered unto her people with a lot more in the way of discretion. If this was indeed a bit of heavenly provenance . . . well, thanking Them wouldn't hurt if it wasn't, and it might help bring more good luck into her life if it was.

As one hour became two, then three, the rain clouds passed overhead, thinning and ceasing their downpour. Serina's stomach rumbled with hunger. She could only imagine how the prisoners felt, since no one had offered them any water, let alone fed them during the entire time she had been here. But finally, the last string of Mandarites reached the block. Trying not to show her disgust as the bidding grew very heated for "two noble-born sons," and "a Mandarite earl, a highly valuable war criminal," Serina waited impatiently for the final sale of the day.

She wasn't the only one still waiting; the farmers and the fishermen and -women had faded back from the crowd, their purchases made, but the crowd hadn't thinned. Their places had been taken by a sea of mostly women. These were the rich, the wealthy, the noble-born, and the mage-born residents of Port Blueford. Some were merely agents of such denizens, but the rumor of a shackled male mage had clearly spread throughout the city over the past few hours. Port Blueford was too far from Guchere to see male mages all that frequently. It didn't surprise her that the news of one being offered for sale had drawn the women out of the woodwork.

Even if his magical prowess was minimal, bedding a male mage greatly increased the likelihood of young daughter-mages being born in Natallia. Most of the women who had gathered appeared to be of childbearing age, or probably had daughters of that age. And he *was* handsome, despite the poor quality of his garments, the scruffiness of his appearance, and the lingering dirt of his captivity. It never hurt to have a visual feast, where such matters were concerned. She could understand the sales appeal of the man, even if she deplored the fact he was up for sale.

A thought struck her, making Serina wrinkle her nose. *I'm no better than these matrons! Drooling over him for the chance to get my hands on his fertile, magical flesh . . . though at least my reasons are a bit nobler and less selfish. Succeeding with the ritual will restore the damaged balance of magic between the genders in this region, and afterward, I can easily set him free. Of course, that would still leave me with a child to raise . . .*

She hadn't really given the aftermath of the ritual much thought before now, but there was the truth of it: She *would* have a child to raise, afterward. The consequences of the attempt to fix the botched Tantric spell permeating the local Font would be more than just the spell-wrought impact on the aether. Serina would have a lifelong responsibility for rearing a child, once she was done.

Of course, eventually the child will grow up, she reasoned as the scowling, bearded Mandarite earl finally sold for the price of a large ruby ring judged to be worth more than a thousand in gold. Cash in hand, or at least the equivalent in valuables, was considered more important to the slave traders than promises of payment, after all. Serina contemplated her own problem as she waited for the sale to finish being transacted.

Presuming I do a good job in raising him or her, the child should be self-sufficient. At least, I hope they'll be a good citizen of whatever land they might choose for their homeland. I do know one thing: I am not going to raise my son or daughter in this *land.*

A century-plus of war had hardened the Natallians. The Mandarites weren't any better; in fact, she considered them to be culturally insane. She wasn't about to live among the Five Lands—they believed in slavery, and a citizen had to prove they were noble born to be able to enjoy certain freedoms, wear certain clothes, even grow their hair to a certain length. And although she *could* return to the Moonlands . . . she'd lose her magic if she returned as a permanent resident. Serina enjoyed being a mage too much to give it up. Guchere had been a nice place to visit, but it just hadn't appealed to her. It wasn't exotic enough for her to consider making it her home. Certainly its political situation was a little too nervous, stuck between the war-embroiled Natallians and the rigid society of the Draconan Empire.

Which leaves me with finding some other place to live. Perhaps if I could find out where—

Her idle speculation about the foreign mage's birthplace had to be quickly set aside; with the Mandarite earl's services bought and his scowling body being hauled off in chains by his new mistress, the foreigner was being hauled up onto the block. Hers wasn't the only figure to stiffen and straighten, or the only set of eyes to linger on his rain-dampened clothes in speculative interest as slavers prodded him up onto the stone dais of the selling block.

"Who'll be the first to bid on this fine specimen of a Mandarite war criminal?" the slave merchant called out. Several women opened their mouths to shout their replies, but a different voice cut through the others. A baritone voice, sharp with censure, silencing everyone.

"I am no Mandarite war criminal!" The prisoner's blue eyes swept the crowd with tightly leashed anger. "Nor am I some Natallian slave! I am a free citizen of the sovereign Isle of Nightfall, kidnapped unlawfully from my people by the Mandarites!"

"A likely story!" the slaver sneered.

"Bring a Truth Stone, if you doubt me," the mage demanded

coldly, "and place it in my palm! It should work even with these bands that the Mandarites placed upon me. See for yourselves if my words are lies."

"Silence, Mandarite dog!" the slaver disparaged. "The captain who brought you said you were known among the rest of the war slaves for being a liar. Let's start the bidding at—"

"*I* want to see him touch a Truth Stone," Serina called out, tightening her gut to project her voice over the murmur of the others. The uncertainty in the crowd made her mind race. She had to know for certain whether or not he was indeed a foreigner, fulfilling one of the requirements of the ritual. Inspiration struck with that thought. "I want to know exactly how powerful a mage he is, before I'll pay a single copper."

That got the swell of voices to start babbling with some enthusiasm in her favor. Grumbling, the slaver gestured for one of his servants to bring over a Truth Stone from the market's offices. Slapping the white marble disc into the foreigner's palm as soon as she brought it back, the slave trader ordered, "Wrap your fingers around that and tell us your name is Maeve the dancing girl."

The twisting of the foreigner's mouth was too sarcastic, too sardonic to be considered a smile. "My name is Maeve, and I am a dancing girl."

Uncurling his fingers, he displayed the black marks where his fingers had wrapped around the white surface of the stone, balancing the disc on his palm. After a few moments, the stone turned pale again. Squeezing it a second time, the mage spoke.

"I am Lord Dominor of the noble family of Corvis, Lord Chancellor to Her Majesty, Queen Kelly of the sovereign kingdom of Nightfall." Opening his fingers, he displayed the pale, unblemished surface of the Truth Stone. Clutching it again, he continued briskly, his voice sharp with vehemence. "I was kidnapped and imprisoned against my will by the Mandarites and kidnapped against my will by the Natallian Navy. If you do not wish to invoke the threat of serious repercussions for the indignities your people have inflicted so callously upon me, an innocent bystander who has nothing to do with your war, a bystander who *refuses* to have anything to do with your war, then you will set me free immediately!"

Again, he showed the stone. Again, it was clean, unblemished. For a moment, doubt hung thick in the air. Then a woman wearing the Royal Livery nudged aside two of the women at the barrier between the buyers and the courtyard. "How powerful of a mage are you?"

"What does that matter?" the prisoner called back, lifting his chin. "I am not some war criminal to be bound in chains and sold to the highest bidder."

"Answer the question," Serina found herself calling out, "and we'll consider setting you free!"

There were a few disappointed grumbles at that, but not many. Most of the women gathered were still interested in his abilities as a potential father of mage-born daughters, despite the revelation that he was indeed a foreigner.

"Answer the woman!" the slaver ordered him, whapping him in the back of the legs with the loops of the coiled whip he held.

Wrapping his fingers tightly around the stone, the mage answered with an arrogant lift of his chin. "I am the third most powerful mage not only in all of Nightfall, but one of the ten most powerful mages in all of our neighbors to the west, in the Empire of Katan. And I have yet to meet a spell I cannot master . . . including Ultra Tongue, as you can hear for yourselves."

Uncurling his fingers, he tilted his palm outward, displaying the pure, unmarred surface of the Truth Stone.

"A thousand gold!" someone shouted. It startled the chained foreigner into dropping the Truth Stone. Another woman shouted, "Eleven hundred!" A third yelled, "Twelve!", and a fourth, "Twelve hundred and fifty!" From there, the bidding began in earnest.

Most of the crowd had dropped out by the time the bidding reached twenty-five hundred. The slaver had quickly demanded cold, hard proof of the money being offered, which weeded out some of the bidders. The remainder offered jewels as well as gold, some of the wealthiest in the crowd literally stripping the wealth from their necks and wrists as proof of their ability to pay. Serina held back to see just how high the others were willing to push the limit. She had more than enough wealth to—

The woman in the Queen's Livery raised her arm, drawing the attention of the others and silencing the bidding with her assertive call. "One rainbow pearl!"

That caused a startled rustle in the crowd. The slaver, all but visibly drooling at the wealth being offered, shook off some of his avarice in exchange for practicality. "Prove it, and I'll consider your offer!"

"Bring out the sun, and I'll prove it," the government servant retorted. "You know as well as I do that there's no proof without sunlight, or the light of the double-Moons."

"*I'll* do it," Serina called out, as a few of the mages in the crowd began squabbling over who should have that task. Meddling with the weather was a tricky prospect in the best of circumstances; she didn't want to ruin the weather patterns with a permanent change. Not when all that was needed was a brief opening in the clouds, which would suit her own needs.

"Who are you?" the liveried woman challenged her. "Why not let Mage Theresse, here, clear the clouds from the sky? I know her abilities, but I do not know yours."

Mage Theresse, a plump older woman, blushed and cleared her throat. "Because that's Lady Serina, milady Servant. Everyone knows she's a far better mage than I."

"Lady Serina? Guardian of Koral-tai?" the Royal Servant asked, arching one of her dark brows. "What would the Guardian of a nunnery need a man for?"

Trying to not let her cheeks heat, Serina planted her hands on her leather-clad hips. She didn't want anyone in Natallia outside of Mariel and Mother Naima—who could be trusted—to know that she was working on a means of changing the Natallian way of life. "Because I myself am *not* a nun?"

Ribald feminine laughter greeted her words. Glancing up over the roof of the slave market, Serina flicked up her arm. Magic roiled up through those clouds with the wordless gesture, boiling and shifting them apart. Sunlight streamed down out of the northern sky, taking advantage of the temporary aperture. It glinted off of the wet stones of the courtyard, shining at the wrong angle for the Servant to use, since she stood on the northern side of the enclosure, well within the shadow cast by the buyers' roof.

At a gesture from the slave merchant, the Servant vaulted the stone railing and strode into the sunlight; a moment of digging in her belt-pouch, and she offered a tiny white object balanced on her palm.

Serina climbed over the fence, too. The merchant, who was passing his hand over the pearl to watch for the telltale iridescence to vanish under the shadow of his fingers, frowned in her direction. "You are not given leave to enter the yard, milady."

"I enter to offer my own bid," she stated, reaching into her coin purse. "*Two* rainbow pearls."

"I am not some slave to be sold!" the man Dominor protested as Serina displayed them for the slave seller to check for authenticity.

"Be silent!" the Queen's Servant ordered him. The dark-haired woman dug into her own pouch, pulling out a second pearl. "Two rainbow pearls, but of a larger size than hers."

"Three rainbow pearls," Serina countered calmly. The pearls on her own palm were indeed smaller than the other woman's, but three were worth more than two.

"These two, and five thousand gold, to be delivered within the hour," her opponent countered.

Serina fished out the fourth pearl she had tucked into her pouch earlier, proffering it with a little smile. "Four rainbow pearls."

"Two rainbow pearls, twelve sea-pearls, *six* thousand gold, and the right to bear the Queen's Arms above your business sign, as a Royal Slaver!" the Servant countered, her face reddening with the offer. "Her Majesty is looking for a male mage strong enough to sire several powerful granddaughters, to ensure the country's future succession."

Serina knew she was going to lose the bid, if she didn't put her best offer on the table. "*Ten* rainbow pearls . . . each *twice* the size of hers."

The slaver and the government servant both blinked. The slave seller was the first to recover, clearing his throat so that he could speak. "Prove it. *Either* of you ladies. Prove it here and now, and he'll be yours!"

The liveried Royal Servant gestured to someone in the crowd, but Serina was faster. Tugging on the white thong, Serina fished out the plain dark brown nutshell. Cracking it open carefully, she concentrated and shook out not one, not two, but three long chains, each one strung with dozens of pearls. They gleamed with a sea pearl's creamy luster in the shadow of her arm and scintillated with the metallic-oily highlights of a rainbow-pearl in the light of the sun. The pearls ranged in size from the diameter of a very small lentil to that of a lima bean and larger.

The pearls were strung on golden wires with a spiraled loop at one end; a simple, practiced twist was all it took for Serina to remove ten of the medium-sized pearls . . . but it wasn't the bean-sized pearls she selected for the transaction that had fixed the seller's attention. It was the sheer wealth represented in the *rest* of those pearls. Wealth which Serina was silently displaying as proof that she could easily counter any other offer made by the Queen's Servant . . . in the equivalent of cash on hand.

Only the Natallian Queen herself might have this many of the rarely seen, highly prized bivalve-gems this far from the Moonlands. Certainly ten of them would be considered enough of a price to ransom a noblewoman of very high standing, possibly even a Royal Princess. From the pinched look in the other woman's face, the liveried Servant didn't have anything comparable on hand . . . and, judging from the gleam in the slave trader's eyes, having the proffered payment on hand was far more valuable to him than any promises of prestige. He proved it by scooping the ten pearls from Serina's hand, pausing only to shake her palm between both of his to seal the bargain.

"Sold! And if you ever see anyone else in this market that you would like to purchase, Lady Guardian—"

"I sincerely doubt it," Serina dismissed him, extracting her fingers and trying not to grimace visibly. In fact, if she could have prevented it, she wouldn't have bought anyone, let alone someone caught up in the insanity of the gender war between the two local nations.

She had already completed several calculations about her own foreign flesh being gradually infused with the botched spell of the Font, and had discerned that the risk of waiting another year before starting the ritual was a *small* risk . . . but still a tangible one. It would only increase with exposure, too. If the Moons saw fit to drop this particular man into her immediate vicinity like a present, shortly after figuring out that she needed someone like him, she would do her best to use Their Gift as soon as feasible. The expense certainly wasn't enough to make her hesitate, by Moonland standards.

"Thus ends the slave auction for today! Come back in two days' time, when the warship *Dreadful Ice* is due to reach dock; its mages reassured me by mirror that they have a shipment of dock workers and stevedores from the sacked town of Mansright!" the slaver asserted, clutching his gleaming pearls tightly in his fist. The crowd groaned in disappointment but slowly dispersed. Gossip chattered among the departing women; Serina's purchase and display of wealth were about to become very famous news in Port Blueford.

No doubt it will also spread rumors of my wealth to any outlying bandits on the road north, Serina thought. *Perhaps I should just construct a Mirror-Gate to the Retreat for the nuns to take back home. I know the horses don't like it, and transporting the carts across the widened frames without breaking anything will be a pain in the neck as well as magically draining . . . but if it spares me the hassle of dealing with ambush after ambush, it just might be worth it.*

Mindful of the queen's ransom dangling from her left hand, Serina tapped the opened nutshell to the pearl-strung chains, replacing them one by one from public view, then tucked the closed shell back into her cleavage. The thong and its shell were enspelled against theft or breakage, so it mattered not to her how many people had seen her display of wealth, or if they gossiped about it. Those who knew who she was wouldn't be so stupid as to attack, and those not smart enough to ask who she was would not be smart enough to survive her counterattack. It would be a bother and a hassle to protect herself, but she'd do it if necessary.

The important thing was that Serina had potentially just acquired the man she needed for the task at hand. Moreover, he was trapped by those antimagic collars; he couldn't free himself, or he would have done it already, which meant she would be able to barter his freedom for an oath from him to assist her. As the slaver hurried off with her pearls, Serina moved to the edge of the stone block, looking up at the man she had just purchased. Blue eyes bored down into her golden brown ones, narrowed with distaste.

"I *am* a free man. I am no one's slave!" the foreigner asserted in a sharp-edged baritone. If he had been bought by anyone else, Serina guessed his innate arrogance would have inclined his owner to whip humility into his spine. Certainly he had enough pride in his attitude for her to believe he was the Lord Chancellor of some foreign land, even without a Truth Stone to verify his claim.

"I have paid for you, Lord Dominor, for a very specific purpose," Serina informed him as one of the slave market's servants unlocked the nonmagical fetters from his wrists and ankles, leaving behind the rune-marked ones. "You will accompany me to my inn, where you will be cleaned, clothed, and fed, and where we will discuss in private what that purpose is. You will then give me a mage-oath that you will help me fulfill my task and not seek retribution against me for these indignities.

"Once your oath has bound you to not harm myself or my companions, I will release the manacles restricting your power so that you can assist me as I require . . . and, once my task has been completed, I will personally see to it that you are returned to your people, safe and sound, and freed from all further obligations to me.

"Until that time, you will follow me and obey my commands . . . unless you *wish* to be chained to a royal bed, never to see your homeland again?" she added rhetorically, arching a brow. "Those manacles only prevent you from using your power directly. They will not prevent your seed from having its potential spread among Her Majesty's daughters."

He drew in a breath, his blue eyes narrowing, ready to argue the point.

"You would be treated like a bone passed between dogs," Serina informed him bluntly. "Or rather, they would keep you like a prized stud and pass you out to anyone the Queen desires to reward with a crop of potentially powerful mage-daughters, until you were too old and worn out to rise to the demands of their genealogical ambitions. So. Either come with me and determine your own future, or stay here and have no choice in the matter."

Stepping down from the slave block, the foreign mage eyed her warily. "How long will this task of yours take, exactly?"

"Hopefully no more than a year. But we will not discuss it here. Come," she ordered again, turning toward the gate out of the market yard. He followed her, as she knew he would. The man had no choice, really; not if he wanted to have his powers released from his enchanted restraints.

FOUR

At least she had given him leave to follow her of his own free will . . . such as it was. For a moment, Dominor wanted to rebel against her command—Gods, he wanted to balk and rail at the whole of this situation! But at the moment, his position was not just bought and sold like a rug in the marketplace. He was also shoeless, coinless, and magicless. Not exactly a good position to be in, when stranded in a foreign land.

Unlike his two elder brothers, Dominor had not excelled at the fighting arts. He had not failed at his weaponry lessons, and he wasn't the least of his brothers when it came to fighting, but he was not a natural-born warrior like Saber and Wolfer were. Grabbing a weapon and fighting for his freedom wasn't his style, anyway, not when it was against overwhelming numbers.

Of course, padding barefoot through the cobbled streets of a foreign town wasn't his style, either. Not when the refuse-sweepers hadn't been by recently to catch the dung and the shards of broken pottery that made him walk very warily in his purchaser's wake.

The woman, Serina, turned and waited for him at a cross-section among the rows of stalls. Her pale brows pinched into a frown at his slow approach. "Can't you keep up?"

"Not unless I want to cut and infect my feet, woman," Dominor retorted, almost stepping on a rusted, twisted bit of metal lodged between two of the weatherworn paving stones. He almost missed seeing it from the need to look up when he answered her and had to look down again to watch his footing more carefully. An infection in a foreign land was not something he needed to add to his troubles. "How far do we have to go?"

"Five more blocks to the inn." Serina, watching him grimace and maneuver carefully over the cobblestones, paused in thought. She knew he was in desperate need of a bath, because she was currently downwind of the man; he would also need measuring for new clothes, everything from his head to his feet. She had some spells that could create clothing out of fabric, leather, and thread, of course, so she could make his garments herself if necessary. There were just two problems: One, she had to get the materials on the way, since she didn't trust him enough to stay put at the inn; and two, hers was the only room where he could stay.

Between the regular patrons and the nuns, the establishment they had selected to stay in upon their arrival last night was very full. Serina was lucky to have received a room to herself. Certainly, he couldn't bunk with any of the nuns. Not only were they already two to a room, they were from an order that forbade carnal relations with men. It would be cruel to tempt them with the specimen of maleness this foreigner was—most of the nuns of Koral-tai were lovers of women, but not all of them were strictly of that preference. *No, he'll have to stay in my chamber. And bathe there. I might even have to delouse him with a few spells, too . . .*

Moving onward, she turned a corner and headed down a row of stalls, detouring slightly. This street in the marketplace had rows of tailors, milliners, cobblers, and other sellers of garments and their accessories. Some of them held bolts of fabric. Kidnapped as he had been, the man literally had only the clothes on his back. On the one hand, she had him literally in a bind; he *would* spell-vow himself into aiding her before she'd agree to release his final bonds. On the other hand . . . she needed him in a cooperative mood, in order to get that oath sworn before his release. That meant showing him kindnesses in advance, as a show of good faith.

Or as Mother used to say, lead with the carrot and guide with the stick, to keep your unruly goats from straying off the path . . .

Dominor thought she was just pausing again to let him catch

up to her, until she gestured with a sweep of her slender hand at the bolts of cloth displayed on awning-sheltered shelves.

"Why don't you select some fabrics? I'll have them made into garments for you."

These were not inexpensive fabrics, Dominor decided, casting his eyes over the materials. Finespun linens and cottons lined the stall. They weren't the best quality; those kind of fabrics would be found in actual buildings, guarded and measured by the thumb-length. But these weren't shabby, either. They were the sort of materials he wore when he was working, not when he was playing the Court Mage.

For anyone else, though, they would be considered fine clothes, above the cut of the ordinary citizen. He could live with that. There was also no question that the woman could afford it; he'd had a front-row view of her immense wealth, the same as the other woman bidding on him, and the slave merchant selling him, and most of the other would-be buyers back at the marketplace.

If she wanted to buy clothing for him, Dominor wasn't going to quibble. In fact, he felt that she as a Natallian owed him for the indignities he had suffered in the past few weeks. He would push a little to see just how much she would buy for him and see what she intended to offer to entice him to work for her.

He hadn't had much of a chance to escape while trapped on a ship sailing the breadth of the southern ocean. Now that he was on land, he had a few more options available to him, awkward though escape might be while still magically bound. Clothing would definitely help, however.

Casting an eye over the bolts, he studied the selections. Pastels seemed to be in favor at the moment, but there were a few bolts of the darker, richer shades that he preferred. "That dark red, that deep blue, the deep green, and the gray at the back, for trousers and tunics. At least five double arm-lengths of each. The white and the cream, there, ten double arm-lengths apiece, for undershirts and under-trousers. And twenty double arm-spans of that trim there, the fifth . . . no, the sixth one from the left, on the second row of spools from the top."

Nodding her head at the cloth merchant, Serina directed the woman to start measuring out the material he requested. Dominor pushed a little further.

"I will also require socks and footwear, a belt, a pouch, a cloak to shed the rain—a finespun wool with a tight, felted weave, preferably in a dark green—and of course a clasp. A brush and a comb are essential, and some high-quality soap, something thrice milled. Softsoap, if this barbarous land has even heard of such a civilized thing. And some cologne," he pressed. "Nothing flowery, but it should have a clean, pleasant scent, something suitably masculine."

That made her eyes narrow, letting him know he was definitely pushing the boundaries of his requests. They were odd eyes, given her pale tresses; all of her hair was platinum blond, almost albino-white, from her hip-length braid to the brows and lashes guarding her eyes. Her eyes, however, were a tawny, rich brown. Not the blue or pink one expected to see in someone with hair that light and fine. And her skin was lightly tanned, golden from the sun, not milk-complected. She was clad in a sleeveless, tightly laced vest and fitted trousers vaguely like the garments his sister-in-law favored, though these were cut and stitched from travel-worn white leather, not from aquamarine silk.

She was pretty in an exotic sort of way, this wealthy, pale-haired woman. She also didn't look completely like the other women around here. *Maybe she isn't a Natallian by birth . . .*

Dominor's sharp mind mulled over the question of where she had gotten that fortune in rare, iridescent pearls. Sea-pearls were rare enough; they rated equal to emeralds and diamonds in their value, but it was the rainbow-pearl that was the rarest jewel in the world. It was quite possible that this mage knew the source of those pearls, both to own so many and to be so casual about buying him for ten of them. That was a fortune that could have bought the County of Corvis, his former home, and two or three of the demesnes around it as well. *If* they were for sale, of course. Given the sheer number dangling from the chains she had displayed, she could almost have bought a whole kingdom.

She didn't say anything about his arrogant demands, though. Serina just paid for the cloth with several gold coins, handed him the bundled sections of fabric to carry, and led him to another stall farther down the market row. It was a leather seller's; she bought a large, black-dyed hide and a brass buckle, ignoring the premade belts. The next stop was a wool merchant, where she bought a couple arm-spans of a lightweight dark gray wool, and then a stop at the spinner's stall, where she bought a few skeins of finespun thread, a pair of scissors, and a couple of needles stuck through a scrap of paper, all of it wrapped in a scrap of muslin to keep the purchases together.

His arms were rapidly filling up with the burdens she was buying. Serina stopped a passing peddler woman long enough to buy a couple of deep-woven baskets. That allowed her to shift the purchases in his arms into the handled carriers, which in turn allowed him to balance the load and see where he was putting his bare feet. Their next stop was a booth selling a variety of items. One of them was a small leather case containing a tiny pair of trimming scissors, a comb, hairbrush, razor, mirror, tweezers, sea sponge, and even a small lathering-brush-and-cup set. To his surprise, she immediately ordered one from the proprietor.

Along with that, she purchased a pot of softsoap. Dominor felt mollified that she considerately offered the various scented pots for him to sniff since his hands were busy with the baskets. The one he chose with a nod of his head was scented with sandalwood. It seemed to be a more common perfume around here than back home, where it was considered exotic and expensive. Then again, the remarkably busy streets were filled with sellers of exotic-smelling herbs and spices, unfamiliar flowers, and strange-looking fruits. *Sandalwood has to grow somewhere, around the world . . .*

Her generosity made him suspicious about just what, exactly, this woman, Lady Serina, wanted him to do. She was being nice in purchasing such fanciful necessities. All he really needed were a change of clothes, a comb, shoes, and a bar of soap. A toweling cloth of some kind would be nice, too, though he doubted these Natallians would know about the luxurious, nubbly, loop-woven fabric that Kelly had introduced to him and his brothers. Before that, all he and his brothers had known in the way of such things were plain cotton cloths, the same unbleached sheets that the Katani of his former homeland wove.

By the time they reached the inn, he had bruised his feet on unexpected rocks, stepped in things left behind by various animals, been stared at and bumped into by too many foreigners, stretched his arms under the weight of the baskets, and was nearly ready to beg for that promised bath. His stomach growled loudly at the aroma of the food being cooked in the inn's kitchen—he could've eaten stale bread and moldy cheese with relish, he was so hungry. The food during the second half of his journey by sea had consisted of a bland, paste-like gruel, without even the slightest hint of meat for flavoring. The portions hadn't been very big, either, but that hadn't been a bad thing. The gruel had sat in his stomach like a mushy rock, and the stench of his fellow captives had unsettled his stomach enough that even the small servings had seemed dangerous to consume at times.

Letting him into her rented chamber, Serina wrinkled her nose at the stench of the man. It wasn't pleasant without the breezes down in the streets to disperse most of the smell. *Well, that isn't entirely true; some of his odor smells pleasantly musky. Very male.* She fancied the sandalwood he had chosen would go well with his personal odor, once he was clean . . .

The rest of him just stank. Tracing a symbol on the door in chalk to ward and lock it against intrusion, she eyed her guest. He was studying the room in turn, with its small table and two chairs, the double-person-sized bed, the rack of shelves for storing personal goods, and the door in the side wall that led to the refreshing chamber.

Taking the baskets from him, Serina set them on the bed, plucked out the leather satchel with its toiletry supplies and pot of softsoap, and crossed to the other door. "In here . . . Dominor, was it?"

"Lord Dominor, Chancellor to Her Majesty, Queen Kelly of Nightfall," Dominor corrected, feeling filthy and lowly, and desperately in need of asserting his civility and noble-born status. He lifted his chin as he spoke to her. "Thirdborn son of the late Count Saveno of Corvis. I prefer to be addressed by my title."

Serina narrowed her eyes, studying her one and only slave. "Let us get one thing straight between us, *Lord* Dominor, Chancellor to Her Majesty of Wherever. I, too, have a number of titles. I am Lady Serina Avadan, firstborn daughter of the Inoma Ilaiea Avadan, who is the foremost leader of my homeland—my mother is the equivalent of a mage-queen, in other realms, which makes *me* the equivalent of a royal princess. I am the Guardian of Koral-tai, which is an ancient nunnery located at the Heart of Natallia, and from what I can tell, at least one of the six most powerful mages in all of this land." Stepping closer, she tried not to breathe too deeply as she added bluntly, "Now, we can trade titles and ranks back and forth all day long, or you can shut up, clean up, and *put up* with me calling you *just plain Dominor.*"

He blinked at her vehemence. Dominor hadn't thought it possible, but it was: Here was a woman even bossier than Saber's new wife! For a brief moment, his unsettled mind wondered what it would be like to have two strong-willed women running around Nightfall, then he shook it off.

"In return," Serina continued more calmly, stepping back so that she could breathe more comfortably, "you may also dispense with formalities, and call me Serina . . . when formalities are not necessary between us. You will give me respect when and where necessary, however. I am a Guardian, after all, and your hostess during your stay in this land."

Lifting his chin slightly, Dominor inwardly acknowledged her point. Outwardly, he challenged, "Respect must be earned. If it is forced, it is worthless."

"I think I have earned a certain level of respect, already," she returned, looking and sounding as cool as an icicle in her white leather vest and trousers, with her pale hair spilling over her shoulders.

"You *bought* me!" he protested. "How can I respect that?"

"I *saved* you from being bought by someone else! I only need your services for a short while, a year at most. Anyone else would want to bind you to them forever. And they would not be so generous regarding your needs, as I have already been." She lifted the toiletry satchel in her hand, casting him a pointed, tight smile, then thrust it at him. "Now, go into the refreshing room and clean yourself thoroughly. You stink."

Since he couldn't argue with that, Dominor took the satchel and passed through the door she had opened. The room had a water-flushed toilet, a sink with levers next to the spigot . . . and an odd, small stall with an oilcloth curtain, a drain in the floor, a pipe high on the wall that crossed from one side to the other, perforated in several places along its underside, and more levers like the ones at the sink. These were set in the wall of the alcove, not behind the curve of a table-sunk basin. But there was only a very small lip on the near edge of the ceramic-tiled basin, and it certainly wasn't big enough to crouch in, anyway, unless the bather wanted his knees to poke up around his shoulders. Confused, he set the satchel on the counter holding the sink and leaned out of the refreshing room.

"Serina, where is the bathtub? How can I bathe, if there is no tub?"

One of her blond brows quirked. "Have you not seen a show-ering stall, before?"

"Would I be *asking* if I had?" Dominor retorted, uncomfort-able with his ignorance over the local plumbing.

Sighing, she stalked into the bathroom, squeezing carefully past him so that his clothes wouldn't touch her own. Twisting the levers in the stall, she turned on the water, letting it shower down out of the perforated pipe crossing overhead. "This lever is for hot water, this one for cold. Adjust it yourself. The towels are here, and *do* use the soap everywhere."

He made a face at her back as she left, but as soon as the door closed behind her, Dominor was more than happy to strip off his sailor's rags. In fact, he would be happy to burn them, save that he didn't know how soon he'd have real clothes of his own. The door opened again without warning, just as he dropped the last filthy scrap on the floor.

"I'll need to take some measure . . . ments." Serina stopped and blinked. First at his lean but muscular, tall backside, and then at his front as he twisted reflexively to face her. She hadn't seen such a perfect body in a very long time, notwithstanding the dirt and the scraggly beard. Perhaps not even since taking her first lover, which had been almost a decade ago.

But that had been an athletic youth of nineteen. This was a fully grown man, probably in his late twenties much like her, and just beginning to tap into his prime. A tall, dark, handsome, fully proportioned man. He wasn't a hairy man, either, which relieved her; she had never cared for men who were almost as furry as a proverbial bear, never mind a literal one.

On the one hand, Dominor was irritated at having his pri-vacy broached without a by-your-leave. On the other hand, he was rather flattered that he had derailed her train of thought. If he'd had a third hand, he might have used it to cover a certain exposed portion of his flesh that thickened and rose at her bla-tant, head-to-toe perusal . . . but because she was admiring *all* of him, he decided to not bother. He felt justifiably proud of his figure, filthy though it might still be. Hands shifting to his hips as he faced her fully, Dom arched one of his brows at her. "You were saying?"

Serina closed her eyes for a brief moment, regathering her scattered thoughts. Opening them, she fixed her gaze firmly on his face and nothing else. "I need to take a few measurements.

I also need to know what style of clothing your people wear. It will probably not be exactly like what you are accustomed to, but it should at least be comfortable."

His other brow lifted for a moment. She probably knew spells much like the ones his twin wielded. Dominor explained Katani fashions to her; his hands outlined his words, redrawing her attention to his figure as he gestured. "We wear clean, simple lines. Tunics with a slight taper inward at the waist, which fall to midthigh on a man. Trousers with a straight-legged cut and an overlapping, laced front for the men. Outermost tunics can be opened down the front much like a vest or simple doublet, and the sleeves of each layer can be absent, elbow-length, or wrist-length, depending upon the weather, function, and time of year.

"The current style of ornamentation calls for embroidered trim to form swirls and abstract lines over the shoulders and halfway down the chest," he described, tracing his fingers down over his nipples and ribs. A spark of male mischief within him was interested in seeing just how much he could distract her, since it was clear he could distract her at least somewhat. "The cuffs of the sleeves are decorated halfway up the forearm for the longer ones, halfway up the biceps for the shorter ones. The hem is also often decorated for at least a hand-span in depth. Trousers, if not tucked into boots, are ornamented halfway up the calves. There is no collar on an outer tunic, though there may be a short, rounded one for an under-tunic."

Thankfully, Serina had a firm ability to concentrate through most distractions. Part of her mind was puddling in feminine fascination when he trailed his fingers over his chest and tapped the edge of his hand against his thigh, but part was still able to register his descriptions. Nodding when she had a fair idea of what he meant, she turned and left.

As soon as the door was closed between them, however, she sagged back against the panel, careful to not make a sound. It wouldn't do for him to know just how distracting his body was. He was sharp-witted, just on the civilized side of sharp-tongued, and she suspected it would take the threat of leaving his powers in their chains to get this particular mage to cooperate with her plans. Somehow, Serina didn't think a year-long delay before being returned to his home would be appealing to the "Lord Chancellor" standing naked in her refreshing room.

Sighing, she pushed away from the door, moving toward the

baskets of fabric on the bed. Then winced, spun determinedly around, and crossed back to the bathroom, suppressing a groan at her own stupidity. Of course, there was a very good reason for her distracted state . . . A moment of hesitation, and she chose to knock this time, rather than just barge in again. *Not that the view was bad, Moons, no . . .*

The door opened a crack, blue eyes meeting tawny brown. "Yes?"

Her cheeks heated in a blush, making her feel awkward. There was only one way to get around her embarrassment, and that was to brazenly embrace the reason for it. "The view was so distracting, I forgot to measure you. I'll need to be let in for a moment, in order to do so."

Dominor hesitated. He was admittedly out of practice in dealing with women, but even when he'd lived back on the Corvis lands, the local women hadn't been nearly so straightforward as this. It didn't help that his manhood twitched, reminding him that it hadn't exactly gone back to sleep after she had left. If he opened the door, she'd see his continuing, unabated interest in her.

However, whatever she had in mind for him, he didn't think it was for breeding purposes. Given how blunt the other women in this foreign port had been about such matters, surely she would've already said as much without hesitating.

"If you want that fabric turned into clothes, I *will* need to measure you," she prodded him, impatience coloring the edges of her voice.

"Fine." Stepping back, he opened the door wide, letting her see him in all his Gods-wrought glory. Dirty glory, and desperate for a bath glory, but glory all the same. Once again, her gaze slid down over his frame. This time, she wrested it quickly back up to his face again, giving her head a little shake. Dominor took some pride in his ability to distract her. He also found her level of willpower admirable despite that distraction.

Lifting her hand with two fingers raised, the rest curled out of the way, she muttered something. A bright ribbon shot from her first two fingers and flicked itself over his body. The touch of the glowing ribbon tickled as it measured him literally from head to foot, whipping around his scalp, then his throat, both above and below the rune-scribed collar. It slithered across the breadth of his shoulders, down one arm, circling him at elbow, wrist, and

manacle, then snaked its way up the inside of his arm before encircling his chest at several points.

Honey-brown eyes narrowed slightly in concentration, she
kept her fingers extended as she followed the shimmering tape
whipping its way down over his hips. A moment later, Dominor
gasped from shock as the ticklish-cool ribbon first circled his
half-hardened member, gauging its diameter, then measured the
length of it. Before he could do more than blink twice, it slipped
between his legs in order to wrap around his thigh, then dangled
down the side of his limb while taking his inseam. A few more
rapid measurements had it at his feet, sizing them, before it flew
back into her hand, where it coiled itself into a silvery cylinder.
Lifting his gaze back to hers, he found her cheeks sporting distinct blooms of color.

"My apologies. The spell is, um, designed to be very thorough."

Dominor covered his groin with his hands, feeling abruptly
overexposed with *that* little stunt. "What in the Gods' names was
it measuring *that* for?—If you try to make me wear one of those
silly Mandarite cod-things, I'll choke you with it!"

Serina wrinkled her nose. "Certainly not! They're absolutely
ridiculous for one thing. For another, you'd probably get yourself
lynched if you wore one here in Natallia. The spell I used is
just . . . thorough. When I use it on myself, it measures my breasts,
after all."

Unable to come up with a suitable retort that didn't delve into
topics two strangers really shouldn't discuss until they knew each
other better, Dominor grabbed the edge of the door, slamming it
shut between them. Then he leaned forward and thudded his forehead against the solid boards. "Kata's Sweet Ass . . . *don't* think
about her breasts."

It was no use. It was like telling oneself to avoid thinking
about pink pookrahs. The long-fanged, vicious wardogs would
inevitably lope into one's mind, their short fur dyed a spectacu-
larly unnatural shade of pale red. Suppressing a groan, he turned
back to the water still falling from the pipe in the tiled alcove,
snagging the jar of softsoap and the sea-sponge from his new toiletry supplies.

As tempted as he was to touch himself, to relieve some of the
ache caused by her words, her stare, and that extremely friendly
measuring spell, he needed to be clean even more. First he'd use

a liberal application of soap from head to toe, then he'd lather up his beard a second time and shave it off with the razor from the kit. And then he'd probably scrub himself a second time. Maybe even a third.

By preference, Dominor bathed every single day. There was plenty of water on Nightfall, and he could refresh the heating spell for his bath himself whenever it ran out, which was roughly once a year, given the rate he bathed. Going so long without being able to properly clean himself in these last few weeks had left him loathing his situation above and beyond civilized bearing. He had been patient, abiding his time with the other prisoners, but he hadn't been happy about it.

Out in the bedchamber, Serina was berating herself, if for a different reason. She was doing so silently, as she heard him thumping his head and the unintelligible, door-muffled mutter that followed it. *Why did you have to measure his manhood? You aren't measuring him for that silly Mandarite codpiece-thing! You had no reason, other than pure prurient interest, to measure his masculinity! Gods, it's not even been nine months! You are* not *that desperate for contact with a man!*

Well, I do *have the ritual to prepare for, hopefully with his delectable assistance*, she allowed with a thoughtful shrug. Then winced and shook her head. *Get your mind out of the midden heap, and back onto your work! He'll not be in there forever, and he'll need clothes when he emerges.* Snapping her fingers, she started enchanting the scissors, needles, thread, and piles of material to begin measuring out the necessary garments. Trying not to think of everything the tape had wrapped itself around, she pulled out one of her slates to make a sketch of what she wanted the tailoring spells to fashion for him.

With a damp toweling cloth wrapped around his hips, his borrowed shirt and trousers left in a smelly heap on the floor until such time that they could be gleefully burned in a bonfire, and his face as smoothly shaved as a physical razor could manage, Dominor padded into the bedroom. He couldn't get very far; the air was filled with garments assembling and stitching themselves. The sight impressed him; not even his domestically oriented twin had ever bothered to cast so many spells at one time. And not just trousers and tunics, either; there were even a pair of needles plying their way through the black-dyed leather, stitching the second half of a pair of boots as he watched.

It was an intricate dance imbued with subtle sounds as the needles stabbed, the threads unspooled, and the fabric rustled. Another sound also filled the air, the smack and scrape of chalk on a slateboard. It wasn't until the garments finished folding themselves neatly onto the bed that Dominor managed to spot his unusual hostess. She was on the far side of the room, next to a small table. From somewhere, she had procured a large slateboard and was busy marking out a very complex equation. Some of the figures marked on the matte gray surface moved magically, changing positions with each other at her direction; others rotated in place or orbited around their neighbors.

Intrigued, Dominor moved closer. Mathemagics—one of the few magical written languages that was the same wherever one went on their world—was a difficult discipline to master. Most mages didn't bother beyond the basics required to calculate amounts of ingredients and outcome effects for new potions, or the general effects of a new spell, such as its duration or the total mass to be affected. It could be used to great effect in the hands of a talented arithmancer, but it required careful study. Dominor was better than most of his brothers at the discipline, but whatever this woman was working on, it was beyond his immediate ability to grasp. A fact which irritated him.

"What are you working on?"

She gasped and whipped around, startled. With the chalk in her left hand and the fingers of her right tangled in one of her pale, thigh-length locks, she looked like a young student caught writing something naughty on the classroom slates . . . like he and his brothers had once done. Untangling her fingers, she lifted her chin, visibly regathering her composure. "I'm attempting to work you into the final equation. It's only a rough sketch so far, since your powers are bound and thus a mostly unknown quantity . . . but I think you will be able to assist."

Dominor frowned. *She's treating me like a mathemagical formula? Or rather, a variable, nothing more than a component of some spell?* He didn't like the sound of that. "What exactly is this 'final equation'?"

"Erm, yes . . . why don't you put on your clothes, while I order some food, and then we can discuss it while we're eating?" Serina offered, moving closer to the table.

The needles finished their work with his boot and the decorative trim on his jackets, settling neatly on the foot of the bed next to his new clothes. Dominor shifted to join her at the table, but that brought her close enough for him to smell. He wrinkled his nose, lifting his hand and taking a step back. "Why don't *you* go take a shower and change into something clean?"

"What?" Tawny eyes widening, she blinked at him. "What do you mean?"

Debating whether to be subtle or blunt, Dominor settled for blunt. "You reek of horse and sweat."

"What? Oh, my riding leathers! I haven't had a chance to clean them in the last few days. I suppose I should change out of them," she muttered. "I put them on this morning, since the nuns like to have outriders guarding the wagons at all times, and I just never changed out of them. Here, let me order the food, first. What would you like to eat?"

"Nothing too heavy or greasy," Dominor told her. "And *nothing* even vaguely resembling Natallian gruel."

Her mouth quirked up at the corner. "You have my sympathies. Even up at the Retreat, I've heard how terrible the Navy's food can be. How about soup and some greens? That should sit well in your stomach, after being abused for who knows how long . . ."

Nodding, he watched as she opened one of the saddlebags sitting next to the table and extracted a small scrap of paper and a charcoal stylus. Scribbling on it in the angular Natallian script, she pulled some silver coins from her pouch, wrapped them into the paper, and snapped her fingers. The twist of paper vanished. Straightening, she snapped her fingers at the slateboard. The chalked figures faded into the gray surface, and the bed-sized board shrank itself down to the size of a plate. Setting it on the table, she grabbed the other saddlebag and nodded at him.

"Get dressed and answer the door if someone knocks five times. It'll be a server with the food. Don't open the door if anyone else knocks. There might be a few people in this town willing to risk my wrath in order to get their hands on you. They'd be fools to try, but I'd rather not waste my time tracking you down again." A polite nod of her head, and she disappeared into the refreshing room.

Dominor watched her go and was tempted to open the door after a minute or two to try and catch *her* naked. Her slender figure was gently curved, with smallish breasts he suspected would fit easily in the palms of his hands. And that long hair of hers; he liked long hair on women, and definitely liked hair that held the soft shine of silk in its strands. Unfortunately, he was still a prisoner. Bought and paid for. *Somehow, I don't think walking in there and attempting to seduce her will get her to release me from these damned runes.*

She had bought him for a purpose, after all. What that was, he would have to wait until she was ready to reveal.

FIVE

The soup was good, rich with beef and vegetables; the greens were fresh and crisp, and tossed with roasted seeds and small strips of cheese in an odd sort of cream sauce that tasted of mustard and honey. It was a light meal compared to what he wanted to eat, but that was all right. Anything heavier, and his stomach would have probably rebelled. Setting down his spoon, Dominor eyed the woman across from him. She had just finished her own meal, nibbling on a last bit of cheese.

Resting his forearms on the edge of the small table, deliberately clunking his manacles against it, Dominor stared at her until she reluctantly looked up at him. She had clad herself in one of the local outfits, a sleeveless, side-slit dress and leggings that suited the midday warmth of the room. The pale pink shades of the odd garments looked good on her.

"Well?" he finally asked. He lifted one of his dark brows, as she hesitated.

Sighing, Serina gave in. This was bound to be one of the most awkward conversations of her life. She didn't want to whack him over the head with the blackmail of his magic-bound state to get him to cooperate, but somehow she suspected it would come down to that. "First, I want an oath from you that you will *not* discuss with anyone else the conversation we are about to have."

"Why?"

She rolled her eyes. "Because it is a *private* matter? Because I do not wish anyone else to know why I bought you? Because I am requesting it of you, the woman who gave you those clothes and that shower and this meal?"

Dominor bridled a little at her sharp rejoinder. Forcing himself to calm down, he asked, "What, exactly, do you wish me to swear?"

" 'I, Dominor of Whatever, bind unto my powers this vow: that I will not discuss with anyone else beyond the Lady Serina the contents of the conversation I will be holding with her for the next hour, without the Lady Serina's clearly expressed permission,' and so forth," she offered. "I'm aware that the oath-binding magic is the same in all lands that I've encountered so far, so no doubt you're familiar with the conventions."

He considered her wording. She wasn't asking him to bind himself to whatever her task was. There was no obligation on his part to do or say anything, other than to keep his mouth shut. "I, Lord Dominor of Nightfall, bind unto my powers this vow: that I will not discuss with anyone else beyond the Lady Serina the contents of the conversation I will be having with her for the next hour, without the Lady Serina's clearly expressed permission. So swear I, Lord Dominor of Nightfall."

Magic tingled over his skin, as soon as he sealed the vow with the traditional words. The manacles did not stop its progress. Oath-binding was too primal and too personal to be stopped by mere runes. Only the Gods Themselves could alter an oath made by a mage. That was one of the reasons why mage-kings and mage-queens were so popular around the world; when they swore to defend their lands, their magics were literally bound to that task.

"You have one hour. I will listen," Dominor informed her. "But I will make no other promises before I have heard everything and had enough time to carefully consider your proposal."

"Understood." Grateful he was now bound to not discuss anything about her project, Serina started with the truth. "There's a problem in Natallia, and by default, Mandare."

Dominor didn't bother to stop the snort that escaped him. "That's putting it mildly."

"Be silent and listen," Serina chided him. That earned her a dark look from those sky-blue eyes, but her audience subsided.

"The problem began roughly eight hundred years ago, when a pair of mages . . . um . . . copulated and created a sort of botched Tantric spell." At the arch of his dark brow, she tried not to blush. The topic was too serious for such things, but something about the mage seated across from her made her blush at the topic like an untouched maiden. Clearing her throat, she continued. "Anyway, the end result of the botched spell was that, of all children born within the influence of the spell . . . the magical potential of the males shifted into the bodies of females instead . . . thus causing a severe imbalance of mages in the two gender populations."

Both of his brows rose. "A botched Tantric spell created an all-female-mage nation and is the root cause behind the Mandarites kidnapping me so they could have a powerful male mage on their side? A botched *eight-hundred-year-old* spell? Lady, either you're lying to me, or there is something you are not mentioning. *No* spell lasts eight hundred years," Dominor countered brusquely. "Not unless it is a Major Working, one of the rare Permanent Enchantments—and I personally know of only three such spells in all the world." Dominor shook his head emphatically. "*No one* would permit a Permanent Spell to exist, if it were botched that badly. They would dismantle it as soon as they knew what was wrong, even if it took them another year!"

"Then I misspoke," Serina corrected. "Not so much a botched spell, as a . . . as an *inadvertent* spell. One they didn't realize they were creating . . . and since its effects were very subtle, it took literally decades for them to be noticed across the population as a whole. A couple of generations, in fact."

He leaned back, skepticism furrowing his brow. "Now I *know* you lie. Inadvertent spells do not last eight hundred years, either. Tell me another market-tale; this one is *fascinating*."

"They *do* . . . if they were cast in the heart of a Font," Serina confessed, waiting tensely to see how he reacted. Many mages would gladly lie, cheat, steal, and even kill, to have direct access to a Font. Just being around one strengthened one's magical efforts through a proximity-based absorption of magical energies; if the mage was strong enough to tap into the magic directly, it added force and effect exponentially. But he didn't look the least bit covetous.

In fact, he frowned at her in puzzlement. "A what?"

"A Font." Serina couldn't believe he hadn't heard of them.

Sighing, she explained as if to a non-mage. "It's a rare, physical wellspring of magical energy that—"

"Oh, a *Fountain*!" Dominor interjected, rewording her term. Ultra Tongue did allow him to understand the local language, making it sound as if the two of them were simply speaking an accented version of his native Katani . . . but some technical terms didn't always translate. "To my people, a 'font' is either a type of inkwell, or a style of lettering. You were confusing me, calling it a Font."

His mention of vocabulary sidetracked Serina with curiosity. "How is it that you come from a land I have not heard of, yet speak Natallian so fluently? You can't be wearing a translation pendant, or using a spell. Those would be canceled by your runebonds."

"As I said on the auction block, I have yet to meet a spell I cannot master. Including the crafting and brewing of Ultra Tongue," he informed her, pride lacing his tone with a touch of arrogance. He was the Master, after all, according to the Seer Draganna's prophetic verse, just as his twin was the Song. A moment later, her meaning struck him. "Wait—you said this couple *copulated*, and cast an accidental spell . . . in the heart of a *Fountain*?"

"Yes. To everyone in Natallia, I am the Guardian of the Retreat of the Koral-tai Nuns. But the Retreat itself was originally established as a place to hide and guard the Font of Koral-tai," Serina explained, content to know that, without her permission, he would never be able to tell another soul about its existence. "It's a particularly strong Font, too. It saturates the entire kingdom of Natallia, including the lands taken over by the rebel Mandarites. Because the inadvertent spell they cast was done in a, ah, rather *adventurous* location . . . it bound itself to the wellspring's energies and has since permeated and saturated the landscape.

"Now, according to my calculations," she continued, tapping the frame of her reduced slateboard with a fingernail, "it *can* be ameliorated. The balance of magics can be restored across the length and breadth of the land, evening out the distribution of magics across both genders within just a few decades, as is right and proper," Serina admitted. "But it has to be done in a very specific way. The 'botched spell' has to be recreated under very similar circumstances, which means in the heart of the Font, and fixed into place at the proper moments in time, exactly like the original was.

"In order to do that, I need several things," she continued, her left hand twiddling with a bit of her hair as her right gestured in accompaniment to her words. "Because the spell has saturated the local aether and has done so for roughly eight hundred years, it has a lot of momentum and weight. It cannot be easily moved; I cannot use anyone who is a native-born or a long-term resident of the area because their very being is permeated by the original spell. So no Natallians or Mandarites could help me reverse the effects; they're already saturated by the magic, and their very nature is resistant to the necessary changes. In addition, whoever enacts the ritual to change the original . . . well, it takes place in a Font, which causes its own host of problems, even without the saturation factor to consider."

"They'd need to be extremely self-controlled, able to concentrate on the ritual in question with single-minded determination in spite of their own pleasure, as well as being capable of withstanding that much energy during a very vulnerable moment in time," Dominor finished for her.

She nodded, looking pleased he had caught on to the requirements without her having to exhaustively explain anything. "Exactly. Mages who are powerful enough to tap into a Font are rare enough. To find one who is also disciplined and ethical enough to not meddle with the energies any further than necessary to right the wrong that was already done are even rarer. I'm sorry I had to buy you, but your presence as a foreign and potentially very powerful mage was like a gift from the Gods to me. Of course, it remains to be seen if you'll actually qualify, but I couldn't risk letting the opportunity you potentially represent slip from my grasp."

Dom was in two minds about her proposed task. One half of him was deeply excited by the prospect of working with a Fountain and thrilled to possibly work with what was essentially a Permanent Spell, but hopefully without the tedious, exhausting, yearlong buildup that most Permanent Enchantments required. The desalination system on Nightfall was one such Major Artifact; it strained the salt, algae, and other objects from seawater, providing the fresh drinking water that supplied the palace where he and his brothers had lived for the last three-plus years, thanks to their prophecy-imposed exile.

Dominor had long been impressed with the permanent structure and the magical efforts that had been required to create it. He had been somewhat envious, too. A Major Working such as that would make a name for any mage who could successfully complete such a task. This proposed task of hers was similar, in its own way; it was a monumental undertaking that would—if successful—alter the metaphysical landscape around it.

More than that, it was something none of his other brothers had done. He had the opportunity to be first at something; first and best, if he had anything to say about it.

The other half of his mind was very nervous about having to reenact a *sexual* ritual inside the heart of a Fountain. Sex was not only about control, to ensure that neither partner rushed too fast for the other to keep up; it was also about releasing control, in order to find the release of pleasure. The specific term for sexually cast enchantments was *Tantric magic*; some said the word *Tantric* was related to *tantrum*, to release a lot of emotional energy with very little control. It was not an easy discipline to master by any means because of that release. Casting magic successfully and safely was about control, not loss of control. Tantric magic was therefore counterintuitive, even harder to master than the mysterious logic of Mathemagics.

The problem was how to convey his doubts and unease to the woman across from him without looking weak or helpless. Thinking quickly, Dominor asked, "Have you ever performed Tantric magic before? I'm presuming that you—as the protector of this particular Font—would be one of the mages involved to make sure its energies are not abused."

Serina hated to admit it, but she really had no choice. "Not with a partner, no. Just the usual self-pleasuring sorts of charms and spells one does on one's own. Most of my partners haven't been mages, themselves. And yes, I would be one of the two mages involved. I need a strong, self-controlled mage to undertake the ritual with me. A male mage," she added, feeling her cheeks warm. "I'm not the kind of woman to be a Nun of Koraltai, seeking pleasures only among my own gender. I *definitely* prefer men."

Dominor felt his face heat as well. Same-gender pleasure sharing wasn't an unknown activity in Katan, nor an illegal one . . . but it wasn't a widely discussed one, either. Resisting the urge to clear his throat, he returned to his questioning. "How do you think to make this reenactment successful, if you haven't performed Tantric magic before?"

"Practice," she asserted, her cheeks as pink as her clothes. "Lots of practice. I figure at least a month's worth, once we return to the Retreat. Possibly even two. And then, when we have everything as practiced as possible, we enter the Font and re-create the first stage of the spell. Only our version would have the changes necessary to alter the spell permeating the realm."

" 'First stage of the spell'?" Dominor repeated. "How many parts of this spell did the original couple 'botch'?"

"Just the two parts. They didn't realize they were creating a spell at the time," Serina confessed. "At least, insofar as I've been able to tell from my scryings of the past."

That lifted his brows again. "You can scry the past as far as eight hundred years ago?"

She smiled at him. It wasn't quite a smirk, but it did have a slightly superior feel to it. "You forget, I am powerful enough to tap into the Font's energies to boost the extent of my own powers. I also have the mental discipline of an Academy-trained Mathemagician—that's the Drakeshan Academy of First Land, in the Draconan Empire. The Drakeshan Academy is renowned worldwide for the quality of its Arithmancers."

Biting back the urge to brag about his own accomplishments—which weren't nearly as impressive-sounding, given he wasn't a specialist mage like she was—Dominor asked instead, "So, when does this second stage take place, and what does it involve?"

"If everything goes right, it takes place roughly nine months later, again in the heart of the Font, in the form of a blessing."

"A blessing," Dominor repeated.

"Yes, a blessing," she confirmed, face turning pink once again.

Her reluctance and her blush made him suspicious. "What sort of a blessing?"

"Just a . . . a common one used all across the region. In both Natallia and in Mandare. Though not in Guchere, thankfully. By using the same blessing as was used originally, and which is used by everyone across the two lands, Natallia and Mandare," she explained, "it will cement the changes we'll make in the spell, effectively maintaining it like a Permanent Spell, but without needing to actually *be* a Permanent Spell. Or needing a mage to constantly recast it. The Font will provide the energies for the casting, and the blessing will be the trigger for the renewal of the spell.

"It's not going to be a fast cure; it'll be more than a decade before the change will be noticed by anyone," she added, "but ten to fifteen years from now, there should be as many boy-mages revealing their abilities with the onset of puberty as there are girl-mages. Though technically there would be half as many girl-mages in the future as there are now . . ."

"I see." He knew there was more to this than was being revealed, but she seemed to be dealing truthfully with him. "So . . . my part in all of this is to practice and enact a Tantric ritual in the heart of the Fountain with you and then nine months later, repeat the blessing in the wellspring to cement the alteration to the original spell?"

"Yes. And then I will return you to your home—in fact, if you live near a Font, I can send you there directly. To the other Font, that is," she added, making him blink. "I found the spell in an old Aian grimoire the nuns had in their library. It works perfectly well; I've used it to travel safely to the Font in my homeland and back."

That impressed Dominor. "How many Fountains do you know?"

"Oh, everyone knows about the Font back home," she dismissed with a shrug. "It's part of the Permanent Magics sheltering the Moonlands from the rest of the world."

"You're from the Moonlands?" he asked, frowning in disbelief. "I thought they were just a myth!"

"No, they're quite real. We just prefer to remain hidden."

Dominor sat back, studying her. The Moonlands were a place of legend, where dragons frolicked alongside people, where the food was said to be the ambrosia of the Gods, and where . . . where rainbow pearls were said to originate. "No wonder you could pay a fortune for me, if you come from the same place that rainbow pearls are supposed to grow! And the *myjiin* powder, the rarest but most important ingredient for the Ultra Tongue potion—it comes from there, too, doesn't it? That's why you have such a flawless accent!"

"Actually, I didn't drink any Ultra Tongue until after I left my homeland. There's no need for it in the Moonlands," Serina explained, shrugging. "We're very insular; most of us don't travel elsewhere, and we don't allow very many visitors. You have to know how to get through the protections cloaking my homeland, and that usually requires a personal invitation. They're not offered very frequently, as you can imagine."

"If it's such a paradise, with a Fountain and a fortune in rainbow pearls, why did you leave?" Dominor asked her, curious.

"I couldn't be a mage. You see, most of the energies of our Font are tied into a spell much like the Natallian one at Koral-tai, a spell that affects all mages from puberty onward. Their powers go toward the protection of the Moonlands shortly after they manifest. I knew I could be a mage, and I wanted to be a mage, but in order to actually *be* a mage . . . I had to live elsewhere. So, I did," she finished, shrugging.

"And your family did not object?"

"A bit, but I was insistent on leaving," Serina sighed. "I wanted to find my own place in the world, rather than be 'the sister of the Singer' for the rest of my life. My mother was a bit worried about my safety, but she gave me her blessing. And some friends of ours found me a sponsor to one of the Academies in . . . another kingdom." She had almost said, "in the neighboring kingdom." "So I traveled to the Dragon Empire and trained there, since I had already shown a talent for normal mathematics. It was thought by the Elders that I could make the transition into Mathemagics. The rest, as they say, is history."

Ever since the nasty civil war that broke the Sixth Land away from the other Five Lands, the renamed Moonlands had been very careful to hide their continued existence from the rest of the world. To the Dragon Empire, the Sixth Land had been turned into a veritable wall of impassable, barren mountains . . . and the Moonlands were indeed regarded as nothing more than a myth. Which was the way it should be. Certainly her people were very careful to protect the drakes that lived in their land, and the Holy Fruit, and definitely were very chary about letting outsiders get their hands on the rainbow pearls that grew only in the long, broad river valley of the former Sixth Land; her people used those pearls as their monetary system.

She eyed him as he absorbed her words, wearing the soft, dark blue cotton that had been crafted from one of the fabrics selected. She couldn't blame him for wearing the best of the outfits she'd made; no doubt he wanted to reassert his civilized nature after being treated for so long as an object rather than a human being. In his situation, Serina would've been just as needful of reasserting her humanity and her high status. Unfortunately, he was magically manacled, and at her mercy.

If this foreigner were to ever learn I only paid for him what I would've paid back home for a donkey—and a swaybacked one, at that—somehow I have the feeling the "Lord Chancellor" here would explode with indignation . . . The thought made the corner of her mouth quirk upward in a smile.

Dominor let himself enjoy how pretty she was when she smiled, but his curiosity had been roused. "Who or what is this 'Singer' you refer to?"

Uncomfortable at letting him learn too much, she kept her answer short. "The only person living permanently in the Moonlands who can still do magic, and consequently, the woman who is our leader." Changing the subject, Serina returned it firmly back to the task ahead of them. Her jealousy of her younger sister had not made her decision to leave easy, because she did love Kayla. It was just too hard to be merely the "sister of" somebody. "So. Now we come to the crux of the matter.

"I'd *prefer* your willing cooperation, Dominor. That will make it more likely for me to succeed. I could find someone else, but that could take me months, and take me away from my duties. Until I have completed the prophecy of Seer Milon, which is to counter the spell keeping the distribution of magery among the genders so unfairly uneven, I am obliged to protect the Font. But in order to find a foreign mage of sufficient power and control, I would have to travel beyond Natallian borders. That could take more time than my duties would allow me to spend."

Dominor frowned when she mentioned a Seer and a prophecy. *What are the odds I'd get mixed up with a woman who has her own Prophecy?* An unsettling thought crossed his mind. *What are the odds* this *woman is my predestined mate? Weeks have passed since I was kidnapped, after all. It's conceivable that Wolfer has encountered his own bride by now . . .*

A shiver crawled over his skin at the idea, though he couldn't tell if it was from revulsion or not. His situation was bad enough, after all, without throwing in his foretold entrapment at the hands of some unknown woman. He shivered again, this time closing his eyes briefly in a wince.

Kata's Tits . . . I am *trapped by my circumstance, at the hands of a woman bearing the title of "Lady"!* That thought made him eye her warily. She seemed smart and powerful . . . but that didn't necessarily make her "his" kind, as his verse in the Song of the Sons of Destiny decreed. *I'll have to watch her carefully, and my circumstances.*

Serina, seeing him giving her a dubious look, asked defensively, "What? You're here, you're in a position where I can get an oath out of you to cooperate—so that I know for sure you won't walk out mid-effort—and based on my preliminary calculations, you do seem capable of fulfilling the required role."

Based on her calculations? Dominor blinked at that. Her wording offended him. "You make it sound as if this were something clinical and cold, like . . . like dissecting a dead toad for potion ingredients, not lovemaking in the heart of pure magic itself!"

"It may be lovemaking in the heart of pure magic, but because it's pure magic, we have to be *extremely* careful in what we ourselves do," she retorted. "I don't want another botched spell to occur! This stupid civil war is the result of masculine resentment at not having any native-bred males born with magic in their own veins. The imbalance *has* to be corrected, and my calculations are the most reliable guide available for correcting the problem!"

"Yes, and you say I'm a likely candidate to help you correct that problem, but you hardly know me, Lady," Dominor pointed out. "How can you tell I really will be suitable for the task? You certainly cannot measure my power with any accuracy, considering that it's locked up by these Gods-be-damned manacles!"

"That's why they're *preliminary* calculations," Serina reminded him. "I'll know the exact effect once you've vowed to help me and I've removed your bonds."

"Wouldn't it be more useful to remove my bonds, take the necessary measurements, and *then* request an oath that I help you?" Dominor returned smoothly, quickly. "After all, a preliminary calculation might miss something vital, and you wouldn't want me oath-bound to help you, only to find that I'm utterly unsuitable when my abilities are calculated in full detail."

"It's easy to word the oath-binding to include the possibility that you aren't suitable after all," Serina dismissed. "If that becomes the case, you would be free to walk away."

Damn. He was hoping she hadn't considered that possibility. Frustrated, Dominor thunked his manacles on the edge of the table again. "I would *rather* offer to help you of my own free will."

"Because the spell requires a two-part attack, spaced roughly nine months apart," she countered, "I'd rather have you bonded to be there for both phases of the task, if it turns out your inclusion in the ritual is indeed adequate for the task."

Her choice of words lifted one of his dark brows. " 'Adequate'? I am never merely *adequate*, I assure you!"

"Then put your oath where your mouth is, and prove it!" she challenged him.

Dominor opened his mouth, then closed it warily. "What, *exactly*, would you have me swear? And will *you* swear an oathbond as well to remove my manacles, if I find my oath agreeable?"

That made her stiffen a little. "My honor isn't at stake!"

"Neither should *mine* be," he pointed out tartly.

"It is *my* task. I need your magics unbound and functional in the Font," she dismissed. "I'd *have* to release your rune-bonds. It's guaranteed by the very nature of what we'll have to do!"

"But it's not guaranteed that you'd release me any time soon," Dominor argued. "For all I know, you could wait until the moment before we entered the Font to release my shackles."

Serina snorted. "Hardly! I have calculations to make, remember? They will take some time to discern and refine; we will be required to interact sexually *and* magically, so that I'll be able to tell just how closely we'll have to copy the original ritual in order to be effective. I'll have to unbind you before we can practice, and we'll have to practice before we can enter the Font. And the longer I linger in this kingdom, the more saturated I will become with the same problem plaguing the rest of Natallia; I cannot afford to delay this ritual by too many months, without having to start the search for a foreign *female* mage, as well as a male one. You *will* be unbound quickly, if you agree!"

Damn, again. Dom was hoping she'd overlooked that little bit of logic. *Her mind is like a hair-trigger trap, in some ways . . .* As much as he wanted to admire it, Dominor was frustrated by it, and wanted her to know. "Do you know what it is like for me to sit here, kidnapped and taken far from my home, sold and bought like a side of beef, my powers unjustly bound, being *extorted* into obeying someone just to be free?"

"I can well imagine. But *I* am merely trying to be expedient!" Serina returned defensively. "The faster you agree, the faster your powers will be unbound, and the faster we can get on with the task at hand. Call me an opportunist if you must, but I feel like the Gods have dropped you into my lap as the answer to my dilemma!" He drew in a breath to protest, and she cut him off, guessing what he was going to argue. "Just because the Gods do drop the opportunity of you into my lap doesn't guarantee that you'll cooperate. I *want* that guarantee."

Her fingertip thumped into the planks of the table next to her soup bowl.

"Where is *my* guarantee?" Dominor returned, thumping the table with his own finger. "I deserve one, too, if I am to trust you."

"It's in the wording of the oath."

"What, exactly, would be that wording?" he challenged her.

Tapping her slateboard, she enlarged it a bit, summoning words to its surface. "It's all right here. I've calculated it as the base for this part of the equation spells I'll be casting. I've already figured all the angles, but if you can see something I've missed, by all means, make a suggestion."

Taking the rectangle from her, Dominor studied the script. It wasn't written in Natallian; this was a more circular font than the spiky angles he had seen on local shop signs. His eyes blurred for a moment, but within two blinks, he could make sense of the writing. "What language is this?"

"Draconan. Can you read it, or do you need a translation to Natallian?"

That made him roll his eyes up at her in a prodding look. "*Ultra Tongue?* I can read it, now that my eyes have adjusted. I just hadn't encountered it before now."

"Right." She looked away in her embarrassment, giving him the opportunity to read in silence.

The text was just as sharply defined as her verbal logic had been:

I (Name inserted here), bind unto my powers this vow: Provided my powers and abilities are proven mathemagically suitable for the task once they have been unbound and examined by Lady Serina, and swearing to stay long enough for my powers to be examined for the purpose of determining that codicil, I swear to assist Lady Serina Avadan to complete both parts of the Tantric ritual that will restore the balance of inherited magic between the genders born within the influence of the Koral-tai Font, occurring in both the lands of Natallia and Mandare. I further swear that I will not harm the nuns of Koral-tai during this whole process, nor any others residing at or visiting the Retreat at Koral-tai, nor attempt to steal control of the Font from its rightful Guardian, nor use its magic for any purpose not authorized by the Guardian of the Koral-tai Font while I am in residence at Koral-tai as an assistant and visitor. So swear I, (Name inserted here).

Dominor rubbed his razor-shaved chin, soothing the faint sting left behind by the blade. *She certainly has covered all the angles, restricting access to the Fountain, ensuring that I have to stay and be tested . . . and yet, it* is *a fair deal. I have to stay long enough to be examined, and I cannot harm anyone at this Retreat . . . but my powers would be unbound, and I would be free to leave if her calculations prove me to be less than perfect for the task.*

His inner competitive nature roused at that; he was *never* less than perfect, if he could help it. Even if it took a lot of practice.

Of course, his loins tightened at the thought of "taking a lot of practice" to learn this Tantric sex-magic ritual she wanted the two of them to perform. Whether the woman across from him clad herself in a vest and trousers—much like the clothing his sister-in-law Kelly preferred to wear, however oddly unfeminine the style—or in the panel-dress and tights that she now wore, Dominor couldn't deny she had an appealing figure. Slender, yet femininely curved.

Already his mind could envision her hair spilled over the white linens of . . . *Scratch that. She'd look best with that pale mane spilled over dark-dyed bedding, her naked body arching up into her lover's touch . . .*

Marshaling his thoughts firmly, Dominor read over the oath again. This was his chance at freedom, after all. If she didn't unbind him personally . . . he realized he was free to escape, if needed. So she had to hold to her word in order to get him to cooperate, or he wouldn't have to be held to his by his powers.

Clever woman.

He decided he could indeed admire her. Just a little. Picking up the slateboard, he braced himself, inhaled, and began. "I, Lord Dominor of Nightfall, bind unto my powers this vow . . ."

SIX

❧

Relief washed through Serina, though she did her best to not slump visibly in its wake. Certainly her mother wouldn't have approved of bad posture. Nor would her father have cared to see her displaying a weakness in front of an outlander, were he still alive. As soon as the magic of his vow finished rippling over his skin, Serina took back the slate, tapped it clean, and turned to root in her saddlebag.

"You do realize, of course, that if you do not succeed in unbinding these things, Lady," Dominor informed her, "I am not obliged to stay. The locks seem to be warded against any sort of magic used upon them, and as I doubt you possess the original key . . ."

"I don't need it," Serina admitted, digging through her belongings. "While I was studying some advanced courses in Artifact construction at the Magerium in Sul-a-Ven—that's in the kingdom of Guchere, east of here—I made the friendly acquaintance of a young man who was . . . shall we say, a purveyor of preemptively acquired antiquities?"

" 'Preemptively acquired antiquities'," Dom repeated, liking the delicate turn of phrase. "You mean, you made the friendly acquaintance of a *thief*."

"Well, at first it wasn't a *friendly* acquaintance," she allowed, glancing up briefly from her search.

"Oh?"

"Yes, I caught him trying to break into one of the lockers where the half-finished Artifacts were being kept between classes. I hexed him into obedience, made him give back everything that he'd stolen, then made him teach me how to open locks the mechanical way—ah! Here it is. I was worried I'd left it behind at the Retreat.

"Stick out your feet," she ordered him, extracting a rolled leather pouch and a large square of raw, undyed silk. One of his brows arched, but he turned his chair sideways to the table and extended his legs. He hadn't donned socks or boots, though he had donned undergarments, trousers and a tunic in the bedroom while she'd been showering in the refreshing room. Abandoning her chair, Serina knelt, examined the first of the manacle locks, and selected her tools.

It took a bit of poking and prodding, during which her pearl-bought assistant sighed twice in impatience, but she figured out the innards of the lock by touch as she had been taught, and released the first manacle. There were rubbed spots underneath the metal from weeks of wearing the damned things, but she didn't try a healing spell on him just yet. Not when there were four more to go. Oath-bound vows would bypass the manacles, as it was entirely self-contained magic, but healing spells wouldn't be nearly as effective.

Placing the rune-carved leg iron on the silk, she wrapped it in one of the corners, letting the raw silk dampen its antimagic capabilities. It couldn't prevent the runes from draining whatever it touched, but it would dampen the effects, and it would allow her to wrap it in leather to further muffle the iron's properties. A bit of exploratory prodding showed the lock of the other manacle to be made in the same way, which meant it was quick to release.

Straightening from her crouch, she had him put his wrists on the table while she tickled those locks open; they were different from the ones on his ankles, but similar to each other, thankfully. Each manacle was wrapped in a corner of the large square, leaving the center open, waiting for the collar binding the last of his powers.

Peering at the base of his throat, she found the keyhole for the neck collar directly under his chin. It was an awkward spot to work. Dithering for a moment with indecision, Serina reminded herself firmly that they were about to become Tantric co-experimenters and boldly straddled his lap. That made his eyes widen and his hands lift automatically to her hips, steadying her in place. Thankfully, her panel-skirts were slit high enough to make her position comfortable, but it left his wrists resting against her hose-clad thighs.

"Tilt your head back," she ordered him, standing to give him more room to maneuver. "It might help to slouch in the seat a little."

Dominor wriggled a little lower, until he could brace the nape of his neck on the highest rung of the chair's back. She reseated herself and set to work as soon as he held himself still. This lock was a little different from the other two sets, a little trickier, but it didn't take long for Serina to tickle it open with the help of her tools. Remaining on his lap, she twisted and set the collar in the center of the cloth, then tucked the manacles in around it as she folded the silk to insulate it.

An unfamiliar murmur made her glance back at the mage she had bought and freed. His hands had lifted while she was distracted, and now formed a ball of yellowish energy that looked much like a ball of string, if a ball of string had been made out of thin, racing strips of fire instead of fuzzy, winding strands of thread. Arithmancy used the same symbols worldwide, but the language of magic varied from place to place, and she wasn't sure what his intent might be. Especially with her seated right there on his lap, inches from his spellcasting.

He formed a second ball beside the first with another lengthy murmur, letting the first one hover on its own in midair. She knew he couldn't harm her, or the nuns with her here in the city, but she didn't recognize those spells. That made her nervous.

Warily, Serina asked him, "What are you doing?"

Dominor smirked and tapped the first ball. "Lord Kemblin Aragol, former Earl of the Western Marches." Extracting his finger, he watched the ball zip away from them, hesitate a long moment, then zag off to the side, vanishing through the wall of the room. He touched the other one. "Captain Mierran Falleska, of the Natallian warship *Bloody Waters*."

The second ball zipped out through a different wall after only a moment of hesitation.

"What was that all about?" Serina inquired again, even more curious now.

He kept his answer simple, though he continued to smile. Very few people messed with Dominor of Corvis and got away with it. "Vengeance."

"If you've just broken Natallian law—" Serina started to warn him. His smile cut her off, as did the hands returning to cup her hips.

"It's nothing overtly illegal, I assure you. I usually prefer subtlety over blatancy anyway, and this is a very subtle punishment." At her curious look, he smirked. "I just enchanted the two of them to tell the truth, the whole truth, and nothing but the truth . . . for a year and a day. In exchange for lying to me, and lying *about* me, landing me in this whole mess."

Her mouth fell open. Shock gave way quickly to a laugh of delight. "Sweet Moons! That's *devious*!"

Dominor inclined his head in a mock-bow. Serina smiled for a moment more, then remembered the rubbed spots on his skin.

"Here, let me heal you of any lingering harm from your captivity—"

"—I can do it myself," he interjected, brushing her hands away. Her presence on his lap was distracting enough; he didn't need to feel her fondling his chest.

"If *I* do it, then your state of health can be factored into my calculations. Put your hands down," she ordered him, flattening her palms against his tunic. Dominor complied, just as she remembered she needed her slate. Reaching over the bundle of silk, she brought it close, careful to nudge the wrapped manacles well out of the way with her forearm. It wouldn't do to erase the information stored in the magical slate, after all. Tracing the edge of the frame with her finger, she muttered the necessary words to record what would happen, then returned her palms to his chest.

Magic was a matter of focusing the mage's inner energies, shaping them into specific uses. A lot of it relied upon words and gestures, runes and images, for they were ways to confine and define the magic very concretely. Some of it relied upon awakening and stimulating the innate properties of magical plants and animals, usually brewed in potions and salves, sometimes in the materials used in Artifacts. But in the case of chanted spells, it was just what the mage was taught locally, or came up with on their own, that crafted each spell. That was why the language of magic was so imprecise and impossible to translate via Ultra Tongue, even if the precision required by the discipline of Mathemagics allowed Arithmancers to communicate via formulae, regardless of whether they could speak each other's languages.

Some spells were similar, being taught from mentor to pupil, and some were widespread. But some were more personally developed. Because of this, the healing spell she used on the man seated beneath her was just a simple muttering of words that were more a mnemonic to her than an actual spell, with the added impact of a direct touch to ensure that the carefully shaped energies impacted the correct target. Serina wasn't the Healer that Mariel was, but this much she definitely could manage.

She could also manage a discreet check for sexual or other health problems, with an added string of mnemonic syllables. Once again, Dominor's skin rippled with a sparkle of magic, albeit of a more silvery greenish hue than the pale golden ones of before. This time, the sparks lifted up off his skin, forming symbols that glittered for a moment, then darted into the slateboard on the table, recording themselves in chalk marks that quickly vanished, stored for later use. The symbols being revealed pleased her; he was free of disease, quite healthy, and ripely potent with virility. He could definitely sire a child for her.

Already, Serina could see in her mind some of what the arithmantic calculations would most likely be, once proven in chalk on slate. He would definitely be able to handle a Tantric ritual within the very heart of the Font. Provided they practiced said ritual, of course, and provided he had the opportunity to step into the Font under her supervision prior to enacting the ritual. Just being in the heart of pure magic that very first time was a rather giddy and overwhelming experience for most mages. She knew he'd need exposure to the powers beforehand, to know what he'd have to concentrate through when the time actually came . . .

Dominor now felt rather good. The lingering bruises and irritations from his manacles that he'd been forced to ignore along with his unwashed state had vanished. He was clean, neatly dressed, fully healed . . . and he had a beautiful woman on his lap who wanted to practice and perform Tantric magic with his help. The first woman he'd had straddling his lap in more than three years, in fact. All he had to do was see how willing she was to start practicing right away.

He started by cupping her hips. They were nice hips, gently

rounded with the curves of a woman grown, though Dom supposed she could do with a few more meals before they were perfect. *Or maybe childbirth would widen them a little more toward perfection* . . . Dominor blinked. *Sweet Kata—where did that thought come from?*

Oh, of course. Prophecy. "When Lady is the Master's mate" . . . *but what is that bit "Set your trap and be your fate" about? There is no trap here that I myself have set! I'm simply the victim in this particular matter.*

The healing spell ended. Serina didn't lift her hands from his chest, though. It was a nice chest, as she'd seen when she'd walked into the refreshing room, earlier. It certainly felt as nice as it looked, even with the material of his trim-decorated tunic caught between their skin. When his hands slid from her hips to her waist, arousing her with the ticklishness of his touch, she looked at his expression. Those sky blue eyes had darkened slightly. His palms slid to her ribs, making her breath catch. He was touching her intimately, already?

Fair is fair, Serina reminded herself. *You are essentially borrowing him for sex-magic. And he is a man; men do enjoy almost any opportunity to share pleasure with women.* Smiling, she slid her own palms sideways just a little. Right over his nipples. She knew she had the right spots, too, for they tightened enough to be felt through the cotton of his clothes. Lightening the pressure of her hands, she brushed them over those covered nubs, making him squirm and draw in a quick breath. He didn't squirm away from her touch, though. No, he arched into it.

Jinga! Dominor swore, feeling lightning searing between his chest and his groin. She had managed to ignite a fire in his body with the simple act. *Gods, grant me stamina—it's been too be-damned long since I was touched by a woman* . . .

There were . . . certain spells . . . that a male mage could use to crudely simulate the pleasures of sharing a bed. Ones for female mages, too, he was sure. And of course, there was self-pleasuring. But it wasn't the same thing as a real partner, and three years of celibacy was too long to go without a woman's touch. When his sister-in-law had been brought to Nightfall, Dom had worried for a moment that he'd lost the ability to be aroused by a woman out of sheer disuse. Kelly had arrived in her outworlder nightclothes, after all, but nothing had awakened within him when he had looked down upon the redhead that day.

Proximity to the feisty redhead, however, had proven why: She just wasn't his type, intellectually, emotionally, or physically. *Kata, sweet Goddess of Love . . .* this *one definitely seems to be my body's type . . . even if she's almost as thin as my sister-in-law.* Catching her hands, Dominor dragged them up to his mouth, kissing her palms one after the other. "Gently . . . I haven't been with a woman in a while."

"Then why don't we retire to the bed," Serina offered, sliding off his lap, "where you can recline in comfort while I test your responses to pleasurable stimulation. As a part of the testing requirements, of course."

He flicked his gaze up to hers, about to rebuke her for making a romp in the sheets sound as boring as an entry into a ledger, and caught the quirk of her mouth and her brow. She was teasing him. Arching one of his own brows, he accepted the hands she offered, allowing her to pull him to his feet. "Of course. That is why I'm here."

Since she had already seen him naked, Dominor didn't hesitate to remove his new clothes, tossing his tunic at a chair and stripping off his matching dark blue trousers. To his pleasure, she stripped herself just as readily, hauling the panel-dress over her head and removing her slippers, leaving her clad in her pale pink knit hose. Loosening the drawstring as he watched, distracted, she stripped those from her legs, and the abbreviated, legless under-trousers that lay beneath.

He couldn't wait; his chest ached to feel those half-an-apple sized breasts pressing against him. Pulling her close, he lowered his mouth to hers, pleased she was only a finger-length shorter than him. That made kissing her very comfortable. Dom didn't know how Saber managed anything resembling a comfortable kiss with Kelly, given how their redheaded "queen" was shorter than this willowy goddess. Not when this minor difference between his and Serina's height was perfect for embracing.

Looping her arms around his shoulders, Serina returned each nip and press of his mouth with one of her own. Their tongues met and tangled. There were a few brief moments of awkwardness, but they faded quickly enough as each tested and learned what the other liked. Certainly his technique was different than those of her previous lovers. Serina couldn't remember if her prior encounters had included the way he suckled her lower lip. He did so, not at the center, but toward one side. It turned her head naturally with the gentle pressure of his lips, allowing him to nibble his way to the curve of her ear. Shivering, she pressed herself into his body, hungry for more.

Somehow, Dominor remembered something important. Something very important. He couldn't remember when his calm breathing had turned into unsteady panting, or when her fingers had delved below the waistband of his under-trousers, though he did enjoy the way she cupped and kneaded the muscles of his backside. But he remembered something too important to forget. Pulling back slightly, he looked at her as she twisted against him.

"We need to talk . . ." He swallowed and focused as she ground their pelvises together, arching her head back. "We need to discuss . . . contraception. I'm really not interested in being a father . . ." *just yet*, his mind finished for him, his voice derailed by the sight of her breasts lifted almost in offering as she arched back even farther. She stilled in his arms, and he swallowed hard against the dryness in his throat, managing to repeat himself just a little, watching her blush becomingly. "You know . . . contraception? Something to prevent . . . pregnancy?"

Oh, Gods. He doesn't want *to be a father. Third Moon,* that's *awkward . . .* She felt her cheeks flushing with just how awkward the subject was. Composing herself, she straightened and cleared her throat. "Don't worry, Dominor; you won't have to be a father, if you don't want to be. It's my responsibility. I'll take care of everything."

Dominor wasn't sure why she couldn't quite meet his eyes. It didn't mesh, this cool-voiced awkwardness; not when contrasted with the heated passion she had displayed only moments before. "Are you sure? It won't take me that long to craft an anticonception amulet."

"I'm already wearing one," she dismissed. Torn between hoping he was compatible for the ritual, and now having to hope that he *wasn't* compatible, Serina dithered for only a moment, calculating what to do. She finally gave up and pulled him into a kiss, closing her eyes. *Brother and Sister Moon, if all I get to have from him is this one encounter, testing to see if it'll work between us . . . then it'll be enough to immerse myself in a moment of pleasure. Provided it's at least modestly enjoyable.*

You certainly know I've been far too celibate for my liking, stuck for the last two years in Your sibling-Goddess' enclave up in the mountains. You know I've only been free to come down into

*civilized lands a handful of times a year . . . and not always able
to find myself a decent bed partner when I do . . . and now You
send me this man. If he wants to participate . . .*

He lifted her off her feet and laid her on the bed, letting her
know he definitely wanted to participate. A tug at the drawstrings
of his under-trousers allowed them to slide to the floor, and a shift
of his weight permitted him to step free of the undyed cotton. Serina scooted back to make more room for him as he climbed onto
the bed. Catching her amulet-girded ankle as he knelt between
her legs, he lifted her limb, surprising her by pressing a kiss to
her toes. They curled in response, and he kissed the sole of her
foot. That made her leg spasm.

Dominor smiled. "Ticklish, are we?"

Serina didn't trust that smile. "Behave."

"No." Having gained his freedom from all but his oath-
sworn vow, Dominor was feeling naughty. Rebellious. Since he
knew she was freshly bathed and had been wearing clean hose,
he had no compunction against sucking her toes into his mouth,
starting with the littlest one. Sliding his tongue between each
digit, he worked his way to her big toe. From her moan and the
way she arched her back, he knew she was enjoying it. When he
sucked strongly on her largest toe, however, her hand flew to
her groin with a louder groan.

The sight of her playing with herself, rubbing and circling the
peak of flesh between her folds, was too much.

Grabbing her hand, Dom pulled it away. "Don't!"

Surprised, Serina opened her eyes. "And why not?"

He debated internally for an uncomfortable moment before
admitting roughly, "It's . . . it's been over three years since I was
with a woman. Don't tease me like that. I would prefer to last."

Her mind calculated that answer. Serina lifted her brows,
comprehending within moments what his problem really was.
Tugging her ankle free of his grip, she curled her body around.
"Then we'll just have to take care of that."

She made him choke on his own breath, just by wrapping her
fingers around his shaft. Closing his eyes, Dominor gave in to
the sensations she evoked.

Someone had removed his foreskin, Serina noted, mildly curious. She wasn't used to men who were so exposed, but figured it
was probably just a part of his exoticness as a foreigner. It would
have to be noted in her calculations, but it shouldn't harm the task

ahead of them. As much as she wanted to examine that difference in further detail, ask questions about his culture, his experiences, she had a specific task in mind at the moment.

A swirling lick of her tongue dampened the protruding rim, eliciting a sharp breath and an exhaled shudder. That allowed her to suck him into her mouth. He tasted clean, with a hint of salt-musk at the tip. Serina loved doing this; she loved the power it gave her over a man, making him gasp and tremble and bury his hands in her hair like this man was doing. Not to force her, nor really to guide her, just to anchor himself with her pale tresses as she pleased her partner orally.

Knowing that he hadn't been with a woman in three whole years seemed to add its own spice to her actions. Serina felt pleased to be the first one in such a long while to bring him pleasure, though she would have liked to ask why he hadn't been with anyone in all that time. Certainly his size was very nice; neither too long nor too short for a man of his height, and nicely proportionate in its thickness. A proper mouthful.

That thought made her want to giggle. Of course, her mouth was full, so she settled for a happy hum. That made him tense and suck in his breath again, stiffening. Amused, she did it again.

"Gods—!" The vibration wasn't much, but the tip of him had been resting against her soft-palate when she did that. Dominor tightened his buttocks, trying not to climax. This sensual, bold wench was going to do him in if she kept doing that.

Curious, Serina shifted her weight so that she was hunched over on her knees, and used her free hand, cupping his scrotum. He sighed. She bobbed her head and gently tugged on his nether-hairs. That made him groan. Sliding one finger down between his legs, she stroked the root of his manhood, tickling it, then slid her finger back just a little bit farther—Dominor stiffened and groaned roughly, his shaft twitching in her grip. Warm musk with an undertone of bitter sea flooded her mouth. She had successfully taken off the edge of his need, as promised.

Serina had never really cared for the taste of the men living outside the Moonlands. As soon as he finished the subtle but necessary flexing of his hips to bring him to the end of his orgasm and started to withdraw from her lips, she moved away, trying not to make a face. He didn't seem to notice, choosing to sag onto the bed on his side, breathing heavily. Leaning over the edge of the mattress, she discreetly spat her mouthful on the floor, then fluttered her fingers over the mess, banishing it. Twice more she cleared her mouth and wriggled her fingers to scour the age-worn planks, then Serina twisted around, stretching her body languidly beside his on the bedding.

Some outlander women loved the taste, but she just couldn't get used to it. Not when one of the side effects of the men of the Sixth Land eating the Holy Fruit was a distinct sweetening of their seed. Her first two lovers had been fellow Moonlanders, like her, but the subsequent ones hadn't been. Of course, she did have those ripe, stasis-preserved *myjii* in that chest she'd bought . . .

Just because we'll be reenacting the botched ritual doesn't mean our liaison has to stop the moment we're done with the first stage, she thought as he slid his hand over the soft, smooth skin of her stomach. *I don't think it would harm the ritual for us to share the fruit . . . and his seed would taste all the sweeter for a week afterward, if we shared it.*

I wouldn't want my child to be born outside of at least some form of wedlock, either. It's said that a bastard-born is tapped more often by the Left Hand of the distant Threefold God of Fate than with Their Right Hand, compared to those who are legitimate. Not to mention that here in Natallia, legitimate children are always preferred; the cultural unpleasantness toward a bastard-born often turns them into a bastard-by-nature. I wouldn't want that to happen to any child of mine. I don't know how long I would be staying, once the second stage of the ritual is complete; I might end up staying long enough for the local social niceties to be a concern . . .

We could drink and swallow the liqueur of the Holy Fruit from the same cup in front of witnesses when we share the flesh of the fruit; that's the way marriages are formed among my own people—the Gods honor and acknowledge the ways of all lands, in such matters. And after the babe is born, all we'd need to do is drink again before witnesses, and spit it out rather than swallow, breaking the bond between us, she reminded herself as she waited for her partner to recover. *It's the easiest form of wedding and divorcing available . . .* Thinking of divorce—thinking of marriage, for that matter—was an equation she wasn't quite ready to calculate, however. That, and his hand was growing rather distracting, since he was gently playing with one of her breasts.

Dominor wasn't an idiot; he knew she hadn't swallowed his seed. That she had vanished it with her power, however discreetly.

He couldn't blame her. Dom had experimented in his teens, tasting his own flavor out of curiosity. It wasn't awful, but it wasn't that pleasant, either. But what she had done for him . . .

Oh, sweet Kata, that was incredible! I haven't had that done for me in ages. Lying beside her, circling her areola with his fingertips, Dominor knew he needed to return the favor to her. *But first, I think I need to play with a few other areas on this woman's rather delectable body.*

Propping his head on his hand as he lay on his side, Dominor abandoned her breast. The subtle pout of her lower lip let him know she'd been enjoying his touch. He just had something else in mind. Clasping her wrist, he drew her hand to his lips. Kissing her palm, he nuzzled it with the tip of his nose, then licked the underside of her index finger. She sighed in contentment as he did the same to her littlest finger, then drew a short, fast breath as he all but swallowed the slender digit, sucking it to its root. Air escaped her lungs in a sultry moan; yes, she liked that.

Abandoning her hand after a few moments, Dom licked at the inside of her wrist. Grazed his teeth in a phantom-light scrape along her forearm. Suckled the inner bend of her elbow, making her moan softly. She seemed to like it best when he swirled his tongue over the soft skin in a feather-light caress, so Dom traced his tongue up the length of her arm to her shoulder, then pressed a line of kisses to the base of her throat.

Lapping there made her giggle and squirm. Her hands traced restless patterns over his chest and shoulders. Bracing his weight over her, Dominor kissed his way down to her breasts, where he could swirl his tongue over their soft curves, tonguing the passion-shriveled flesh of her nipples. One of her hands left his chest to once again play with her folds while she splayed her knee to the side for better access.

It was a distracting sight. A peculiar kind of jealousy rose up within him; *he* wanted to do that for her, to be the one to please her flesh. Shifting lower on the bed, Dominor nipped at her hand, nuzzling it out of his way. Serina gasped and moaned, arching up into the lapping of his tongue, twitching her other knee out of the way to give him greater access.

This was something no charm could adequately simulate. Serina had certainly tried to find one. Flicking and nuzzling, licking and suckling, he settled himself more comfortably between her legs. Holding her folds open with his hands, he exposed her delicate flesh for a gentle attack of his tongue and lips. When he used one of his fingers to penetrate her, curling upward, Serina found herself moaning aloud. Her whole body twitched when he nudged a certain spot inside; her eyes rolled behind her eyelids, her moan rising sharply in volume, forming itself into fervent words. "Oh Gods—yes, touch it! Touch me there! Moons, *yes*!"

Dominor blinked, pausing in his ministrations. She was being rather . . . vocal. Loudly so. Arousingly so, as she complained that he'd stopped. When he pressed and rubbed on that spot inside of her again, she groaned so loudly, someone banged on the wall separating them from the next room over, startling both of them with the wordless demand for quiet. Flushing, he freed his hand, quickly licked it clean, and snapped his fingers, muttering a charm for a sound-dampening ward. Instantly, the noises of the coastal city muted, from the rattle of carts traversing the cobbled streets to the cries of gulls fighting over the midden bins in the alleys.

Diving back into his task, he suckled her fiercely, rubbing his finger once more up into that spot Trevan had explained to him, back when they'd lived on Corvis lands and had been in the mood to swap stories of such techniques. She cried out again, straining into his touch. Her words weren't entirely coherent, but she did react enthusiastically, raking her fingers through his hair and tugging on his scalp. It wasn't until she almost broke his nose, yanking him into her rhythmically, that he realized he had reduced her to making a single, frustrated demand.

"Take me! Take me! Take me!"

Disentangling himself from her fingers, he shushed her frustrated groan. Settling himself over her—with her very enthusiastic help—Dominor sucked in a sharp breath as she caught him by his shaft, positioning him in place. With her knees raised and splayed, with her hands shifting to cup his backside, she was in the perfect position beneath him. Perfection was the only word for it, too; sinking into her slowly, gently, Dominor had to rock only a little bit to seat himself fully within her tight, welcoming heat. His partner groaned as he did so, a long, low, husky sound of need. She accompanied it with the sting of her fingernails, biting into the flesh of his buttocks just enough to stimulate his nerves, if not enough to break his skin. Breath hissed through his teeth as he fought with his baser instincts for control. Only when he knew he wasn't going to thrust like an animal did he risk moving slowly and carefully within her.

Ohhh, yessss . . . This was what she missed, what Serina couldn't find with a makeshift phallus charm. There was no mistaking the warmth, the strangely blended contrast of hardened softness, the feel of a flesh-and-blood man in her arms. The warmth of skin against skin, the play of muscles under her hands as she groped and caressed his back, sliding her hands up his spine. Even the puff of his breath against her cheek, the tickle of his dark brown hair along the side of her face was a sensual composition one just didn't get with any of the charms she knew for self-pleasuring. That his breath was sweet, his body attractive, and his movements slow yet skillful only added to her bliss.

Now that he was inside of her, filling her, some of Serina's urgency had diminished. It was as if the heat remained, but the flames weren't burning her flesh; Dominor of Nightfall had managed to bring her to a plateau of sensual pleasure. Languidly, she slid her hands up to his shoulders, maneuvering one around his arm so that she could cup the back of his neck. Pulling him down, she lifted up off the bedding to meet the descent of his lips.

SEVEN

·❧·

Their sudden languor, when moments before had been passionate urgency, helped Dominor. She had taken the edge off his earlier need, allowed the dam to burst on his reservoir of exile-imposed celibacy, but her heady responses had revived his interest sharply. To suddenly go from a mad race toward the finish line to this carnal version of a stroll should have diminished some of his enthusiasm . . . or at least made him question his sanity. Instead, Dominor found his blood simmering at a steady soft boil. Each time he pressed into her, each time he retreated and then returned again, it was with the steady force of waves lapping at a shore. When she tugged him down into a kiss, it added more to their mutual pleasure.

But they were only flesh and blood, bound to the laws of their nature. Desire increased between them with each stroke, rising from a slow, gentle bubbling to a full, vigorous boil, as Dominor instinctively increased the speed and strength of his thrusts. Serina lifted one knee, doubling it up almost to her chest. Both of them moaned as that changed the way they connected. Slipping his arm under her calf, he braced himself over her as he thrust harder. Her other leg lifted as well, and he paused just long enough to catch that one and hold it up, too.

Her ankles weren't quite on his shoulders—she wasn't that flexible—but she was open to the full depth of his strokes. When one particularly vigorous stroke reached the bottom of her depths, Serina squeaked at the unexpected jolt. Stopping, he blinked down at her, sweat glistening on his brow.

"Are you all right?"

Nodding, Serina looped her arms over his shoulders. They couldn't quite kiss in this position, but—*no, sorry, I was wrong about that*, she thought distractedly as he indeed managed to dip his head to hers. It was the way his arms braced half his weight and his feet the rest of it; he wasn't resting on elbows and knees as one might think. The athletic position left his hips free to piston smoothly, quickly, deliciously, and allowed him to dip his head far enough to meet hers.

Unfortunately, Dominor couldn't hold the position for long. For weeks now, he'd been locked up in both a small cabin and a dank hold. He'd had some leeway in his chains to move and work his muscles once the *falomel* had worked its way out of his system, regaining some of his strength, but it wasn't the same as being free to move as he normally did, walking around the island, sparring with his brothers. Forced to drop to his elbows and knees after only a dozen or so strokes, he broke the kiss, focusing on trying to find that one spot again with experimentally angled thrusts. Freeing his arms from her legs, he used one hand to brace himself and the other to lift her into him. He knew he'd located it when she shouted hoarsely in surprise, lifting and tilting her hips farther into him.

Adjusting his stance, Dominor rubbed against it with each stroke, enjoying her throaty cries; once again, she was loud enough to need the silencing spell still wrapped around their room. It also didn't take long for her to clutch at his shoulders and demand raggedly for more, for faster, for deeper and harder and all that he could give her. Caught up in his own mounting need, Dom gave it to her. As hungry as Serina was for the pleasure they were sharing, he felt equally starved.

In the quiet of the rented room, their gasping breaths and groaning cries mingled with the rhythmic creaking of the bedstead. Dominor was determined to outlast his partner, but his long-deprived body wasn't cooperating.

For her part, Serina wasn't really thinking; in fact, at the moment, thinking was not only highly overrated with the way he kept nudging that *spot* within her on each passing stroke, she was all but growling ferally.

For a moment, his rhythm faltered and broke; pausing, Dominor held himself very still over her, halfway withdrawn. Serina keened in her disappointment. Before it could turn into a full-fledged whine, he slammed back home . . . breaking her with pleasure.

Thank the Gods! It was the only coherent thought he had left. He'd stopped to prevent himself from exploding without her, but had failed. Thankfully, in that unavoidable thrust back into her, just before erupting and losing himself to his body's urges, he had triggered her orgasm. Though he had hoped to outlast her, a tie in their sexual race was an acceptable outcome. Or at least he would consider it such in a few minutes. After collapsing onto her in a sweaty, panting heap.

Serina was blissfully mindless. Thoughtless, too, and almost unconscious. Her normally racing mind had been deliciously silenced in the force of her climax. Slowly drifting back to awareness, she found herself rubbing at his back with soft strokes of her fingers. He was heavy, but not in a bad way. Certainly he had managed to keep at least some of his weight off of her with his elbows and his knees, enough to let her breathe, though she wasn't exactly going anywhere, either.

A humming, contented sigh escaped her. All of her muscles felt like they had been clenched excruciatingly tight—which they had—and only now had the chance to slowly relax—which they were—and it lent a heavy lassitude to her limbs that echoed the languid relaxing of her mind. With his face buried into the curve of her throat, his heart pounding in the chest pressing into her breasts, he definitely wasn't going anywhere. Licking her lips after a few more moments, she managed speech. Not very coherently, but she managed it. "Wow . . . Gods . . . you . . . *fabulous*. Absolutely fabulous. You Nightfallers . . . wow."

The use of the term *Nightfallers* penetrated Dominor's mental relaxation, prompting a snort that was halfway a laugh. *Considering most of us "Nightfallers" are men, and that, excepting only Koranen, the lot of us have definitely enjoyed the delights of the bed many times before our exile . . .*

The sleepy, incoherent woman under him definitely did not qualify as shy or retiring, either, an observation that pleased him. "You took the words from my mouth, my lady."

"Mm, 'Serina.' I think we can definitely dispense with the formalities by now."

Dominor considered her words as she caressed his shoulders. If she was the Lady he was Destined to meet—and at the moment, sated with a depth of sexual bliss he hadn't felt in over three years, he was able to view the idea calmly—Dom didn't have a problem with addressing her as such. *There's no guarantee that Wolfer has to be the next in line to fall in love before me, sequentially . . . and if our sexual compatibility isn't perfect for Tantric enchantments, what was that comment Kelly liked to use? Ah, yes. "I'll eat my underwear."*

Easing off of her, though it meant easing out of her body and losing the delicious softness of her curves, Dominor sagged onto the bedding in a pose reminiscent of earlier, when she had suckled the impatience from his flesh. This time, he was on his other side; this time, she wasn't spitting quietly on the floor. It was rumored certain fruits could make a man's seed sweeter to the taste, but Dominor had yet to hear *which* fruits could do so. Until and unless he learned otherwise, he wasn't going to force any woman to swallow something unpleasant to her senses, if there was no way to cure the problem.

Dragging in a deep breath, he let most of it out. Then asked, "Well? Are we compatible, or do I have to eat my new underclothes?"

Serina opened her eyes at the odd non sequitur. Unable to figure out what he meant by that, she sat up—with a groan—rested a moment while her sated body finished protesting the need for movement, then stood and crossed to the table. A glance at her slateboard made her frown. A prod of her finger, a tap of the frame, and she hung her head with a groan. "Moons! I cannot believe I did that!"

"Can't believe you did what?" Dominor asked, stretching with a yawn as he eyed the sweet curve of her rump. She was leaning over the table, arms braced so that one knee could hang slack, and that made her backside look even sweeter. Her second groan as she straightened contained aggravated words.

"I forgot to record our sexual compatibility!"

Strangely, that made Dominor laugh. It made him laugh heartily, squeezing his eyes shut in the depths of his mirth, though he quickly ran out of energy. It wasn't until the mattress shifted as she returned and settled next to him, propping the side of her head up with her palm, that he opened his eyes and glanced at her. "I'd be delighted to try again in a little while. I hate admitting it, but my trials at sea have left me with a little less stamina than usual."

Her mouth curved in a feminine smirk. "Perhaps it's just as well. You said you've been without a woman for a few years, and it showed; you clearly needed the edge taken off of your desires. From here on out, your responses should be more typical of your normal performance capabilities. Though I am curious as to *why* a man as handsome as you—if a tad arrogant—went for three years without a bed partner. Is it because of some Nightfall custom?"

Dominor started to snort and agree, however much of a stretched truth it would be to say it without giving away that it was "customary" for men to be exiled to the isle without companionship. A rapid thought made him reassess his response. *If she is indeed intelligent—as her Arithmantic abilities suggest— and if she is my Prophecied Disaster—my foretold wife-to-be— then even I know it wouldn't be smart to tell her a lie and have her uncover the truth after she meets my family.*

She *would* meet his family, eventually. Dominor did *not* want to get involved in the war between Natallia and Mandare. Not any farther than he'd already been unwillingly dragged. He couldn't return to Katan, being in exile, and he loved his brothers too much to abandon them for long; he was competitive against them to a fault, but they were his family. With the loss of his parents, his siblings were all Dom had left.

Which led to thoughts of their fledgling little kingdom. Somehow, Dominor didn't think Kelly of Doyle was the sort of woman to ignore her claim to be queen of the isle. Of course, that had been done mostly just to impress upon the Mandarites that they couldn't just sweep in and take over the island without facing some sort of serious opposition. And yet, discretion stated that he was still a long way from home, a long way from his brothers' help, and a long way from being returned to them, if this two-part ritual was supposed to take nearly a year to complete. If he lied outright, it could lead to awkward complications, later.

"It's a long and complicated story," he finally dismissed. "Suffice to say, I haven't really had the opportunity, or the inclination in those few instances where an opportunity was available."

That was the truth, after all; being in exile had restricted his opportunities until Kelly had arrived, but Dominor hadn't been interested in her when she had shown up. There had been other times in the past when Dominor had competed against his brothers for the attentions of other women. Mostly, he had competed against Trevan, the acknowledged lover among them, before being thrown into celibate exile.

Serina wasn't a fool; his evasions told her there was more to the story than that. A strange thought crossed her mind, making her blurt out, "You're not married, are you?"

Blinking, Dominor quirked a brow at her. "If I were, I would have told you when you revealed your plan for me. I certainly wouldn't have given any oath to help you sexually."

Relief coursed through her. "Good. I, um, just realized I hadn't asked you, that's all."

"Are *you* married?" Dom returned. He had no idea what the morals were for such things here in Natallia, never mind in the near-mythical Moonlands.

"*Definitely* not." She didn't mean to sound quite so vehement, but Serina was of the same belief as him; if she'd been married, either she would've done it with her husband if he were sufficiently powerful as a mage, or found a pair of mages who could take over the task.

At the sharpness in her reply, Dominor wondered briefly if Serina was against marriage. He knew some women were, the same as some men. *Maybe that has something to do with the "trap" I must set? Sweet Kata—I'm going to go insane if I have to keep second-guessing whether or not this woman is my Prophecied Destiny!*

Covering his face with his forearm, he blocked out the sight of her svelte curves. All he could do was go with the flow—an annoying circumstance, given how he preferred to plan his daily life—and improvise as things arose. The bed dipped. Rather than the expected warm brush of her skin against his, he felt the cool texture of his tunic being dropped on his chest.

"Let's get out of here for a little while, Dominor. We could walk the markets for a bit, while we both recover. There's bound to be a few more things you wouldn't mind having while you're here, and I do have a list of items I wanted to shop for while we were down here—the nuns and I, that is," Serina added to avert any confusion. "I certainly wasn't expecting to run across you!"

Dominor lifted his arm from his eyes, glancing at the pale-haired mage. "I'll express my gratitude for the rescue later, if you don't mind. I'm not exactly happy about being here in Natallia . . . however pleasant the current company."

"I can understand that," she acceded, shrugging. "I'm actually rather pleased you're not in a towering rage about all of this. Your capture, your sale, my bargain . . ."

"That wouldn't be mature," Dominor returned, sitting up and shrugging into his tunic. "I've had to deal with untenable situations before. Getting mad would be pointless."

"I throw vases," Serina found herself admitting. At the arching of one of his dark brows, she shrugged again, this time sheepishly. "When I get frustrated, I throw vases. I don't throw them at anybody, of course; I'm not inclined to actually hurt a person if I can help it . . . but I like throwing and smashing vases. It's noisy, and messy, and it helps calm me down. They're just cheap ones, of course; no Sundaran vessels or Dragonware. I wouldn't want to smash something beautiful or valuable. What do you do when you get frustrated?"

The question was unexpected. Caught in the act of reaching for his under-trousers, Dominor thought about it. "I usually only get frustrated when I'm not doing well in a competition. So I go over what I did wrong, what I did right, and how I could do it better. I've never really thought about it, but I suppose I just get more competitive." Stepping into the undergarment, he laced the strings over his hips. "Was there a reason why you asked?"

"I'm just trying to get to know you," she returned, reaching for her own clothes. "And to let you get to know me better. Unless your magic and your ability to concentrate completely fail to be up to the task, I'm fairly sure you and I will be compatible. Certainly the lovemaking part seems good enough."

That lifted both of his brows. " 'Seems'?" he challenged her. "It only *seems* good enough?"

The sly look she slanted his way caught him off guard. "Well, I'll definitely need to sample your technique at least a dozen more times before I can make any sort of official judgment on the matter."

Caught off guard indeed; Dominor laughed at her brazenness. "Spoken like a true scholar."

"Or an imperfectly satisfied woman," she quipped, tugging her tunic-dress over her head. Her jest earned her a scowl.

"I *distinctly* remember satisfying you, Lady!" Dominor retorted, offended.

"Oh, you did," Serina agreed quickly, forestalling any further argument as she popped her head through the neckline of her dress. "You satisfied me to the point where I'm now craving *more*."

Mollified, Dominor considered the idea. "Shall we skip the visit to the market, then?"

Serina nibbled on her lower lip a moment, then shook her head. "No, I really do have a few things I need to buy. And you could probably use a constitutional after being cooped up at sea for so long."

"A what?" Ultra-Tongue translated most things, but not all things, unfortunately. Like colloquial meanings for words that normally meant something very different.

"A walk. It's good for your constitution, ergo a 'constitutional.'"

"Ah." Dominor considered her point. He did need to exercise his body more than he'd been able to . . . but on the other side of that coin, he was out of shape, and wasn't sure how far he'd be able to walk before becoming exhausted.

The mage was feeling pleasantly tired from their lovemaking, but whether that was exhaustion or just satiation, he wouldn't know unless he tried. *Then again*, he rationalized, *if I don't try to prove myself physically fit, she might think less of my stamina and, therefore, of my abilities.* No man liked admitting to a weakness, and Dominor was even more reluctant. Sitting on the edge of the bed, he pulled on his new socks.

"Then by all means, let us dress and stroll through the marketplace."

Marching through the marketplace barefoot and in the shackles and rags of a prisoner was decidedly different from strolling through the marketplace in good boots and fine clothes as a freed man. Doing so with a lovely woman at his side who was as bright as she was beautiful lifted Dominor's spirits even more than their lovemaking had done. As she stopped to smell some herbs being sold by a farmer, Dominor felt disappointed by the way she released his elbow in order to move closer to the baskets. When she held a bundle of multiply lobed, narrow leaves up to his face, he obliged her with a cautious inhale.

"It's spicy, but sweet. And a bit lemony. What is it?" Dom inquired, curious.

"Lemonhart—the leaves form antler-shapes, see? It's good for blood disorders when distilled, and the macerated pulp is used as a plaster for sunburns. The Mother Superior requested I bring back a fresh bale of it, since her Order uses it in certain purification rituals."

"Does it have any magical properties?"

"Mostly in the distilled form, though some spells require it burned with incense. The scent changes when that happens, though. I don't like it, so I try to avoid using it."

"If you avoid everything about magic that offends you, then you'll never be much of a mage," Dom pointed out. "It's a messy, smelly, dangerous practice at times."

She shook her head. "No, I don't mean like that. There's something in the smell of it when it's burned that makes me sneeze repeatedly."

"Ah . . . which makes it difficult to complete whatever ritual you're enacting."

"Exactly."

Dominor considered her words. This wasn't the first time she'd revealed something personal about herself. In the mage-run political world of Katan, admitting to such a weakness just wasn't done; there was no telling who might be listening, or whether they were an enemy or a friend. "You're revealing quite a lot about yourself. If I considered myself a rival to you, I might try to buy some of these plants at a later date to make you sneeze at an inopportune moment."

"You're pledged to bring no harm to me, for one," Serina returned calmly, setting the small bundle down. "For another, that would be the action of a rival mage. We're not competing for an education, or for a career opportunity."

"Not right now," he reminded her, "but eventually the oath will be fulfilled. And there is the possibility of some rival wanting to know your weaknesses so they can take over the guardianship of Koral-tai. Even if I weren't under the oath, and weren't interested in your position, I could still sell the information to someone who needed it, were I inclined to do so."

Her mouth twisted wryly. "Trying to teach me how to be cautious?"

"I'm merely protecting your best interests," Dominor averred.

"Which are in my best interests, given the vow between us. Anyone could be listening to us speak, for that matter."

"True, but I'm not in any danger," she dismissed. "No one would mess with the Guardian of Koral-tai."

"You're carrying a fortune beyond most street thieves' wildest dreams, which you displayed rather blatantly earlier today," Dominor pointed out. "That's enough to tempt at least some of them into considering some sort of rash action."

"I'm warded against such things," she dismissed. Seeing he was about to argue the point, Serina tucked her hands once more around his elbow, pressing her breasts against his upper arm as she leaned her head back a little, coquettishly. "But if anyone attacks, you have my permission to defend my person, if you like."

"I'd be honored," Dom found himself agreeing. Then, considering her previous, pragmatic statements, offered wryly, "And at the same time, you'll be gauging my magical abilities, I trust?"

"Of course; it would be more efficient that way."

Somehow, that amused him. Releasing a soft laugh, Dominor shook his head. "Are you hoping for such an encounter while we're out and about? Or perhaps an attack by brigands on the journey back to the Retreat?"

"Not hoping, so much as ready for it, should one occur." She debated a moment whether to tell him her plans for the return trip or not, and chose to refrain. When the time came would be the time to speak of it. Releasing his elbow, she turned back to the farmer. "How much lemonhart do you have available, sir?"

"This is only the early crop, milady," the farmer informed her. "I'm expecting my sons with a cartful by week's end, though."

"I trust it was sown in the usual manner?" Serina asked.

"Of course; I butchered and drained the sheep into the seed-bin myself, and my sons did the mixing by hand—say, you wouldn't happen to have a need for a strong, strapping young man in your life, would you?" the Natallian inquired.

Dominor took exception to that. Tucking Serina's left hand around his right elbow, he leaned in close and stated firmly, "She has *me*."

The suntanned farmer wasn't impressed. He looked over Dominor's frame, much like he would've looked over a sheep for butchering, and snorted. "You're too refined and scrawny-looking for good farmwork, milord. Now, my sons are for hire, and seeing as how most of our harvest is naught but early crops this year, two of the younger lads are looking for employment elsewhere."

"I don't have any use for farmhands, sorry," Serina demurred, biting back the urge to laugh. It was clear the mage at her side thought the farmer was offering his sons' *other* services as strapping young men. "Though I'll come back for a look at that lemonhart. I'll need three bales, full-leaf cut, if you can. I'd like to get some extra for the Mother Superior, if you have it available. And if it's as good in quality as you say it is."

"I'll send word back to fix you up three of the finest, if you like," the herb seller agreed and held out his hand. Serina dropped a couple of silver coins into it for his trouble, and he touched the brim of his conical straw hat with his other hand. "Check back here each day or so, milady!"

"I'll do that." A tug of her fingers on Dominor's elbow allowed Serina to guide him farther down the row of stalls.

"What was that bit about the sheep's blood?" Dom asked her, curious.

"If you mix the seeds with blood before sowing them, it's a form of sanctification. That makes the leaves usable in priestly rites, once they're full grown. It also acts as a sort of gruesome fertilizer," Serina added, wrinkling her nose. "The leaves grow a thumb-width longer when germinated that way. The locals in this corner of Natallia have a bit of a blood cult. No ritual sacrifices of sentient beings, thankfully," she allowed with a dip of her head, "but some rituals and rites do require the spilling of blood."

The thought unsettled him. Spilling blood often meant the person doing the spilling was seeking the power released by such an act. If it wasn't willingly given, it wasn't supposed to be used by a good and lawful mage. "Does *our* two-part ritual require blood to be spilled?"

"You have nothing to worry about," Serina reassured him. *She* was the one who would be spilling blood, but only placental blood in the birthing half of the ritual ahead of them. "There's nothing unnatural in any of it . . . aside from doing it in an unusual location, that is."

"That's more than enough to worry about," Dominor observed dryly. "But not today. Which reminds me; how long will we be in this city?"

"About two weeks, give or take. It depends on how quickly the nuns' stock sells."

"Do they always sell it here in . . . what is the name of this place again?" he asked.

"Port Blueford. And no; the Mother Superior sends them to various cities. The Retreat is located in the heart of Natallia—that is, the heart of the land before the Mandarites started this civil war with their asinine beliefs. Because it's situated in the middle," she continued, returning to the original topic, "there is a road that rings the base of the mountains around the Retreat, and from it spring the roads that lead to all the corners of the realm. The Threefold God of Fortuna had a Hand in bringing you to Port Blueford, and a Hand in Mother Naima's choice to send the nuns down here in time for me to see you being marched to the slave market. We could've been sent to a dozen other locations, easily."

Dominor narrowed his eyes thoughtfully. "You believe our meeting was Destiny?"

"Fate, rather," Serina countered, not quite sure why he was staring at her so intensely. "Destiny is what we make out of our allotted Fate. The Hands of the Threefold God touch all, whether or not a person worships that far-flung God . . . but those Hands only touch; they do not control. I didn't *have* to pursue and purchase you, after all. So our *meeting* was Fated . . . but my purchasing you and your agreeing to the oath between us is what became our Destiny, after I chose to act upon that meeting."

It was an elegant piece of logic, and difficult to refute. He still didn't know how the line "*set your trap and be your fate*" figured into his future with this woman, but Dominor couldn't deny the touch of the Gods in their fortuitous meeting, today. *And to what the Gods touch, mortal man should pay close attention. So let us examine the line "You seek she who is your kind"* . . .

He was certain she was strong-willed and strong-minded. A person who left her homeland to forge her own destiny, who had secured for herself a suitable education and a rarified position, surely possessed both qualifications. She was definitely focused; he couldn't deny that.

There were two different paths for approaching magic: the mystical; and the scientific. Coming from a background in arithmancy and mathemagic, Serina's approach was decidedly scientific. Dominor's approach was slightly more pragmatic than scientific: He accepted the mysticism when necessary, but he preferred concrete answers. It was easier to modify spells when one grasped the underlying theories of how magic worked. Modifications led to innovations, and innovations made a mage's reputation. At least, it was that way back in Katan. It wasn't enough to merely be strong in magical ability; to be powerful, one had to be versed in the many uses of magic as well as possess the energy and stamina for spellcasting.

"You're deep in thought," Serina observed, studying his profile. She had been braiding her hair as they walked, and tied the end with a bit of string. He wasn't looking at the glasswares stall they had stopped next to, but instead at some undefined point beyond it. "Copper for a glimpse?"

"What? Oh . . . just thinking about the nature of magic," he dismissed.

"Ah. My favorite," she admitted, smiling wryly. "I would've starved my soul, had I stayed at home. I never knew how much pleasure could be found in delving into the mysteries of the mystical universe until I went elsewhere."

"Indeed," Dom agreed, thinking of the research and special projects he had crafted since his exile.

"What is your specialty, as a mage?" Serina asked him, curious.

"My specialty?" he repeated, caught off guard by the question.

"Yes—like mine is mathemagics. Or do you have one?" she added. "I mean, if your work as a Lord Chancellor keeps you terribly busy with politics . . ."

"No, my duties are rather light in that regard," Dominor told her truthfully. *Considering the position was created and held for only a couple of days . . .* He considered the question more carefully, and finally offered, "I suppose you could call what I do a specialization, but not in a traditional sense. I take special orders from clients, creating and modifying various artifacts to their exact specifications. I mean, my eldest brother makes enchanted weapons of all sorts, but his are usually made first, and then sold to an interested buyer—of course! Why didn't I think of it?"

Serina was puzzled by his sudden change in topic. "Why didn't you think of what?"

Rather than answering her, Dominor held up his hand. *"Zathras!"*

Nothing happened. Disappointed, Dom lowered his arm. It was too much to expect, given the distance invol—

EIGHT

❖

*B*ang! A silk-wrapped hilt filled his hand. Pleased, he lifted the long, narrow blade, displaying it to Serina's widened eyes. "This is one of my brother's creations. I helped him research a way to forge a summoning spell into the metal, several years ago."

"Hey! Watch where you're pointing that thing!" someone protested as they moved past the pair.

Serina pushed Dominor's arm down. "Blades aren't to be bared in the marketplace, unless you're testing the edge at a weaponsmith's stall. Keep that point down at your side. Where's the scabbard for it?"

Dominor grimaced. "That's the drawback to the summoning spell. It only fetches the blade. We'll need to get one for it."

She rolled her tawny eyes in the expressive way that said he shouldn't have summoned his sword at all, if he couldn't summon the scabbard as well. "There should be a weaponsmith somewhere over here, if I remember my trip through the market earlier; she might have something for it," she consoled him, guiding him to the right as they reached a cross-path in the market. "Why would the spell summon only the blade? Isn't that impractical?"

"Not if you're summoning it to defend yourself from an unexpected attack," Dominor returned. "And the spell is forged into the steel of the blade, not stitched into the leather. To summon the scabbard as well puts a distance-limiting factor on the sword, as well as requiring a steel-forged sheath."

"Are attacks common, in Nightfall?" Serina asked, curious about his homeland.

"It's 'on Nightfall,' not 'in Nightfall,'" Dominor corrected her. "And . . . no, not common. We're a peaceful people by preference. We're prepared for war, but we'd rather have peace, even if it's a contradiction."

"The contradiction isn't insurmountable. Of course, the Moonlands are so well-hidden, we're not exactly prepared for war, because we have no need to be prepared for it," she told him. "We don't let a lot of outsiders know the secret of how to enter our land."

Dominor nodded. "Given the fabled nature of your homeland, I'm surprised some outlander with the secret hasn't been tempted to spread it to others."

She shook her head, her braid sliding over her back. "It wouldn't work. We guard our secrets too carefully. You have to be told by a native-born how to get past the barrier, otherwise they're just meaningless words."

"You use a limited-exchange spell modifier?" Dominor asked, intrigued. "A so-called first-generation limitation, one that I presume can be used by non-mages? Or can the barrier-use be extended under the use of an outlander mage?"

"It's limited to a native-born generated explanation, with a one-shot use by any one outlander. It's woven into the barrier itself, not into the words used."

"One-shot?" Dominor asked. "But that would mean you would have to be retold again and again, to be able to access the Moonlands a second or more times."

Serina shrugged. "We like it that way. We select our visitors, allow them inside once, and if they behave themselves and prove trustworthy both within the borders and without them once they've left . . . we'll consider retelling them how to enter."

"But . . . why?" Dominor eyed the woman at his side. "Why are the Moonlands so insular? What made them that way?"

"A nasty civil war with our neighbors. It was over the rights to some rare resources that needed to be protected, rather than exploited," she explained vaguely.

"What do you do about the urge for conflict inherent in human nature?" Dominor asked, curious. "Mankind must compete, after all, whether it's for food, resources, mates, prestige . . ."

"We have games that we play. Formal competitions on the local and regional levels," she admitted. "Some are in weapon-sports, others are in noncombat matters, from embroidery to equestrian skills, food preservation to falconry. Like a local harvest-faire has competitions, only ours are larger and more formalized."

"Were you any good at them?" Dominor couldn't help asking. He might not be a swordsmaster like his eldest brother, preferring to focus on his magic, but he did enjoy physical challenges.

"I wasn't expected to be. I was just expected to be 'the sister of the next Inoma,' " she self-mocked. "And to find some sort of useful occupation wherein I could support the Inoma's work, whether it was her or my mother. A number of my aunts and great-aunts had turned to the healing arts in recent generations, and it was half-expected for me to do the same. Or to take up some sort of useful, educated profession like being a law-mistress, or maybe an architect. And of course, as the sister of the next Inoma, I would have a better chance at becoming a Moon-lands Elder once I was old and gray . . . but even then, I'd still be 'the sister of the Inoma.' Only my children would escape the stigma of merely being a 'sister of.'

"Even my little brother wouldn't have had a problem," she added with a rough sigh. "There's no disappointment inherent in merely being 'the brother of the Inoma,' because only a girl can be born with the mark. Boys are exempt from the weight and the responsibility, in my family line. But I was born a female, yet born without the mark, so I'll always be a sister-of, and never completely respected in my own right," Serina complained. "Not in my birth-land; not as an individual. Ah! There's the weapon-smith."

Dominor considered her words. There was an old bitterness underlying her otherwise calm revelation. He could understand her decision to leave, to make a name for herself far from the reputation of her family—even if he still wasn't quite sure what set an Inoma apart from a regular Moonlander—but he didn't have the same sort of bitter rivalry with his brothers that Serina seemed to have with her sister. A rivalry, yes; a bitter one, no.

"I *am* glad you left your homeland, and that your ambitions to be more than just a mere sister-of for the rest of your life brought you here, Serina. I don't think I'd care to be a royal stud," Dom demurred.

She smiled at him as they reached the stall. "I'm about as close to royalty as you'll probably get in your life . . . unless your queen is unmarried?"

"No, she's definitely married," Dominor quickly asserted. "And I wish my brother Saber all the happiness he can find with her."

"You make her sound like a harridan," Serina observed dryly.

"More like a virago. They're good for each other; they have a lot in common in their temperaments and opinions," Dominor corrected. Lifting the sword by its hilt, he showed it to the stall owner, a muscular woman manning a portable forge-pit with the help of a teenaged girl nearly as muscular as she was. "Do you have a scabbard for a blade like this?"

The woman signaled for her apprentice to cease pumping the bellows and came over. "Never seen a blade that thin, milord. Whereabouts did you get it?"

"Katan. It's a dueling blade." He handed it over for the woman to have a better look. She gripped it, turned it to peer down the edge, and shook her head.

"One good blow from a broadsword would break this blade. You should have one of my swords," the craftswoman asserted.

"It's spell-forged, Milady Smith," Dominor enlightened her. "You could lay it over a gap between two tall stones and drop your anvil, there, onto it from a third-floor window, and it wouldn't break."

"Still seems a bit silly to me," the woman muttered doubtfully. "Where's the weight you'd get with a broader blade? How would it cut through armor without any heft to it? It doesn't even weigh half a stone!"

Dominor didn't know what a stone was in terms of local measurements, but he knew his preferred style. "It's not meant for battle with armored opponents. It's meant to fend off thieves in the street, wielded against people who aren't wearing armor and aren't likely to be carrying huge blades of their own."

"Well, I don't have anything sized for something as skinny as this—you could practically shove it up the back end of a sausage for roasting, like a spit!" the woman disparaged. Then shrugged and amended, "Well, it would have to be a particularly *fat* sausage, to not split it in half . . ."

"The point is, can you *make* something for it?" Serina asked. She turned to Dominor as the smith considered her words. "I don't know any spells for stitching scabbards out of leather. Just boots and belts. Otherwise, I'd just do it myself."

The smith took offense at the thought of someone else making the sale. "I didn't say I couldn't make something! Just that I don't have anything ready-made. A scabbard out of leather, for something of this size? I don't have any strips that are long enough at the moment, unless you want to buy and bring me a hide. I'll grant you, this blade's a full finger-length longer than most, and reach can be important, but all my spare stock is cut for a shorter blade. But you could bring me the leather, as I said.

"Or my girl, here, has a fair hand at carving wooden scabbards, and we do have some boards that are long enough. Some stout oak, sturdy enough to use as a parrying wand." The smith eyed the lengths of wood her daughter obediently fetched for display and nodded. "We could have something carved up for you by this time tomorrow, if you like. Leather would take a little longer to size, stitch, and rivet for fittings, not more than two days."

"Wood will suffice," Dominor decided.

"You need an Oathstoning, to make sure I'll give this overgrown table-knife back, milord?" the smith asked him with a teasing grin, gesturing to her apprentice. The girl moved toward a small chest near the back of the stall in anticipation.

"No, I'll trust you," Dominor demurred.

Serina could guess why he could afford to do so, if the slender blade was spell-forged to come to his calling. Certainly, it impressed her that the blade would come over the length of both an ocean and part of a continent. It would take a powerful warding to prevent the blade from appearing when summoned; frankly, she didn't think either the smith or her apprentice had enough magic to try. Without studying the forged magics, she wouldn't know in advance if she could, either.

It did make her curious about his brother, though. As soon as he finished making arrangements to pick up the scabbard the next day, she pulled him toward a watering fountain centered in the next junction of market aisles. The afternoon was growing late, which meant it was growing muggy in this warm climate. The moisture around the fountain, at least, was slightly cooler than the rest of the increasingly cloying air in the city. It would make a good resting point while they talked.

Gesturing for him to sit beside her, Serina fluttered her fingers, throwing up a small, simple sound-warding charm. Like the one used earlier in her room at the inn, this one cut back much of the noise around them. It would allow them to speak and hear freely as well as decrease the chances of being overheard.

Curious about the purpose for her use of the spell, Dominor arched a brow at her. "Anything in particular you wanted to discuss?"

"Your brother. I'm curious about him. You said you're the thirdborn son; I take it he's not your only sibling? Does he work for your Queen, or is he an independent magesmith? Are all Nightfall blades shaped like that?" Serina asked. She blushed when he blinked, taken aback by her barrage of questions. "Forgive me, but I'm insatiably curious about other lands. Once I've completed the ritual ahead of us, I'm thinking of moving on to another kingdom. I could go north to Sundara, which straddles the Sun's Belt, and keep going north . . . but if your land is interesting, I might want to visit it, instead. Um . . . that's not to insult by implying that your land is automatically *boring* . . ."

Her fumbling made him grin. "Oh, it's not boring. And Saber, my eldest brother, doesn't just work for our Queen; he's married to her. I witnessed it myself . . . two days before the Mandarites kidnapped me."

"What horrible timing!" Serina commiserated. It did allow her to sate more of her curiosity by asking, "So . . . what are Nightfaller marriage rituals like?"

"Much the same as Katani ones," he admitted. "Most of our culture still has its basis in Katani ways, though they're changing here and there."

"Were you originally part of the Empire of Katani, then?"

"Katan, and . . . sort of," Dominor hedged. "Our independence has been fairly recent, I'll admit."

"Was there a civil war, like Natallia with Mandare?" Serina asked.

"No. It was just that Katan wished to have nothing more to do with the inhabitants of Nightfall, seceding all claim to its jurisdiction, and so we claimed independence for ourselves in the wake of their dismissal. Of course, Nightfall Isle is just that: a modest-sized island not much more than fifty miles long and maybe twenty miles broad at its widest points. It's sort of shaped like an hourglass, too," he continued, searching for ways to tell her the truth without revealing the vulnerabilities and weaknesses of his siblings' home. "The main settlement is up in the pass between the northern and southern mountain ranges, flanked to the east and the west by two coves. The eastern cove is a beautiful, sweeping curve of sand, while the western cove is made of rock and stone. It has deep waters close to the shoreline, suitable for merchant ships with deep drafts to pull up to the docks without trouble at low tide."

"You know something about sailing, then?" Serina asked next. "I'm not exactly a sailor myself, but I grew up in a port city, so I picked up a lot simply by proximity. I like the smell of the sea, the bustle of the docks, and seeing all the exotic goods flowing back and forth."

He grimaced inside, hating to admit a weakness. "I don't know very much about ships, myself. Just enough to know what's good for the traders who come to visit."

"As Lord Chancellor, I'm sure you've had to deal with your Harbormaster a few times, though, and maybe even some of the merchant-captains who come through."

He didn't feel right about lying to her, though he didn't want to reveal the whole truth, either. "Actually . . . my brother Saber has been in charge of most of that."

Serina gave him a bemused look. "It sounds like your brother holds many jobs on Nightfall: consort to your Queen; magesmith; trade-overseer . . . Is there anything he doesn't do?"

Dominor took exception to that. "Not much more than that! As the eldest of us, and the former Count of Corvis over on the mainland, it only made sense to let him continue to those sorts of things. But most of the time, the decisions were made by a committee of all of us."

That was an interesting revelation. Shrewdly, Serina asked him, "So, just how *many* inhabitants does this modest island hold?"

"Why do you want to know that?" Dominor returned warily. He'd slipped up somewhere, but wasn't sure where, just yet.

"Because you make it sound like the only inhabitants are you and your siblings."

Damn. Hiding his wince, he narrowed his eyes. "And again,

I ask you why you want to know how many Nightfallers there are? What business is it of yours? There could be four, there could be forty, there could be four thousand, or four hundred thousand on the Isle. What difference does it make to you?"

"Because your answers are very sparse and unsatisfactory, because you're very evasive for a government official, and because there are dichotomies between what you are saying now, and what you said when holding that Truth Stone, earlier today."

"If I am a government official, why should I trust an outlander with potentially sensitive sovereign information?" Dominor countered smoothly.

"You have a point . . . but I'm the woman who might have enough power to find a mirror within your homeland that I can send you through, with the backing of the Font to empower me. A woman who's looking for the next realm to travel to, once my obligations at Koral-tai have been completed," she returned calmly. "I'm the woman who is trusting you to help me with an extremely delicate and difficult ritual—even if you are Oathsworn to help me—and because I am the only friend you have, here in Natallia.

"If you play me false, I'll not be inclined to trust you . . . and *that* means, if you get into trouble, I won't be as inclined to help you. Like you almost did, bearing a naked blade through the market," Serina reminded him. "We're lucky no Royal Servants saw you carrying it like that. I might have enough money to bail you out, and a need to bail you out . . . but once the ritual is complete, we'll only have how we treated each other to maintain a friendship between us. Or not."

He wanted to argue the matter further, but she had a point. "I would rather not reveal any of the weaknesses of my home. Suffice to say that everything I have told you is the truth . . . from a certain, incompletely explained perspective. The more of my trust you earn—because this works both ways—the more I might be inclined to tell you."

That lifted one of her pale blond brows, but Serina let it stand. "All right . . . tell me more of these 'incompletely explained perspectives' on your homeland, then."

"What exactly do you want to know?" Dominor inquired cautiously.

"Let's get back to your siblings. How many do you have?"

Giving her question a moment of thought, he answered directly.

"I am the thirdborn of eight . . . so you can see I have as much an urge to compete and make a name for myself as you ever did, faced with your sister's fame. I have one sister-in-law so far . . . though it's been long enough, my secondborn brother, Wolfer, might've met a female of his own, now that Saber has married. The fourthborn, Evanor, is my twin brother. Fraternal, not identical," he explained. "We look alike in our features, but he has fair hair. And he's not very competitive, compared to me. He's also Her Majesty's Lord Chamberlain, being the sort to enjoy overseeing domestic affairs."

"What does he like to do, when he's not being a Lord Chamberlain?" she wanted to know.

Caught off guard, Dominor cobbled together an answer. "He, ah . . . well, he sings a lot. And lately, he's been working on sewing projects in his spare time . . ."

"Is he a follower of the ways of Karan-ten, then?" Serina asked.

"I have no idea what that means," Dominor returned dryly, "so I have no idea."

"Uh . . . the monks of Karan-ten are like the nuns of Koral-tai, in that they, um . . . prefer their own gender."

Dominor choked on his own breath. "Jinga's Ass, no! Gods and Goddesses . . . no, he's just as interested in women as I am! In fact, the two of us used to get drawn into fights with others about that when we were in our teens, back at the ancestral home. Some of the local youths thought he was, um . . . inspired in the ways of Koral-ten."

"*Karan*-ten," she corrected, smiling.

"Right. Anyway . . . home-tending just makes Evanor happy. He's a romantic soul, I suppose you could say," Dominor added with a shrug. "Love, happiness, domestic bliss. He's always longed to be a father, more so than the rest of us brothers. I have faith he'll be great at it, too, once his turn comes."

" 'Once his turn comes'?" she repeated.

"You know, once his turn to walk the eight altars comes along. His turn to get married, whenever that will be," Dominor explained, avoiding the topic of his family's Destiny.

"Eight altars? You have that many Gods?"

"It's the wedding custom of my people for the couple to walk around the eight altars found in most Katani chapels, each signifying one of the four seasonal aspects of Jinga and Kata, the God and Goddess of Katan. As they do so," Dominor explained, "the couple pledge their vows to each other, with each of the facets of Jinga and Kata being witness to each section of their vows, as well as being witnessed by those gathered there."

"It must have been a fairly recent split, to still have chapels and altars for what is now essentially a foreign pair of deities," Serina observed shrewdly. "The Laws of God and Man state that each kingdom must have a patron deity to watch over it, to guard and guide its people spiritually. It's extremely rare for the Gods to be shared among two or more lands. Even the Mandarites have found an Aspect of Divinity to worship, in their crude, discriminatory way."

Dominor hadn't considered that. He and his brothers were definitely reverent, but not particularly religious. It hadn't bothered them to not have some sort of clergy on the Isle; when they wanted to pray formally, they just went down to the chapel and did so. As for Kelly's beliefs, at one point she had explained during their marathon palace-cleaning sessions the many, many different religions of her own world, but she had admitted that she herself wasn't devoted to any one particular faith. Of course, she also admitted that in her universe, the Gods and Goddesses almost never made physical manifestations, while miracles were rare at best and often subtle—her realm being miracle-poor as well as magic-poor.

Personally, Dominor thought it was a horrible world in which to live, compared to the marvels of his own.

Clearing his throat, he shrugged. "We have no official religion as of yet . . . but frankly, the vast majority of us are very reverent, but not very religious. We could pray to Jinga and Kata out of habit . . . but we could just as easily pray to the Threefold God of Fate, or to the God-King of Aiar, or even to Brother and Sister Moon, and it would all be one and the same to us."

"What is Her Majesty's view on religion and the Gods?" Serina asked.

"She's open to anyone worshipping anyway or anyone they want," Dominor related with some confidence. "Provided their form of worship doesn't harm anyone, and provided it doesn't condemn the rights of others to worship as they themselves please."

"How odd. Usually the ruler of a nation leads that nation in worshipping the local deity. She doesn't follow the ways of the Katani Gods?"

Dominor shook his head. "That's not the way of her people. They're very tolerant by nature."

"She's not a Katani, then?"

Hesitating briefly, Dom gave her the truth. "She's an outworlder."

Serina blinked, her freewheeling questions drawn to a halt. "Your Queen . . . is an outworlder? Someone not even from this world?"

"Yes."

"How extraordinary . . ." Serina wondered if she could meet this outworlder Queen . . . and then remembered that the Lord Chancellor didn't want children. It would be a bit awkward to visit Nightfall after both halves of the ritual were finished.

A white-clad woman hurried up to them as fast as she could wend her way through the crowd, her braided hair confined under a tight coif that had been tied under her chin. It was the only tidy thing about her appearance, since part of her tunic-dress had split higher than it should be at the side seam, and the stitches at the opposite elbow had been torn out. Dirt stained her skirt-panels at the knees, and a bruise reddened her cheekbone.

Seeing her approach with a worried look, Serina sighed heavily. "Moons! Can't they go more than a single day without running to me with every least little complaint?"

Dominor arched a brow at that, but she canceled the sound-dampening spell with a flick of her fingers, negating the opportunity for a quick inquiry. The nun halted before them, panting as she braced her hands on her knees.

"Brawl . . . in the stall . . . lightfingers . . . broken boards . . . accused of . . . cheating—"

Rolling her eyes, Serina shoved to her feet and stalked in the direction of the nuns' stall. Dominor followed at her heels, leaving the nun to recover her breath by the fountain. It only took a moment to reach the stall, which showed signs of damage in the way some of the wares had been scattered about, along with a broken strut two of the nuns were struggling to support to keep the canopied roof from collapsing. A crowd of at least fifty people had gathered a short distance away to watch the mayhem, which was mostly verbal at the moment.

Three men in a simplified version of the livery worn by the Royal Servant who had almost bought him were arguing with the nuns, who had collared two lanky, half-grown youths with the patched clothes and sullen faces of street urchins. Dominor tried to follow the mass of confusion inherent in so many voices raised in counterargument, but the babble only increased when some of the nuns spotted his hostess approaching. A quartet of them hurried over to her, while the others continued to hold the youths, support the roof, and argue with the city guard.

With Serina distracted by the need to make sense of what they were saying, Dominor focused on the most immediate need. Lifting his hand, he scribed a burning rune in midair. *"Shalcoloth!"*

The rune flared and zipped straight at the broken post. The damaged pieces leaped back into place, making the nuns supporting the upper half gasp with relief. They staggered back as the support glowed for a moment, then solidified. With that little display of magic, the constables eyed him warily, breaking off their argument with the nearest cluster of nuns in the longish market stall.

The urchins were still grumbling under their breath, and the knot of white-clad women surrounding Serina was still babbling away, while the frustrated mage tugged on her braid, trying to get them to quiet and speak one at a time. She wasn't succeeding very well. With the roof taken care of and the constables quiet, Dominor waded into the nuns, pulling them back by the elbow from their Guardian. His efforts silenced them, although they cast him shocked, affronted looks for being literally manhandled; somehow, given the preferences Serina had revealed to him, he guessed the nuns of Koral-tai didn't get hauled about by any males all that often.

Catching the last one by the shoulders, he silenced her with a firm, quelling look as she glanced back at him, and pushed her back among the rest, moving to stand beside Serina. In the relative quiet—since the rest of the marketplace was still noisy—he pointed at one of the women. "You. Describe what happened. The rest of you, stay silent."

Serina, listening with half her attention to the explanation of how the urchins had attempted to stampede a horse and rider into the stall and then make off with some of the spilled goods in the confusion, marveled at how quickly he had taken charge of the bedlam. She wasn't upset at his high-handedness; far from it, in fact. Sometimes the nuns were like an overwhelming flock of magpies, all chattering at once, all making demands on her time.

They were used to looking up to strong-willed women to guide and lead them. She was strong-willed . . . but she also found leadership positions tedious. Mariel usually provided a buffer from the nuns at the Retreat, but Mariel was still up at the Retreat. Smiling gratefully at Dominor, Serina turned her full attention to the explanations the singled-out nun was giving.

"We made sure the rider and horse were all right; he took off in that direction, being a messenger, and that's when my Sisters brought back these miscreants. That's when they started yelling about wrongful imprisonment," the nun finished.

"We ain't got nothin' on us!" the taller of the two youths protested.

"We's clean!" the shorter, redder-haired one added with an indignant sniff.

One of the nuns nearest the pair shook her head. "They don't have anything on them *now*, but they bumped into a couple of youths in the crowd right before we caught them. They could've passed off what they lifted from our stall."

"We'd need a Truth Stone, to get to the bottom of this," one of the city guard spoke. "Which is why we want to take these boys to the gaol."

"They disturbed the sanctity of our stall, which is considered holy ground," one of the older sisters protested. "By rights, their punishment is to be meted out by our own hands—and that one stomped on my foot!"

Serina played with the end of her braid with her fingers, trying to remember if she had a spell suitable for discerning the truth of the matter. "I suppose I could cast a tracing spell, to see if any of the amulets were indeed stolen."

"First, a Truth Spell," Dominor interjected, before she got any further sidetracked.

"I don't exactly have a piece of white stone, let alone the herbs to coat it with," Serina reminded him. "Nor are the Moons both full, at the moment."

"There's another way to reveal the truth from a lie," he assured her. Then realized this wasn't his jurisdiction; she might be able to do an interrogation as a Guardian, but he was an interloper. "If I may?"

"Please," Serina conceded, gesturing for him to proceed.

The spell Dominor had in mind required sympathetic magic to work. Crossing to the two youths, he reached up and plucked a hair from the taller boy's head. The urchin yelped and glared at him.

"Whacha do *that* for?"

Dominor muttered a word, twisting the short hair into a loose knot; it was too short for him to tie with his fingers, but that didn't matter. The spell-word was required for this bit of magery. Keeping it visible between them, he asked, "Did you steal any of the nuns' wares?"

"Of course not!" the boy protested.

The hair unknotted itself. Dom glanced at the constables. "He lies. He stole something all right. If he were telling the truth, the hair would have tightened into a full knot."

"Prove it," the constable who had spoken before demanded, eyeing Dominor skeptically.

Plucking a hair from his own head—glad that his hair was now clean, along with the rest of his body—Dominor knotted it with the same word, and stated, "My name is Dominor." The dark brown hair knotted itself tightly. "My name is Maisie, and I am a dairymaid." The hair correspondingly unknotted itself, standing stiff and straight in his hand. Dropping it, he looked at the constable. "Proof enough for you?"

"That's a spell I ain't seen before," one of the other constables muttered. The crowd behind him muttered similar comments among themselves, arrayed in a semicircle around the longish front of the nuns' stall, still watching the drama unfolding.

"Use it on the other one," the first city guard ordered him.

Dom obliged, though the youth tried to dodge his fingers. The nuns holding him tightened their grip, making him yelp from the pressure of their hands. Plucking the hair from the boy's head, Dominor knotted it with his power and asked, "Did you steal anything, or assist in stealing anything, from this stall?"

The youth sealed his lips together, refusing to answer.

"A sign of guilt for certain, if he doesn't want the truth of his words to show!" one of the other nuns stated, folding her arms across her chest in satisfaction.

"We'll take them into custody, now," the third constable asserted.

"Certainly not!" the nun with the folded arms protested. "They've committed offenses on Koral-tai property; they will suffer Koral-tai judgment!"

"They committed their crime on city property; they will be dealt with by Port Blueford justice!"

"Please!" Serina interjected. "Stop arguing over who should do what to whom." Giving her braid a last tug, she tossed it over her shoulder. "Now, I can geas them to replace everything they stole, which would be restitution by Koral-tai standards, according to what the Mother Superior told me about such things . . . and *then* they can be handed over to the City Guard for further punishment. Will that satisfy *both* groups? Sister Amerith? Guardsmen?"

The nuns and constables looked at each other. Finally, Sister Amerith nodded and unfolded her arms. The lead guardsman nodded curtly, gesturing for her to proceed.

"Good! Now, let's get this over with, so I can go back to what I was doing," the pale-haired mage muttered.

NINE

·⊰⊱·

Dominor watched as she moved around behind the boys.
Placing a hand on the back of each of their necks, she sent
them to their knees with a Word of Power, pulling them from the
nuns' grip. Magic shimmered in a flickering golden light that
played over their bodies as she muttered under her breath. The
nuns dusted each other off, though their hands left prints; a few
more smudges wouldn't matter either way, but they seemed to release some of their stress with the activity, giving each other
comforting touches. Same-gender relationships didn't interest
him, either male-and-male or female-and-female, but Dom couldn't
deny them the right to a little physical reassurance.

It was rather like watching a clutch of tan-and-white birds
grooming each other after having had their flock unsettled.

The magic slowly darkened over the urchins from a pale gold
to a dark brown. Releasing the boys with a slight shove, Serina
stepped back. They stayed kneeling for a moment as the darkness
seeped into most of their bodies, lingering only at wrists, ankles,
and throats. Then they jerked upright and stumbled into the next
stall, where they dug out a few hidden amulets, returning them to
the nuns.

They did the same on the other side, as both stall owners eyed them warily, then one of the boys crossed the street and rooted around there. The other one took off at a lope. That made one of the constables shout.

"He's getting away!"

"No, he's not," Serina returned calmly, if with a smirk. "He's hunting down his partners in crime to fetch back the rest of the stolen goods. The geas laid upon him will lead him straight to whatever is missing, and then he'll come right back here with it. When the last piece has been returned and they're back on their knees in the position where I released them, the bands around their limbs will finish lightening, then vanish . . . and at that point, they'll be free to do as they please. I suggest you be ready to clap them in irons and march them off to the courts."

Even as she spoke, the dark bands around the one remaining youth were indeed lightening. He, too, took off down the street, vanishing into the crowd. The nuns watched him go, then clustered around Serina again, patting her shoulder, stroking her arm, babbling words of praise for their clever, powerful Guardian. One of those hands caressed and patted her pink-clad backside, making Serina jump in wide-eyed shock.

Dominor could guess why she had started so violently and moved in to rescue her. Clearing his throat, he pulled the nearest ones away, giving them a firm but polite look. "That's enough praising; you don't want to give her a swelled head. *Enough*, I said."

As soon as he had the ones on her near side cleared out of his way, Dominor slipped his arm around his hostess' waist, pulling her against his side. Out of the nuns' hands. They stared in a mixture of surprise and affront at the possessive move, then in confusion and disgust at the way her body relaxed against his, accepting it. Disappointment showed on more than one face, but they backed down, returning to the task of straightening the merchandise in their stall.

"Thank you," Serina murmured in his ear. She was only a few inches shorter than him, so she merely had to turn her head and tilt it to do so. "That isn't *quite* the way Mariel would have done it, but I do appreciate your help in extracting me from their clutches."

"Mariel?" Dominor asked under his breath, turning his face toward hers. That caused her lips to brush against his jaw, making her blush a little. She got over it quickly, pressing her mouth to his cheek deliberately before answering.

"She's the widow of the previous Guardian, and my dearest friend. She stayed at the Retreat after Milon's passing because she's a better Healer than what the nuns have, and because she wanted to help me settle into my duties. I'd be swamped with constant petty requests, if it weren't for her efforts in keeping them at bay."

"You sound as if you dislike being their Guardian," Dominor observed quietly.

"I don't dislike it, so much as I would rather be able to spend large blocks of my time on my work. The nuns seem to think I should be interrupted every half hour or so. Arithmancy requires solid bouts of concentration, at the levels I calculate," Serina explained. "That, and while I'm strong-willed when I want to be . . . I'm just not that interested in being a leader. If they could make me a sort of assistant-Mother Superior, I think they would . . . and I'd go screaming mad."

Now that things were settling down, some of the gathered crowd had dispersed. Others were stepping up to the long front of the nuns' booth, looking over the displayed wares as they gossiped with the white-clad women about what had just happened. Dominor couldn't blame them; gossip was gossip wherever one went around the World, it seemed . . . and gossip was often good for business. In fact, if word spread about this little incident, it was likely more people would come to chat, and if they came, some of them were bound to buy something.

It reminded him of the merchants who stopped at the Isle. More would've come to Nightfall, if it weren't for the Katani Council's edicts against visitors. *Now that we have our own government—since I like the thought of being an independent nation—we should definitely see about getting more traders to come by . . .*

"Excuse me, but . . . who are you?"

He pulled his attention back to his surroundings. The woman Serina had named Sister Amerith was peering at him dubiously. Dom started to release Serina, but at some point she had slipped her arm around his waist as well and carefully kept him at her side.

"Sister Amerith, this is Lord Dominor; I've hired him to help me with a very important project. As such, he will be returning to the Retreat with us. I give you my assurances, however, that he won't be bothering any of the nuns and will in fact remain mostly in the Guardian's wing with me."

Sister Amerith eyed the male mage skeptically. "How do I know he won't accidentally wander toward our sleeping cells some night?"

"Because we'll be working on Tantric magics together," Serina returned smoothly, though her cheeks flushed a little bit. "Trust me, he won't have the energy to spare."

Dominor's cheeks heated a little. Slipping his hand down from her waist, he lightly pinched her backside in retaliation for that particular comment. She twitched a little, glancing sharply at him, but he kept his face smoothly, neutrally polite. With seven brothers to get into trouble with, and a sharp-eyed mother to have to explain things to, he had learned long ago how to dissemble in the face of an interrogation. "I am aware, madam, that your Order is not inclined toward an interest in men. As far as I'm concerned, you are all nothing more than sisters to me . . . in the sense of being born into my family, as well as spiritually."

The nun studied him carefully, then made up her mind and nodded. "Good. Keep that in mind, and we'll get along. Though if the Mother Superior says you're not to stay, out you'll go!"

"Provided Lady Serina agrees, of course," he returned smoothly. "*She* has hired me for a specific task, after all—now, if you gentlewomen are settled back into your business, Lady Serina and I have matters to attend to elsewhere."

Hand back around her waist, he turned Serina away from the stall before the other woman could come up with a reason to keep them there. It was clear the geas spell would complete its work without needing their presence, thankfully . . . and he did have that comment about his hostess wearing him into nightly exhaustion to address. Preferably in private, as his sexual energies now felt reasonably recovered enough for a second attempt at "gauging compatibility."

ꟿmmph . . . mmmfop . . . stop—stop!" Pulling back from that all-too-distracting mouth, Dominor held Serina away from him by her shoulders and tried to regain his breath.

She frowned at him in confusion. "Why do you want us to stop?"

Licking his lips, Dom tipped his head at the small slateboard still lying upon the table in the rented chamber. "You forgot to set the spells to measure our compatibility, didn't you?"

Wincing, Serina tugged sharply on her braid and moved away from him, crossing to the table. "Stupid . . . stupid!" She let out a short, sharp chuckle. "Normally it's my *work* that consumes me to the point of neglecting the more mundane details of life. Yet here I am," she sighed, peering over her shoulder at him as she picked up the slate, "neglecting that work just to share pleasure with you. That's a definite turnabout on the usual order of things." She smiled wryly at him. "Somehow, I doubt we'll be incompatible."

Sinking onto the edge of the bed, Dominor watched her expanding the board with a muttered spell and a tap of her hand on its frame. Stooped over the table, her backside had been outlined nicely by the lightweight material of her tunic-dress. *Distracting* was definitely the word for it. "Is there a danger in our being *too* compatible?"

"Possibly, but in theory, we'd just need to practice until our lusts were sated enough to be placed under our control. Enough familiarity would breed a certain level of boredom, if nothing else."

"You prick at my vanity, my Lady," Dominor muttered as she found a piece of chalk and started marking mathemagical runes on the expanded board. "I may have gone awhile without the company of a woman in my bed, but I do have enough experience to ensure such things wouldn't be *boring*."

"I meant, from having to do the same thing over and over again," she returned somewhat absently, most of her concentration on the figures she was marking.

"You mean we have to perform in the *exact same way* as the long-dead couple whose work we're attempting to ameliorate?" he asked, dismayed by the idea of a rote performance. "I'm not some sort of machine, content to do the exact same thing the exact same way every exact, awful time!"

"Actually, I'm not completely certain. There's a bit of leeway in the calculations," Serina admitted, checking her runes carefully. "It depends on who I partner with, of course, as to how closely we'll have to follow the original couple's copulations. Calculating passion may be fascinating from a purely theoretical standpoint . . . but in practice, it's rather difficult to pin down without hard, recorded facts close at hand." Marking a last bit, she tossed the chalk onto the table and dusted off her fingers, turning to him with a feminine smirk. "The question is, are your hard facts still close at hand?"

Dominor knew an innuendo when he heard one. Reaching out to her, he caught and interlaced her fingers with his, tugging her close enough to stand between his knees. "If it is *your* hand, my Lady, I think so . . ."

That made her frown softly. She even leaned back slightly, staring down at him with a puzzled look. "Are all of you Nightfallers so formal, even when you're about to romp around in a bed?"

He couldn't think of a good reason to tell her about his foreseen Destiny just yet. Not when he still wasn't quite sure if she was the Lady he was supposed to seek. Standing, Dominor caught and held her against his frame, keeping her balanced, since the movement made their bodies bump closely together. "Would you rather have me roll like a rude barbarian in the bedding with you and then disrespect you come the morning?"

"Well, no," she agreed, looping her arms around his shoulders. "Respect is good. Respect can be fun, so long as it's not taken to a stodgy level of form . . . mmm . . ."

There was nothing of "formality" in the way Dominor kissed her. Plenty of respect, but very little formality. Not when it involved the challenge of seeing who tasted better. The only way to judge that, Serina knew, was by both of them sampling as much as possible; not just of their mouths, but of the softness of her cheek, the edge of his jaw, the curve of her ear, and that soft-rough spot beneath his chin where he needed to apply a shaving charm. And of course, tasting all the other spots bared as they once again stripped away their clothes.

Tumbling onto the bed, off-balance from trying to remove half-forgotten footwear, they found themselves laughing as they extricated and sorted out their limbs. As soon as they were completely stripped, Dominor stretched out on his back. Hands reaching for his bedmate, he pulled Serina up over his chest, urging her to straddle him.

She did so with a quirk of her eyebrow, wondering what he had in mind. Catching the end of her somewhat ragged braid, Dominor unbound what he could reach of it. Her fingers worked to free the rest, but when she started to pull it forward over her breasts, he shook his head.

"No. I want it down your back. And then lean back a little," he instructed the woman astride his ribs.

Serina eyed him doubtfully, but did as he asked. Shaking the pale mane back from her shoulders, she grasped the hands he offered and arched herself backward. A moment later his fingers tightened on hers, accompanying a hiss of pleasure . . . and a buck of his hips. Twisting her head, she saw where the ends of her thigh-length hair had pooled, caressing and tangling around his arousal. That spread a grin over her lips.

Tilting her face so that she stared at the ceiling again, Serina jiggled her head, tickling him deliberately with her long locks. He sucked in a breath, then tucked her hands behind her back, bracing them on his hipbones. That freed his own hands. It didn't take long for her to find out where they had gone: to play with her breasts. It was her turn to sigh in pleasure, enjoying the way he traced the seam along the underside with his fingertips, then circled up over her small curves, spiraling in toward their tightening peaks.

He surprised her with a muttered word, shifting his hands from her breasts to her hips. Magic lifted her body, lightening her mass. Pulling her up and forward, he held her in place with one hand, tugged a pillow more firmly under his head, and kissed the inner curves of her thighs. Between his hands supporting her hips and her arms supporting her upper body, she felt oddly suspended. And titillated; this wasn't the usual position for such things. If anything, she was used to straddling a man facedown, sharing such pleasures mutually. However, this Nightfaller seemed content to let the braiding-kinked waves of her hair pool and dangle over his lap.

Dominor lifted his knees, propping up his thighs a little. It gave her a backrest for her shoulders, though it ended much of the tickling sensation of her pale tresses. He had something else in mind, however: delicate torment.

Expecting him to devour her with the same enthusiasm as before, Serina discovered after the first few minutes of feather-light licks that this was *all* he was going to give her. She squirmed in his grip, trying to inch closer. Thanks to his spell, it was difficult for her to fight against the steady grip of his hands under her buttocks. She had some of the necessary strength, but none of the mass to enforce it. Finally, it was too much, even as it wasn't nearly enough.

"Dominor, please!"

Dom paused between licks. "Please . . . what?"

As if he doesn't already know! That frustrated her, even as it made her want to laugh. This particular man was definitely arrogant. *If he wants me to speak my mind, I'll* speak *my moon-riddled mind!*

"Please make my brain explode!"

Well, he'd never quite heard it put *that* way . . . but it was as apt a description as any other he'd encountered. Pulling her a little closer, he prepared her with one last, slow, teasing lap. She growled in frustration, until he suckled on the little sentinel-peak of flesh before him. The growl shifted to a gasp, her body arching in his grip.

It didn't take long for him to make her buck and cry out, straining against his lips. Twisting free, she flopped lightly onto the bed, twisting her head to one side as she lay face-down recovering. After a minute or so, Serina regathered enough of both energy and wits to push herself up onto hands and knees. The caress of his hand along her hip made her shiver, but it was the sight of his manhood, engorged and proud, that held most of her attention.

Intimate kisses such as those were quite enjoyable, but they didn't *fill* her the way that intercourse did. Scrambling to straddle him once again, Serina settled this time over his hips, not his ribs. A helpful mutter from him canceled his weight-lessening spell, which allowed gravity to assist as she positioned herself and sank down onto him. *That* filled the emptiness inside of her, and she let it show in a smug, feminine smile.

It looked to Dominor like she had plans of taking over their interactions, at least for a little while. Deciding he would let her work her lascivious will upon him—and that smile was decidedly lascivious—he tucked his hands behind his head. That allowed her to ride him however she liked. It was quite enjoyable from his perspective, too; there wasn't any vigorous thrusting, but she did circle and shift her hips in delicious ways as she gently rode him.

Once again, he lifted his hands to her breasts, teasing their soft, small curves with feather-light touches. Her hands came up and covered his, showing him that she liked having her nipples gently plucked. Dominor improvised by rolling one beaded tip under the edge of his thumb, and she moaned in appreciation, letting her head fall back. With each circling stroke of her pelvis against his, the strands of her long, pale hair teased his knees, calves, and inner thighs. Soon his muscles began subtly flexing, thrusting up into her downward strokes.

Gentleness transformed into a greater enthusiasm. Leaning forward, Serina braced her palms on the bedding, giving her a better angle in which to thrust, and a way to pull her down into his strokes with his hands gripping her hips. She knew it had been a long while since her last lover, but never had she felt so quickly at ease with a new partner. They were like two equations that completed each other, like the calculations for determining the energy required and the area to be affected when enlarging or shrinking a particular type of spell: magic, to her way of thinking. When his hand shifted from her hip to the nape of her neck, tangling in her hair and pulling her mouth down to meet his, she didn't resist.

Their tongues entwined even as their loins did, a steady coupling rhythm that felt very much like a dance. But like some kinds of dance, the tempo couldn't stay steady as they neared the end; it speeded up between them, keeping time with the increased pace of their hearts and their lungs. Breaking off their kiss, Serina sat up a little, arching her back as the new position stimulated her nerves just that necessary bit more—

"Dominor!"

"Gods yes!" he agreed as her inner muscles clenched and spasmed, tightening around him. Clutching her hips, he thrust up into her three, four times—her short nails raked lightly down his chest, stimulating him unexpectedly, but not unpleasantly. A grunt escaped his clenched teeth, heralding the spasming of his loins and the pouring of his seed into her anklet-protected womb. Three releases on the same day, and none of it by his own hand; he could definitely grow fond of his vow to assist her Tantrically . . .

Serina collapsed on top of him. Her sagging frame, though slender, almost made him wish she still wore that mass-lightening charm he had applied earlier, but only almost, and only for a moment. When she muttered something about possibly being heavy, Dominor wrapped his arms around her, letting her know he was quite capable of supporting her weight.

Both of them were damp and sticky with sweat, but the air in their chamber was cool enough to allow their skin to dry. He suspected the inn had some sort of cooling charm laid upon it, for its walls were made from wood, which normally retained heat in such a warm climate. There were two reasons why the palace-like castle back home was crafted mostly from plastered stone: one, for fortification; and two, for climate control. Wood held and retained heat; stone cooled and dispersed it.

One went with what was available, however. Nightfall had a lot of wood, but it also had a lot of stone in the form of its two granite mountain ranges. This land seemed to have a lot of hardwood trees, given the sheer number of wooden structures that composed the port city. That made him think about possible trading materials, since Nightfall's forests were wild-grown orchards, fruitwoods. Those sorts of fruits didn't grow around here as far as he could tell, based on the samplings he had seen offered in the market stalls. A pity Natallia and Mandare were too hardened into their so-called civil war to be effective trading partners.

Your wits are wandering, Dominor chided himself. *You have a beautiful, sensual woman in your arms, and your wits are wandering to matters of trade—though if you're to ever be a Lord Chancellor, I suppose cross-oceanic trade is one of the things you'll need to think about.*

"Pardon me," Serina mumbled, squeezing him with her arms before lifting her head with a sheepish smile. "I forgot to say 'thank you.' That was wonderful."

Dom smiled back. "You're welcome, and yes, it was." He started to say more, but one of their stomachs rumbled; he couldn't tell whose it was, since the sound told him *he* was hungry, and the quick flush of her cheeks told him that *she* was, too. "I think supper would be in order, don't you?"

"Mm, yes. Let me go tidy up in the refreshing room, then I'll place another order with the kitchens. Unless you want to go downstairs to the dining hall for supper?" Serina asked him, summoning enough energy through her post-satiation lethargy to climb out of the bed.

"Not tonight, I think. Tomorrow will be soon enough to handle crowds again." A thought crossed his mind, making him frown softly. "Serina . . . where is that shell-necklace of yours? The one your pearls were stuffed into?"

"Oh, I'm still wearing it," she confessed, scooping her hands between her breasts. A moment later, the shell materialized on the same bit of thong as earlier. "It's just enchanted to hide whenever I'm naked. And whenever I'm showering. I almost had it stolen when I took it off for a bath, one time. So long as it's on *me*, however, it cannot be stolen. It's only visible when I'm clothed." She flashed him a smile, as she paused in the doorway to the refreshing room. "It's a spell I came up with myself!"

That pricked his competitive nature, but Dominor wasn't quite sure how to go about proving he could be creative, too. He preferred to create tangible, useful things, a habit encouraged by his brothers' need to produce objects for sale so that they could buy the things their island exile didn't provide. With all those rainbow-pearls in her possession, she didn't need anyone to buy *things* for her, nor even create them. *Which leaves me with . . . what?*

Rising from the bed, he stretched his limbs, pleased with the aches and twinges of muscles that hadn't been used in those particular ways for some time. He was a little out of shape, thanks to his ordeals; now that he was no longer a captive, he could get himself back into proper trim within a few weeks. Moving over to the waist-high window to brace himself against the ledge while he stretched his calves, Dom peered through the mesh keeping out the bugs, but not keeping out the early evening breeze.

They had been smart enough to erect another silencing spell before tumbling onto the bed, so the view below his window was eerily quiet, considering the number of carts heading away from the market sector. Dominor thought he saw the farmer-merchant they had stopped and chatted with earlier. *She needs to check daily for those bundles of plants she wanted picked . . . what were they called? Lemonhart, that was it. And we'll need to stop by that weaponsmith's stall for my sword and its new scabbard—she's right, it's a silly thing to summon a weapon without summoning the sheath for it as well, though there are more times when having a bared blade is direly important than there are times when you need to summon sword and scabbard both.*

Perhaps I can speak with my brothers about that; we could create Summonable sheaths that would bring themselves and whatever is stuck within them when commanded by a wielder-coded word . . . Ah, there are some of those nuns, from earlier! He peered down at them through the mesh, though the angle made it hard to see through the dark-dyed gauze. *They still look like a flock of noisy, nosy birds, to me.*

It had been nice to know that his efforts at controlling their chatter and managing the situation earlier were appreciated by his hostess. If there was one thing he could do well, it was taking charge of a group. Not his brothers, of course, but back in their homeland before the exile, Dominor had organized the servants more than once. It had been a way of competing with his eldest brother, Saber, whose job it would be by birthright, commanding the servants of Corvis Castle and the farmers who tilled the county's lands.

If he hadn't been born with enough ability to grasp magic at the level of a Councilor, Dom could've been employed as a seneschal or castellan, placed in charge of some other lord's or lady's lands. That was the best an educated thirdborn son could expect to achieve, if he didn't have enough power to go into politics. Well, that or marrying into wealth and power.

If we keep up the pretense of Nightfall being a sovereign isle, and make *it sovereign in the eyes of all . . . better for me to be Her Majesty's Chancellor. Even if Saber is her Consort and thus her closest advisor, it's far better to have a great deal of influence in a tiny kingdom, than a modest bit of influence at best in a much larger empire . . . assuming the Council of Mages would allow a Son of Destiny to serve alongside them.*

"Refreshing room's free. I'm going to start those calculations, now that we've remembered to get our interactions recorded," Serina told him as he turned around. She was blithely naked, still. Dominor quirked a skeptical eyebrow at her, making her eye him defensively. "What?"

"Shouldn't you first send a note down to the kitchens for our supper, and then get dressed so that you're decent when the inn servant arrives with our meal?"

"Oh, right—sorry; I was just eager to get started on those calculations," she apologized, flashing him a smile. "Note first, clothes second, and *then* I can have my fun. Mental fun, that is," Serina added, catching him around the waist as he passed her on his way to the refreshing room. She pulled their bodies together for a not-quite-quick kiss, then released him. "I've already had my physical fun for the day."

"You can say that again," he muttered as she turned toward the table. Three times already today, and his manhood had just now tried to stir again, thanks to the feel of her curves pressed against him. He retreated to the refreshing room, deciding on a quick use of that rain-shower stall to remove the sweat from his skin, as well as the inevitable sticky residue from lovemaking.

By the time he emerged wrapped in a damp toweling cloth, she had donned only her tunic-dress, her legs bare, her feet padding over the wood as she tapped and slid a small brick of chalk over the surfaces of two fully enlarged slateboards. Pulling on a pair of trousers, Dominor studied her work. Most of it he could follow, but some of it was a little confusing, for her notes were being written in some personal shorthand that the Ultra Tongue he had imbibed couldn't decipher.

He didn't know what the capital letter *P* stood for, for one. *B* was another, though it seemed to not be quite as important, or at least it seemed to enter into the equations much later than *P* did, and seemed to supplant it. *No, wait,* B *is there in what looks like the earliest part of the equations, if she's scribing in the standard left-to-right pattern. Some kingdoms around the World write differently than we do in Katan, of course, but since most people are right-handed, it makes sense to move the hand across the blank part of the page, so that the ink does not smudge . . .*

Five knocks at the door let him know the servant had arrived. His hostess didn't look away from her work. Dominor cleared his throat. "Serina . . . shouldn't you be getting the door?"

"What? Why?" she asked, finally glancing over her shoulder.

Dominor gestured at it. "To pay for our food?"

The first time they had eaten, she had sent money down to the kitchens with a note requesting their meal. This second time, Dominor hadn't seen her do so. Somehow, he didn't think the server on the other side would just leave the food without first receiving payment this time—the woman was very distractable.

"Oh. Um . . . I have a coin-pouch in that satchel, there," she told him, gesturing at one of the saddlebags on the floor by the table. "Just pay them whatever; I trust you."

Dominor shuddered, internally. She *trusted* him? Oath-bound or not, how did she know he could be trusted with her money? This woman had very few self-preservation instincts, compared to him! The knock came again as he rummaged in the satchel, finding the coin-purse by the feel of the discs inside. Opening the door, he accepted the tray and set it on the table, paid out the three silvers and two coppers the woman asked for, and shut the door again.

Removing the wicker domes revealed identical plates of fresh-baked fish on slabs of cheese-covered bread, raw but washed vegetables, and leafy greens lightly drizzled in some sort of sauce. A carafe of chilled white wine had been provided along with two ceramic cups. Sitting down, Dominor reached for the cutlery, glad it wasn't too different from the kind the Katani used, though the tines of the forks were a little shorter. He stopped before taking his first mouthful, glancing up as chalk continued to scrape softly against slate.

"Supper is here."

"Mmm." She didn't look away from her work, though she did tug on the ends of her hair, dusting it with some of the chalk smudging her fingers.

He tried again. "Serina, come eat your supper."

"I'll be right there . . ."

He almost fell for it. Almost, except her tone seemed rather . . . rote. Absentminded.

"Serina!"

She jumped and turned around at his sharp use of her name. "What?"

"Sit," he ordered briskly, pointing at the chair across from him, the chair that was a single step away from her position, but which she had yet to use. "Eat. *Now*."

Rolling her eyes, she dropped the chalk into the scoop-shaped bottom of the nearest chalkboard frame and pulled out the chair. A muttered spellword cleansed her hands. "Fine. I'm eating! You're as bad as Mariel." A pause, fork in hand, and she gave him a sheepish smile. "Not that this is a *bad* thing, since I do tend to get a bit immersed in my work. At least, when I'm guaranteed a nice stretch of uninterrupted ti—"

A knock on the door and a muffled but feminine voice calling her name from the hallway beyond their room made her groan. Serina dropped her fork in favor of bracing her forehead in her palms. "I can't *wait* until I can get this stupid ritual finished, and I can go find somewhere *else* to live!"

Rising, Dominor crossed to the door. He readied a defensive spell just in case it was a trap, but when he opened the door, it was the nun who had questioned him before. "Sister Amerith."

She didn't look too happy to see him, especially in his shirtless state. "Er . . . I came to see Lady Serina, actually." The nun tried to step inside, past him, but Dominor didn't budge. Given that he was taller and more muscular than the older woman, she didn't get very far. "Do you mind? I'm here to see the Guardian!"

"What do you want, Sister?" Serina asked, not budging from the table.

"Well, there's that strange chest you brought by, earlier; it's still in the stall and we can't get it to move. Sister Merina thought it was important enough to be guarded by a couple of us until we could speak with you, to see if you really wanted it left there overnight, but with that mess we had earlier today with those thieves . . ."

"I'll go fetch it myself, Sister."

"*After* you have eaten," Dom asserted over his shoulder upon hearing Serina rise from the table. He returned his attention to the nun, and spoke under his breath. "I'll not have you depriving her of her supper. I will also make sure that anyone guarding it is escorted back to the inn safely. Thank you for bringing this to our attention."

To make sure she understood the dismissal in his words, Dominor closed the door in the woman's face. Keeping his weight against it just in case, he turned to see Serina's reaction to his high-handedness. She was staring at him with a peculiar expression, making Dom wonder if he had gone too far.

"On the one hand," the pale blond mage stated slowly, "I should be upset with you for being so . . . so . . ."

"High-handed?" he offered.

"Well, yes," Serina agreed. She studied Dominor, lean enough from his kidnapping ordeal that he could stand to put on a full stone in weight, but very capable looking, regardless of his trials, and sagged back into her seat. "But on the other hand . . . you're every bit as good at that as Mariel is. I'm going to miss her terribly once I'm free to leave, unless I can convince her to come with me."

A terrible thought crossed Dominor's mind as she poured herself some wine. "This Mariel . . . is she . . ." He didn't quite know how to phrase it. "Is she . . . your lover? In the sense of Koral-tai?"

Serina nearly choked on the first sip of her drink. Setting it down quickly, she delicately wiped at her mouth with the edge of her hand. "Oh, Moons, no! She's *very* interested in men. Well, sort of, considering she's been in mourning for her husband for the last two years. You know, she *did* urge me to go out and get tumbled into a bed, but she hasn't done so herself. I really should find someone for her. Even if it's only an itch-to-scratch sort of person, she could use a spot of physical fun in her life . . ."

Moving away from the door, Dom joined her at the table. "Less talking, more eating. You're getting sidetracked again."

She straightened and thumped her fist against her chest in what he thought was probably a Moonlands salute—a mockery of one, given her earnest but overblown, wide-eyed expression, which she followed with an expressive, sardonic roll of her eyes—then picked up her fork and dug into the greens.

TEN

⦁❧⦁

Politeness made Dominor offer to carry the chalk-marked chest, after they had dressed and returned to the market-place. Unfortunately, when they were no more than a third of the way back to the inn, the street was partially blocked by a not-so-small group of men. Five stepped out of the shadows in front of them, four more behind them. All of them had weapons—cudgels, knives, even one with a length of rope. More ominous, two of them raised hands that glowed with mage-fire, a visible warning that their victims would face magical as well as physical danger.

The four nuns, though startled, quickly spread themselves out, two to face the front, two to the back. They angled their hands in a way that was both odd and yet oddly familiar to Dominor, but did nothing else. Dom hastily set the chest on the ground, needing his hands free. Serina merely rolled her eyes, sighed with heavy, audible disgust, and planted her hands on her hips.

"What do *you* so stupidly want?"

"We want that chest there, and them pearls of yours," the rope-wielder stated. The robe writhed in his hands under some sort of enchantment, its ends lifting and displaying loops that could ensnare and strangle the unwary. "We're not afraid of Koral-tai fighting, an' we've more mages than you."

"Hardly," Serina snorted. None of the four nuns who had accompanied her and Dominor were mages, though several of the others on this expedition were. But she doubted any further mages would be needed to handle these idiots. "Numbers do not necessarily equal strength. And if you try to press an attack, you will be badly injured."

More figures moved into the half-shadowed light. Several of them also had further signs of arcane ability, from shape-shifting limbs, to a pair that literally hovered over their companions' heads, suspended in the night air by the force of their magic. Rope-man grinned at Serina, his teeth gleaming in the light of a nearby lantern. "Not when we've got twenny o' us magickers, and there's only two o' *you*."

Dominor parted his lips, ready to offer to dispatch them; if any of them had even a tenth of his ability, they wouldn't have to join forces with a street gang to be a genuine threat. Serina stamped her foot before he could speak, however—and as fast as a dashing cat, the cobblestones around them *jumped* underfoot. Dom staggered, as did the nuns, but that was the only effect within an arm's reach of the ragged, defensive circle they had formed. Beyond that arm-length point, the cobblestones *changed*. The worn, weathered blocks shifted abruptly from their flattish, rounded contours, jutting up as swift, sharpened spikes.

The ranks of would-be thieves screamed, jerking and stumbling, toppling to the ground . . . where they screamed as more than their now bloodied feet encountered the hand-length stone spikes Serina had created. Dominor almost missed his own cue, startled by the strange piece of magery. The two floating mages screamed in anger; one hurled a ball of fire, the other a bolt of lightning. Reflex took over for Dominor.

His left forearm whipped up in front of his face, the gestural habit erecting a dome-like shield; the flames spilled over and vanished, and the lightning grounded itself upon the magic, draining into the smooth cobblestones under Dominor's feet. His right hand jabbed forward in time with the lowering of his left forearm, shooting a bolt of his own back at the pair. It struck the flame-hurler as he was summoning a second fireball; unable to contain the flames in the face of the shocking jolt, he crisped his own clothes, lost control of his levitation spell, and dropped from the sky.

The one who was using lightning had dodged out of the way and now readied a second blast of his own.

The thugs really had no chance, given that this was the sort of magery-combat he and his brothers practiced along with the ways of wielding physical weapons and shields. *He should've been preparing his second spell immediately*, Dom thought chidingly. *Spell combat is just like physical combat; the faster and more accurate mage will usually win.* And though it was more a dirty trick of the sort Trevan would've pulled, Dominor had no compunction against using this particular counterspell, as his opponent began crackling.

A mutter, a sharp gesture—and a conjured allotment of water splashed down out of the sky. The mage spluttered and lost control of his lightning, which zapped and crackled over his drenched body in an uncontained dance of writhing white lines. He, too, dropped to the spike-sharpened ground, adding injury to such a sopping-wet insult.

Serina stomped her foot again. The ground beneath them jumped once again in a fast, outward ripple. This time, the spikes vanished, leaving the men groaning in pain on flattish, rounded, blood-soaked but otherwise ordinary-looking cobblestones. To Dom's surprise, the four nuns dug into the pouches at their waists, each casting a handful of copper and silver coins out over the groaning, whimpering bodies.

"Here," one of them stated with a derisive edge to her voice as she echoed her Sisters' actions with a fistful of her own funds. "Some coins, so you can pay the Healers for your troubles."

At the foreign mage's confused look, Serina smirked. "The nuns of Koral-tai are known for their charity toward those less fortunate—or even less intelligent—than themselves. By giving them some money to pay a Healer, it also keeps the city's Guard from hauling them up in front of a judge for causing an 'unnecessary burden' on the Port's medical resources."

A parting gesture of her hands and several of the whimpering, would-be bandits slid out of their way, clearing a path to the far side of the aborted ambush. The street was still red and damp from the metallic tang of blood, but at least they wouldn't be tripping on anyone.

Dominor shook his head, stooping to pick up the chest again. "This is a very strange land."

He had said it in his native tongue, so as not to offend the four pale-clad nuns moving around him. Serina shrugged and matched his native accent as best she could. "Tell me about it."

"Yes, but you've been here for two years," he pointed out, sticking to Katani. "I haven't even been here for two days, yet, and already I've seen more than I wanted to know about Natallia."

"I'll try to keep you out of too much trouble," she teased, smiling. The curve of her lips softened and broadened into a warmer smile. "Thanks for your help, by the way; you have very fast reflexes, for a mage."

"I have seven brothers, all of them mages, my Lady," he reminded her. "All of us are trained for attack and defense, as well as for more peaceful, creative forms of magery."

"It's rare for so many siblings to all have the Mage-Gift," she observed thoughtfully. "Most of the time, it's maybe two out of every five children, if one or both parents has the ability, with only one in every forty or fifty families having it in their blood at all . . . and it's only one in every ten born with the gift who have it in any real strength."

Since that was about the same ratio as Katan had, he merely nodded in agreement, concentrating on not soiling his new boots too much as they left the injured idiots in their own blood for the city Guards to find. He didn't wish them dead, exactly, but he wasn't going to stop to bandage their wounds, either. "Are we going to be fighting every would-be pickpocket and roadside raider from here to this Retreat, once we leave Port Blueford?"

"No. I've already thought about it and decided against it," Serina admitted. "Instead, I'll open a mirror-Gate from here to the Retreat, widen the frames, and just transport the carts and goods across the frames. It'll be a pain to keep the horses and the cart wheels from touching the frames and risking a collapse of the link, but if you can levitate them for me, I can concentrate on keeping the mirrors steady. There's a dozen two-horse carts, and twenty more horses."

Dominor found that impressive. "Levitating carts and horses I can do, easily. Widening a linked pair of mirrors . . . that's impressive. I *can* do it myself, but it's still impressive."

The way he phrased that made her laugh. "I'll actually have help from the Mother Superior; she's a fair mage herself. But tell me: Are you always this arrogant, in regards to your skills?"

"Why must everyone think that a simple, bold statement of *fact* must automatically be a sourceless spouting of *arrogance*?" Dom countered, though he smiled as he did so.

"Because most societies prefer for those who are powerful to demure and say they are less so, in order to keep from frightening those who lack a similar level of skill?" Serina returned, answering his rhetorical question as if it were real.

"Probably," he agreed. And decided he definitely liked this woman, if she could understand at least some of his personality. *Now it only remains to be seen if she is my Destiny . . .*

They stayed in Port Blueford for nearly two weeks; Dominor spent his time either with Serina in their room at the inn—and in more than just bedsports, for she was eager to learn what he knew of foreign magics and mathemagics, and he was interested to know what she knew from her own travels—or in following her around the town. Part of that was spent in keeping track of her somewhat absentminded errands, and part of it was spent in keeping the nuns from being too much of a nuisance. Thankfully, by the middle of the second week, the flock of nun-hens had finally grown accustomed to his interventions, and he had learned which of their impositions were actually important.

The grateful looks she sent his way mollified the part of him that was annoyed she didn't deal with these things herself. It wasn't that she couldn't—she *could* and did occasionally take matters into her own hands, and successfully. It was just that Serina of the Moonlands was so *focused*, she clearly disliked having that focus shifted . . . and when it did shift, things got forgotten, or abandoned, or muddled in the wake of whatever disruption had occurred.

It wasn't so much that she needed a keeper, Dominor discovered, as much as a manager. More than that, he discovered he *liked* managing her day: It gave him a sense of accomplishment. Of course, part of it was that the more she could focus on her calculations, the more she could get her work done, and get them that much closer to the ritual they were contracted to perform together. Once that was out of his way, Dominor would be free of the oath-obligation and could make up his mind what to do with her on a more permanent basis. Another part was that he really had nothing else to do with his days; they were merely biding their time here in this city until the nuns finished their selling and buying.

The only fly in the ointment was the fact that she *was* unevenly focused: Serina seemed to think her calculations were vastly more important than common necessities such as eating. She would eat of her own free will . . . but only one meal a day, that being breakfast. And maybe some sort of snack in the late evening if he didn't make her stop and have an actual lunch and supper. Her focus on her calculations seemed excessive to him, actually. Make-work, while they were waiting for the nuns to finish their trading and purchasing. They couldn't make love every hour of the day, after all.

But their time in the port city did come to an end. He followed her to the city's Mage Guild and watched her negotiate for the use of a mirror. She used it to contact the Retreat, where a nun in a slightly more elaborate uniform than the rest cast Gatingpowder on the mirror, turning it from a communication tool into a traveling tool, but only long enough to toss a pair of pots through. Dominor knew it wasn't that different from the powder his youngest sibling used to contact other universes. A second casting of powder closed the connection.

He also knew of the salve that Serina and the other woman rubbed onto the frame in carefully arranged synchronicity, once the Gate was closed; it made the wood pliable. That came from one of the pots passed through the mirror. Together, Serina and the woman she addressed as the Mother Superior stretched the frame until it was a double hand-span wider than the carts waiting in the Mage Guild's courtyard. The surface of the mirror was now thinner; that meant the plane where the two surfaces intersected was correspondingly thinner. They had to make sure the mirrors were carefully stabilized before reopening the link; if the aether between the two locations was disturbed, the connection could be lost . . . and the mirrors could be shattered.

Mirror-Gating *could* be done without a second mirror involved, but *any* modest disturbance in the aether could cause the Gate to collapse, unless the mage casting it was willing to spend great amounts of power to stabilize it. Dominor and his brothers suspected that the mage who had been plaguing them with those frequent invasions of nasty beasts wasn't averse to using unpleasantly illegal means to acquire enough outside energy. Whoever their enemy was, he or she clearly didn't care about legalities, given how frequently they plagued the brothers in their exiled home. It was only thanks to Kelly's influence and Morganen's inspiration a few months ago that they'd altered their residence too much for anyone to successfully scry from a distance.

But that was there, and this was here. Dominor's job was simple; passing the carts and horses through from one side to the other without letting them touch the frame. If they touched it, they could jolt the mirrors out of sync, and that would mean shattering the connection and severing in half whatever was passing through them at the time. *If* they were lucky. A bad jolt could cause the item—or living being—in transit to explode from the torquing of the disrupted spells.

The simplest way was to wrap each beast in a firm, floating bubble to keep it from struggling successfully beyond the bubble-spell's—and thus the mirror's—confines. Because the connection couldn't stay open forever, the horses had to be hitched to the carts so that, once released from their prison, they could be led away from the mirror frame by the nuns on the other side, leaving room for another cart and horse to cross. That meant wrapping beast and cart in the spell, for the horses that were hitched to the heavily laden wagons. Thankfully, the spheres were fairly easy to cast.

Floating them was another matter; horses and carts were heavy, requiring energy. Serina bartered with the Mage Guild for Dominor to tap into their reserves of magic. That meant he worked under the watchful eye of three Guildmistresses. He had the feeling, as they watched him with stern, wary expressions, that if Port Blueford had been just a little bit closer to Mandare and thus their stupid war, they would've refused him their permission. Even if he was a foreign mage with a clear and reasonable grudge against their national enemy.

Magic came mostly from within a mage; the more powerful one was, the greater spells one could cast, and the greater efforts and deeds one could perform. Magic *could* be garnered from the life force of others, but unless the mage was attuned to gathering ambient energy, other means had to prevail. Either it required a cooperative effort, usually between two or more mages pooling their resources, or it required a blood sacrifice. Some blood sacrifices were willingly made, usually by the mage in question; most, however, were garnered from torturing and murdering highly unwilling victims.

Those were anathema to most mages, and a blood-magic practitioner often found him- or herself with a lot of wary watchers, if they took the route of willing sacrifice, and a lot more of enemies if they took the path of psychotic evil. Even just killing a chicken for roasting had to be carefully done, if it was done by a mage; it was considered dangerously close to the wrong sort of blood-magic, if the mage doing the deed collected that little bit of life force without *some* form of appeasement to the Gods, and to the chicken's spirit for the use of its energies. Dominor and his brothers didn't bother with capturing that energy; they all had enough energy in and of themselves to begin with, plus they knew each of them could call upon any of the others for assistance, so there was no point in risking a downward spiral of temptation in grabbing the wrong kind in the quest for more power.

Natural energies could be converted as well, such as the electricity found in a lightning storm; it took some of the mage's energy to convert it, however, and wasn't very cost effective, unless the mage in question had an affinity for that type of energy. Rydan invariably charged himself during storms before going off to make Artifacts for sale, and Koranen usually ignited a physical fire in his forge, converting that into extra magical energy for his own works. Fonts and Fountains were another source of energy, but they were usually kept secret and guarded fiercely against misuse.

The most common way to collect energy was to gather it into special containment spells and artifacts, usually held by the masters of a Mage School or Mage Guild; it could be gathered from natural or living sources, or even by blood sacrifice, though that left a taint in the energies. The most common source was from the mages themselves; they shed energy near constantly when awake, like miniature Fountains.

When trained properly, most mages could pool their energies back into their own bodies, carrying around within them a large reservoir of magic to draw upon. Unfortunately, Dominor had been shackled by magic-draining manacles; his reserves were still severely depleted even two weeks after their removal. Thus he needed to draw upon the Guild's reserves to complete his task.

There were ways to get around that, however. He had the nuns on the Port Blueford side drag the horses up to within a body-length of the mirror and only then encapsulated them in his shield-bubble. A lift and a carefully but quickly aligned shove sent them straight through the mirror to the other side just a hand-length above the edge of the frame, which rested on the court-yard ground. Once across the intersection plane, he set them down just as quickly about a body-length from the far mirror. As soon as the bubble collapsed, nuns on that side of the connection hauled the disturbed horses quickly out of the courtyard hosting the far mirror.

The same happened with the riding horses. They were brought up to the mirror with their riding tack and the nuns' belongings strapped firmly to their backs, encapsulated, lifted and shoved through, then released and led away. One or two tried to buck on the far side, disliking the enclosed space and the abrupt jolt, but he had chosen a spot too far from the mirror to be a threat to either it or the Mother Superior standing next to its frame, occu-pying more or less the same spot at the Retreat that Serina did on this side of the Gate. Following them were the nuns them-selves, though he thankfully didn't have to enclose them in a floating bubble. Instead, they hitched up their tunic-dress hems and hopped through the broadened frame two at a time, where they staggered into the arms of yet more white-clad women waiting on the far side.

Dominor didn't follow the last of the nuns, however; he needed to rest for a moment, though he never would have admitted it aloud. Serina closed the Gate with another casting of powder, though she left open the scrying link. Carefully wiping the frame in tandem with the Mother Superior, she reduced the size of the mirror to its standardized, door-sized proportions. Only then did she cast another handful of powder and step carefully, if tiredly, across. Dominor followed her, sparing just a moment to thank the mages for their energy and mirror before stepping across the immeasurable distance.

The intersection plane was like stepping through a cold, glass-thin spill of water, only this was a waterfall that poured straight through skin, muscle, and bone and added a bit of dizzying dis-orientation, too. It was different each time, depending on the state of the aether when Gating, and the distance to be traveled. Cold was unpleasant, but at least it didn't feel like a thousand needles stabbing through his nerves. And only the seventhborn of his brothers enjoyed it when Gate-travel felt like stepping through the flames of a bonfire; only Koranen would. Some-times, one felt nothing, or one became inured to the side effects;

the disorientation was the only consistent complaint regarding mirror-Gating.

That inevitable dizziness wracked his body as he staggered free of the mirror's vicinity. It had been a long while since his last Gating. Dom struggled with his stomach, breathing carefully through his teeth until he wrestled his innards back under his own control. The cool air around him helped, though it was thinner than expected, making it a little harder to feel like his lungs were getting filled properly. Only when his stomach ceased its rebellion did he look around—had he Gated into enemy or unclaimed territory, he would have forced awareness out of sheer caution, but this was a nunnery, presumed to be secured and safe.

It was a nunnery carved out of dark gray basalt, livened—if one could call it that—by white. The pointed frames of the windows and the arches of the sheltered walkways were dark stone, hewn from the equally dark mountains around them, but the walls of the courtyard and the main shafts of the pillars, had been whitewashed. Everything was either white or gray or black. With the nuns' hair covered in veils and the horses now out of sight, only the deep red of his garments and the green of Serina's splashed any life into their surroundings.

Only their clothes convinced him his eyes hadn't lost the ability to see in color, for even the overcast sky seemed to leech the warm hues from their skin. Dominor turned around, surveying the rows of windows carved into the very rugged peaks around them, and faced his hostess. "*This* . . . is where you live?"

"For now, yes," Serina agreed. She had braced her hands against her knees for a little bit, recovering from her exertions, and now straightened. "You'll get used to the thinness of the air after a few days."

"It's not the elevation I object to," he told her, gesturing at the whitewashed walls and dark gray flagstones. "It's the . . . the *starkness* of it—haven't these nuns heard of color?"

"The Retreat has been this way for aeons. The exterior lack of color allows it to blend into the mountainsides, as well as clouds, and especially the snows of winter—this is one of only three places in all of Natallia, and now Mandare, where it snows," Serina told him. "The nuns of Koral-tai . . . well, their quarters and halls are rather ascetic in many ways, but they do have some

color in them. They use it sparsely, as a focal-point for their med-
itations.

"Thankfully, they're sequestered in the Nunnery. The Retreat
may technically include the Nunnery, but the place where you'll
be staying is where the Guardian traditionally lives . . . and that, I
assure you, has plenty of color once you're inside," she finished.
Catching his hand, she tugged Dominor after her as she headed in
a direction opposite to the ones the nuns had taken. She headed
for the nearest staircase, mounting it easily despite the thinness
of the air. Dominor had to release his hand from hers and climb a
little more slowly, pacing himself so that he wouldn't run short of
breath.

She climbed the equivalent of three floors to an upper ram-
part, following the covered walkway around a bend in the mountainside. Once on the other side, they entered a hall that became
another stairwell, climbing even higher. Dominor was grateful it
didn't rise too much higher than the previous set; by the time the
corridor leveled out and headed for another open-sided walkway,
he was feeling the effects of the altitude.

"It's not much farther now," Serina reassured her partner as he
lagged behind a little more. The far end of the walkway termi-
nated in an arched door. Pushing it open, she led him into the solar, a broad, arch-roofed chamber with a wall of windows along
one side.

It was not decorated in shades of black, gray, and white, unlike everything up to this point. This room was painted in subtle
golden hues that complemented the wood parquetry inlaid in
geometric patterns on the floor. The furniture, which mostly
grouped itself around either the windows or a pair of fireplaces
on the opposite wall, was crafted from polished golden woods
upholstered in reddish-hued leathers. Narrow silk panels in pale
shades of blues and reds, greens and purples, hung on the walls.
True, they mostly depicted the rugged landscape visible beyond
the windows, but they had been painted in darker shades with
subtle variations to their tones; the ink-drawings were decep-
tively ascetic in their simplicity, but clearly aesthetic in their
beauty.

Doors led into the mountainside from this chamber; like the
floor, they were inlaid with different hues of wood, ranging from
the palest mountain birch to the darkest ebony. Large, brightly

glazed urns held flowers constructed so cunningly, Dominor first mistook them for fresh blossoms. It took a closer examination as they passed a vase on one of the tables to realize they were made from some sort of sculpted, colored clay, though it had more of the resiliency of leather than the brittleness of the dried porcelain he was expecting to feel in such a fine sculpture.

"Bright Heavens, but you're back early!"

The woman who bustled into the room was all smiles and curves. It took Dominor the length of the room and her enthusiastic embracing of Serina, to realize just how *short* the woman was, a full half foot shorter than the pale-haired Guardian. This woman had the ripe curves of a well-fed adult, marking her clearly as a fully grown woman despite her modest stature. She also had rich brown hair full of thumb-sized curls that had been drawn together at her nape by a brass hair-clasp.

Surprisingly, her clothes were even darker than Dominor's, a strange sight after seeing so many people wearing pastels down in Port Blueford; the tunic-dress she wore was a deep walnut brown that complemented her hair, and the hose encasing her legs were even darker, more of a burnt umber. Her skin was the same tanned shade as most of the Natallians he had seen so far.

After the two women finished embracing, Serina pulled back and held out her hand toward Dominor.

"Mariel, I would like you to meet Lord Dominor, Chancellor of Her Majesty, Queen Kelly of the sovereign isle of Nightfall . . . a mage of most suitable ability and power." She smiled at him as she said that last bit, her amber eyes gleaming with feminine knowledge. "Dominor, I present to you the Healer Mariel Vargel nii Milon, widow of the previous Guardian of Koral-tai, and my dearest friend in this land."

This was the woman who normally managed Serina, then. He had a lot of respect for someone who could keep the taller woman on track. Dominor moved forward with the smooth, courtly grace of a nobleman's son, catching and lifting her hand in his as he bowed over her fingers. "A pleasure to meet you, Lady Healer—a great pleasure indeed."

He pressed a light, courtly kiss to the backs of her fingers in Katani fashion. She blushed and started to say something, but a young voice interrupted them, scattering Dominor's wits.

"Hey, if you're kissing her, does this mean I get to have a new father?"

"Mikor!" Serina snapped, even as the woman Mariel flushed and Dominor jerked his hand away, shocked at the boy who was staring at him in undisguised hope. Words tumbled out of Dom's mouth as he hastily backed up, mindful of his oath-bound liaison with another woman.

"Good Gods, no! I didn't come here looking to be a father!"

It was the wrong thing to say, for the youth's face fell. He clearly had the look of his mother: a heart-shaped face and curly brown hair, though his was dark and cropped to the length of his ears. But where his mother was flushed yet serenely composed, the boy was clearly dismayed, lower lip trembling. Dominor scrambled for the words to ease the boy's disappointment.

"I came here in the company of the Lady Serina. It is to her that I'm . . . well . . . I was just greeting your mother in the fashion of my people. I'm sure you'd make a *fine* son for the next man to capture your mother's heart," Dominor stressed quickly. "And if I weren't, um, otherwise occupied at this point in my life, I would be *very* flattered to consider being that man. But . . . I'm not."

Green eyes dropped to the floor, echoing the drooping of young shoulders in an equally green tunic. "Oh. Stupid me."

"No, it wasn't stupid," Serina quickly corrected him. "It was just . . . an understandable misreading of the situation. The customs of Natallia are not the same as the customs of other lands, after all. That's why they're other lands."

"I found this foreign custom of his rather flattering," Mariel interjected quickly. "We've lived a little too long here at Koral-tai since your father's passing; I had forgotten how nice it was to be paid such courtly attention by a gentleman, with only the nuns around for company."

The youth, Mikor, recovered his spirits with a mischievous smile, his green eyes gleaming. "Yeah—especially since you're not their type!"

"Mikor!" This time, Serina's use of his name was edged with disapproval. "How many times have I told you to leave the—"

"—Leave the nuns *alone*," he echoed with the weariness only a youth reciting a rote-learned lesson could impart. "*Yes*, Aunt Serina."

"Impertinent boy!" she scolded him. Then ruffled his curly hair, making him duck in protest. "Since I'm back earlier than expected, you don't have to have your scrolls ready just yet, though you *were* supposed to have them done by the time I returned. But I strongly suggest that you don't dawdle any further in preparing your essays."

"I wasn't dawdling!" the boy protested.

"Oh, yes, you were!" his mother retorted, aiming a swat at his backside, which he quickly dodged. "Back to your studies, youngling! Supper is not for another two hours!"

He hurried back through the door he had used, shutting it behind him. Serina, suppressing her ache of guilt at Dominor's anti-fatherhood protest, turned to face her oath-bound guest. He might not want a child, but he had bound himself to help her. She'd just arrange things so that he didn't have to deal with any of it, other than the initial conception, and the brief necessity of confirming the ritual blessing.

"Well. *That* was Mikor. The only other male in residence at the Retreat—you can't really fault him for wanting a male influence in his life," Serina added to quickly gloss over that awkward moment. "Speaking of which, while you're here, Dominor, please try not to go back beyond that door we just entered, unless you're accompanied by one of us."

"Only part of the rest of the Retreat is officially dedicated to the Nunnery of Koral-tai," Mariel added, "but in practice, it's everywhere else that's monochromatic. The Order is rather ascetic when it comes to living quarters."

"I'll be quite happy to stay where my eyes will not ache from the lack of hues," Dominor reassured her. He wanted to get away from the awkward moment of the boy's interruption, too. Somehow, he didn't think that admitting he was here only to tumble on a bed with the boy's honorary aunt would go over all that well with the boy's mother. Or his honorary aunt. "Did the nuns already bring our baggage up here?"

"Certainly; that's how I knew to break off the lesson," Mariel answered him. "There was a bit more to it than I'd expected, and they were chattering about the problems of hosting a fully grown man so close at hand, and since I already knew that you . . . um . . ."

Serina smiled as her friend flushed in the awkwardness of not knowing for certain *why* Dominor was at the Retreat with her, though her knowing the correct answer was highly probable. "And, knowing why I'd gone out, you thought it was highly probable I had found what I was looking for, and brought him back with me for that particular reason. Which is the absolute truth. I'll tell you the story of how I ran across him—"

"I'd rather you didn't," Dominor interjected reprovingly.

Serina smiled wryly at him, but didn't say anything more on that subject; she couldn't blame a man of his pricklish dignity for not wanting it known he'd been sold as a war slave.

"So . . . which lesson did we interrupt?" she asked Mariel instead.

"Animal husbandry. Which is probably why he was thinking of fathers and mothers just now," Mariel added with an expressive roll of her hazel eyes. She eyed her friend with an amused twist to her mouth. "Care to join me in explaining the proper breeding and maintenance of horse lineages . . . after you've settled your own stud in his quarters, that is?"

"Mariel!" Serina gasped, blushing furiously. She flicked a quick, nervous glance in Dominor's direction—he seemed a little flushed himself at the shorter woman's comment—then glared at her friend, hissing, *"Be nice!"*

"Oh, *please*," Mariel tutted, fluttering a hand in dismissal. "He's clearly very handsome, even somewhat exotic with those facial features. And he's also clearly used to taking charge, but does so with good manners, which means he's not a huge pile of macho droppings. All of which combine to make him an excellent specimen of manliness. I'm only widowed, after all, not *dead*."

Cheeks flaming, Serina wished she had a vase or two at hand, so that she could throw them in her friend's direction. A cheap vase or two; Mariel had laid down the law about that after Serina had broken the third fancy one. Unfortunately, thinking about it reminded the mage of what she had forgotten. Wincing, she tugged on her pale braid and groaned, "I *knew* I forgot something!"

"What did you forget?" Dominor asked, seeking any subject other than a discussion of his potential as breeding stock. "We remembered my scabbard, the lemonhart, the *cinnaron*, that chest of yours . . ."

"Vases! I forgot to buy a bunch of cheap throwing vases," Serina explained. "I *would* have remembered if we'd ridden the way home, instead of taking the mirror-Gate. The road out of Port Blueford goes right past the Potter's Guild."

"Why *did* you come home via the mirrors?" Mariel enquired,

puzzled, as she walked with Serina—and perforce, Dominor—
toward one of the other doors along the walls of the solar.

"Oh, I waved a bunch of my wealth in the faces of several
overly eager ladies down in the slave market," Serina dismissed.
Dominor tried to clear his throat and catch her attention, but she
continued blithely, "It was the only way to get one of Queen
Maegan's Royal Servants to back down. The merchant wanted
wealth-in-hand, and I wanted to make sure he knew I could provide it. As a consequence, we had a minor problem with a rather
large gang of would-be thieves ambushing us in the marketplace
later that evening."

"Somehow, I cannot reconcile the words *minor problem* with
rather large gang," Mariel retorted dryly. "You . . . Lord Dominor, was it? Can you clarify what happened?"

"They attempted to surround and intimidate us, Lady Serina
cast some sort of spell that pierced their feet and crippled most of
them, I finished off the rest, and we continued on our way," he recited.

"I take it you were the person she bought in the slave market?"
Mariel asked next, proving herself uncomfortably perceptive.
Dominor flushed and sought a way to preserve his dignity without technically lying. She beat him to it. "Oh, don't bother denying it, milord. That's the only reason why Serina would go into a
nasty slave market: to find a foreign mage so she can complete
her purpose in being here. And here you are, a foreign mage; it's
the only explanation that makes perfect sense."

Dominor didn't bother to confirm it, for all he couldn't exactly deny it. Because of his oath, he couldn't even address the
truth compelling his presence here, until Serina gave him permission to speak about it. Mariel opened the door in front of them as
she continued.

"Of course, now that she's back, she'll be nigh-impossible to
organize. The nuns will want to chatter with her day and night
about all that they did down in the city—never mind that she was
there when it happened—and of course, they'll question her
bringing a *man* into *their* precious Retreat," Mariel mocked in a
wry drawl, "but *she'll* only want to bury herself in her work.
Which leaves poor me to run interference."

"I've noticed," Dominor muttered, earning him a startled but
keen appraisal from the petite woman. "I seem to have taken over
many of your purported duties in the past two weeks, in that regard."

"Oh, really?" Mariel asked, her tone light enough to suggest she didn't find the idea too terrible after all.

"Excuse me, but I'm right *here*," Serina interrupted, cheeks tinged pink.

Dominor ignored her. "I do wonder why you've allowed her mathemagic work to consume her so deeply. She clearly needs a more balanced approach to life. Surely what she does isn't all that urgent?"

Mariel stopped. As did Serina, but the petite woman hadn't clenched her fists like the taller one had. Instead, she planted her palms on her fully curved hips. "Lady Serina is working on a piece of Permanent Magic, young man. With *your* help, no less. I'd bite my tongue and apologize, if I were you."

He had forgotten that. An apology was indeed due—and if he didn't give one, presuming his mother didn't rise from the dead and box his ears herself, if his sister-in-law Kelly ever heard of it, she'd pinch his ear for it. An unpleasant experience he didn't intend to repeat. Turning, Dom addressed his hostess politely. "My apologies, Lady Serina; I spoke without thought, which is a very bad thing for a man of my station and responsibilities to do. Will you forgive me?"

Folding her arms across her chest, Serina studied him for several seconds. "You *did* keep the nuns off my back while I worked out most of the preliminary equations. So you have *some* use outside of the one for which you gave that little oath of yours."

That little retort forced him to bite his tongue against an appropriately scathing response; he couldn't afford to antagonize her, given how she was still his hostess in a far-flung, foreign land. Instead, he said with a touch of the smoothness that he'd used on his Mandarite kidnappers, "I am pleased I can be of such multiple assistance to you."

Mariel let out a low whistle. "And with *that*, I think the two of you should kiss and make up, while I go make sure my son isn't spending too much of his research time trying to look for pictures of animal husbandry in action. If you will excuse me?"

A bow of her dark-curled head, and she bustled away, leaving the two of them alone in the corridor.

ELEVEN

❖⟡❖

Serina inhaled, then let it out slowly. "My apologies as well. I shouldn't have suggested that your value as a human being is so . . . trivial. It isn't."

Apparently he hadn't been sincere enough, though Dom admired her for realizing her words hadn't exactly been appropriate. Taking her hand, Dominor lifted it to his lips. Without an accompanying bow, the act was more romantic than courtly. Pausing with her knuckles an inch from his mouth, he murmured, "And yet I am still pleased you find me valuable."

Serina blushed, feeling her nerves thrill equally from his words and the press of his lips to her skin. Still, the moment was an awkward one. Turning, she freed her hand so that she could gesture at the recesses above their heads, cones carved into the pastel-painted walls around them. Crystals filled the cones, glowing brightly with daylight, though they were fully inside the mountain. The golden tones of the walls echoed the feeling of sunlight, brightening the chamber despite the obvious lack of windows.

"If you have problems with claustrophobia and require actual windows rather than the daylight provided by these suncrystals, please let me know; we have a number of guesting rooms within the mountain, but a very limited number of chambers that have true windows."

Dominor gave her comment some thought, looking up at the glowing crystals. "I would prefer windows, since I ~~will~~ be staying here upward of a year. What sort of lighting does your own chamber hold?"

"Windows and suncrystals both. If you want your own bedchamber, and if you want it with its own windows, we only have one available at the moment. It's farther away than the inner guesting rooms, which are these two rooms here," Serina told him, gesturing at the two doors offset from each other by a few feet, flanking either side of the corridor they were in. "That door there leads to Mikor's and Mariel's quarters, and this one over here leads to my own. Each has its own hearth and its own refreshing room, and it won't take long to put out fresh linens and such."

"If I am to be sharing your bed, shouldn't I be *staying* in your bed?" Dominor asked her, arching one brow. He gestured at the last door she had indicated, waiting for her to open it for them.

Pleased, and yet nervous—though she didn't know why—Serina opened her bedchamber door. Gray light filled the room; the sky beyond the windows to the right was still leaden with clouds. The walls had been painted in soothing shades of blue and violet, trimmed with silvery gray. The four-poster bed, draped in a burgundy duvet and half hidden by the freestanding bookshelf at its head, faced that wall of windows. To the left sat two chairs and a table that, from its cluttered state, was serving as a desk, and across from the entrance were two doors.

One of those doors opened, emitting two white-clad nuns. They were murmuring to each other, but stopped as soon as they saw Dominor standing next to Serina. He didn't recognize either of them, so they had not been in the contingent that had traveled to Port Blueford. Both were young, but only one was somewhat pretty, while the other one was plain. Disconcertingly, it was the plain one who eyed him like he was her favorite meal, presented unexpectedly.

"Well, who have we here?" the nun asked, crossing the distance between them. "Don't you know it's dangerous for men to come to Koral-tai?"

"Yes," the better-looking nun added, joining her Order sister as the first one circled around the male mage with an assessing stare that made Dom feel like he was back on the auction block. "Very dangerous . . ."

"Oh, please!" Serina snorted. "Tassia, Berenga, you're not fooling anyone—they're as attracted to males as I am to females," she added in an aside to Dominor.

"Not true!" the plain-faced one protested. "I'm only sixty percent attracted to females. That leaves forty percent to admire a handsome man." She adjusted her stance as she faced Dominor, hands going to the generous swell of her hips, her equally generous breasts lifting up in white-clad invitation. "And there's nothing in the Order's Charter that says I can't have a handsome man admiring *me*."

Dominor raked his gaze down over both nuns' figures, noting their curves. A flick of his eyes toward Serina allowed him to compare her slender figure against the more opulent charms of the other two women. "I prefer to look at the Lady Serina's charms."

The plain-faced nun blinked, then snorted and stalked out of the chamber in a huff. The pretty-faced one eyed him skeptically, but left as well, hurrying after her friend. Crossing to the door, Dominor shut it firmly. "Perhaps we should check the other room as well, to make certain we are alone?"

That made Serina laugh. Crossing to the room the nuns had been in, she flung the door wide, calling out, "Anyone else in here?"

Dom followed her into what turned out to be a fairly large changing room. His belongings had been placed on one set of shelves, and hers on another. Well, the *clean* garments were on the shelves; the things that had been separated into a sack were in a wicker basket, he saw, to await the next chance for laundering them. It was a task that he knew all too well. "Who cleans your clothing?"

"Mariel, when she has the time. Usually once a week. She can do yours, too; it shouldn't be too much of a burden. I enchanted a washtub and wringer for her," Serina added, rummaging through the saddlebags placed on another shelf.

"You take advantage of her good nature, presuming she'll want the added burden of my own clothes. I'll do the laundering for the two of us," he stated.

"I couldn't ask you to stoop so low," Serina protested. "Or do the other Lord Chancellors of Nightfall regularly wash their own clothes?"

"I grew up with seven brothers and a mother who insisted that we all learn how to perform household chores. That way we would not take the efforts of our servants for granted," Dom revealed. "I was particularly good at scrubbing laundry, especially after my magic came into play, making the chore that much easier." He hesitated a moment, then added with a wry twist of his lips, "And, being something of a fastidious fashion-hound, compared to my brothers, I quickly insisted on doing the laundry myself so that they wouldn't shrink my woolens, or leach the dye from a blue shirt onto a red one."

"Ah. Well, feel free to work out the laundry arrangements with Mariel," Serina agreed, her slates extracted from her saddlebags and stacked in her hands. "I need to get to work, integrating these equations into the master formulae. Would you like to see my workroom? If you want to do any magic on the side while you're here, I suppose we could find you a chamber of your own. Or you might just want to sit and read all the books in the Guardian's Library; it's quite a collection. I still haven't read it all, in my spare time."

"Workroom first," Dominor decided, taking the slates from her fingers. "You lead the way; I'll carry these."

Serina reached for them, frowning. "I can carry them."

"You know where you're going, and you can open the right doors to our destination," he reminded her, keeping the slates out of her grasp.

"Dominor, don't be silly! They're *my* chalkboards; I should be the one to carry them."

"And I am in essence your swain, am I not? Bound to please you in all ways? Don't the youths of the Moonlands offer to carry the slates of their favorite maidens?" he countered smoothly. "We may not be schooling-aged anymore, but I don't see why that should stop us."

She blushed at the comparison and let him keep the framed rectangles. *If only our relationship* were *that straightforward and simple*. "As you wish."

Permitting him to carry the stack, she led the way out of her bedchamber. It really wasn't worth fussing over. And it was nice of him to offer, though she could wish for him to have asked rather than assumed. Even if it was nice that he seemed willing to play Mariel's role by tending to her wants and needs, it would be better to ask.

Maybe, Serina admitted to herself with grudging honesty as she led the way back through the solar to the door Mikor had used and down the stairs that lay just beyond. *I do get rather distracted at times, such as whenever it's time for a meal. Mariel has despaired of ever* asking *me to come eat, when* telling *me gets far better results.*

The problem was, her work was just too fascinating, too absorbing, to disengage from easily. She smothered a self-aimed sigh. *My problem is, I* need *someone who is willing to make sure I don't lead an unbalanced, work-focused life. But where am I going to find someone like that?* Opening the door into the library, she led him to the right, glancing behind her to make sure he was following. Dominor was handsome, intelligent, a passionate lover . . . and fully capable of *telling* her when to stop and eat. But she would soon have a child from him. *Correction: Where am I going to find someone like that who wants to be a father to the child I will soon have?*

"You said this library is extensive," Dominor stated, following her as she threaded her way between the two large fireplaces along one wall and the reading tables on the other side.

Mikor sat at one, poring through no less than six different texts laid open in front of him. His mother stood behind the youth, pointing something out in one of the volumes. Beyond those were several stacks of floor-to-ceiling shelves; the other three walls were lined to the ceiling with more bookshelves, all laden with tomes of various sizes and ages, but while the room was very large, it wasn't huge.

"Just between my brothers and I, I am sure we have more books than this. Never mind the palace library."

Gesturing at the right-hand of the two doors she was aiming for, Serina corrected his misconception. "Beyond that door are two more chambers, each roughly the size of this one. Those are the archives, containing tomes and scrolls too old, too worn, or too precious to place on shelves with books that get more frequently handled. The lighting in the archives is also dimmer, meant mostly for just finding books, not reading them. The shelves are also carved with many more runes against insect predation, mildew, and other forms of decay. Some of the books . . . even Ultra Tongue has a hard time deciphering them, they're just that old. The library is one of the things I'll really miss, when I finally leave this place."

"Am I permitted to make copies of anything?" Dominor asked, curious. That could definitely be a project worth his time while he waited for his obligations to pass.

"The religious texts aren't kept here, so I don't see why not. Apparently, there are secrets of the Order of Koral-tai that men are not supposed to know," she stated, rolling her eyes at the male-female nonsense of it all. Opening the left-hand of the two doors, she led him into another corridor, this time with stairs that went up. She gestured at a door they passed on the left. "Through that chamber—which we're using for storage of my spare slates—is the salle, if you want to practice with that sword of yours. The pells are a bit old and rather worn-down with use; you might want to repair them with magic, or ask the nuns for some blocks of wood to fashion new ones. We wrap rope around ours in the Moonlands to cut down on the wear and tear, since rope is easier and cheaper to replace, but that isn't the fashion here in Natallia."

" 'We'?" Dom asked her as they mounted the steps. "Do you fight, then?"

"Mariel has been teaching me the art of *tai*, which is the weaponless fighting form the nuns practice," Serina told him. She pointed at the right-hand wall at the top of the stairs, digressing for a moment. "To orient you, my suite is on the other side of that wall, as near as I can tell. The room ahead used to be the Guardian's suite, but I wanted actual windows, so I turned it into my workroom instead." She returned to the previous subject. "I'm not as good as she is—don't let her height or her soft curves fool you; Mariel is almost as good at *tai*-fighting as any of the older nuns. I'm better at throwing things, though. We've been teaching Mikor some weaponless techniques, mostly defense moves, and I've been giving him lessons in throwing knives, but if you . . . well, if you could give him basic lessons in swordwork, it would be nice."

"I could find an hour or two, I suppose," he agreed, then attempted a joke. "It's not as if I'll have anything better to do when I'm not busy assisting you."

Knowing her smile would be strained, Serina turned her attention to the door before them. Opening it, she stepped into her sanctum, taking a slow, deep breath, enjoying the dusty-dry scent of the chalk that permeated so much of her work. She often did that when entering this room; doing so invigorated her, setting her mind on the tasks that awaited her.

The first thing she did—aside from forgetting the presence of her male guest—was to cross to the boards along the eastern wall, checking their calculations. Her arithmancy spells had continued their assigned task in her absence, and she was eager to see if any new data had been presented by her collaborators. Six chalkboards had been enchanted to collect information from around the world, using the Fonts as a link between several disparate points. They didn't quite cover the six facets of a cube, since the Fonts weren't mathematically laid out, but they did cover enough of the globe to give a reasonably accurate view of how magic was being affected on a global scale.

Looks like Sheren, Tipa'thia, and Kelezam have nothing new to add . . . but to the west of here—

"Serina!"

Jumping, she lowered her hand from the frame she had been about to caress, manipulating its rune-controls. Her eyes blinked and focused on Dominor's face, echoing the effort of her mind to return its attention to his presence. "Oh! Sorry . . . This is another big project of mine. Technically I don't have to be a Guardian to work on it, but it definitely helps, since it's interconnected among several cooperative Fonts around the world."

Dominor, still holding her shrunken slates, wanted to return her attention to the task that was his reason for being there. The sooner she attended to it, the sooner he would be free to return home and think about inviting her to come with him. But she crossed to another board as she spoke, tapping its rim. A diagram of their world formed itself out of the marks that had covered the dark gray surface moments before. Overlaid on it were rippling patterns in colored chalk, somewhat crazed and chaotic, like a web spun by a hallucinating spider.

"You see, with access to the Fonts—to your 'Fountains,' " she elucidated, "I am able to get a clearer picture of just how badly the shattering of the Aian Empire warped the aether in regards to the formation of the great Portals. The oscillations of magic are on a larger scale than the more local mirror-Gates usually operate, so they still *do* operate. It's the larger-scaled, larger-distanced Portals that we lost, a couple hundred years ago."

Tapping the drawing of the globe, she rotated it a little, displaying a neatly aligned grid in the midst of the wavering lines.

"As you can see here, the aether-flow in Fortuna is stable. They had an advanced level of shielding on their Portals to begin with, enough warning to shut all of them down before Aiar was shattered, and the Hands of their Threefold God to smooth out the disturbances right after the sundering occurred." Another tap, and she shifted the view. "This is Katan, Nightfall's neighbor, I believe you said. You can see a number of the energy lines are still unstable. That's because they got *most* of their Portals and lesser Gates shut down when the capitol of Aiar blasted itself off the maps, but not all of them. Over here . . . on this side of the world, is the data from the Font in Mendhi; its Portals and Gates were all closed as a part of a holy celebration, so it was stable, but in Mekhana to the northwest, theirs were wide open, and blasted the region with warped energies both large and small.

"You can see how some of the intersections here and here match intersections at other points around the world, including in your direction," Serina explained, twisting the two-dimensional picture with a few more taps of her fingers, which were beginning to smear with chalk. "Some with greater severity than others. These instabilities make it impossible to establish medium-range Portals anywhere except in Fortuna, Mendhi, and one or two other regions around the world. Shorter distances can be spanned by mirror-Gates, especially if they work in tandem, but because of these key disturbance-loci, long-range Portals cannot be established."

Dominor nodded, shifting to set her slates on the desk in the back half of the chamber. "I know of this; it's been the despair of mages since the fall of Aiar. No one has been able to quell the disturbances outside of the unaffected kingdoms. The cracks in the world's aether are too deep to be healed."

"Ah!" Serina exclaimed softly, raising the forefinger of one hand while she tugged on her braid with the other one. Snatching up a piece of chalk, she scribbled on the board. The globe-circle of the world shifted, changing into a flatter, zigzag projection map, the kind that showed all of the pieces of the world as a series of wedge-curves. "But *I* have deduced that it isn't broad-ranging cracks that are rifting the space-time flow of the aether, so much as there are *pitons* of cracked energy *causing* the problem! Like spikes driven into stone or ice, if you get enough of them lined up just closely enough in a row, they will create cracks that stretch *between* these damaged energy-poles!"

Her stick of pink chalk danced over the green, blue, and white lines drawn on the dark gray slate.

"Removing the stress points will permit the aether to heal naturally, as it is wont to do under normal circumstances; magic is very much like a living entity in that regard. The key is to figure out how these stress poles are so stressed; why they're not healing themselves. The key to *that* came when I realized that Portals functioned sort of like miniature Fonts— they are created from wellsprings of energy that come from magic-imbued archways, yes, but they reach out and affect the landscape much like the botched spell on the Koral-tai Font— *that* was what gave me the clue of what to look for and what to tell the other Guardians who have agreed to help me with this."

A scrawl of chalked runes and orange spots surfaced on the map, which restored itself to a rotating globe-drawing.

"I only have six of them who are willing to work with me, but then each of them has a Portal located near their Font, one that has been adversely affected by the sundering of Aiar, though their problems range from a nexus of three Portals that had been opened in the same location, the energies for all backlashing into that single, fourth Portal point, being this one here," she revealed, touching a spot on the far side of the globe where the chalked lines seemed blurred, they writhed so much, "to a simple case of the energies being transformed into a potent, centuries-old Curse, which is this one here."

The sphere rotated again, orienting on an oblong island off the east coast of a larger oblong that formed a narrow continent. A very familiar continent, and a very, very familiar island. Dominor, mind already dazed from the implication that this woman might very well have found the key to quelling the disturbances around the world that prevented long-distance transits, blinked and sharpened his gaze on the spot where she pointed as she continued.

"The first one requires the Guardian in question casting a Permanent Magic from the safety of the nearby Font. It's a technique vaguely similar to what we're doing, in order to calm and heal the aether, but doesn't require Tantric magic to implement, of course. The other one requires the conditions of the Curse being met, which it hasn't been for a couple of centuries, now. Though when I last chatted with the Guardian for this Font, he said he might have found the release-conditions for the Curse."

That observation sharpened Dominor's mind. Thoughts raced and collided, putting together his own family's Curse. "Would this particular Guardian be named 'Morganen,' by any chance? Or 'Morg,' perhaps?"

Serina eyed him for a moment, shaking her head slowly. "No."

Disappointment flooded Dominor, along with confusion; she continued blithely before he could ask for more information.

"He calls himself 'Rydan.' "

"*RYDAN?*" Dominor gasped, then choked on his own too-rapidly drawn breath. Coughing, he struggled to regain control of his lungs. A last cough to clear his throat allowed him to speak roughly. "The Guardian calls himself *Rydan*?"

"Yes. Do you know him?"

Dom almost choked again. He nodded as he cleared his throat. "Jinga's Divine Ass, *yes*, I know him! He's my sixthborn brother!—Rydan is a *Guardian*?"

Serina nodded slowly. "Yes, he is. Presuming we're discussing the same person, of course. Guardians don't actually *see* each other, you must realize; we're blinded by the flow of energies pouring out of the Fonts. I would definitely recognize his voice, though, for all he doesn't say much."

"*That* sounds like him," Dominor muttered. He snapped his fingers, enchanting, "*Bossidula locum ferens Rydan!* . . . Does he sound like this?"

His voice had shifted a little lower and softer-spoken than normal. Dominor wasn't a high-voiced man, but neither did he have a deep one. Even though his brother was younger by two years, Rydan's voice was deeper than Dominor's. Dom suspected it was because Rydan rarely spoke and thus rarely exercised his vocal cords.

Serina tugged thoughtfully on her braid, her head tipping to one side. "Try saying, 'The Portal energies were modified by a Curse,' and I'll listen again."

"The Portal energies were modified by a Curse," he dutifully repeated.

Nodding, she released her braid. "That's Rydan, all right."

A snap of his fingers removed the alteration spell. Dominor struggled with the instinct to demand that she take him straight to the Fountain to speak with his brother. For one, the terms of his oath were such that he would have to ask her permission to use the thing to communicate with his brother. For another . . . it was still more or less early afternoon, here. Back on Nightfall, it was probably closer to midmorning than noon, given the curvature of the world. Rydan wouldn't be awake at that time of day, let alone near the Fountain he apparently Guarded. A fact which Dominor intended to thoroughly discuss with his younger sibling.

A frown creased Serina's brow in the next moment. "But, that can't be right! Rydan stated quite clearly a couple months ago that there were only ten people living on the island where his Font is located—and at that, two of those ten had only arrived recently. But you said you live on Nightfall as the Lord Chancellor of . . . oh sweet Moons!" Her eyes widened. "You *tricked* me! You tricked *all* of us at the slave market!" She wasn't shocked in the sense of upset, so much as startled and confused. "However did you manage that with a Truth Stone in your hand?"

Cheeks flushing, Dominor defended himself smoothly. "Because it is no lie. I *am* the Lord Chancellor of Nightfall. My sister-in-law is Queen Kelly of Nightfall; she declared herself our ruler when Katan—who nominally ruled over the island—decided to cut us adrift. She also happens to be the only female on the island at the moment, but that was merely an omission, and thus technically not a lie."

Staring at him, still dumbounded by his audacity, Serina found herself asking, "And is your magical prowess also a lie—sorry, an 'omission of truth'?"

"I *am* the third most powerful mage on Nightfall. And I am probably the fifth most powerful mage in Katan—I like to tell my brothers that I'm the third-ranked mage in all of Katan, but it is only true in the sense that I rank as close to the equal of three of the other Katani mages as you can get without actually pitting our magics against each other in a formal ranking contest." Wry disappointment twisted his lips. "I never got the chance, at that level of competition; my brothers and I were all exiled over three years ago to Nightfall, for fear of our powers . . . and fear of the Curse that plagues us."

Her eyes widened. "So, *you* know what this Curse means! The one that is attached to the Portal on your island. Of course, it all makes sense, now!"

Whirling back to the chalkboards, she moved to the next one

in the row and scribbled something on its corner. Words filled the board, words written in a handwriting—and indeed, a language—that wasn't her own. Dominor recognized his younger brother's sharp scrawl. Somehow, she had acquired this poem from Rydan, written in his native Katani. He read the words, frowning in recognition.

> *"When doomed is delighted*
> *And royalty has reigned*
> *When cautious is bold*
> *And wildness is chained*
> *When dominance submits*
> *And submitted is free*
> *When sound has been silenced*
> *And alone now is three*
> *When swiftness is slowed*
> *And bound to please one*
> *When dark is enlightened*
> *And nothing's undone*
> *When passion has burned*
> *And quenches its thirst*
> *When returned is match-made*
> *Thus ends this Curse!"*

"And here it is," Serina pointed out, turning to him with a smile. "When royalty has reigned—your sister-in-law has declared herself Queen! The Curse of the Portal is coming unraveled! Once it does," she said, moving back to the other chalkboard and scribbling on it; the wavering lines of the disturbed aether settled down around Nightfall and half of Katan, "we only have two more key points to soothe in this area to the west and the north—and they only need soothing and not a major magic-working, which can be done on-site in a matter of months once this anchor-point here on your island is quelled and is no longer keeping them agitated—before Katan can establish its Portals again!"

The globe spun, showing the rest of the world as she tapped on it with her piece of pink chalk. Dominor stared, absorbing what she was showing him. Mages around the world had struggled with the failure of Portals for centuries, with failure after failure after failure, for generations. And this slender, somewhat absentminded young woman had found the key for curing the aether's ills?

"Once *that* happens, they can connect themselves to Dracona and Fortuna; the reestablishment of open, functional Gates between these three key lands will realign the aether connecting all of *these* kingdoms along these lines, here, here, here, and these two over here! *That* cuts in *half* the greater disturbances keeping us from reestablishing a network of Gates and Portals around the world!" She grinned at him. "And all *you* have to do is help your brother get the rest of your family's Curse fulfilled!"

That broke him out of his trance . . . just in time to catch her as she flung herself at him. Catching her, Dominor held Serina as she squeezed him tightly in her exuberance. He returned her embrace, enjoying the feel of her soft, supple frame against his muscles, but pulled his head back after a moment. The action caught her attention.

"There's just one problem, my dear," Dominor informed her as she leaned back in his arms. "That is *not* my family's Curse. That is what we call the Curse of Nightfall. We have our own Prophecy to deal with."

"It's not?" Serina blinked, then frowned in confusion. She pulled free of his arms, turning back to the board with his brother's writing. "But Guardian Rydan said that the first two lines of the Curse were already being fulfilled by his family . . ."

Realization lanced through Dominor's thoughts with an almost physical jab of pain. "Oh, Gods," he muttered, lifting a hand and rubbing at his temple. "Why didn't I see it before? Why didn't any of us see it before?—I take that back. Why didn't any of us *other* than Rydan—and probably Morganen—see this?"

"See what?" Serina asked, glancing between him and the board.

"That both Curses are intertwined! It says so in the second to last line, the part about 'match-made'! That's my youngest sibling's Curse; he's Destined to match-make the rest of us," Dom growled, disgusted with how the Threefold God of Fortuna was playing with all of them. "Whether we *want* to be, or not."

He wanted to control his destiny, never mind having a Destiny shoved upon him . . .

Her brow pinched together for a moment, then she turned away. Clearing her throat, she asked, "So, what is this other

Curse? I mean, if the two of them really have a congruence of Destinies, then a side-by-side analysis needs to be performed, in order to calculate what the—"

Dominor covered her lips with his finger, stopping not only her words, but some of the rising mathemagical fervor in her eyes. He'd seen it a number of times down in Port Blueford; whether it was in their room at that inn where she'd snatch up her chalk, tug on her braid, and scribble on her board; or down on the docks, where she'd sit on a crate, haul out her slate, and ignore the stevedores trying to move whatever makeshift furniture she had just appropriated. Genius came with a price, and that was the unbalanced focus Serina could and did apply to her work.

"You may save that particular analysis for when you can discuss it with my youngest brother, Morganen, since that is *his* Destiny. *Your* Destiny is to fix the botched spell linked to the Fountain here at Koral-tai." She started to speak, and Dominor pressed his finger a little more firmly against her lips, quelling her again.

Holding her in his arms had the predictable effect on his body. After two weeks of making love with her nearly every single day—and often more than once a day, at that—he would have thought he would grow tired of her. She wasn't classically feminine, with all the lush curves of her friend Mariel. Kelly had been thinner when she had first arrived, but the redhead also had more curves to begin with; a steady diet had regained some of her lost weight. Serina was neither of these women; she was her own unique self. Leaning in close, Dominor tilted his head just enough so that he could inhale her sweet-musky scent from the soft skin underneath one ear.

"Dominor," she whispered against his finger.

"Shh. No, wait," he corrected himself, pulling free of both her embrace and her allure. Turning her gently around, he pushed her toward her desk. "Set up your slates to record us making love together."

She glanced over her shoulder at him, then reached for the small stack of chalkboards. Expanding them into their full size, she settled them into the gaps in a row of several others opposite the ones holding her Gate calculations. Scrawling runes on two of them, she set the chalk down, dusted off her fingers, and faced him expectantly.

"Good," Dominor praised her, admiring her graceful movements. "Now, if there is anything breakable on your desk, I suggest you set it somewhere else, and quickly."

That arched her brow in silent, confused inquiry.

He decided he liked the way confusion made her look more gamin-cute than feminine-beautiful, like the way she looked when she was waxing poetic about her work. "I find intelligence in a woman to be very arousing. Your little dissertation on your projects just now was very . . . stimulating. You have maybe a minute before I throw you on that desk and do my best to sexually nail you to it."

TWELVE

◆❧◆

Shock held her still for two, maybe three seconds, just long enough to blink and struggle to comprehend. Serina spun around in the next second, hastily surveying her desk and shoving several papers and spare slateboards to one side. Turning to face him again, she hitched herself up onto the cleared space and smiled, spreading her knees. That made the front panel of her light green tunic-dress fall between her darker-clad thighs.

"Remove your shoes and hose," Dominor instructed her, his tone soft but implacable.

Complying with a smile, Serina shoved off the low boots she was wearing, then hopped off her desk long enough to unlace and peel down the soft, lightweight tights that were fashionable in Natallia. Dropping the green material to one side, she scooted onto her desk and parted her thighs again. Some women—influenced by their cultures, their parents—were taught that a *lady* didn't show that she enjoyed pleasure, like some light-skirted tavern wench. Thankfully, *she* was from the Moonlands; Lady Serina Avadan was someone who could be a lady born and bred, enjoy her sexual playtime thoroughly, and not consider herself a whore.

Her quick mind had already caught onto the third verse Guardian Rydan had shared with her, *When dominant submits /*

And submitted is free . . . Dominor had admitted he was the third son of his family. If his eldest brother had married their self-proclaimed Queen, fulfilling the first verse for both Prophesies, then it was not improbable that he, having submitted to an oath binding him to her, was the person to fulfill that third part of the Portal-Curse.

So long as he continued to show respect for her, she didn't mind if he wanted to get a little dominant around her. Lifting her legs, she braced her heels on the edge of the desk, as she lay back on its partially cleared surface. Even with her knees raised and spread, the view was still at least somewhat demure, thanks to the fall of her panel-skirt. Feeling the ache for him that had not gone away since their first encounter—which had only subsided for a while when sated—she reached for her dress without prompting. Her fingers slowly bunched the material upward an inch or so at a time.

The sight of her participating willingly in his plan pleased Dominor. He had ideas on what he wanted to do, however. Moving up to the edge of her desk, he touched the backs of her hands, stopping her before the skirt was more than halfway raised. "I did not say you could lift your skirt, my Lady."

Serina stilled her movements, quirking one of her pale eyebrows. His fingertips rested lightly on the backs of her hands, nothing more. No physical coercion to match the chiding command buried in his words. Deciding she would play along, she released the bunched fabric, letting it fall back toward the ground. "Apologies, my lord. . . . What would you like me to do?"

Yes . . . The primitive thought rose up within him without conscious volition. Dropping to one knee, he gave her a one-word answer. "Enjoy."

Lowering her head as he dropped below her view, Serina thought, *Now, there is an order I can wholeheartedly obey!*

He started with a light, feathering touch that made her feet twitch, caressing their tops. Skimming his fingers up along her shins, Dominor crested her knees and slid down the tops of her thighs. He used a light, teasing touch that circled the outsides of her legs, tracing what he could of their undersides, doubled up as they were. Reversing course, he reached her hips and circled around to the insides of her legs, then returned and tickled the front of her legs as he traced his way back to her feet. A soft twist of his torso allowed him to press kisses up the inside of one ankle to the knee; a twist the other way allowed him to salute the other leg.

"Mmm, that feels nice," Serina praised breathily, one of her hands idly stroking down the plane of her stomach and back up again.

Dominor smiled. "Put yourself in my hands," he promised her, "and I will give you pleasures untold."

"Confident, are you?" she chuckled.

"Lift your skirt," he directed her, choosing to give a command rather than a reply. She complied, bunching it up with her fingers once again. Just as her flesh came into view, Dom ordered, "Stop. Hold it there."

"Any particular reason why?" Serina asked, feeling oddly vulnerable, even though less than half of her delicate parts were currently exposed. His fingers answered her, tickling the underside of her thighs, and the bit of curve down at her buttocks that was exposed between the table and her skirt. His feather-light touch made her squirm after a moment from ticklishness.

"Just a little higher . . . stop," Dominor commanded, shifting his hands to play with more of her exposed skin, though he stayed to the edges of her labial folds, avoiding the treasures between them. "A little higher . . . higher . . . stop."

That left her pubic mound covered, though it bared the full length of her slit to his gaze. Again, he caressed most of the flesh exposed between her thighs, but not all of it. Kneeling before her, he could smell her musk and see a hint of moisture beginning to seep from her core. He resisted the urge to touch her there, however; he had a better game in mind. One of the few sexual games he had learned *before* his younger brother Trevan. Women were slower to rouse to sexual pleasure than men, but once they were warmed up properly, they stayed excited and excitable for a longer span of time.

"Now, lift your skirts up past your navel," he directed Serina. When she complied, he stroked the pads of his fingers upward, over the soft skin of her lower belly. She squirmed, but allowed him to tease her, circling her bellybutton with the edge of his thumb. Keeping his left hand on the playground of her abdomen, he brought the right one back down between her thighs to tease the soft, pale-haired folds of her flesh.

It felt so good, she just had to moan. But when all he did was tease, Serina squirmed, shifting her hips to try and make more substantial contact. He didn't allow her that relief. Instead, his fingers skipped over the bits she wanted stroked, straying to the crease between her hip and thigh, where he stroked far, far too lightly for her tastes. She bucked away from his touch and protested, "Hey! That's *ticklish*!"

Grinning, Dominor adjusted his position between her thighs and tickled her again. She squirmed and tried to get him away by closing her legs, but he had wedged his arms and shoulders in the way. He tormented her a few moments more, then dropped down and *licked*. Air rushed into her lungs, half-choking her with the sudden contrast between the two different styles of stimulation.

It escaped her as a moan in the next moment as he did it again. Her hands delved under the edge of her dress, rising up to her slender breasts. Caressing her nipples added to her pleasure, while he licked her a third and a fourth time. Unfortunately, he caught on to what she was doing, pulling back from his ministrations.

"*Stop*. Take your hands out from under your dress. *Now*."

Pouting, Serina complied. "Why?"

"Because *I* will be the one to give you pleasure," he returned arrogantly. "In its fullest measure."

If he hadn't reassured her on that last bit, she would've protested. Instead, Serina subsided, permitting him to direct her into standing and removing her dress. He remained on his knees as she did so, one hand cupping her mound in a light caress, the other working underneath the hem of his tunic. His pose should have been one of submission, of supplication, kneeling at her feet as he was; instead, he was still fully clothed while she was completely naked once her gown was tossed aside. She wasn't Mariel and thus didn't need any form of breast-binding, and her undergarments had been removed along with her hose.

Serina felt her breasts aching with need; a glance down showed them pebbled and taut at their dusky pink tips. "May I play with myself *now*?"

"Not yet," Dominor chided her.

Rising, he lifted her back onto her desk, then stripped off his tunic. Stooping, he caught his forearms under her knees, tilting her back. Serina had enough time to notice that he'd unfastened the lacings of his trousers before she lost sight of anything below his waist. A pity. It was a lovely view, considering just how aroused he appeared to be. He leaned over her, prodding at her body with his jutting flesh, but only lightly. Teasingly. No, it was the dipping of his head, the brushing of his dark brown locks against her ribs, that held her attention. The way he deliberately breathed on one of her breasts, tightening its nipple even further despite the warmth in each steady gust.

"If your intent is to drive me mad with wanting, Dominor—"

"My intent," he murmured, lifting his head just enough to look into her eyes, which required his lower body to press just a little bit more into hers in order to keep his balance, "is to show you that when you give yourself into my hands, I will take every possible care with your well-being. Trust me, my Lady; I have your best interests at heart."

Serina blinked at him. *What can I say to that? If I say no, I'll offend him. And I can't afford to offend him when we're potentially going to be working in the heart of the Font—note to self, I must get him into the Font so that I can see how self-controlled he is—but if I say yes, that'll leave me with* having *to trust him. . . . He did swear all those mage-oaths to me . . . but he* had *to swear them, to get his magic free . . .*

Choosing silence for a conditional sort of assent, she relaxed against the desk, ready to let him work his will upon her. Within reason, of course. His idea of reason was to blow once more on her nipple, then flick it with the tip of his tongue several times, while the tip of his manhood pressed into her core just enough to tease, but nowhere near enough to satisfy. Shuddering, Serina let go of her inner demands and mental expectations, giving herself fully into his hands.

As if he could sense her capitulation, he caught the peak of her flesh in his lips, suckling it. That seemed to be a signal that he would eventually reward her, for he nudged a little deeper into her body as he did so. A shift to her other nipple pressed him deeper still. Sighing in pleasure, Serina arched her back, giving him better access to her breasts.

Dominor kept his proddings shallow, confining himself to slow, short movements that only permitted the head of his manhood to penetrate her folds, and nothing more. Not yet. Of course, the soft, almost popping sensation of her entrance scraping against his tip each time he breached her flesh was quite stimulating. It made him want to lunge deeper, to sate his own needs.

That would not do, however; not just yet. Not when he intended to make her shudder and cry out his name before he took her.

Withdrawing, Dominor ignored her quiet moan of disappointment. Instead, he concentrated on tickling his fingers over her ribs, following it with soothing kisses from his lips, and teasing licks of his tongue. She squirmed under his touch, enjoying it if her breathy sighs were any sign. He certainly was enjoying his task, which was to drive her sexually mad.

Her hands finally fell on his head, tugging on his hair. "Stop teasing me, Dominor, and start *pleasing* me!"

She pushed at his head, sending him back onto his knees between her upraised thighs. But when she pulled him forward, he resisted, bracing himself against her desk. Only the tip of his tongue played with her folds, tormenting her. Releasing his hair, she reached up to play with her nipples. At that, Dominor surged back onto his feet. It took only a moment to position himself, and another moment to catch her wrists, pulling her hands away from her flesh. At the same time, he pushed his way deep inside her body.

The long, drawn-out groan that escaped her lips rewarded him with her approval. "Ohhh Moons, *yes! Yes!*" Rocking against him, Serina encouraged him with her voice, since he had effectively manacled her arms in place with his fingers. "Gods, yes! Give me more! Give me harder! Give me deeper—deeper, yes!"

Releasing her hands, he gripped her hips instead, steadying her. A shift of his stance to secure his footing was briefly interrupted by his trousers falling, pooling around his ankles. Ignoring it, Dominor firmed his grasp and thrust into her again, giving her what they both wanted. Shifting his grip a little, he managed to get one thumb down between her folds. With a circular press of his thumb and a thrust from his hips, Dom established his pattern. It started slowly and built gradually, but that wasn't a bad thing; he still wanted to tease her until she sobbed his name, after all.

It was tantalizing. It was maddening. It was wonderful, too. Since her hands were free once more, Serina caressed her breasts. He surged into her with harder strokes that made her desk creak faintly. Dark hair tickled her chest, as Dominor displaced her fingers with his lips. Everything coalesced within her, twisting her muscles with spasms of pleasure and tightening her voice with an inarticulate cry.

It wasn't quite his name, but Dominor decided he didn't care. He had given her pleasure; that was enough for him. It was also a form of permission for him to seek his own, which he did by straightening and thrusting as deeply as he could, while the hand splayed low over her abdomen twisted and pressed down just a little. No more than half a dozen strokes was all it took for her to shout his name, her inner muscles clamping around his length, milking pleasure from his flesh.

He groaned, the sound wrung from his throat with the gut-tightening force of his climax. Slumping over Serina's sweat-damp flesh, breathing heavily, Dominor enjoyed the last few shudders twitching through both of them. Especially the way her post-pleasure twitches tightened her flesh around his . . . and the way her fingers sifted through his dark brown locks, stroking the strands back from his forehead.

I could get used to this, he admitted in his mind. *Intellectual stimulation leading to physical passion. Jinga, I'll bet she decides to investigate the data we just "collected," too, as soon as she gets her energy back . . . and I'd love to help her, if there's any of it that isn't beyond my comprehension.*

It wasn't easy admitting that some of it *would* be beyond him, but Dominor was more of a generalist when it came to magic; Serina was a true specialist. She might also share her thoughts and her feelings far more openly than he did, but it was just a part of her focus, he realized. Whatever she was doing, whatever she was feeling, she *did* it, and she *felt* it. Intensity was her middle name. That approach to her life and her work left her unbalanced in the sense of skipping meals and such, but he could be honest and admit he liked organizing her day for her. It gave him a sense of purpose here, so far from his home and the work that awaited him there.

Which made him think as he braced some of his weight on his elbows to ensure he wasn't crushing her against her desk. *If she is my Prophecied mate, I would be bringing her home with me. I would have to reconcile her need for someone to bring her life back into balance, versus my own spellcastings and enchantments . . . versus Nightfall's impending status as a true independent, sovereign state, my duties to our incipient nation and our virago of an outworlder-Queen . . .*

Another thought drifted through his post-bliss mind. More of an image, really. Serina trying to teach a child of Mikor's age the basics of plain mathematics, her belly rounded with the swelling that marked another child on the way. It wasn't a true Prophecy; Dominor was a mage, not a Seer. The Gods hadn't touched him

with the power of Foresight . . . but his imagination provided
such a strong image that he wanted nothing more than to slide
down her body and press a kiss to the flesh just below her navel.

Jest as he might that children were the last thing on his
mind . . . Dominor wanted to be the first of the brothers to beget
an heir. Of course, the odds were that Saber and Kelly had likely
managed that feat already; he had been gone long enough from
Nightfall, even if he wasn't quite certain *how* long, thanks to his
drugged stupor. But surely long enough for his randy eldest sibling and sister-in-law to tackle the possibility with plenty of enthusiasm and opportunity.

Withdrawing reluctantly, Dominor stooped and pulled his
trousers up, hastily knotting the laces so that he could assist Serina off of her desk. She staggered forward into his embrace with
a contented sigh. Then thumped her head against his shoulder.

"You have just totally and completely ruined my ability to
concentrate in this room," she chided him, turning her head so
she could nestle her face against his throat, her arms looping
around his shoulders. "I'm going to be haunted by thoughts of
you taking me on my desk, now, thanks to your annoyingly mar-
velous competence—oh! Speaking of competence, I should
check my formulae!"

Dominor grinned, pleased he had predicted that exact
reaction—even if it meant her pulling out of his arms so that she
could find her slates and start organizing her information. The
chamber was warm enough, but he cleared his throat anyway,
catching her attention. "Shouldn't you get dressed again?"

"What? Oh, right! You, too," Serina ordered her oath-bound
lover, reaching for her discarded clothes. "Just because you're
handsome is no reason for you to go flashing all those muscles at
Mariel and the nuns. Or at me, for that matter. You're far too distracting when you're undressed."

Dominor complied, smirking; it was good to know his potential future bride found him so attractive.

Dinner was different, some sort of flour-paste cut into strips,
boiled, and served with thin slices of dove meat in a creamy,
garlic-laced sauce. Doves were an easy source of meat for the
nuns to raise, it seemed. Dominor hadn't tasted dove since leaving Corvis lands to go into exile with his brothers.

It wasn't the nuns who had cooked the meal, however, but Mariel.

"Milady," he praised her as she nibbled on a strip of steamed carrot, "you are as good a cook as my twin Evanor is—that is high praise, for those who do not know him."

She blushed and dipped her head in acknowledgment. "Thank you, Lord Dominor. Mikor, if you eat your nasty greens first, I'll let you have a second helping of pasta."

Sighing, the youth complied, one hand propping up his cheekbone. He reminded Dom of Koranen at that age, though Mikor's brown mop of curls was nothing like Kor's deep auburn locks. Knowing he should set a good example, Dominor ate some of his own. Most of his thoughts were circling around Serina, however, and the work they had done after making love on her desk.

He had been able to help with some of her equations and follow along with at least half of them, but the rest had gone over his head. If he had more time to study them, he knew he could grasp most of it, but his pale-haired lover had moved at too fast a pace for him to keep up. It was disquieting to acknowledge. When it came to sheer power, he held more than she; Serina had gauged his powers with a talisman and compared them in her figures to her own, and that much had been clear. He just wasn't the true mathemagician that she was.

For a man used to competing with his brothers, for a man who felt the need to *prove* himself . . . it was even more difficult to realize that, envious though he was of her sheer ability, he didn't feel *pressured* to compete with her. It would be like trying to compete with sunlight in order to make plants bloom and thrive. The sun did a far better job of it, so why should he waste his efforts on that particular task?

It was a new mind-set for him.

It also left him at something of a loose end. Aside from the occasional pesky nun-pecking to ward off, he didn't have much to do. They had attempted to see her three more times this evening, two of which he and Mariel had foiled, the third being a visit from the Mother Superior who had wanted to reassure herself that Dom wasn't going to cause trouble for her nuns.

He liked Mother Naima; she was as practical a lady as one could wish, for someone who had spent most of her adult life in a mountaintop cloister. The Mother Superior possessed graciousness, a good sense of humor, and a solid education in both magic and mathemagics. She had also muttered to Dominor that *she* was lost whenever she tried to follow Serina's arithmantic leaps and bounds, wishing him good luck in keeping up with the younger woman. The nun was a competent mage herself, though; it made Dominor wonder why she wasn't the Guardian, if the Order had indeed lived here at the Retreat for centuries, as had been implied.

His curiosity prompted him to ask just that. "Serina . . . if Mother Naima is such a competent mage herself, why are you the Guardian, and not her? Why was a Seer the last Guardian? Aside from being God-Touched, Seers don't have any magic of their own. One would think a mage would make a far better Guardian."

"I can answer that," Mariel interjected. "For generations, the Mother Superiors *have* been the Guardians of the Retreat. But there was a dry stretch for a while, wherein there weren't any mages powerful enough to go anywhere near the Font, let alone protect it. Outside protection was sought. When the last Guardian before Milon was in his last year or so of life, my late husband had a Vision of coming here. We had just married, and I hadn't even learned yet that I was carrying Mikor at the time."

Mikor made a face at the thought of his mother being pregnant, but didn't say anything. With the last of his greens eaten, he was free to serve himself more of the pasta dish. He occupied himself with that task, ignoring the adults.

"So we came up here, Milon presented his Prophecy, the Guardian tested him, and Milon passed the requirements. Don't ask me what those were," she added, smiling ruefully. "I never knew. Anyway, at that point in time, Mother Naima was still merely Sister Naima, and her predecessor, the previous Mother Superior, wasn't a mage at all. Milon had more than enough ability to Foresee threats to the Retreat and the Order, and how to counter them, and that was really all the nuns needed to muster their own protective forces. Which can be quite formidable, since there *are* mages among them in this latest generation of Order-members."

"Mother Naima is strong enough to be a Guardian," Serina stated, "and has the requisite highly trained will. But Milon Prophecied that I would be the next Guardian. Until I'm ready to step down, I will remain here as the current Guardian . . . and in the meantime, I'm keeping an eye on her, and on the woman she's training to be *her* successor, both as Mother Superior and as

Guardian, to ensure they remain suitable candidates for the position."

"Can we go with you, when you leave?" Mikor asked in the silence following her words. His tone was plaintive, wistful.

Mariel and Serina exchanged looks. Serina answered him. "Well, I'm not sure *where* I'd be going, after I leave here."

"*Anywhere* would be better than *here*," Mikor stated with all the glum, bored conviction a nine-year-old could summon. "There's no other boys for me to play with, here! No males, since Father died—and *he* doesn't like me!" he added, glaring at Dominor.

"Mikor!" Mariel chided sharply.

"I didn't say I didn't *like* you," Dominor protested. "I don't *know* you well enough to like *or* dislike you. But . . . your aunt suggested I could give you lessons in sword work, so at least that's something we could do together to see if we can both tolerate each other while I'm teaching you to use a blade."

Mikor looked up at that, one brow arching in surprise.

"After all, you might not like *me*, once we learn more about each other," Dominor offered logically. "I'm not the easiest man to be around—any of my brothers would tell you that. I'm far too competitive, for one thing."

"Brothers?" Mikor asked him, perking up. "How many brothers do you have?"

"Seven," Dom stated, reaching for his wineglass.

"*Seven!*" Mikor repeated. "Mother, why does *he* get seven brothers, and I don't get any?"

Dominor wasn't the only one to choke and turn red, at that. Mariel coughed hoarsely, trying to clear a bite of something from her throat, while Serina's shoulders shook with something that was probably more akin to laughter than horror. Clearing her throat, Mariel addressed her son.

"Mikor, I told you that your father and I tried a couple times to have more children. And that I miscarried, the one time we were successful—remember our discussion in Animal Husbandry this afternoon, about cows miscarrying calves?"

"Yeah, but you're not a cow," he shrugged.

A *snort* escaped Serina, who had wilted over her plate, her elbows on the table so that she could prop up her head in her hands. Her shoulders shook so hard with silent laughter, the dining table quivered . . . and it was not a small, lightweight table. Mariel gave her friend a dirty look.

"Oh, stuff a pair of hose in your mouth! Mikor, that's not the point. Your father and I were just Destined to have only you, together. Eventually, I might find another husband, and if things turn out favorable for it, I might have another child or two, so you can have some siblings. But that is in the future. There certainly aren't any available males running around here at the moment. So we *might* accompany your aunt when she leaves the Retreat."

"What about him?" Mikor asked, poking his thumb at Dominor, seated to his right. "Why won't he do?"

"Because he is *mine*," Serina stated firmly, lifting her head from her fingers. The only trace of humor still lingering in her face was its flushed state. "Your mother knows he is mine, and she knows it is impolite to pursue him while he is still mine. Besides, who says that either of them are the right person for each other?"

"Yes, something like that takes time to decide," Mariel agreed. "And it's up to Dominor and Serina to decide if they like each other, without interference from anyone else. So your mother, here, is just going to have to remain single for a while longer."

Sighing, Mikor returned his cheek to his palm, using the fork in his other hand to play with his pasta. "I just want a father in my life again. I know I can't have *my* father back, but I want *a* father, that's all . . ."

Mariel patted his forearm in sympathy, then changed the subject. "Speaking of sword lessons . . . I trust you do have the necessary knowledge and skill to instruct my son safely? I don't want him wielding an actual edged weapon until he has enough skill to keep himself from getting hurt when he swings it about."

"I'll be using a Katani spell that my brothers and I used to learn swordplay ourselves. It transfigures a stick into a soft-edged weapon that has the look and weight of a real blade in the hand, but is cushioned and charmed to prevent anything worse than bruises—no broken bones, in other words. If he trains diligently with it for about a year, he'll be capable of handling a real weapon with very few problems."

"Yeah, but you won't be here for a year, will you?" Mikor pointed out, joining the conversation again. "We do get some male visitors every once in a while, but they never stay for long."

"He'll be here for about a year, actually," Serina informed him. "That should be plenty of time to teach you before he'll return home. *If* you apply yourself."

"Of course I'll apply myself!" Mikor protested. "I want to learn sword fighting! I'll be great at it!"

"We'll see," Serina temporized. "In the meantime, strong swordsmen have to eat their greens *and* their vegetables, not just pasta and meat."

Mikor glanced at Dominor. The older male didn't need the pointed looks from the two women at the table to know what his duty as an adult was. Spearing a tender slice of carrot with his fork, he ate it without hesitation. Words were good, but actions were better when it came to being a good example.

He did not, however, insult the boy's intelligence by feigning extra enthusiasm for the root vegetable. Dom merely ate it as matter-of-factly as he ate anything else. Sighing roughly, the boy followed his example, spearing a slice and eating it dutifully.

Serina threw herself into the chair behind her desk, which had resumed its usual messy state. Dominor, ensconced in a leather-padded chair he had appropriated from the library, looked up from the tome he was reading. She tugged on her hair and sighed.

"About ready to retire?" Dominor inquired. From what she had told him, it would be best to reach Rydan through the Font around dawn here in Natallia, when it would still be night back at the island. His younger brother would still be awake and aware, but not yet involved in his assigned chore of making breakfast. That meant retiring early so they could wake early.

Serina slumped in her chair. "Just about." Her gaze fastened on the far edge of her broad desk, which still had a cleared spot just big enough for her to have sat upon, though she'd covered up too much with her slates and scrolls and papers to have laid back. "Dammit . . ."

"What's wrong?" Dom asked, curious.

She laughed softly, ruefully. "You've ruined my concentration. I can work well enough, *if* I don't stare at my desk for too long—I can see that smile, Lord Dominor!"

He didn't deny the smug curving of his lips, just finished the paragraph he was reading and turned the page. "If you don't want a second distracting memory, may I suggest we retire to your bed-chamber?"

"Actually, I want to save our energy for tomorrow. We already have a number of spontaneous variations for my calculations, but we'll need to do a set of sexual experiments that follow the couplings of the original pairing, to see which would work better at manipulating the energies, duplication, spontaneity, or something in between the two extremes. I—ooh!"

She flinched, curling over and pressing a hand to her stomach. Dominor closed the book, rising and crossing the room in a single, swift motion. "Are you all right?"

"Uh, yes . . . yes, I'll be all right. But, um . . . our session tomorrow will be abrogated a bit," she added, blushing. "It's, ah, that time of the moons. Ow." She winced, then continued. "Or it will be, in six or seven hours. I always get this sharp twisting in my guts about that far in advance. No pain the rest of the time, which is blissful, but it's a good warning system, so I put up with . . . ow . . . with it."

"Is there anything I can do?" Dominor asked, thinking of the potion his twin had helped to concoct for Kelly for a similar, if lengthier, problem. He touched her shoulder, and she used it as an excuse to lean her head against his side.

"Draw me a hot bath?" she asked, glancing up at him wistfully. "With bubbles? I have a jar of softsoap that makes lovely bubbles."

An involuntary smile escaped him. "You look like Mikor, pleading for dessert."

She smacked him for that, but only lightly.

Dominor retaliated by pulling her chair back and scooping her up into his arms. The refreshing rooms here at the Retreat had both rain shower stalls and bathing tubs. "A hot bath—with bubbles—it is. Here, or in our quarters?"

Hearing him use the word *our*, Serina let her head rest against his shoulder with a wistful sigh. "In our quarters, please. Dominor . . ."

"Yes?" he asked, muttering a spell that opened the workroom door, since his hands were occupied with carrying her.

"Thank you for taking care of me. Both now, and back in Port Blueford. I really *can* do it; I don't need a keeper . . . but I do appreciate it."

"My pleasure, my Lady." He stayed quiet, though his mind raced with thoughts and feelings. *She feels* right *in my arms. If I continue to take care of her, surely I can coax her to come with me when it is time to leave this place. . . . Would it be setting a trap of sorts, if I subtly trick her into believing she's better off living with me, as my mate? Of course, the converse is also true;*

the longer I stay with her, the more I could be lulled into wanting to stay with her, wherever she goes. She needs me, there's no doubt of that in my mind.

It was a good feeling, being needed. About as good as winning a competition. Better, he amended silently, since the way she snuggled into him as they passed through the library on their circuitous way back up to her quarters made him feel as if he'd won her trust. A heady prize, indeed.

THIRTEEN

•❁•

S o," Dominor asked as she closed and warded her workroom
    door, "where is the Fountain you guard?"

"The *Font*," she stressed, giving him a small smile to reassure
him she was merely teasing, "is in a safe location, of course."

Slipping behind the row of chalkboards that held her Tantric
equations, she fussed with one of the bookshelves there. Dominor peered around the edge of one of the full-sized slates to see
what she was doing, just in time to see a section of shelving slide
back and then up into some hidden recess. The space revealed
was shrouded in near-darkness, compared to the bright light of
the recessed ceiling-crystals in her workroom, which were refracting the light of the rising sun into the depths of the Retreat.
Glancing his way, Serina stepped into the darkness. Her hand
curled in a beckoning motion, gesturing for him to follow her.

His eyes took a moment to adjust as he crossed the threshold.
Her pink-clad body was just visible enough to see and follow, of
course, but it was with relief that he noted the stone-carved
handrails and circular platform that lay at the end of the short
bridge. The room, somewhat squarish, didn't have a conventional
floor, just the platform and its tenuous bridge. And the four stat-
ues bulging out of the walls, carvings of some female, possibly of
the local Goddess.

Everything was carved from the dark blue-gray basalt of the mountain range however, which made it difficult to discern details. There were tiny pinpoints of light; a glance down over the rails showed them stretching down into unknown depths like stars in the night sky. A tilt back of his head showed that they stretched up overhead as well, though only by a dozen body-lengths at most.

As soon as he stood beside her on the circular pad, Serina lifted her hand, looking up. The platform rose, obeying her silent command. Catching his balance, Dominor watched the tiny spots of light slide down beneath them. They also twisted, adding to the slight, swaying sensation that told him the platform was rotating as well as rising. Those lights slowed, then stopped. They had reached another platform. More half-seen figures ornamented the chamber, and a cluster of artificial starlight directly overhead cast a small pool of light on the platform.

If this is meant to make a certain impression on visitors, Dom thought, following Serina across the new bridge and through a narrow set of double doors, *I must confess that it's impressing* me.

The chamber beyond was short and simple, forming a sort of foyer for whatever lay beyond. Dominor managed to pass close enough to one of the walls to see that the "stars" were indeed artificially constructed; they were tiny suncrystals embedded in equally tiny recesses, no doubt refracting outside light the same way the much larger ceiling crystals did in the rest of the Retreat. But in here, the walls, the ceiling, and even the floor had these tiny crystals, set flush so they didn't present a hazard to walking across the floor. The only spot that didn't have a veritable heaven-full of the things was a rounded, gaping patch of darkness across from the door they had entered. A gesture of Serina's hand, barely visible in the gloom, and the darkness parted, revealing itself to be a broad pair of doors set in a squat, oval archway.

As they parted, light spilled through the opening, making him raise his hand defensively despite the statue-shaped pillar blocking the center of the view. Compared to the darkness of the foyer, the chamber beyond was brightly illuminated. Stepping inside, Dominor moved to a better vantage and stared at his very first Fountain.

It was beautiful, a fountain in form as well as in terminology, one consisting of several levels all cascading down from a central point above his head. It glowed modestly to his physical vision, but when he invoked mage-sight, it radiated like daylight, illuminating the glittering, magic-imbued walls of the chamber. Scintillating hues in a thousand pastel shades, globules and ribbons tinted at their edges in deeper jewel tones spurted and flowed from a singularity that hovered over what looked like a rough-hewn basin. Or rather, he noted as he squinted against the glowing, surging magic, a rune- and figure-carved basin. The whole of the cave-like chamber was carved in strange symbols and stylized figures, Dom realized, glancing to either side.

They weren't magical runes, just very ancient ones that took his Ultra-Tongue-altered mind effort and time to translate. The chamber had been carved to depict legends of gods and heroes from a time long before this land was called Natallia, well more than eight hundred years ago. It certainly explained how some of the texts in the archives could be so old, if the Retreat had been established here so very long ago.

It seemed almost a sin to break the silence of the chamber, for the Fountain made no sound as it splashed its energies into the main collection pool, which then drained away through several raised, spout-like channels that poured mist-like ribbons of magic into tiers of smaller basins that in turn drained into the floor. Where it drained to from there, Dominor couldn't have said. But he had to ask in hushed tones, "How dangerous is it for me to say anything, while we're in here?"

"Not very, so long as you stay out of the Font itself when you speak," Serina reassured him, equally quiet. The Font had that effect on her, too. At least for the first few moments, each time she saw it. Clearing her throat, she spoke a little louder. "It's only when you're standing within the Font that a carelessly spoken phrase, backed with a mage's intent and will, can cause accidental magic to happen."

"So how do we safely communicate with my brother?" he asked her.

"The basins are more controlled than the Font itself, less dangerous for inadvertently enspelling anything; the main pool collects and calms the energies," Serina enlightened him, gesturing as she lectured. "It quiets some of the turmoil in the newly formed magic; the *gargoyles*, or carved spouts, blend and filter the energies. Each Font is different, of course, with its various tiers sculpted for a specific purpose. Some are permanent fixtures, while others can be changed by the effort of the Guardian, based on his or her current needs. The one in the Moonlands filters the vast majority of its energies into the protections hiding my homeland from the rest of the world, including weather manipulation so that rain and snow can fall through the guarding shields.

"This Font's main pool blends most of the magics into general use, though there are a few gargoyles that filter out the energies best used for things like manipulating the weather, quelling earth-tremors, and of course, communication. The ones that are copper-colored are for communication. Each one connects along those lines I showed you yesterday on the chalkboard, so you have to pick the right basin to communicate through," Serina directed him, gesturing toward a set of slowly spilling, multicolored basins off to their left.

"How do they work?" Dom inquired, finding the pool she indicated.

She shrugged. "You stick your hand in it, and you're connected to the next nearest Font in that direction. The magic blinds the inner eye, of course, but you can hear everything quite well."

"And how do you know when someone is calling you, if you don't have your hand in the energies?" he challenged. "Or what if you want to talk to several Guardians at once?"

"The energies will roil upward in a little miniature fountain with the vibrations of speech, visually . . . and you'll actually hear the words being spoken," Serina explained. "I have certain set-spells that alert me to when someone is trying to contact me that way, triggered when the roiling reaches a certain height above the normal level, or the noise above a certain threshold. As for multiple communications, that requires using a special spell that lifts and intertwines the energies into a combined, lenticular node, with streamers flowing both in and out again. At that point, it's the same as any pool; touch it, stick your hand into it, and you can talk. With practice, you can even tap the streamers for private side conversations by using your free hand and a subspell, but it takes a lot of practice to do so successfully.

"Why don't you put your hand into this pool here and call your brother's name?" she offered, gesturing at the energies in question. Stepping back so that he would have room, she helped position him. "If I'm going to be talking a while with someone,

I like to kneel or sit sideways on one of these outcrops here. It's just a little low for true comfort, but if you sit on your calf, it should be tolerable—don't put your hand in that green pool; it'll interfere with your virility."

Dominor eyed the greenish mist warily. "It won't shrink my manhood, will it?"

"More like the exact opposite effect," Serina confided with a soft laugh, and kissed his cheek. "It's a side-project I'm tending for the nuns, filtered energies meant to increase the seed yield for their herb crops. Go call for your brother. He has similar alert-me cantrips for his own Font, I'm sure."

Bracing himself, Dominor dipped his left hand into the swirling, coppery red mist. It boiled up into his nerve endings, a tingling rush of magic that quickly blinded him in bronze light and shimmering sound. *"Rydan? Rydan!"*

His voice echoed strangely. Dom waited several seconds, then withdrew his hand, blinking to clear his vision. Serina had moved over to another pool, prodding delicately at the surface of something indigo, yet glittery.

"How long do I wait for a response?"

Coppery red roiled up from the surface of the pool in front of him, even as she drew in a breath to speak.

"Who is that?" Rydan's voice demanded, sharp and commanding. Foreboding, even, but very familiar, for all that it echoed with strange harmonics. *"Where is Guardian Serina? Speak, or suffer my wrath!"*

"Oops—I forgot he might be a little protective of me," Serina apologized, leaving her spot so that she could hurry to join him.

Dominor felt a stab of jealousy at her words. "Do you mean he has *feelings* for you?"

"You have five seconds to answer me!" his younger brother thundered, spouting the surface of the magic pool even higher than before. Serina quickly dipped her hand into the roiling energies.

"Oh, calm down, Guardian Rydan," she retorted sharply, her voice echoing just as oddly. Dominor realized that the main fountain pulsed in time with her words, as it had at a milder rate for his brother's. *"If you'd pay attention, you just might recognize who was calling to you!"*

"Guardian Serina?"

"Who else? I'll let him call to you again." Withdrawing her

hand, she blinked a few times to clear her vision, then smiled at Dominor. "He's all yours, now."

Dom caught her hand as she started to move away. "Just what is he to you? A would-be lover? Have you traveled through the Fountain to visit his bed?"

The wrinkling of her nose and the rolling of her eyes told him he was being a jealous idiot. "*Hardly*. He's simply a fellow Guardian. And something of a casual friend, for all we've never met. He made it very clear to several of us female Guardians that he is not interested in any sort of relationship with the rest of us, outside of being a colleague."

"*Guardian Serina?*" This time, Rydan's voice was more cautious than angry.

"Go on, answer him!" Flipping her hand at the ruffled contents of the basin, she moved back toward the one she had been viewing before being interrupted.

Mentally calling himself an idiot—*he* was the next one Destined to fall in love, not Rydan, after all—Dominor stuck his hand back into the misty not-waters rippling in the sink-sized pool. Once again his vision clouded over with too many energies to see anything, but he could still hear. "*Hello, Rydan.*"

Silence met his greeting. Then, "*Dominor?*"

"*I'm pleased to see that, though you clearly forgot to tell your brothers about your little pet* Fountain," he chided the sixthborn of his siblings, "*you haven't forgotten the sound of my voice while I've been gone.*"

"*Dominor! Kata's Sweet Ass—where the—what the—*"

Dom couldn't help the smile that curved his lips. He couldn't recall the last time he'd managed to make this self-possessed, brooding brother of his sputter so incoherently. Not since they were young boys, at the very least. "*I wound up in Natallia, where Guardian Serina . . . well, I suppose you could say she rescued me from durance vile, in exchange for agreeing to stay here and help her for the next year, give or take a few months.*"

Silence again. No doubt his brother was regaining his composure, assimilating Dominor's words. Sure enough, when Rydan spoke again, his tone was controlled. "*I don't think you should wait a full year to return, Brother.*"

"*What?*" Dominor blinked, though he couldn't clear his vision of the coppery static fuzzing his view. "*What do you mean?*"

A hesitation, then Rydan spoke. He wasn't the type for long, drawn-out speeches, normally . . . but what he revealed needed explaining. *"All those creature-attacks we suffered were caused by our unlamented uncle-in-law, Broger of Devries. His niece, Alys of Devries, came to the isle mere days after you were stolen away."*

"Little Alys? The one who was always tagging after Wolfer?" Dominor asked. He remembered her, a little girl with curling dark blond hair who had at times been painfully shy and surprisingly bold, but who mostly had gone along with whatever his next-eldest brother had wanted to do. She had always tagged along whenever Wolfer was around, and he in turn had always encouraged her to join him. Comprehension dawned in the next moment. *"So, little Alys came to the island and finished snaring Wolfer's heart, I take it."*

"Very perceptive of you. Unfortunately, her uncle decided to attack us directly. He had protective spells that would backlash against anyone attempting to kill him directly. We managed to reflect one of his own lethal spells back upon him, so that the backlash shouldn't have any serious effect . . . but in doing so, Evanor lost his voice. Literally."

It was a good thing Rydan didn't pause right after saying Evanor's name, or else Dominor might've thought Evanor had lost his life. As it was, Dom felt his heart spasm sharply with fear. He couldn't quite assimilate what Rydan was saying—Ev, without his voice? No vocal cords, no sounds, no singing at all? *"Is he all right? Aside from the loss of his voice, I mean."*

"Despairing, though he tries to hide it. The others' attempts to reach a regenerative Healer on the mainland haven't succeeded yet. The sooner you can return, the better he will be, and the more stable . . . though he will not be truly well *until his voice is restored."*

That caught his attention, about Ev not being completely stable.

"Suicidal?" Dominor asked quickly, fearing the answer.

"Not yet. But his hope for a cure fades a little with each passing day. It will cheer him up a little to know that you are unharmed."

"It will cheer him even more to speak with me . . . well, to listen to me speak," Dominor corrected self-consciously. *"Can you wake him and bring him to your end of things, as soon as possible?"*

"No."

"No? Why not?"

Dominor could hear Rydan release a frustrated sigh. *"Because I said so. I am the Guardian of this Fountain, and I will not allow anyone else access to its powers. Nor to know its location. Nor even its existence. Not you, not your twin, nor anyone else. Do not press the matter, Dominor. Do whatever you can to return home swiftly, instead. Evanor needs you."*

Frustrated, feeling like he was about to be dismissed by his brusque younger sibling, Dominor asked anxiously, *"How bad is Evanor's condition, exactly?"*

"His vocal cords are missing. He can whisper, but he can no longer sing . . . and what little magical ability he has left fluctuates with his distress. What is your own condition?"

"Healthy, of course. The only thing holding me here is the mage-oath I swore. How are the others?" Dom asked next.

"Trevan was wounded by one of those gun-things, but has recovered."

Dominor flinched at that; he remembered the demonstration of Lord Aragol's gun-thing, and Kelly's advanced version of it. He could still see the unshielded, half-exploded melon in his mind's eye, and how deeply the pellet had penetrated even with a tight shield to protect the fruit. *"I'm glad he recovered. Those were nasty weapons. The others?"*

"Kelly's finger was severed during the recent battle, but Morganen reattached it in time. Wolfer and Alys were finally married about a week ago, and act like it. Saber and Kelly also act like they were married a week ago. The rest of us endure. And Koranen nearly burned down the chicken coop two days ago when he sneezed. Kelly was disappointed that he didn't succeed."

Dominor laughed at that. His eldest sister-in-law's disdain of the chickens had rapidly become a family joke. *"Send her my sympathies and tell Saber to import some doves, or maybe partridges. Pheasant would be good, if you can get it."*

"Actually, we're ordering cows. The ladies want fresh dairy."

"Fresh beef will be nice, too, a good change from venison," Dominor agreed. *"If we could get past the civil war problem, this land has some rather nice trade-products in its markets."*

"If we can get past their war. How did you meet Guardian Serina?"

Dominor flushed, his cheeks heating with a warmth that rivaled the magic blurring his vision. *"The Mandarites were blown off-course by a storm and overcome by a Natallian warship. I was in mage-chains, so they kept me as a prisoner of war, and took us all to a Natallian port to sell as war slaves. Serina saw me and decided to buy and free me, in exchange for assisting her in a certain matter . . . which I am oath-bound to complete, before I am free to return home."*

"And you couldn't coax your way out of it?" Rydan asked, his tone dry.

Taking comfort in the fact that his sibling had the faith that he *could* do such a thing, Dominor sighed. *"It was either be bought by her, or be bought by an agent of the local queen to be used as breeding stock for the rest of my enslaved life. Not a fate I care to contemplate. To be freed of the manacles, I had to swear to assist Lady Serina for the next year or so."*

"Lady *Serina?*"

He didn't have to ask why Rydan emphasized the title. *"Your turn will come, Rydan,"* Dominor chided instead. *"Be gentle on those who fall before you, or we'll give you hell when* you *finally do."*

"I will not fall." A pause and he added tersely, *"I have other things to do, right now; I must go."*

"We will talk later, right?" Dominor asked quickly. He hadn't realized just how much he missed his brothers, even the taciturn Rydan, until now.

"Later, yes. Tomorrow."

The pool fell silent. Dominor waited a few moments more, then extracted his hand. Rydan had never been one to say "goodbye." He came and went like a shadow at night. Annoying, but Dom did care for his sibling in spite of Rydan's quirks. As his vision returned to normal, he found Serina studying him, her long braid halfway unraveled in her hands. She had a habit of doing that when stressed, he noted.

"Is something wrong?" he asked her.

"What?" She started, blinked, then looked at her hair, replaiting it. "No, no, nothing's wrong. If you're done here, I have a few tasks that have been pending in my absence; I'll escort you back to the workroom, since the lift is keyed only to the Guardian."

Dominor almost fell for it. His stomach twinged, however, reminding him that neither of them had eaten anything, yet. Rising from the edge of the basin, he folded his arms across his green-clad chest. "You are not getting out of eating breakfast that easily. Or lunch. *We* will descend, eat breakfast, then I shall find that lovely book I was reading last night and accompany you back up here. I can sit and read in a corner while you work, and remind you when it's time to have lunch."

Amber eyes narrowed at him. "You don't trust me, do you?"

"Not when you lose yourself in your work. To the platform, woman," he ordered her. She arched a brow, but sighed and complied grudgingly. Dominor joined her, and swatted lightly at her bottom when she glanced behind her. "Move. So long as the world isn't coming to an end, you have no excuse not to take care of yourself."

"Bully." There wasn't any heat in the insult, however.

"I am simply overseeing your best interests," he countered as they passed back through the foyer, the doors opening and closing silently around them. Stepping onto the platform, surrounded by pseudo-night, he slipped his arm around her waist, tucking her close as she made the lift descend. "Is there anything below the next level?"

"One or two hidden passageways that lead to other points around the Retreat, and an escape tunnel," she confessed. "But the former lead to the Order's quarters, and the latter hasn't been used in generations; the one time I went down there, it was covered in ancient cobwebs and dust more than an inch thick, though there's very little that generates dust, down here. Only a few footprints marred the dust, from past Guardians exploring and checking the tunnels to make sure their protections were still empowered by the Font, I think."

The platform stopped gently, allowing them to exit the hidden lift. Someone was knocking on the workroom door. Mikor's voice floated through the panel as Serina closed the hidden entrance in the shelving.

"Seriiiiiinaaaaa! I know you went in here! Mother's not going to let me eat until *you* come and eat, and I'm *starving*! Wake up, Aunt Serina! Breakfast is ready! Come on—I'm just going to annoy you until you answer me, you know!"

Crossing to the door, Dominor opened it. Mikor stopped mid-knock and blinked. He shook his shaggy curls out of his eyes and grinned up at the older male.

"Hello! Can we have that sword lesson after breakfast?"

"After lunch," Dominor compromised. "I must help your aunt this morning."

Out of the corner of his vision, he watched Serina roll her eyes. She came forward, ruffling Mikor's hair as she passed through the doorway. "Time for breakfast, you two. Don't make me drag you to the table!"

As if Dominor hadn't just bullied her into abandoning her work for said meal, and Mikor hadn't come to nag her until she complied. Dom smiled wryly, shutting the door behind him before following the other two. *If I am indeed falling, Rydan, can you fault me for enjoying my Prophesied flight?*

The door to the second-floor dining chamber opened. Rydan glanced up from his nearly finished plate as a smiling Alys and a smug Wolfer entered lazily. The sun was already up; knowing this, the secondborn brother arched his brow at his younger sibling before settling his wife next to him at the table. The others, like Rydan, were nearly finished with their breakfast; the last entrants had nearly missed the morning meal entirely.

"Now that you are all *finally* here," Rydan stated, startling the others since he rarely spoke if he could avoid it, "I have spoken with Dominor."

That caused a babble of questions from the others. The only voice that didn't add to the interrogation of what and how and why was Evanor's—but not for lack of trying, since the blondest brother's lips were moving just as much as the others'. Who, what, how, it all tangled together, aimed at him.

Rydan lifted his hand, silencing them. "He is well, but is occupied with a task."

Koranen glanced at his twin, Morganen. "I thought *you* were keeping an eye on him, not Rydan."

"I still am, and as I told you previously, Dominor is well," Morganen returned calmly. "This only confirms what I have been saying all along."

"Yes, but *how* did Rydan find out these things?" Kelly asked, seated next to her husband, Saber. She looked around the table, seeking an answer.

The remaining brothers and her new sister-in-law all looked at each other. Saber and Kelly, Wolfer and Alys, the silence-frustrated

Evanor, Rydan's twin, Trevan, and the youngest twins, Koranen and Morganen, stared expectantly at their black-haired kinsman, waiting for his answer. Morg arched one of his light brown brows in silent inquiry.

Of all of them, the youngest of the brothers *might* know how Rydan had pulled off the trick of communicating with their missing sibling. Rydan hoped not. Lifting his own black brow, the sixthborn mage drained the last of his cup, then set it on the table and murmured, "I have my sources. His kidnappers were captured in turn by their enemies, and all were sold as war slaves. His purchaser has agreed to free him after a year's oath-sworn service, but he is otherwise well."

Kelly tipped her strawberry-blond head thoughtfully, but her tone was decidedly amused. "Tell me, Rydan, is his purchaser *female*, by any chance?"

Smiling ever so slightly, Rydan stood, bowed slightly to her, nodded to his brothers, and left without a word. Without confirming *or* denying that fact. Her chuckle followed him out the door.

FOURTEEN

❧❦❧

"Readjust your grip, Mikor, and keep it firm; don't shift your hand so much," Dominor instructed his pupil. "The sword is rotating in your palm. You won't be able to strike true with the edge if the blade is twisted partway around. The edge has to hit with the proper alignment, else you'll be spending far too much energy per blow."

"It's heavy," the youth protested as he adjusted what had been a simple stick before the mage had enchanted it into a practice blade with the proper spells. "Even with two hands, it would be too heavy."

"Be glad I only enchanted a small sword for you. Were you to try and use mine, you'd not be able to wield it for more than a moment or two. You'll build up your strength and stamina soon enough, though. Five more rounds of the pattern, and then you can set it down," Dominor reminded him. "Remember: one, three, five, two, four, six."

Dutifully, the nine-year-old did his best to hit the battered pell in front of him, striking more or less at head-height, waist-height, and knee-height on the same side as his sword arm—his left arm, as the boy was left-handed—then switching the angle of his blows to hit the other side. None of the blows was striking fast or hard, but then his teacher had instructed him to worry more about accuracy and form right now. With the battered, rope-wrapped pole set up in front of a long row of spell-protected mirrors, Mikor could see himself striking each time. It was a little distracting, though; he was supposed to be focusing on where to hit the pell, right now.

Watching him, Dominor noted how the boy's aim wobbled a bit worse than usual by the third set of "taps." "You can do it," he encouraged. "Just two more sets. Don't worry about speed, don't worry about force, and don't worry about weight. Just tap the pell with the blade at the right angle . . . five . . . two . . . four . . . six. One more set! Yes . . . watch the sword twisting! Good."

With a sigh of relief, Mikor dropped his arm, letting the hilt slip from his fingers. The blade thumped onto the sand-packed floor of the salle. Ignoring it, he rubbed with his other hand at his upper arm. "Am I ever gonna be strong enough to really do that as fast as you?"

Giving the boy a chiding look, Dominor pointed at the weapon. "Not if you discard your weapon. Doing so right after you *think* you've won a fight will only encourage your foe to strike at you after he's surrendered."

Mikor flashed him a gamin grin. "Not if he's dead!"

"But what if he's only *pretending* to be dead?" Dominor countered smoothly. "And here you've let go of your only weapon. How would you defend yourself and make sure he really was dead, if he suddenly got up again, and he'd kept hold of his own weapon while he was down? Or what if you were under orders to take your enemy alive for questioning, and couldn't kill him?"

A blink signaled the boy was considering his words. Pointing again at the blade, Dominor waited until Mikor picked it up again, then nodded approval. Abashed, Mikor gave him a small smile.

"You're not so bad, you know?" the boy praised him. "I mean, when we first met, I wasn't sure, after you said you didn't want . . . you know."

That made Dom grin. "Your mother's a lovely woman, and I do like you . . . but I'm here for Serina's sake."

Wrinkling his nose, Mikor rested the edgeless practice blade across the back of his neck, gripping it with both hands. "I know . . ."

"You know, if things between her and me progress like they might," Dominor found himself offering slowly, "and if I can convince her to come live with me . . . there *would* be room for your mother and you to come along as well. I do have five more brothers."

"I thought you said you had seven brothers," Mikor retorted, frowning in confusion.

"Two of them are married. The other five aren't. And your mother *is* a lovely, charming woman," he added.

"But you happen to like Aunt Serina more," Mikor observed shrewdly.

"Yes, I do." Dominor had no reason to hide that from the lad. "She's an extraordinary woman."

Mikor shrugged, then scratched through his mop of curls. "She's kind of scatterbrained, actually. There was this one time she shrieked late at night, and Mother and I came out of our rooms just in time to see her running down the hall to get to her workroom, babbling something about, 'I figured it out!' . . . and she was *naked*! Didn't stop to put on a dress, or anything."

Dominor choked on his laughter at the expression of disgust on the youth's face. He hid it behind a hastily raised hand, clearing his throat. "Well, yes, I could see why that would disturb you."

"Dominor?" Mikor asked, a funny look wrinkling his nose again. "What is it that boys do with girls, when they're alone together? Mother just said that when a boy and a girl are all grown and they love each other, they do adult stuff together."

Cheeks flaming, Dominor sought for a tactful way to reply. "Uh . . . well, they hug each other, and they kiss each other, and they, well, touch each other. While they're naked."

Thankfully, Mikor's reaction was everything the older male could've asked for. Dropping the sword from his shoulders, he made a horrible face. "EWW! I didn't want to see *Aunt Serina* naked! What makes anyone think I'd want to see some dumb *girl* naked, one that I don't even know? Why do grown-ups want to *do* something like that?"

That, Dom could answer. "Because when boys and girls go through puberty and change into men and women, the Gods change their bodies and their minds enough to think that it's fun."

"Nuh-uh!" Mikor swore, shaking his head hard enough to

make his curls bob around his face. "No way could watching some dumb girl get naked be *that* much fun! Sword lessons are *fun*, even if it's hard. Holding a girl while she's naked?" A shudder swept through his frame. "Can we change the subject, please?"

Carefully refraining from pointing out that it was the boy who had started the conversation, Dominor nodded and complied. "I think, if you start practicing at least a little bit, you could learn to wield your sword in your off-hand, which would be your right hand."

"Can a warrior wield two swords at the same time?" Mikor asked with rising excitement, his imagination snared by that possibility. With the mental flexibility of youth, he had discarded the last topic and was now firmly focused on this new one.

"With lots of practice, yes. Since you've had the chance to rest, why don't you switch hands, and we'll start with the first pattern I taught you. Only this time, we'll tap the three strike-zones down the right side of the pell," Dominor instructed his young pupil, "which would be the same side as your sword arm in this case, just as the left side was our starting side, before."

Time for bed, Serina," Dominor informed his hostess, closing the book in his hands.

When she merely grunted and exchanged the blue stick of chalk in her hand for a purple one, he rose out of his chair, crossed the room to stand behind her, and cleared his throat again. Loudly. She jumped, whirled, and faced him, blinking owlishly. "Dominor?"

"It is time to go to bed now, Serina," he instructed her gently. "And wash your hands. You left chalk-marks on the bedding last night."

That made her scowl briefly. "I did not! . . . Did I?"

He smiled at her. "You did. You also look enchanting with your cheeks flushed with indignation."

Serina flushed harder at his compliment and tried to refocus on what she had been doing. "I just have this one equation to finish . . ."

"We're going to bed, now," Dominor asserted a touch more firmly. "Your work will wait until morning."

"But it's still fairly early in the evening!" she protested. The suncrystals recessed in the ceiling still glowed, but it was a cooler, almost blue light than the warmer glow of sunlight. It came from the Font, of course; there was certainly enough energy to spare. "Why should we retire so early? I mean, when I can't exactly *do* anything with you, right now."

"For one reason, we don't have to *do* anything," Dominor reassured her, pulling her into his arms. "I'm quite content to just hold you, tonight. And tomorrow night. And perhaps another night after that, though more than that would be a bit much to ask. I could use a *small* rest from your lustfulness," he teased her, leaning in so that he could rest his forehead against hers. "But not much more than a small rest. For another reason . . . I want to wake up early again, tomorrow, so I may speak with my brother once more. I'm . . . not happy with my twin's condition. I'm not sure how much you heard of our conversation—"

"All of it," Serina reassured the man, slipping her arms around his waist as well. She carefully did her best to not think about his lack of interest in being a father, or his comment about not wanting to be treated as breeding stock.

"Well, my twin's magic is almost entirely steeped in sound. Singing, for the most part. For him to lose his voice would be . . . would be as if you could never use another chalkboard, sheet of paper, notebook, or scroll. As if graphite, chalk, and ink all suddenly stopped working for you."

She wrinkled her nose, suggesting where Mikor had picked up that habit. "That does sound rather terrible. I suppose we can get up early again, tomorrow . . . though I'd rather stay up all night working."

"Bed. *Now*," Dominor ordered her, shifting one hand to swat her bottom lightly before releasing her.

She gave him a mildly annoyed look, but didn't protest. Setting down her chalk, Serina headed for the refreshing room attached to the workroom. Aware that she wasn't in the mood for anything at this turning of Brother Moon, Dominor contented himself with watching her slender hips sway.

The only thing spoiling his mood was the lingering worry over his twin's state of health. He would have to interrogate Rydan in the morning and see if there was some way of convincing the most reclusive of his siblings to let him speak to Evanor somehow. They were two different men, yes, but Ev was his twin;

Dom would have moved heaven and earth to save his womb-mate from his current fate, had he the opportunity.

Instead, he had to find an opportunity to fix what his twin had lost.

Dominor shook his head, even though Rydan couldn't have seen it. Once again, he had his hand sunk wrist-deep in the coppery red mist that connected Serina's Font with Rydan's Fountain. *"That's not good enough! Dammit, Rydan—if it were Trevan and you in this position, and you couldn't talk to him any other way, wouldn't* you *be demanding the use of any and all means to communicate with your twin? Why can't you unbend that damnable attitude of yours long enough for me to speak with him?"*

Silence met his demand. It stretched on for a minute as Dominor made himself wait for his sibling to think it through. Finally, Rydan spoke, his voice echoing through the magic. *"I may have an idea. It will take a few days to implement, however. And no guarantee it will work, though I will do what I can. We will talk again in five days."*

"Rydan—!" Frustrated, Dominor extracted his hand from the basin, shaking off the tingling feel of the filtered energies. When his vision cleared, he found Serina tugging on her braid once again. "This is *very* frustrating. I hate the fact that my twin has been injured; I hate the fact that I don't have the skill to Heal him; I hate that I cannot even *talk* to him, because our younger brother is being a—!"

He broke off before finding a word suitable enough to describe his pigheaded, obstinate family member. Running his hands over his scalp, Dominor sighed roughly, bracing his elbows on his knees. It didn't help that he was stuck here, bound by his own magics to assist Serina for the next year or so.

"He's my *twin* . . . We're nothing alike, but he's my twin, my constant," Dominor muttered. "My anchor—he does for me what I do for you, grounding me in reality when I get too steeped in my own work to pay attention to more trivial things. No wonder he couldn't Sing to me, shortly after I was kidnapped. He has no voice, and with it, no magic anymore."

Serina bit her lower lip. The results from her calculations

were proving Dominor to be a highly compatible partner for the ritual awaiting them—an almost perfect match, in fact. The remaining piece of her arithmantic puzzle was to test their compatibility in a situation where they were following as closely as possible the pattern of sexual congress that the original pairing had used in the Font eight centuries ago, fine-tuning to see which actions on their part would maximize the effects of their repair work to the embedded Permanent Spell.

That Permanent Spell had to take priority, too . . . but it could be attempted in roughly two, maybe three weeks, when she cycled into fertility.

Only a couple of weeks to go, with time and the removal of her contraception amulet to help realign her body's humors, a touch of the green energies in the basin near Dominor's elbow to finish the job, and she would be at peak fertility. After that . . . it was sit and let the proverbial bun bake in her oven for nine months. Technically, she didn't need Dominor around for that aspect. If she called him back in the last week or so, to be around for when labor came upon her and the birthing of the baby could take place in the Font to seal the alterations to the spell with the birthing-blessing . . . he *could* go home in the interim to help out his twin.

As much as she disliked being considered merely the sister of the next Inoma, and not an important person in her own right . . . Serina knew that if her sister truly *needed* her, she'd go back to the Moonlands for a while, too. *I can't blame him for being distressed over his twin's injury. And maybe Mariel has the skill to Heal his brother. I can survive for a little while without her—I could even finish training Mother Naima to take over my duties as my pregnancy progresses, though there's really not much left for her to learn. She knows what my task is and approves, though no one else in the Order does . . . and few would. They like lording it over males too much, magically.*

Setting aside his melancholy with a sigh, Dominor stood, smoothing his clothes. "The sooner we get your calculations performed, the sooner all of this will be over. Did you have anything else you needed to do while we were up here?"

Serina shook her head. "No, I took care of everything important yesterday. Shall we descend, then?"

"Yes, please." He managed a wry smile. "I prefer brighter

illumination for reading than this place holds, extraordinary though it may be."

The scroll landed in his lap. Dominor looked up from the latest book he was reading—and more than reading. Serina hadn't jested when she said there were more books here than a mage could find the time to read. With her permission, he had begun searching for and copying certain of the texts, skimming through the pages of each tome to see if it was something he wanted for his personal library.

In her opinion, books shouldn't be kept secret and solitary, but duplicated and disseminated far and wide, to make sure that if one copy was damaged or destroyed, other copies would survive. Given the loss of access to the Corvis family library, and the books he and his brothers hadn't managed to bring with them into exile, Dominor was inclined to agree. She had left him to go have a "*tai*-practice" with Mariel while he worked in the library; the scroll was unexpected.

"What is this?" he asked.

"Your instructions," Serina informed him. She had a toweling cloth draped over her shoulders and a small stack of shrunken slates under her arm. "I'm going to go set up our bedchamber, then take a thorough bath. Think you can memorize that in roughly an hour, or will you need more time?"

Untying the ribbon holding it shut, Dominor unrolled the parchment. The instructions were a step-by-step, detail-by-detail listing of what he suddenly realized were the exact sexual maneuvers the original pair of mages had made in the Font, all those centuries ago. One of his brows arched as high as it could go. "We're supposed to follow this? As exactly as possible?"

"Yes. I have a lot of data for spontaneity, which *could* work well enough according to my formulae, but I need to know if it's better for us to follow the original couple's activities as closely as possible. The tighter we can refine the process, the more potent the impact will be in altering the magic," she explained.

Dominor smiled ruefully at her. "I think I'm going mad."

That made her frown in confusion. "You are? Why?"

"Because that was the most technical discussion of lovemaking one could probably have without reducing it to 'insert rod *A* into cog *B'* . . . and yet I'm aroused by it." Shifting his chair back a little, he caught her wrist and tugged her closer, then pulled her down onto his lap. "Or maybe it's just you."

Serina blushed, then kissed him. Thoroughly, but much too briefly. Rising with a sigh, she shook her head. "It may be me, but I need to bathe. I'm ready for lovemaking again, but I need to feel clean and sweat-free after my workout, before we try anything. Is there any particular scent I should don?"

"What, it's not already covered by this?" Dom challenged her wryly, lifting the scroll.

She made a face at him. "Scents aren't exactly conveyed by the past-scrying spell I used. Can you follow it, or do you need more time to memorize the instructions?"

"I'm a highly trained mage, my Lady. Memorizing the steps in a ritual spell is a requirement of the job," he dismissed. "I'll take a quick rain-shower in a little bit—perhaps I should join you?"

"In the bed, not in the bath. Conserve your energies for the task ahead," she reminded him mock-sternly.

"Oh yes, please; use your instructions to sweet-talk me," he joked, earning a shake of her head and a roll of her expressive amber eyes.

Step four was difficult to disengage from. They had done the kissing, caressing, and breast-play for the first three activities on their list of what to do and when to do it, but this one—mutually applied pleasure with their mouths and hands to each other's loins—was intense. But they had to move on to the next stage.

It wasn't easy; Serina craved the feel of him in her mouth. The taste was so-so, a bit salty and a little bitter, but the texture of that soft, sueded-silk feel of his skin, the firmness beneath it, and the peculiar, exotic lack of the usual little cowl fascinated her. He was appreciative of her explorations, too, moaning into her flesh. But she was ready to move on to new things. Penetrative things.

The hunger this man stirred in her body was incredible. Pulling free reluctantly, she twisted her hips. His fingers flexed, trying to hold her in place for more. She could have sworn he had used some sort of spell to lengthen his tongue, and where the man got his *linguistic* stamina—well, that certainly didn't come from Ultra Tongue!

A groan escaped her. "Dominor! Pay attention! It's time for phase five!"

Her words almost didn't penetrate. She tapped his penis with a fingernail, and the sharp sting caught his attention. "Mmm?"

"Step five?"

Step five . . . step five . . . oh, sweet Kata, yes! One last lap to ensure she was wet, and Dominor hauled her willing body around, into position. Thighs splayed, facing away from him at a perpendicular angle. With her own hands, she positioned him just so. Once she was ready, he used his own fingers to pull her onto him. It was a delicious sensation, warm, wet, and snug. Slowly easing her back, he pulled her onto him again, enjoying the frictionless way they came together, floating in midair as they were.

It was good, but position six would be better, he knew. Catching her hip-length braid in one hand, he gently tugged her backward in relation to him—they were actually floating on their sides at the moment, but a judiciously cast spell had negated gravity. The Font, Serina had informed him, negated gravity by sheer virtue of its overpowering energies, so his gentle tugging wouldn't actually hurt her as it might have, had they been affected by the normal tug of the world beneath them.

They wouldn't need the spell once they stepped up into the main basin, but they needed it right now, to achieve similar freedom of movement over her bed. She was fairly confident she could filter out the effects of levitation in her calculations, based on previous gravity-free encounters they'd had. And feeling him pulling her back by her braid, prickling her scalp just a little bit with the sensation, wasn't unpleasant.

Sliding his hands from her hips to her breasts, he cupped them. Without his hands on her hips, though, he couldn't thrust up into her as effectively as before. Serina did what she could to help, wrapping her legs around his thighs, but it was an awkward position. Tapping his hand to make him stop, she squirmed carefully free. A twist in midair, and she managed to catch his arm and use him to finish her rotation to face him. They pulled each other together, free-floating as they repositioned themselves.

Pressing into her shouldn't have felt so good. Not after they'd been making love for weeks. Even with the short break to wait for her menses to pass, he should have been growing . . . not exactly bored, and not exactly comfortable, but *used to* her. Dominor reflected briefly that she was like itch-vine residue to him; at first, the tingling sensation was bearable, easy to ignore. But once touched, once rubbed, each successive scratch only made his body itch even more.

Eventually, he'd grow accustomed to her effect on him. And his on her, he knew, enjoying the way she bit her lower lip when he sunk into her as far as he could go. Her eyes were closed and her head tilted back in her abandon. Curling in close, Dominor kissed the exposed skin of her throat. It wasn't on their list of instructions for this session, but he couldn't resist the delectable view. Pulling back a little, she gave him a chiding look, though he wasn't fooled; she had enjoyed that.

Anchoring her fingers in his dark locks, Serina showed him what they were *supposed* to be doing as they coupled midair. Kissing. Mating mouth-to-mouth as they mated loin-to-loin. His lips were warm, male, and still flavored somewhat with her own essence. Delicious, in combination.

As fun as the other things they were doing might be, she enjoyed kissing him. If they'd been in a real relationship, and not just Tantric partners in her quest to fix the local aether, she would've given in to her urge to kiss him several times a day, by now. For a few moments, Serina allowed herself to pretend. To imagine that they were more than just Tantric partners; that they were lovers . . . beloveds. The thought of him *wanting* to have children with her, of him wanting the child they were going to have to make—bittersweet though the fantasy might be, compared to reality—was enough to clench her insides around him, enhancing her pleasure to the point of an orgasm. Shattering with a low moan, she clung to him as her body shuddered and bucked.

Caught off guard by her climax, Dominor felt his self-control escape the moment her inner muscles pulsed around him. Three, four thrusts, and he trembled, too, pleasure searing down his spine and up his shaft, pouring into her. They clung together for a little bit, then Dom relaxed and pulled back slightly.

"Mmm, as good as that was . . . is that all there is to this ritual?"

Serina flushed at his question. She didn't want to lie to him, but she didn't want to upset him, either. *At least I'll be able to edit out of the equations any parts where he throws a fit, after this point . . . and he is oath-bound to help me, whether he likes it or not.*

She shifted her upper body back from his, though she kept her calves clinging to his buttocks so that they remained attached at the hips. Taking his wrist, she shifted his hand to her lower abdomen and flattened his palm against the skin just below her navel. Covering his hand with her own, she cleared her throat.

"We wait a few minutes, enjoying the, um, post-bliss lethargy, then you place your hand here, and we state in unison a variation on what the original couple said, focusing all your will on *believing* what you say."

"And what is this variation we have to recite?" Dominor asked indulgently. She was right about enjoying the 'post-bliss lethargy,' because he was certainly feeling it right now.

"Um . . ." A hesitation, and she cleared her throat again. " 'Give us good sons and daughters with all of their own powers.' "

The warmth of the post-bliss lethargy in his bones froze at her words, turning to ice. It took him a moment to find his voice. In that span of time, his manhood shriveled at the implications, withdrawing from her depths. Serina gestured, ending the levitation spell that kept them aloft. It faded gradually enough that they could finish separating and settle on the bed across from each other as gravity slowly resumed its normal pull.

"What . . . was the original version?" There, that came out without squeaking. Or yelling the words. He waited for her answer, kneeling across from her on her bed.

" 'Give us fine daughters with all the powers of their brothers.' " She rushed onward, doing her best to explain. "I think their intent was to ensure equality in the distribution of magical ability between the genders . . . but the Font took them literally and stripped away the powers of the sons and gave them to their sisters, or rather, to any nearby in-the-womb or newborn female."

Dominor stared at her.

Uncomfortable, Serina blurted out, "I've got it all figured out, though; you won't have a single thing to worry about. I mean, just because the original pair were married and attempting to start a family together doesn't mean that we have to do all of that ourselves. I'll take care of everything."

He frowned in thought. Serina almost held her breath, then forced herself to inhale and exhale normally, quietly. Not knowing what he was thinking, she felt compelled to add more reassurances.

"I was even thinking, right after we go through the first part of the ritual, I could just send you on home to Nightfall, to the Font that your brother guards. We should be ready to go through the ritual in about twelve to fourteen days from now, once I've examined my calculations and come up with an idea of what our exact actions should be during the attempt. I mean, now that we have the 'more or less as they did it' stage recorded."

She was babbling, and she knew it. Biting her lower lip, resisting the urge to tug on her hair, Serina waited for him to assimilate her offer.

"And you'll take care of everything?" Dominor wanted to confirm.

Serina nodded, trying not to hold her breath. "My word of honor. You, um, won't have to be a father."

The possibility of the two of them having a child wasn't unpleasant to him, but it had been unexpected, realizing it could very well be a part of this ritual of hers—if she hadn't found a way around it, as she implied. It certainly wouldn't take place outside the bonds of marriage, as far as he was concerned. Their father, Count Saveno, had dented a sense of honor into his eight sons' heads, Dominor included. No scion of Corvis would be born a bastard, not when there was a safe, reliable way to prevent out-of-wedlock pregnancies. Such as the contraceptive amulet still safely tied around Serina's ankle. He could even see it right now, since she was resting on her hip, her legs folded to one side.

But . . . he *did* need to return to Evanor's side, and if she had to remain the Guardian of Koral-tai for at least nine and a half more months, Dominor couldn't exactly bring her over to Nightfall with him. A marriage wherein the two of them were separated and out of communication with each other was no marriage worth speaking of. Rydan certainly wouldn't bend on his stance to allow him to use the Fountain to communicate with his wife. No, taking her as his bride would have to wait at least until after Evanor's voice had been Healed and he could convince Rydan to send him back to the Retreat. *So it is a very good thing she says she's found a way around all of that . . .*

"All right, then," he agreed absently, his mind more centered on the logistics of getting his twin Healed and himself back to her. Children *could* come later, after all. So long as she had everything calculated around that particular problem, he was fine with it.

Relieved that he hadn't made a fuss—and disappointed—Serina crawled off the bed, heading for her chalkboards. "Well. Um. With that settled, I should get these back to my workroom."

Dominor studied her at that statement, arching his brow. "Shouldn't you put on some clothes, first? You've already traumatized young Mikor once before, running through the halls without a stitch to your name."

She blushed at the reminder. "I'd just figured out something important—I'm sure you've gone running about at one point or another, all excited over something in your own work, and in the process, forgetting something else that's almost as important."

"Yes, but until recently, I lived on an island with only my brothers to worry about seeing me naked."

"It's not Mikor I'm worried about," Serina retorted, crossing to the changing room to fetch fresh clothes. She paused just past the doorway, leaning out to give him a pointed look. "He's at that stage where girls are still icky things. It's the *nuns* I don't want seeing me in my natural glory. *They'd* think it was an engraved invitation!"

Dominor chuckled, enjoying her sense of humor as she ducked out of sight.

Inside the changing room, out of his immediate sight, Serina allowed herself a few precious moments to crumple. Curling over, face buried in her hands, she suffered in silence. *He doesn't want children . . . he doesn't want responsibility for our child . . . and I'm forced to hedge and lie so that he won't throw a huge fuss. Which he'll probably do if and when he finds out—and if he does, he'll make my life miserable with his loathing and disdain for fatherhood. Oh, Moons . . .*

She didn't stay curled over for long. Inhaling deeply to regain her composure, she pulled herself back together, hiding her distress as she pulled fresh clothes off the shelves and donned them. Hose and undergarments, tunic-dress, soft-soled slippers . . . she felt somewhat armored in her clothes, almost ready to face him.

If I keep him too busy to notice the contraceptive amulet is gone, and I send him straight to Nightfall after the end of the ritual . . . and I arrange to keep him away until it's time to bring him back for the birth of the child, he won't have any chance to get mad at me. The oath he swore will force him to assist me with the ritual blessing at the end, and then I can just send him back, and he won't ever have to deal with me again. That's what I'll do, she decided. *Just . . . keep him away, and not tell him a thing that I don't have to.*

It's a form *of keeping my word. That he won't have to worry about anything, that he'll have no lingering responsibilities from the consequences of what we'll have to do . . .* Squaring her shoulders, she plastered a light, teasing smile on her face, heading back out into the bedroom to collect her slateboards. She had work to do, something she could bury herself in thoroughly enough to escape her misery. Somehow, she even managed to throw him a wink as she shrunk the full-sized boards, enjoying the sight of him stretched out on her bed in all his naked glory. It was an enjoyable sight, after all.

Moons, don't let him see me cry.

FIFTEEN

◆❦◆

Within moments of Dominor placing his hand into the communications basin and calling his brother's name, Rydan replied; the rapidness of the response startled Dom, though his brother's words clarified as to why.

"About time you crawled out of bed, Your Laziness. I have something for you. Inform Guardian Serina that I am sending a large object through the Fountainway. I don't want it destroyed by any defenses she might have in place."

A hand brushed against Dominor's. He couldn't see its owner, but he could hear her voice. *"I'm right here, Guardian Rydan. What are you sending across?"*

"A very special communication mirror. Try not to break it. Sending in ten seconds . . ."

Dominor hastily extracted his hand, as did Serina. They both quickly moved away from the tiered layers of the Font, Serina lifting her hands and readying her magic to catch the incoming present. As Dominor watched, the pulsing singularity above the main basin brightened and then expanded, turning first into a sphere, then into a sort of broad-edged torus of energy.

Light flared brightly at the center. When it faded, an oval mirror in a silvery frame the length of a torso hung in the center of the slowly throbbing ring. The communication pool boiled upward with Rydan's voice.

"It's not going to be capable of transporting a person at the distances involved, but it should be capable of communication without needing the Fountains. We got the trick from something Alys told us about her uncle, how he used a pair of twin mirrors as a Portal between his home and his menagerie; twinned mirrors double their effective distance."

"And their communication use is twice that of transportation use," Dominor murmured, forgetting for a moment that his brother couldn't hear him.

"Stick your hand in the pool, if you have something to say to him," Serina reminded him, her tone a little distant; she was distracted with gently extracting the mirror from the heart of the singularity. There was a plane of transition between the edge of the Font's energies and the rest of the chamber, and she didn't want the mirror flexing the wrong way.

Complying, Dominor dipped his fingers into the roiling notwater. *"We're extracting it now. We'll be able to test it in a moment."*

"The other mirror is here with me. I suggest you test it as soon as it's outside the heart of the magic, then remove it from your Fountain Hall and find a good location for it. I will bring the other with me to breakfast, provided they both function."

Muttering a spell, Serina conjured a stand for the mirror. Positioning it so that it didn't face the Font, she settled the mirror in place. "You can extract your hand now, Dominor. At least, I presume you'll be the one testing it?"

"I'm going to test the mirror now, Rydan," Dominor informed his brother. *"Anything special about it that I should know?"*

"Just that it is keyed solely to its twin; you will not be able to shift the focus elsewhere. Touch the frame and speak your standard Word to activate it, as you would any other mirror. Once it is awakened, a simple touch to the frame is all that will be needed to turn it on or off. I shall be waiting."

Lifting his hand from the mist, Dominor blinked the coppery haze from his vision. Pushing to his feet, he moved over to join Serina. The frame was remarkably plain, just a thumb's width of silvery steel. The mirror itself was the glazed kind.

With a deep breath to steady himself, he lifted his hand, caressed the cool metal, and spoke the word he used to activate any other communications-enchanted glass. *"Anan!"*

The mirror flared and shifted from a reflection of Dominor and Serina, the dark basalt carvings of the wall behind them, to the reflection of a pale face floating in the midst of darkness. It was so dark on the other end, in fact, that Rydan's hair vanished into the void behind him. The younger mage's mouth twisted into a smile.

"Congratulations. It works. Presuming you can both see and hear me, of course?"

Dominor grinned at his sibling, ecstatic at finally being able to communicate with his family. "If you call that darkness you love so much 'seeing' anything, then yes."

"Good. I will be blocking this end in a moment. It'll reopen in half an hour or so, once I have hung it in its place, though I will be returning to my work until breakfast," Rydan added, the expression in his dark eyes shuttered. "I will hang it in the dining chamber, so that anyone who wishes can speak with you. Do remember the time difference; breakfast won't be served for another three and a half hours, here."

"Still as taciturn and solitary as ever?" Dom quipped, in too good of a mood now to let Rydan's demeanor spoil it.

"Of course. But . . . I will see you again at breakfast. Guardian Serina," he acknowledged the blond woman. A polite nod of his head, and the mirror darkened fully, then resumed its normal appearance.

" 'Taciturn' is right," Serina muttered, eyeing their reflections. "I was hoping he might warm up a bit when talking with one of his family members, but apparently not. Is he always like that, even at home?"

"Always," Dominor agreed dryly. He gestured at the mirror. "Where should we put this?"

"In our own dining hall?" she offered with a shrug. "I'd suggest the solar, since it has a beautiful view of the rest of the Retreat, but the Mother Superior might object, since its windows could be used for scrying the location of Koral-tai. Not that I think your family *would*; it's just a matter of precaution."

Nodding, Dominor lifted the mirror with a muttered phrase and a pass of his fingers; he would be far less likely to drop the precious artifact when it was floating than if he carried it physically.

I also had them install a chime-spell," Kelly explained to Dominor, "so that if no one is in the immediate vicinity of the mirror, it'll ring loudly enough to hopefully catch someone's attention. It's basically the same as the ringer on a *telephone*, back in my old home. You just say 'ring-ring'—"

Chimes interrupted her, clanging melodically but loudly; Dominor, Serina, and Mariel winced, while Mikor clapped his hands over his smaller ears.

Kelly smiled and continued once the tone died down. "—And they'll ring, just like that. So basically anyone in either household can call upon the other, whether or not they have magic."

"Ring-ring!" Mikor retorted, hands still over his ears. The youth had the satisfaction of seeing the redheaded woman wince and wiggle a finger in her ears, as did some of the others in the background.

They had decided within a few moments of establishing the connection to hang both mirrors sideways, like a landscape painting rather than a portrait one; it permitted several people to be seen side-by-side. The normal ability of a scrying mirror to refocus and pan its view had been sacrificed in order to span the severe distance between the two locations. Thankfully, the orientation of the mirror had no effect on the scene it scried, unlike the device Kelly had described to Dominor and his brothers, something called a *television*.

She extracted her finger from her ear, smiling ruefully. "Yes, well . . . try not to do that if someone is actually standing right there, okay? I'll let it pass since it did need to be tested, but any more would be impolite."

"You heard the lady," Mariel reinforced, tapping her son's shoulder to ensure he paid attention to the admonishment.

"So," Saber stated; he was standing behind Kelly, his head just visible below the edge of the mirror-frame. "Now you're up to date with our side of all the excitement on our side of the Eastern Ocean. What have you been doing?"

"In specific," his twin Wolfer rumbled, also standing behind his own wife, Alys, and to the left of Kelly and Saber, "what is this task you have that is going to take you a year before you can return?"

Dominor slid his gaze to Kelly's other side, to where his own twin, Evanor, stood. Being reduced to mere whispers placed his voice almost completely below the threshold of what the mirrors could detect and transfer. Rendered mute, Evanor was forced to be content with just staring at his closest brother, unless he wanted to stand close enough to the mirror to fog its surface and block all view of the others. His brown eyes, darker than Serina's, begged him mutely for a reason as to why Dom couldn't come home.

Unfortunately, he literally could not say why. "I'm under an oath. I cannot say why."

Evanor's brow creased. He started to say something, then scowled and leaned over, whispering in Kelly's ear. Straightening after a few moments, he folded his arms across his blue-clad chest, still frowning unhappily.

Kelly lifted her chin slightly, taking on an imperious air. "Evanor wishes to know why you have been placed under this oath . . . and I myself demand to know."

"You *demand* to know?" Mariel returned, one hand bracing on her hip. "And just who are you, to make any sort of demand?"

Nobody had formally introduced themselves, just exchanged a few names casually. Dominor quickly intervened. "Kelly is also known as Her Majesty, Queen of Nightfall. Ruler of some of the most powerful mages in existence, including myself."

"Beloved ruler," Saber quipped, wrapping his arms around his wife from behind.

Serina tugged on the end of her hair for a moment, then lifted her chin. "I will not release him from his vow of silence until after the first stage has been completed . . . and only then will I grant him permission to speak *discreetly* of what he has vowed to help me do. And only to those who are trustworthy enough to keep a secret. It's too dangerous to risk word getting out among the Natallians and Mandarites before our task is complete."

Dominor felt her words sweeping through him like a subtle, tingling wind, altering the mage-oath binding him to silence. It was a relief to know that he would be able to speak of at least some of what he was going through. If nothing else, he could distract Evanor from his own troubles with the details of his twin's salacious quasi-captivity.

Evanor's lips moved. Kelly leaned close to him for a moment, her strawberry blond hair looking very red in comparison to his paler blond. She spoke for him as she straightened. "Ev wants to know just how long you'll be keeping his twin from coming home, and if there is any way to shorten that time."

"Um . . . actually . . . he can probably go home in another ten days or so."

Dominor whipped his head around to stare at her.

Serina shrugged as casually as she could manage, though her insides were a knot of nerves. "I don't really *need* you in the interval between the first and second stages. I can manage everything on my own; I gave you my word on that already. So long as you come back in time to complete the second stage of our task, I see no reason why I shouldn't release you from my presence so that you can go home again. And with these clever mirrors, here, I can just call for you when it's about time for you to come back."

"Evanor says that's a splendid idea," Kelly stated, smiling at them from the other side of the mirror. "You are, of course, welcome to visit. Just let us know when you're coming through the looking glass, here!"

"Kelly, they can't exactly step across the mirrors," the golden-blond mage holding her stated. "The distance is simply too far to hold any sort of Gate stable." Saber lifted his gaze from his wife to his brother. "Exactly how will you be returning?"

Dominor, mindful of their darkest brother's vehemence, shrugged. "I have several options. I'll probably pick the fastest available to me at the time."

"Perhaps I should tell you boys the tale of Aladdin and his flying carpet," Kelly quipped.

"'Flying carpet'?" Mikor repeated. He looked up at the pale blond woman next to him. "Can I ride on a flying carpet, Aunt Serina? That sounds like so much fun! Please?"

"No!" Mariel stated.

Serina, however, was caught up in the idea. "It would have to have a dozen safety charms woven into the material, and of course it would have to have an altitude limitation, since the air thins too much for comfortable breathing when you rise too high . . . and warming charms, and—mmphf!"

Keeping his hand firmly wrapped over her mouth, Dominor gave his sister-in-law a dirty look. "Kindly do *not* plant any further ideas in her head. She already has enough projects on hand. Besides," he added, loosening his grip and looking into Serina's amber eyes, "I was thinking I could take on that particular idea myself. *You* have plenty of projects as it is."

Cheeks turning pink from his manhandling of her in front of his family, Serina eyed the faces on the far side of the mirror. Evanor—who was as pale as his twin was dark, almost as pale-haired as she was—smiled warmly at her. Kelly smirked, one brow quirked upward as if daring Serina to question why. The red-head's husband had a mild look of exasperation in his gaze, and *his* twin and his wife, Wolfer and Alys, were grinning. There were two more redheads in the background, males who were also smiling, and a fellow with light brown hair who hadn't said anything yet. That last one smirked almost as badly as their erstwhile queen did. But not one of them looked at Serina with the least bit of cruelty or hostility in their gazes.

Pulling Dominor's palm down, she smiled back. "Speaking of which, I should get to work. The exact timing of the first phase still needs to be calculated. If you'll excuse me?"

"Of course," Kelly acknowledged, her smirk melting into a smile. "It's time we all headed off for our various tasks, anyway."

"Yes, I have some books to copy this morning, and then I'll have a sword lesson to teach," Dominor added as Serina escaped, her skin still flushed.

"*You*, teach swordwork?" his eldest brother quipped. "Are you trying to usurp my specialty?"

"No, I'm trying to keep this young man, here, out of trouble. Since you're too lazy to come all the way over here and do it yourself," Dom mock-sighed, "the responsibility naturally falls to me."

"Remind me to beat you around the courtyards four or five times, when you get back. Milady," Saber added politely, turning to Mariel. "If you'll excuse us, in turn?"

"Of course," she murmured. "I have work to do, myself."

Dominor, glancing at the petite woman's face, noticed she was sneaking looks at his twin. His twin, Dom also noted, was studying her in turn. In fact, Ev looked rather fascinated with Mariel, his brown eyes gleaming with a mixture of curiosity and appreciation edged with hints of frustration. A tug on the darker twin's sleeve made him glance down.

In a whisper that hopefully didn't carry as far as the mirror, Mikor asked wistfully, "Is *he* one of the ones that isn't married?"

"Mikor!" Mariel gasped, flushing bright red. Dropping her hand on his shoulder, she shoved him only somewhat gently away from the mirror. "It's time for your lessons, young man! *And*, I think, a surprise essay test!"

Evanor watched them leave with a smile twisting his mouth. He moved up close to the mirror as the others on his side left as well, and mouthed something into the mirror. Dominor, distracted by Mikor's trudging footsteps, didn't catch it. Shaking his head, he held up his hand until the door had closed behind them, then looked at his twin.

"What did you say?"

"*I said,*" Evanor hissed as loudly as he could, "*he's rather precocious, isn't he?*"

"He's on the hunt for a new father," Dom explained. "His mother, Mariel, has been a widow for over two years now, and since the only other occupants of this place are a local Order of nuns . . . Oh, get that look off your face. They're more interested in playing bed-games with other women than with men."

Evanor's smirk turned wistful. He muttered something, only half of it picked up by the mirror's scrying spell. "*I had a . . . two women.*"

It looked like one of the missing words was *chance*, from the movements of his twin's lips. Dominor shook his head. "Serina is mine. Or she will be, soon enough. Mariel . . . she and Mikor *might* come with Serina, when she's ready to leave this place. Which will be in about nine or ten months, if everything goes right." A pause, and Dom asked teasingly, "Would you *like* me to convince the estimable young widow to move to Nightfall along with her best friend?"

Evanor nodded vigorously, then sighed: "*Hopefully . . . my voice back by . . .*"

The mirrors just weren't sensitive enough. Frustrated himself, Dominor could only imagine what his twin was suffering. Still, there was no denying that just being able to reassure Evanor that he was well and unharmed was enough to relieve some of the strain his younger brother was suffering. "Hopefully, indeed. And I will search for someone who can help you on this side of the Eastern Ocean. Even if I have to kidnap *them* to get them to help you—which would only be fair, considering how they kidnapped *me*."

Grinning, Evanor said something.

"What was that?" Dom was forced to ask.

A frustrated look crossed his twin's face. Normally a placid, even-tempered man, Ev showed signs of definite stress with his situation. Scowling, he spat something vulgar in his frustration that was loud enough for the mirror to pick up, then repeated himself, straining to be heard. "*I said, I take it you're happy with your Destined mate!*"

Dom smiled slowly, and gave his twin a singular nod of his head, almost a bow. "And I'm falling with far more grace than our idiot eldest brother did. How did Wolfer fall for little Alys?"

His twin held up his hand and snapped his fingers. *"That fast . . . though I think they started their fall long before our exile."*

"Well, I am happy for them."

"You've certainly . . ." Evanor observed with an arch look.

"What was that last bit?"

"Mellowed! Love suits you, Brother," Ev repeated, exaggerating his words. Again, a frustrated look crossed his features. His hands raised, fisted for a moment, but then they uncurled, his fingertips rubbing lightly at his temples. *"So glad when this . . . over!"*

"Kata watch over you, Ev," Dominor told him. "Ten or twelve more days, and I should be coming home. Just hold on for that long, all right?"

Sighing roughly, Evanor nodded. He lifted his hand in a farewell gesture, then tapped the edge of the mirror, terminating the link. Dominor found himself staring at his own reflection once again.

He did have work to do. Turning away, he left the dining hall, descended a set of steps, and passed through the solar. Since it was midmorning, the sun was shining down through the windows in columns of light, warming the pastel hues of the room. The dark gray of the mountains and slate rooftops of the rest of the Retreat formed an almost grim view in contrast. It made him long for the green-covered slopes of the two mountain ranges flanking his castle home, back on Nightfall.

Descending farther into the library, he found Mariel giving her son a few last instructions, a stack of paper in front of him, along with a quill and an inkpot. She followed him into the rows of shelves at the other end of the chamber. When he crouched and extracted the next book on his list to skim and see if it was worth copying, she cleared her throat.

"I, ah, wanted to apologize for my son's brashness, earlier," she offered hesitantly. "I've been trying to teach him good manners, you see, and his curiosity about such things . . ."

Dominor stood and opened the book in his hands. Without lifting his gaze from the pages, he stated calmly, "Evanor thinks you're beautiful."

Out of the corner of his eye, he watched her flush a decidedly flustered shade of pink. She stammered, too. "Well, I . . . that is . . . um . . . well . . . yes, ah . . . I mean . . ."

"When Serina comes to live with me on Nightfall, you and your son will be most welcome to come, too. There is certainly plenty of room . . . and if Evanor is not to your taste, there are four other bachelors among my brothers."

She sputtered and flushed even more. Looking up from the book, Dominor dared to wink at her. Mariel caught her breath, glared at him . . . and then relaxed, chuckling.

"And here I thought my son was an over-eager matchmaker. We'll see," she temporized, in the way of mothers everywhere. "In the meantime, I have an essay to oversee."

She started to turn away, then turned back.

"Dominor . . . was there a particular reason why your brother wasn't able to speak?"

"He lost his voice. Literally," Dominor admitted, gesturing at his own throat. "He has no vocal cords anymore, thanks to an enemy's spell a few months ago. My brothers are trying to find a Healer capable of regenerating the missing tissue, but . . . we're not exactly in good standing with the Mage-Council of Katan, our western neighbor."

"Oh." She chewed on her lower lip for a moment, looking like she might say something, then shook her head. "I have things to look up. We'll talk about your brother later."

With that curious statement, she left him, returning to oversee her son's education. Shrugging it off as something he could question her about later, Dominor paid attention to the pages he had been leafing through. If he had his way—and a big enough stack of blank books, beyond the handful of ones he had transformed from spare firewood—he'd copy all of the works in this library. As it was, he had less than ten more days to select out the best of what he could find.

If he could find some way of blackmailing Rydan into cooperating, he might be able to come back through the Fountains to this place, visiting his lady as they waited for the requisite nine months to pass. Something about that, however, made him stop and examine that thought. *If I can blackmail Rydan . . . what does he have that he doesn't want the others to know about, other than the Fountain he's been hiding from us? It is a risk, as he is the stronger mage . . . especially with a Fountain to tap into . . .*

but I could blackmail him into sending me across. And if I can be sent across, what's to stop me from claiming Serina as my wife now, rather than at some nebulous point later?

The idea appealed to him. He didn't think he would be able to do so with impunity, however; she seemed a bit skittish in regards to the relationship they had formed. She retreated behind the walls of her work whenever things started to get too non-sexually intimate between them.

Of course, that would be the way to approach her, he decided, crouching and reshelving the volume where he had found it. *Through her work. I need to think about how to go about this . . . and how amusing it will be, to "set my trap and be my fate" . . . with marriage as my reward, as well as my hidden bait. But these things must be done delicately. You scare away the deer by charging right up to it, hunting bow in hand . . .*

He found his opening four days later. Serina had finished her calculations and had explained to him how the phases of Brother and Sister Moons would be at their most optimal positions in six more days. *If* they abstained from sex for the five days prior to their target-hour.

"And of course, we'll need to follow most of the original pairing's sexual steps, in order to invoke the strongest sympathetic vibrations in the Font, which will exponentially increase our effectiveness. We can substitute this awkward pose here with turning me around a step early in the intercourse process—" She broke off and smirked at him. "Am I exciting you, with all of this technical talk?"

"Of course," Dominor returned, only half-jesting. He took the opening she had given him. "You say that, the more closely we align our actions and timings with what happened originally, the more easily we will be able to effect the desired change in the Font's future emanations. Yet we are not married to each other, while the original couple were. How will that lapse affect our efforts?"

Serina blinked at him. His question had just bucked her thoughts right out of the proverbial riding saddle. *Marriage? He's actually suggesting marriage between us?* Well, he wasn't suggesting it *directly* . . . but she *was* somewhat concerned over the legitimacy of the child she would be bearing. *If I can show him that it will have a discernible effect, I might just coax him into marrying me . . .*

Turning to her chalkboards, she quickly scribbled the necessary changes into the equation. It didn't take long; she'd hauled in extra slates and expanded them into full size, linking them to her original calculations so that she would have the room to test any number of possible variables—it was simply a matter of plugging in the specific values on the sideboards, while the main boards held the original algebraic equations. Setting up something like this took time, but once it was established . . . it only took a few strokes of the chalk in her hands to input the data, and a few more moments to watch the mathemagic altering the results.

"We could see a five percent increase in efficiency. Now, I know that doesn't seem like much," she admitted quickly, "but even so much as a one percent variable is significant, in this scale of an enchantment. The reason why we can't follow the original step six-*a* is because our personal awkwardness and discomfort form a greater negative impact than would switching to step six-*b* as an alternative position for copulation. Six-*b* only gives us a point three percent increase in efficacy, but it's worth every tenth of a percent. Comparing that to the five percent effect of getting married . . . it's worth any conceivable inconvenience . . . yes?"

Dominor watched her moving across her workroom, gesturing at the various formulae on her slateboards. It was difficult, but he managed to hide the urge to smirk; she was doing all the convincing herself as to whether or not they should wed. *This is almost too easy . . . barely even a month together, and already I know you too well, my Lady!* Folding his arms across his chest, he affected a thoughtful look. "Would we have to wed according to Natallian custom?"

"Oh, no, any God-sanctified custom would suffice; it's the sanctified union of marriage itself that is important. Actually—I just happen to have available the Moonlands method of sealing a marriage," Serina offered, struggling to hide her nervousness under the blasé offer. "It's in that chest I brought back from Port Blueford."

"Moonlands method?" Dominor asked, intrigued. *If we wed by the customs of her people, it will bind us together all the more thoroughly in her mind.* "What is this method?"

"We, um, drink the liqueur of the sacred fruit. From the same cup. Together, in front of witnesses," she explained, hands worrying at the end of her braid. Realizing she was giving away her nervousness, Serina clamped her fingers around the end of her locks to still them, then slid her hands free. Clasping them in front of her, she offered, "It also has the advantage of being the quickest form of sanctified divorce; the process is the same, sharing a cup of the sacred fruit's liqueur, only we spit the liquid back into the same cup, each in turn. In front of witnesses. So that once everything is all over, after the second stage no longer requires a marriage tying us together . . ."

"We'll get to that when we get to it," Dominor asserted, privately deciding he'd not go anywhere near a second cup of whatever-it-was that they had to drink. "This sounds a lot simpler than the Katani ceremony, which would require eight altars sanctified to the aspects of Jinga and Kata, the patron God and Goddess of Katan. Which we don't exactly have available here in Natallia."

"No, we don't have that," she agreed, smiling slightly. "And I'm not too keen on the Natallian version of marriage, which for outlanders like you and me, requires getting permission from a Royal Servant of Queen Maegan to oversee the nuptials and sign as a witness on a legal contract—it's all very tedious, from what I hear. What sort of ritual or tradition does Nightfall itself have?"

"None, so far . . . unless you count lingering Katani ones," he admitted.

"Ah, that's right; you're still a brand-new kingdom," Serina remembered. "You really should start looking around for a God or Goddess to be your Patron Deity, if you want true political recognition. Even I know that's how the various substates of shattered Aiar are pulling themselves out of the lawless chaos of barbarism."

"Well, we're not exactly lawless barbarians," he returned. "I'll take it up with Her Majesty and the rest of our family when I return. You can even assist in the search for a Patron Deity yourself, if you like."

"Oh, I'll be very busy with my own projects," Serina quickly hedged, blushing. Somehow, she didn't think he would be too happy to have her showing up for a visit pregnant with a child he didn't want. She quickly returned the subject back to the marriage between them. "When would you like to go through the ceremony? Now? Sometime over the next week? Or on the day we attempt the ritual?"

Dominor opened his mouth to say *today* and paused. Even if they weren't going to marry by Katani custom, he didn't have a marriage-torc ready for his bride. With Mariel's help, he could get one made in the next few days. "How about the day of the ritual itself? If we have to be celibate for the five days beforehand, I'd rather not be married to you and *not* be able to assert any conjugal rights."

She blushed, managing a smile. "All right, then. I have the fruit wrapped in stasis charms, so it will keep just as well until then. Mariel can stand as one of our witnesses. Mother Naima can be the other, since we need two adults. I should, um, go over my calculations some more, to make sure the timing of everything will be right, now that we're, um, going to be married . . ."

"And I have tasks of my own," Dominor agreed, shifting to head for the door. He wondered what he could use to make their wedding-torcs, as he didn't exactly have access to his usual resources on this side of the ocean. He paused at the door to glance back at her. She was a beautiful sight to behold, tugging on her braid, strolling from one board to the next as she studied the marks on her slates.

Six more days until she was his bride; Dom turned away with a smile. He would have to stop loving her shortly, but tonight . . . they could store up enough pleasure to hopefully last for those remaining five days. A thought crossed his mind, making him stop again. "I just remembered something."

"Yes?" Serina asked him.

"I haven't gone into the Fountain yet, to see how well I can handle it beforehand."

"Ah, yes! Thank you for the reminder," Serina told him, seizing on the topic since he did need to know what he would have to face. "It's not *too* terribly difficult to handle, if you've a strong sense of self-control and willpower. Would you like to go up there right now, and try it?"

"Sure." Any excuse to spend more time in her company was a good excuse, Dominor decided. Closing the door again, he followed her to the bookcase.

SIXTEEN

❧

ou," Mariel stated, startling Serina out of her mathemagical daze with a jump, "are unhappy."

One hand pressed to her racing heart, Serina turned to study her friend. "Uh . . . what makes you say that?"

"You have a handsome block of masculinity at your lascivious beck and call, and you've buried yourself in your work," Mariel observed. "That, and your braid is fraying. If you were angry, you'd be searching for spare vases to throw, but you're not; you're trying to tug your scalp bald. Ergo, you're unhappy."

Serina gave her a wry look. "We *can't* pounce on each other; we have to abstain for five whole days, and that means the last four days have been an exercise in frustration—don't even think about suggesting we take care of the problem ourselves—I had to explain to Dominor that he couldn't do *that*, either."

She flashed her friend a quick grin.

"He stopped me before I went into the technical details of why, said it was making things even more difficult for him." Her smile didn't last long, however. Tugging on her pale braid, Serina returned her pensive stare to the chalk marks shifting and moving in their gracefully enchanted dance.

Mariel stepped all the way inside the workroom, shutting the door behind her. "So what's bothering you?"

Sighing, Serina shook her head, looking away.

"Don't you give me that attitude," Mariel chided her friend, folding her arms across her bosom. "You have a man who clearly cares for you, to the point where he finds your mathemagical babble *arousing*, and you can only sigh and *mope*?"

Crossing to the chair Dominor often used to read in, Serina flopped into its leather embrace. "He's wonderful! He's charming, he's intelligent, he's witty, he's caring, he's masterful, he's sexy and perfect for me in almost every way—except for the glaringly huge fact that he doesn't want children."

Comprehension dawned in Mariel's green gaze. "*Oh.* And you have to . . . yeah, *that* is a little awkward. Enough to mope over." Moving over to the chair, Mariel perched on the armrest, embracing her friend in a one-armed hug.

Serina leaned into her side with an unhappy sigh. "And he's perfect for the ritual, too. Only, in order to complete it, I have to lie to him. Well, sort-of lie to him. I don't *want* to lie to him, you see . . . so I've been *creatively* hedging around the truth."

"I see. Well, maybe he's not as adamant against children as you might think," Mariel encouraged her. "He's been getting along like cards in a deck with Mikor. If he didn't like children, why would he be so interested in teaching my son, day after day? And in being a good role model, too?" She laughed softly, squeezing Serina's shoulders. "I've never seen Mikor eat his vegetables without complaining, before, until His Lordship came to stay with us. *And* his greens."

Serina smiled slightly. "Maybe . . ."

"Look, let's go practice some *tai* in the salle. Mikor and Dominor are in there right now, going through a sword lesson. There's plenty of room for us to do some practicing ourselves . . . and you can see for yourself just how well he gets along with your honorary nephew, all right?" Mariel coaxed, encouraging her friend.

A nod, and Serina extracted herself from the comfortable chair. "All right. I do need something physical to do to burn off all this sexual energy I'm not expending . . . and can't expend until tomorrow afternoon."

"That's the spirit!" her petite friend teased, patting her on the shoulder. "Let's go get changed and show the boys how a pair of real women defend themselves!"

Dominor glanced away from his opponent long enough to take note of the two women entering the salle. The door was located at the midpoint, but he and Mikor were working at the end near the pells and mirrors; the other half of the large, sanded floor was wide open for their own use. They were wearing short-hemmed tunic-dresses that only came to their knees, and footless hose. *Tai*-fighting clothes.

Returning his attention firmly to his pupil, Dominor pushed away the thought of how sexy Serina's bared ankles and toes looked. They had one more day to *endure*—which was the right word for it, considering he wasn't even allowed to do anything to himself—and then they would be making love within the heart of the Fountain. An exhilarating, unnerving prospect to consider. Especially with her lithe body doing some preliminary stretches a handful of body-lengths away. *Your wits are wandering again—focus on your pupil!*

"All right, Mikor, you've practiced the rote counters and blocks long enough. We're going to do what is called a three-twenty. I will defend, and you will attack. You will get twenty strikes against me, and you should focus mostly on that, but don't forget to defend, too, for I will get to pick three times that I may strike back. Understood?" he asked the youth.

Mikor nodded, shaking out his left arm for a moment before raising it again. Unfortunately, they weren't working with shields, as the only shield-transforming spell Dominor knew formed one too large for the boy to lift. In a real fight, Dominor would pick a shield for himself to get whatever defensive advantage he could, but this was just a practice. He wanted to be fair to the boy . . . or as fair as he could be, given the boy simply wasn't skilled enough to get through his ability to parry Mikor's still clumsy blows.

"Begin!"

Out of the corner of his eye, he saw Serina and Mariel closing. He blocked the first few of Mikor's somewhat hesitant swings, distracted by what he was seeing at the other end of the field. Their arms swung and struck, lifted and blocked. Their legs kicked . . . and Mikor backed him around with a flurry of mostly ineffective swings. He glanced down to strike inward in an opening in the boy's nonexistent defenses, thumping him lightly on the hip.

It *might* leave a bruise, but not much of one. Dominor had too much control over his weapon and the force with which he applied it; in fact, *he* was in more danger from his pupil's efforts. Mikor gritted his teeth and swung harder, clacking his transformed weapon against Dominor's. In the mirror behind him, Dominor saw a swirl of pale color and glanced up reflexively, just in time to see Mariel's reflected image *thudding* into the sand-covered floor with an audible *oof*.

Facedown.

Serina . . . can make someone "eat dirt?" Just like Kelly ca— PAIN!

Breath strangling in his throat, Dominor dropped his sword, his hands, and his body, grabbing and curling protectively around the shattered fragments of his family jewels as he landed awkwardly on his side in the sand. Red waves of blood-streaked agony blurred his vision, alternating with sparkles of lightning-white.

"Gods—Dominor, I'm so sorry! Mother?" Mikor shouted, his voice sounding strange through the frantic pounding in Dominor's ears. "Mother, HELP!!"

Pounding footsteps matched the pounding in his groin. Sand kicked against his back, a minor inconvenience, then hands were gingerly trying to turn him over. "Let me see—what did you do, Mikor?"

"I . . . I struck him in the *you know*! I was expecting him to block it, but he didn't!"

"Dominor, can you hear me? How bad is it?" Mariel's voice coaxed him.

He didn't know where he found the strength, but somehow Dom managed to make his voice work. He couldn't even see her, the pain had clouded his vision to the point of nearly blacking out. In a gravelly, undignified squeak, he gasped, "I am never . . . *ever* . . . going to have children . . . *ever*!"

Footsteps pounded across the floor, and the door slammed shut.

"I'm really, really sorry!" Mikor babbled. "I didn't mean to hurt you, honest!"

"Mikor, I need you to back up a little and give me room to work, all right?" Mariel's voice was calm, soothing, though mere tone alone couldn't do much to alleviate Dominor's agony. "In fact, why don't you go wash up, since I think your sword lesson has been canceled for the rest of today."

"Yes, Mother." Shuffling sounds accompanied the promise.

A hand lightly splayed itself over Dominor's protectively cupped fingers, though with his legs drawn up, there wasn't much room for her to touch. The other one laid itself on his chest. A moment later, the most amazing sound caressed his ears.

She was singing. Like an avatar of the Gods—or a feminine version of his twin—Mariel was Singing, infusing him with Healing energies. Cool, soothing relief poured into his veins. Agony receded, draining away the mixture of darkness and rippling waves of light clouding his gaze.

With the subsiding of his pain came the relaxing of his protectively hunched muscles. Once his legs relaxed onto the sand, she gently shifted his hands aside, cupping his groin through his trousers. Pausing in the midst of her delicate, crooning melody, she offered, "Pardon the familiarity, but it's rather necessary . . ."

"No, please!" Dominor managed to gasp, blinking up at the ceiling as the last of his vision returned. "Keep Healing me, by all means!"

She chuckled and resumed her crooning. The magic she was pouring into him soothed more than just his groin; it relaxed the pain-induced tension in the rest of his limbs. By the time she ceased Singing and removed her hands, Dominor could barely move, he felt so comfortable. And, thankfully, *not* aroused by her touch, despite the location of her hand mere moments ago.

"That's an incredible gift you have," he murmured, breathing deeply to restore some of the energy subdued by her Healing powers. His gaze sharpened, and Dominor pushed himself up onto his elbows. "Are you strong enough to regenerate lost tissue?"

"Strong enough . . . yes, I am," Mariel confessed, resting beside him on one hip and one hand. She gestured with the other one, waggling it horizontally. "*Skilled* enough . . . well, let's just say it's been over a decade since I last practiced that particular set of skills. I did train in such things at the Sanitorium in Lombeza, which is a Healing School just across the eastern border in Guchere, but that was before I married and moved here.

There's not many opportunities for people to lose body parts in a nunnery, either, so I'm out of practice."

Mind racing with possibilities, Dominor asked, "And what if you did practice? Say, on chickens? Remove a wing and practice regenerating it?"

She wrinkled her nose at him. "Wouldn't that be a bit cruel to the chickens?"

"You don't know these chickens," Dom only half-joked. He sighed and sat up farther, running a hand through his hair. Then grimaced at the sand he tracked through his locks. Brushing it out of his scalp, he shook his head. "That's the one thing we *don't* have on Nightfall, a true Healer. Some Healing spells, yes, but none of my brothers specialized in Healing magics."

"What about your sisters-in-law?" Mariel asked him, curious.

"Alys . . . she was never very strong with magic, though she did have the same feel to her powers as my next-eldest sibling, Wolfer. He's a shape-changer," Dominor explained. "And Kelly has no magic whatsoever."

That raised her brows. "No magic? And *she* is your Queen? There aren't more than a handful of nations outside of maybe shattered Aiar that have non-mages for their rulers. She must be an extraordinary woman."

"Considering she was responsible for my distraction and sub-sequent near-fatal maiming . . ." Dominor muttered. At Mariel's frown, he twisted his mouth ruefully. "She has this ability she calls *kungfoo* that I think is very similar to your *tai*-fighting, the ability to make a man 'eat dirt.' Which she refuses to teach to me. Realizing it . . . distracted me."

"I think I can see why, if she feels the need for an edge over you mages," Mariel chuckled. Catching the look in his blue eyes, she shook her head quickly, making her curls bounce. "Don't even think of asking me. *Tai*-fighting is designed for females and only sanctioned to be taught *to* females. I'm afraid you don't qualify."

Dominor studied her, then shook his head. "Women and their conspiracies."

"Dominor, I'm a little confused," Mariel stated, her brows pinching in a thoughtful frown. "You seem to get along just fine with my son; you're as patient and caring with him as any man who is capable of becoming a good father . . . yet you claim you will never, ever want any children of your own."

"What?" Startled by that, Dominor stared at her. "When did I claim that?"

"Just now, when you were huddled on the sands?" she reminded him dryly, arching one of her brown brows.

"No, I was bemoaning the fact that I thought I *couldn't* ever have any children," Dom corrected her. "Not that I didn't *want* any. I do. It's just that your son nearly gelded me . . . or so it felt."

"So, you *do* want children?" Mariel asked, studying him carefully.

"Of course," he shrugged. "Mikor's a wonderful boy; I'd be proud to be his father . . . except I'm not interested in his mother, that way. Sorry, but it's not *you* that I'm madly in love with."

She beamed at him. "Well, then that's settled! Tomorrow, you'll wed Serina, complete the first stage of her project, and live happily ever after!"

That made him laugh. "You make it sound so easy. It'll take a bit more effort than that, I think—*will* you consider coming with us to live on Nightfall?" he asked her, switching from amusement to seriousness, since it was a very serious question. "Or at least come for a visit?"

"And a Healing?" Mariel added lightly, though Dom had the impression she wasn't treating the offer that lightly. "I'll consider it . . ."

"Good. Now, if you'll excuse me, I think I should go reassure your son that he didn't kill me and that I'm not about to kill him in retaliation for what he did, either." Rising from the sand, Dominor helped her to stand, gave her a formal bow, and headed for the door. He wondered idly where Serina had gone, dusting himself off as he went in search of her honorary nephew.

At the bottom of the Font access shaft, huddled with her arms around her knees in the mouth of the dusty escape tunnel, Serina let her tears fall in sniffle-broken silence.

She couldn't blame Dominor; being whacked *there* that hard was enough to make *her* flinch and want to protect her loins.

No, you knew he didn't want children from early on . . . you knew it was a risk when you ran your initial calculations. He's oathbound to help you, so his own magics will compel him to comply with the requirements of the ritual, in both halves. All you have to do is make sure he doesn't know *he's impregnating you, tomorrow.*

*That'll cut down on any fuss. Then just . . . just not let the mirror
show you from the waist down, or something. And ask Mariel and
Mikor to not say anything to him when you start to show . . .*

It was cold comfort to know that she *felt* strong enough as an
adult to bear and raise a child all on her own; it just wasn't the
same as knowing she could have had someone to share the burden and responsibilities of parenthood with her . . . someone
whom she loved very much, in spite of himself.

At least they were already sleeping in separate beds. To quell
the urge to cheat against the no-sex stricture, she had conjured a
bed for herself in the changing room attached to her workroom.
Cuddled up together, they would have been too tempted each of
the past four mornings to do something together. She didn't have
to go back and see him again until tomorrow, if she didn't want
to. She could even transform the dust around her into food and
water, if she wanted to hide here all night long . . .

You're a coward, Serina Avadan, she chided herself, sighing.
Her inner coward retorted quickly with, *Yes, but at least this way
you won't break your heart even further, wanting something he
cannot give either of you: an interest in being a father.*

So, what exactly does this marriage ceremony entail?" Mother
Naima inquired as the last of their quartet entered Serina's workroom, deemed the most practical place to hold the somewhat impromptu wedding.

There was an abandoned chapel on this side of the Retreat
complex, but neither Serina nor Dominor had felt it wise to invoke the Natallian Gods. Neither of them were Natallian, and
neither of them cared for the traditions and beliefs of this land.
Respect was there, of course, but no real belief in the local
deities. Serina picked up a gold-rimmed goblet unearthed from
one of the storage rooms. She had found it in a case someone had
opened, probably Mikor. Two of the faceted crystal cups were
missing, and she would have to remember to question her honorary nephew about it later, but for now, the cleaned and polished
cup would suffice.

"I break open the sacred fruit," she stated, pointing with her
other hand at a covered, sealed dish she had found to transport
the *myjii*, "pour its liqueur into this cup . . . and then we drink
from the same cup, swallowing what we sip. Divorce is very

similar, only we each spit the Sacred Liqueur back into the cup without swallowing. In front of witnesses, of course."

Eyeing her askance, the Mother Superior of the Retreat slowly shook her head. "That is the *strangest* form of wedding ceremony I have ever heard of! What if . . . what if you're just drinking in a tavern, and someone grabs your cup and drinks from it, too? Does that make you married? Or what if you choke on a laugh, and you spit into your goblet—does that divorce you?"

Serina shook her head. "No, of course not. For one, it's only the liqueur of the Sacred Fruit that counts. For another, no one in the Moonlands would dare be that rude without an invitation. If they attempt to do so, the person they offend spits the liqueur into their face, not the cup . . . and the rude person is banned from any attempt to legally marry another person for a full ten years. If they try to 'steal a mate' in this fashion a second time . . . they are exiled permanently, with all memory of how to return stripped from their mind."

Dominor, cradling a square box in his hands, eyed her warily. "I sincerely hope you aren't going to be spitting in my face, anytime soon."

She flushed at his words, mumbling, "Nor you in my own." But she didn't meet his gaze. Instead, she changed the subject, gesturing at the box he held. "What's in that?"

"A custom of my own people. Wedding-torcs." Dominor dipped his head wryly at her goblet. "I see you found the same crate I pilfered. With Mariel's permission."

His comment confused Serina. "But we can't drink out of two different cups, Dominor. It has to be the *same* cup, or it doesn't count."

He grinned. "*Torcs*, not goblets." Unlatching the case, he opened it, revealing two spell-crafted curves of glass. They were enchanted to be shatterproof, yet just flexible enough to slip around their throats. The ends and part of their curved shafts had been gilded with a thinly traced pattern. "We wear them around our necks."

"Oh. Well." She blinked and stared at the objects, saying the first thing that came to her mind. "They're beautiful. But won't they break?"

"I *am* a mage, my Lady," Dom reminded her archly. "And craftsman enough to ensure that only the best will encircle your throat."

"Enough with the flirting!" Mother Naima interjected, lifting her hand. "I have other things to do, this afternoon. Let's get on with it."

"Marriage-cup first," Dominor suggested as Serina dithered, still eyeing the torcs in his box. He was pleased that she found them so lovely she couldn't stop staring. He wasn't the artist in glass that Rydan and Koranen were when they put their black and auburn heads together, but he could give them very stiff competition when he put his mind to it.

"Right . . ." Turning her attention to the sealed bowl, she touched the lid, then looked at the others. "Um, just to warn you all, this is going to smell disgusting at first."

Before they could ask her what she meant, she released the spell-sealed lid. It took a few moments for the smell to reach the others. Serina was prepared, but Mariel cried out, covering her nose, and the Mother Superior staggered, her face turning almost as pale as the white cotton of her habit. Greenish, but pale. The stench reached Dominor last, making him cough and lift the lapel of his tunic-jacket to cover his mouth.

"Gods above, that's *awful!*" Mother Naima moaned, shifting as far back as she could without knocking over Serina's chalkboards.

"It smells like someone clogged up a refreshing room under a hot sun and then tossed in the contents of a rotting garbage pit!" Mariel agreed, grimacing as she tried not to breathe too deeply— the taste of it on the tongue was even worse than in the nose, if that could be believed.

Dominor had to admire Serina's resilience. Aside from a certain pinched look to her tightly sealed mouth, and the way her nostrils flexed, as if she could keep out the scent by sheer willpower, she didn't flinch. Indeed, she reached into the bowl and picked up the ugliest so-called fruit Dominor had ever seen. It was an oblong oval with a leathery, hard green skin that looked like it had been stretched outward at a dozen or more points along its surface by jabbing thumbs. The blunt-ended spikes, each about an inch or two long, studded the surface as she turned it over in her hands.

Finding just the right spot, Serina carefully pried two of the closest-set spikes apart with her thumbs, exerting control as well as strength. The flesh cracked open along a nearly invisible seam. She waited two seconds, then breathed deeply, a beatific smile curving her mouth.

The others eyed her askance, until the new odor reached them, too. It wasn't as fair as the previous stench had been foul; it was *better* than that. It scoured away all lingering traces of unpleasantness, an indescribably sweet yet subtly spicy scent, that faint hint of a bite keeping it from being cloying. The other three breathed deeply, and breathed deeply again, enjoying it. While they did so, Serina finished prying apart the fruit. It parted into two halves, one side hollowed, the other holding a bulging, jiggling membrane-sac.

Setting the empty half on the table, she carefully tipped the sac into her hand. Setting down the second shell, with its creamy white, divinely scented flesh, she snatched up the goblet and wriggled her fingers around the sac, searching for the right spot. Finding one of the six seeds hidden at the center, she used its sharp, almond-shaped tip to puncture the sac. Golden liqueur spilled out, bringing an even thicker, headier version of that mouth-watering smell with it.

The sac deflated while she caught its contents in the cup, until the last drop had been drained. Setting the now shriveled, lumpy membrane in one of the fruit halves, Serina turned to Dominor, goblet in hand. The gleam of the liqueur in the goblet, he noted, matched the shade of her amber-gold eyes uncannily.

"Will you drink with me, Lord Dominor of Nightfall?" she asked him softly, smiling.

"I will drink if you will drink, my Lady," he agreed, stepping close to her. Cupping her hand in his own, he lifted the goblet to his lips with her assistance. Liquid summer spilled onto his tongue, tasting of honey and sweet mint, *cinnin* and feminine musk, a thousand favorite flavors distilled into a single moment. And for all it contained not a single drop of alcohol, it was as intoxicating as twice-distilled spirits.

Blinking, he lowered the cup and swallowed cautiously. It felt like he'd swallowed a ray of sunlight, glowing its way into his gut. Aware that it was her turn, Dominor helped guide the cup to Serina's lips, watching her swallow. She kept her eyes on his as she did so.

There was still some of the liquid in the goblet when she lowered it. Bringing it to his lips, her hand still cupped in his, Dominor finished half of it. Without a word, he urged her to drink the last few swallows. The flicking of her tongue over her lips was a beacon to his instincts.

Leaning in close, he captured her lips with his own, kissing not just her, but the taste of the Sacred Liqueur, seeking it with his tongue. They were a perfect blend, Serina and the liqueur. Intoxicating.

When he pulled back, he licked his own lips, enjoying the way she blushed. Clearing her throat, Serina set the goblet aside and reached into the box still cradled in his other arm. Selecting the larger of the two rings, she lifted it to his neck. It didn't take more than a gentle pull for her to discover the glass had been enchanted to be elastic, bendable . . . but she was going to put it on him the wrong way.

Quickly setting the box down, Dominor covered her hands with his, helping her turn the torc around. "It sits this way, with the opening in the front."

"Ah. Right." Stretching her arms behind him, she fitted it carefully around his neck, letting it settle in place. The rounded, gold-swirled ends rested just to either side of the hollow at the base of his throat. The weight of the decorative knobs would help keep it in place.

She picked up the smaller one and handed it to him, awaiting her turn. There was no need to lift her usual long braid out of the way; a few judicious charms in front of a mirror had coiled the lot around her scalp, spell-pinning it in place. Dominor fitted the slightly smaller torc around her slender neck. It looked good against her skin, the subtle play of gold echoing the highlights in her amber eyes. Once it was in place, he cupped her arms and kissed her gently, just a brush of his mouth against hers. Pulling back slightly, he rested his forehead against hers, feeling unusually tender.

"Serina, my wife," he murmured, testing the words on his lips. They felt good, making him smile.

"Dominor . . . my husband," she returned softly, almost shyly. Firming her attention, she pulled back from him, giving him a reassuring smile. "We have much to do. I trust the two of you are satisfied, as our witnesses?"

"If you're satisfied that this . . . whatever this was . . . constitutes a marriage rite," Mother Naima returned dryly, "then yes, I will stand witness to it."

"And I will happily stand witness," Mariel agreed, smiling at her two friends. She wished she had found Serina earlier; the taller woman had vanished since yesterday, not reappearing until just now. No doubt the blond mage was still suffering under the delusion that Dominor didn't want children. Knowing that it was quite the opposite, she held her peace; there would be time to straighten out the misunderstanding between the two of them once their task in the Koral-tai Font was finished. Right now, they had to concentrate on what they were about to do. "You'd better get going and keep your minds firmly on the task at hand. Don't let yourselves go straying into side thoughts, or we'll have another piece of Permanent Magic to have to untangle."

"Yes, *Mother*," Serina teased her friend, rolling her eyes.

A flick of her hand shooed the other two women out of her workroom. Not that Naima and Mariel didn't already know where the secret door was hidden, of course. She simply didn't want an audience waiting for their return. Once the door had shut behind them, Serina bolted it.

At a questioning look from her husband, she shrugged. "I don't want either them or Mikor getting in here while we're occupied. Clear your mind. We cannot risk doing this if you cannot concentrate fully and solely on the task ahead."

"I *am* a fully trained mage," Dominor reminded her. "I could thrust my hand into a fire without protective shielding, and grasp a burning log with my bare fingers for a count of one hundred without hesitating, if I must. The pleasure of making love to you will be well within my capabilities."

"So long as you make love to me *without* saying anything other than the required phrase at the end," she cautioned him, "we should do fine."

" 'Give us good sons and daughters with all of their own powers,' " Dominor recited from memory, blue eyes gleaming with the thought of one day seeing her swell with a child. He almost asked her if they *could* create a child in this ritual, but two reasons stopped him. One, it would ruin her efforts with all of those lengthy calculations, and two, he wanted to coax her into making their marriage permanent. The last thing he wanted to see was her spitting out a mouthful of that divine juice. Or spitting it into his face.

Serina nodded, glad he remembered. "Yes, 'give us good sons and daughters with all of their own powers.' Just keep that in mind, and we'll do fine. Shall we?"

Bowing, Dominor gestured at the bookcase-hidden door. She fetched a shrunken slateboard, then turned to open it, looking like a shaft of sunlight in her cream tunic and yellow hose. He had opted for his dark blue tunic and trousers, selected from the clothes she had created for him. They weren't matching wedding clothes, like his sister-in-law had insisted on, but he thought they complemented each other nicely, light and dark. Joining her as she passed through the opening to the platform beyond, Dominor caught her hand, lacing their fingers together.

Her palm was damp with sweat. He arched a brow at her before the hidden door finished closing. "Nervous?"

"A bit." Lifting her free hand, Serina silently directed the platform to rise.

"Perhaps I should remind you as well to relax and concentrate only on the task ahead?" he gently teased.

They docked at the upper level and walked through the foyer, hand in hand. Entering the Font Chamber, Serina led him to the edge of the tiers, then freed her fingers. "I must warn the other Guardians and ward the Font against external interference."

"Anything I can do?" Dominor offered as she expanded the chalkboard, readying it to record their attempt.

She flashed him a smile of gratitude, but shook her head. Deciding he would ready himself, he stripped off his clothes while she walked around the room, touching each of the coppery red basins. Streamers of mist rose in the wake of her fingers, spiraling after her until they linked together in an ephemeral railing surrounding the central pool. Touching, it, she spoke, her words echoing in that same odd way as before.

"This is Guardian Serina. I am about to commence a Major Enchantment and will be sealing my Font against outside interference."

A female voice, one Dominor didn't know, echoed out of the mist. *"What exactly are you going to be doing, young lady?"*

Serina blinked. *"Oh! Um . . . hello, Mother. I didn't think you'd be near the Font."*

"Gods-touched coincidence, at best. Now answer my question. What do you think you are doing?"

Dominor didn't envy her position; from the struggle he could see on his wife's face, she was uncomfortable with confronting her mother. He didn't have that problem. Of course, he didn't have parents, period, for they had died before he and his brothers had been exiled.

As he watched her, she stiffened her spine and her tone. *"I am*

*not the 'daughter of the Inoma' anymore, Mother; I do not answer
to you, and I do not have to answer to you. I love you, but I will
not bow to you, nor will I answer your demands."*

"*Poor Serina, still jealous of me?*" a second female voice interjected, similar to the first, but lighter in tone.

Serina extracted her hand from the mist encircling the Font. Gritting her teeth, she restrained her temper carefully. Her eyes met Dominor's steady blue gaze; he had moved up beside her, wearing not a stitch of clothing but looking powerful and supportive all the same. She appreciated that support. A deep breath allowed her to return her hand to the mist and speak in a gentle tone.

"*No, Kayla. Jealousy no longer touches me. I have all of my
own powers, and I know how to wield them very well. I have a career that I love, friends who love me, the support of my husband,
and the honor of crafting a Permanent Magic that will affect millions. I stopped comparing myself to you ages ago. I will love
you, but I am not you. If you wish to burden yourself with trying
to compare the two of us, you will only harm yourself with envy.
As I used to. Now, get out of the mists. I'm about to seal the lines,
and I don't want to injure you.*"

Extracting her hand, Serina waited three heartbeats, then clenched her hands, muttering under her breath. The rippling mists stiffened, then lowered and flattened. Stepping up onto the mist proved it was as solid as it now looked. She used the hand-wide ribbon as a walkway, stooping and touching the next row of similarly hued basins, a pale aquamarine. She had to step around solitary pools that weren't repeated at regular intervals in order to do so. The next tier she formed was butter-yellow, and the last one a rich plum. That gave them a set of steps all the way up to the mouth of the main basin.

Descending, Serina found herself on the far side of the Font from Dominor . . . and near the communications basin that tapped into his brother's Font. Stooping below his level of sight, she cupped her hands, scooped out some of the rippling green mist from the basin next to the coppery red one, and half-inhaled, half-drank the contents. She had already removed her anklet five days ago; now the fertility-magic realigned the rest of her bodily humors, tingling through her in a very arousing manner. Ripening her for what was to come.

A check reassured her that her hands were clean of energies, though there were visible signs she was affected. Two of them, in fact, poking through the front of her tunic-gown. Straightening and moving to the side, she found Dominor staring up at the heart of the singularity, no doubt contemplating what it might feel like as they made love. "Dominor, come here, please."

He blinked and complied, pulling his gaze down to hers. She gestured at the pool, trying to ignore the scrape of her dress over the taut peaks of her nipples. "I'm, um, a bit concerned about the blow you received, yesterday. Mariel is a good Healer, but I want to be sure you're at your physical peak. If you could sip a handful of the green mist from that basin, there, it'll ensure that you're more than capable of functioning . . . if you don't mind humoring me, that is?"

Dominor glanced down at his groin. He felt quite capable; rampantly so, in fact. But to indulge her, he scooped up some of the mist in his hands, breathing in the energies. His erection stiffened further when his body absorbed the mist, warming him from bone to skin and back again with a rush of heady desire. Glancing at Serina, he watched his newly made wife removing her garments. Lithe and lean, she was perfect for him, a pale-haired foil for his darker locks. Their skin, however, was similar in hue as she twined her fingers in his.

Lifting her finger to her lips, signaling for silence, Serina led her partner up the step-like rings encircling the Font. Her body ached for more contact than just their fingers, but that had to wait. Planting one foot on the rim of the basin, she tugged him up beside her, then reached up with her free hand and touched the pulsing magic of the singularity, *willing* them to be lifted up into its sphere.

A gasp jerked air into his lungs, the moment Dominor felt the sheer power spilling from her body into his. It was just like the previous time, when she had pulled him up into the Font for a practice run. Fully clothed, though, with no intention of making love. It was a familiar shock, but it was still a shock to his system when the magic struck.

He was still struggling for breath when the sphere pulsed, lifting them off their feet and sucking them into its depths. Immersed in the chaos of pure magic, it was hard to breathe, period. The only sensations that anchored him, just as they had the previous time, were the fingers tightly entwined with his.

Seizing on that as a lifeline, he pulled her to him. Their limbs collided with a gentle bump and tangle. His free hand found the braided hair at the back of her head; a thought literally was all it took to unbind the pale strands, sending them floating into the flow of energies caressing their flesh. Mouth sought mouth, nipping animalistically; there was supposed to be a progression of acts, a set pattern to this literally enchanted seduction, but with pure magic playing over their bared skin, there was no thought free to process anything beyond overwhelming sensation and purified instinct. This was his mate, and he intended to mark her and claim her as such.

Serina had more practice in dealing with the overwhelming power at the heart of the Font, but this was a different sort of experience. The fertility-energies she had sipped had brought out all of her procreative instincts. Her conscious, rational mind knew that this was what they were supposed to be doing, so she released the brakes on the cart of desire hurtling toward the bottom of their hill. Returning his kiss with equal enthusiasm, she caressed his body, freeing her fingers from his only so that she could entwine her limbs around him.

Unlike the free-floating of the levitation spell they had practiced with, the Font itself provided them with a certain stability, literally at a thought. It was something like moving through a mist that solidified wherever they needed support, be it a hip, a knee, or a shoulder. Energy surrounded them like an effervescent jelly, for the magic throbbed and tingled, flowing outward through the sphere cocooning them.

They could see, unlike the communication, but they could see only each other; whatever lay beyond the Font was curtained by the energies pulsing around them. Dominor used his vision, pouncing on the tip of one of her breasts with his lips like a hawk stooping on a mouse. She squeaked like a mouse, too, when he sucked the tip between his teeth, before she locked her throat against any further sound. It didn't matter to him; Dom was too intensely focused on the taste and the feel of her to waste his time with a groan.

Her hair had taken on a life of its own, rippling in the not-wind of the energies enveloping them. It caressed his skin like a cooler version of her hands. His own hair was equally animated, though it was shorter, chest-length rather than thigh-length; the dark brown strands whipped in the not-wind of magic fountaining into existence around them. His locks tickled her breasts, collarbone, and abdomen as he switched between her nipples, enjoying both of them.

Catching his hand, Serina drew his fingers to her lips, kissing them. She suckled his fingers, savoring the salty taste of his skin. A swirl of her tongue made him cease his torment of her breasts in favor of shifting her upward in relation to him. That put her within reach of the heart of the singularity, and as she twisted in his grip, panting at the swirl of his tongue against her navel, her wrist drifted through the source-point.

A not-quite-electric shock seared through her flesh. Gasping, she jerked her arm free reflexively; that was too intense to tolerate. Not this early in their lovemaking. Her breath choked in her throat a second time as Dom buried his face in the folds of her mound. It felt incredible, the soft stroking of his tongue against her nerves, versus the pulsing of magic in her veins. She had to reciprocate.

A twist of her body managed to get herself turned around and oriented the right way, long strands of hair tangling in the perturbed aether. Grasping his shaft with one hand, she used the other to pull his hips closer, until her lips could close around her goal. The moisture seeping from his tip tasted delicious, sweetened by the juice of the Sacred Fruit they had drunk together. Greedy, Serina suckled more from his flesh, making him moan against her.

Conscious thought didn't matter; only pleasure. The energies skittering rhythmically through their nerves both enhanced and disrupted their efforts. It wasn't enough to orally please each other; it only went so far before leaving them suspended at the edges of their desire, lacking enough cohesion for that final push and plummet.

Without conscious agreement, though moving almost as one, they rearranged themselves with a scrambling spin; now he floated on his back and she straddled him, her legs splayed to either side as she guided him up into her body. *This* was what was missing; that fullness, that connection, that completion of male-female energies that only came when their loins were slotted together in the correct manner. Riding her mate, Serina focused on the pleasure of sheathing him over and over.

Sliding his hands down her calves to her ankles, Dominor focused on the pleasure of piercing her slick warmth, claiming the space within her body that was now reserved solely for him. Their bodies fitted themselves together to the pulsing rhythm of the magic cocooning them from the universe. Primal energies fluxed and flowed around and through them, driving the urge to procreate. Primitive, yes; primal, yes . . . perfect, yes . . . In unconscious choreography, they increased their pace; he caught several strands of her hair, tugging her forward against his chest.

The air around them pulsed and shimmered with its own increasing beat, though whether they were responsible, or if the magic was speeding on its own, dragging them with it, neither cared. They tumbled midair, inverting, until the singularity stung him in the small of his back, precipitating the final plummet as it sliced through his flesh, exiting through his loins along with his seed and his breath in a harsh groan. It stung her flesh, too, rippling her gut in a clenching, mindless spasm of need. Clinging to each other, they stilled midair, orgasmic energies flooding every muscle and nerve.

Clarity filtered into the aftermath of their mutual orgasm like sunlight burning through a morning's mist. Gradually, thought replaced instinct, though it was disrupted every few seconds or so by the pleasurable cramping of an aftershock. Limp with repletion, Serina clung to her husband; he held her just as tightly, his fingers stroking in slow, soothing circles against her back while hers slipped up and down.

Her abdomen tingled. Instinct warned her what was about to happen. Pushing back a little, she caught one of his hands, dragging it to the soft flesh just below her navel. Blue eyes blinked at brown. His tongue came out, moistening his lips; her own echoed the act, wetting and readying them for speech. A nod of his head, a nod of her own, and they spoke in unison.

"Give us good sons and daughters with all of their own powers . . ."

The singularity, still lodged deep within her abdomen, pulsed and spiked with raw power. Serina gasped, *feeling* his seed finding its home in her fruitful loins. The thought of that, the knowledge that she was now pregnant, reminded her of what she had to do. Quickly disengaging, she ignored the mute frown of questioning confusion in his blue eyes and reached into the magic between them, opening the Fontway.

Between one breath and the next, Dominor of Nightfall vanished, cast through the heart of the aether, abruptly sent home.

SEVENTEEN

❦

The sudden cessation of energies searing his nerves was replaced by a wild masculine yell. Dominor twisted, frantically trying to protect himself from his abrupt fall. A klaxon overpowered his ears, making him wince and clap his hands to his ears . . . or rather, attempt to clap his hands to his ears. Something seized his flesh, stopping him.

Since it was also preventing his fall to the pale granite floor just below his left shoulder, he couldn't complain too much. Except that he had just been shoved from Koral-tai to . . . well, the color of the granite told him it was most probably Nightfall, somewhere inside one of the two mountain ranges. At a guess, the northern one; that was the side that Rydan had his tower along the outer wall of the palace, and it made sense that he might've found some sort of hidden passageway leading to the otherwise unknown Fountain occupying the island.

The klaxon mercifully fell silent. Dominor tried moving, once the last of the echoes died down. The effort was futile; whatever had gripped him held him securely in the air, unable to see much beyond the polished, seamless stone floor and a bit of a column off to one side. It was only just visible through the tangled curtain of his hair at the edge of his vision, since he couldn't even move his eyes. He had "landed" in the net of energies holding him with his face and body tilted mostly down, his head slightly lower than his heels.

He couldn't understand it. *Why* had she shoved him through, like that? *She could have at least allowed me enough time to get my clothes on, before sending me through to my brother!* Dominor thought, frowning internally. *Gods, I'm never going to hear the end of this, when Rydan shows up and sees my naked ass in his precious Fountain Chamber . . .*

Something smacked him in the back, soft and crumpled, just as the klaxons blared a second time. It felt like his clothes, though he couldn't twist and look behind him. He was fairly sure the edged object that was tickling his left buttock was the edge of a boot sole, too . . . so apparently his wife *had been* kind enough to send his clothing through. Just not while he was wearing it.

It didn't make sense, though. It wasn't as if she couldn't send him through the Fountainway at any point in time; she was the Guardian of Koral-tai, and the energy was available for her use in any way she reasonably saw fit. Guardians were carefully screened so that they weren't the type to abuse so much overwhelming power . . . and so it doubly didn't make sense as to why she wouldn't at least give him enough time to wish her a proper good-bye.

Unless . . . she was concerned for my twin's sake, thought to just send me through while we were conveniently already in the Font . . . and didn't want me saying anything aloud that could jeopardize our efforts to cure the last botched piece of accidental magic?

That made as much sense as anything, though it still left him suspended over the floor at an angle that was threatening to make his head rush from the blood that was starting to pool.

Footsteps raced toward him, pounding louder and louder as their source approached wherever-he-was. Only one set, of course, but then Dominor didn't expect Rydan to invite anyone else into his hidden domain, arrogant, black-haired bastard that he was. Bastard-by-nature, of course; they did share the same mother, after all.

Those racing feet skidded to a stop somewhere close by, accompanied by a panting set of lungs. And a furious roar. "*GOD-DAMMIT, DOMINOR!* How *dare* you come here?!"

Magic jerked and tingled, dumping him abruptly onto the hard, cold floor. Unable to stop his fall, Dom felt the edge of his forehead crack against the pale granite. Another inch lower and farther back, and he would've been stunned by a blow to his temple. As it was, he twisted his wrist, trying to stop his ignominious fall.

"Ow, dammit!" Twisting onto his hip, Dominor craned his head, finding and glaring at his younger sibling through the tangle of his hair. "Did you have to *dump* me like that?"

Rydan, clad only in a pair of black sleeping trousers, clenched his fists. Energy crackled tangibly around him, he was that visibly furious. "You are *forbidden* to be here! How *dare* you invade my sanctum!"

That made Dominor gape. How dare *he*—? Shoving to his feet, snagging and clutching a scrap of blue fabric to his loins—his wedding-tunic—Dominor glared back at the younger mage. "How *dare* I? I didn't have any *choice*! My damned wife shoved me through without a by-your-leave, as soon as we finished having sex in the gods-be-damned Font! She didn't even let me put my clothing on first—in case you haven't *noticed*!"

Baring his teeth in a grimace, Rydan clutched his hands to his head, flattening his black, sleep-mussed locks. "There is a *reason* why I haven't told any of you about this place—and now you've *sullied* it with your energies, ruining my one source of peace! Go—go back to wherever you were!"

Dominor turned toward the Fountain to do so—it was a lacework of ribbons and streams, rather than pour-spouts and basins—but found himself blocked. By his own magics, no less. Groaning roughly, he faced his brother again. "I cannot!"

Rydan blinked at that. He scowled in the next breath. "What do you mean, you *cannot*? I am throwing you back out of here! You'll have to find *another* route home!"

"I cannot go back, you cold bastard-by-act, because I am Oathbound against using her Fountain's magics *without* her permission," Dominor growled. "Which includes returning the way I came—and like a cold day in a Netherhell, I'm going back only to try to find another way home! I am *home*, Rydan, and I *am* going to go see my twin! Now either you get out of my way, or you get in line for when the Healer comes!"

Rydan blinked again, taken aback at his older brother's ferocity. Dominor took advantage of the other mage's confusion to sort through his tossed clothing. He was stepping into his undertrousers when his younger sibling recovered.

"*Fine*. But you will *not* speak one word to the others of whatever you have seen here. And you will *not* deviate from the path I will set for you. If you do—brother or not—I will rip out your tongue and cast such spells that no Healer on this Gods-Given World will be able to repair the damage I will do to you!"

Dominor stared at his moody sibling. He wanted, very badly, to retort that Rydan needed a roll in the blankets with a willing wench. Since it was probable that such a comment would send the Storm on a literally thunderous rampage, he refrained. It did require him literally biting his tongue to do so, however. Hurrying through the donning of his clothes, Dominor barely had enough time to stamp his feet into his boots before Rydan's hand flicked, and a sizzling ball of energy appeared, hovering between them.

"Follow this, to find your way out. You will have to run to keep up with it . . . and if you deviate, *you* will be the one needing a Healer's services," Rydan growled. "Do *not* presume that you will ever be allowed here again. This place is forbidden to *all* of you!"

A slash of his hand, and the ball zipped away from the Fountain. Dominor lurched into a run after a startled moment. The mage-ball barely waited by one of a dozen ornate, slender, oval openings at the edges of the vast, columned chamber before it vanished beyond, giving him just long enough to orient on which path to choose. A glance behind him just before he darted into the indicated corridor showed his younger brother crouched by the Fountain, hands rubbing at his temples and grimacing as if he were in deep pain.

There wasn't time to explore the enigma that his brother had become, however; the energy-ball was zipping out of sight ahead, giving Dominor barely a glimpse of which turn to take. Running through the halls after it didn't help; he barely noticed the architectural details of this place, long, graceful lines of geometry intermingling with elongated leaves carved on equally thin vines. It was a style unlike most of what Nightfall's architecture echoed. As much as Dom longed to study it, to try and make sense of who or what had carved this place out of the mountains, he didn't have the time.

All he could see clearly were the pools of crystal-fed light that illuminated his path, reminding him forcefully of the Retreat, despite the mottled white of the unplastered, unpainted granite walls. And an impression of many turnings that he wasn't allowed to take, a veritable underground palace of passageways and chambers. The light led him onward, however, relentless in its race to extract him from his brother's underground hall.

Stumbling up and down tiers of stairs, he raced down a final, rougher-hewn corridor, narrow and darkened with age, and up a set of stairs. The ball of light splatted against a trapdoor, bursting it open with a loud crack as the heavy wooden panels met the stone of the floor in the chamber above. Slowing his ascent, panting heavily, Dominor emerged in a basement chamber much like one of the ones in his own outer wall tower. No sooner had he cleared the trapdoor, however, than it slammed shut.

Several locks *snicked* into place, glowing with energy that warned him of the futility of trying to open the underground passage. Bracing his palms on his thighs, Dominor struggled to catch his breath. He glanced around as he did so. In *his* tower, the basement was a storage space for various infrequently used pieces of equipment and some of the less commonly used materials for his experiments. This chamber, though . . . this basement chamber was completely empty. Not even a cobweb marred the corners of its ceiling.

Dominor remembered all too clearly his bossy eldest sister-in-law demanding that he and his brothers scrub their palace home from attic to cellar, leaving only their tower workrooms untouched. This chamber was clean enough to satisfy her picky outworlder standards. Straightening, he moved toward the only door in the whitewashed chamber. Opening it led to a stairwell that curved up through the tower.

He ascended slowly, checking the rooms as he passed each floor. Every single one of them was empty, their windows shuttered against the daylight, save for the chamber that lay at the level of the top of the outer guard wall. That one held black velvet curtains in its windows and the summoning-gong, centered in the room on its lacquered stand. As soon as he passed through the final door to this chamber, it slammed shut behind him, making Dom jump. A *snick* told him that the door had locked itself from the inside, too, a final barring of the thirdborn mage from his younger brother's "sanctum."

Upset with Rydan's rudeness, Dominor flipped an obscene hand-sign at the door. It was undignified, normally beneath him, but he felt the need for some show of defiance. Of course, Rydan wasn't around to be insulted by it, which wasted the effort, but it did make him feel somewhat better. Heading for the door out onto the ramparts, Dominor left the northernmost tower behind.

Judging by the light of the sun streaming down on the

courtyards beyond, it was close to midday, here. Instinct told him that, magic or no, Evanor would be in the kitchens at this time of day, preparing lunch. The kitchens were located at the base of the northern wing, one of the four Y-split wings of the palace. They had been built close to the donjon, the octagonal hub at the heart of the castle-like structure, just two floors below the room the brothers had picked to be their dining hall.

Crossing one of the drawbridges connecting the upper floors of the palace wings to the outer walls, Dominor went in search of his twin. A moment later, he slowed, craning his head to look at his shoulder. The dark, tangled locks of his chest-length hair had caught his attention. They looked . . . odd. Pinching some of the strands, he lifted them into his line of sight, and blinked. His hair, his straight, dark brown hair . . . glowed with iridescent highlights? It was the strangest thing he had ever seen. Not unattractive, but strange.

It also only showed in the sunlight, he noticed, crossing into the shade of the palace doorway. Stepping back, he watched his hair iridesce again, a faint rainbow of shimmering hues playing along the strands . . . save for where he covered them with the shadow from his fingers. *Odd. It must be a side-effect of some sort, from our coupling in the heart of the Fountain. I'll have to remember to ask my wife about that when I see her again.*

She almost forgot to send him his clothes. It was probable that at this time of day, Guardian Rydan was asleep, but he would likely have the same sort of alarms on his Font that Serina had on hers. That meant he would catch Dominor unclothed.

Rather than huddling in a ball of misery at the bottom of the Font basin, Serina bundled up Dom's things, climbed up to the top again, and tossed them through the Fontway, willing them to travel to Rydan's Font. She knew she had to gather up the rest of the garments she had made for him and send them through, too, but as soon as the last boot swirled into the vortex that briefly opened, she relaxed the extra protections.

Donning her clothes, Serina restored the Font to its normal functioning, shrunk her chalkboard to portable size, and wearily returned to her workroom down below.

Oddly enough, she felt too tired to cry. Not physically tired, nor magically tired. Just . . . emotionally tired. Slumping back in her chair at her desk, she buried her face in her hands, rubbing at her eyes. Her hair was a tangled mess. Normally, Serina would either manage it herself or ask Mariel for assistance, but since her hair echoed her thoughts, she left it alone. Leaning forward, she braced her elbows on her desk and stared across the room at nothing for a while. Not even her equations interested her, right now.

She was alone, impregnated, and facing a lengthy future without the man she had grown to love.

I am strong . . . I can do this. Serina rubbed her temples as she thought her way through these self-assurances. *I don't need anybody . . . but I need him—no, I don't need him, I just want him in my life . . . and I can't have him. So I have to be strong. Besides, you won't be alone for long, Serina Avadan. You have a little one on the way.*

One hand slipped down to her abdomen, touching it through the fabric of her tunic-dress and underlying hose. Her stomach felt flat, but that wouldn't last for long.

I'm a mother. I'm going to be a mother . . . I'm going to be the best mother I can be. And if—when—the little one asks about his or her father, I'll just say that some people think it is best if others be the mothers and fathers, rather than risk harming a child through lesser parenting skills . . . though he was *good with Mikor . . . as far as I could tell.*

At least he'll be there for the birthing. He can spit the myjii *juice in my face afterward, if he likes—which is likely, when he finds out I hedged completely around the part where I actually do have to get pregnant—but the little one should be born within the bonds of marriage; I can make it a condition of his service-oath to me. I'll not shame the family name in that much, at least.*

The confrontation with her mother and sister, though unexpected and stressful, had been a good thing. It was Dominor who had shown her, in a roundabout way, that she didn't need to kowtow to her family. He and his brothers had broken away from their home government, Katan, boldly forming their own island nation. He supported that independence wholeheartedly, as witnessed by the Truth Stone's purity when claiming himself Lord Chancellor of Nightfall. He didn't *need* approval from others, or even from the Gods, to know that what he and his family were building was the right thing for them to do.

It was the same with her. She didn't *need* her family's approval to know what to do with her life and to know it was the right thing for her to do. *I am an island of my own. I don't know where I'll go after the little one is born, but wherever it is, I will make a place for myself in the world. I am strong. I* can *actually do this.*

Drawing in a deep breath, she rose from her desk and crossed to the right-hand slates, carrying the slate that had been up in the Font Hall with them. It was time to begin her calculations on how successful their Tantric efforts had been. Everything seemed to have gone more or less according to plan, though there hadn't been nearly the same sexual activities as the first couple had engaged in, and that *could* alter the outcome in any of a dozen negligible to highly potent ways . . .

The main kitchen chamber was empty, but reeked of fresh meat. One of the preparation nooks held the sounds of whacking, thumping, and muttered words. Following ears and nose, Dominor stepped into the side chamber. A scene of industrious carnage greeted him: Wolfer, a youngish woman with curly dark blond hair, and Evanor were processing what looked like an entire, if disjointed, cow; Wolfer and Evanor were wielding cleavers, and the woman was fine-trimming and spell-preserving the pieces they carved apart.

He recognized the girl, of course. Alys of Devries, childhood playmate of his siblings and him. Only she wasn't a little girl anymore; her figure had finished filling out, and now she and his elder brother wore matching wedding-torcs. She was the first one to look up at his entrance. Her gray eyes widened a moment later in belated recognition. "Dominor!"

Wolfer glanced up from his work, but didn't stop carving apart the ribs on his butchering table. Evanor, working on one of the haunches, whirled around, hair caught back by a cream-colored headband that blended into his blond hair, a cleaver clutched in his hand. Wild brown eyes met blue, and his lips moved, hissing something. Dominor flinched in the next moment, as Ev threw himself at his twin.

Thankfully, Evanor kept the cleaver out of the way as he embraced his twin hard with his other arm.

Dominor returned the embrace just as fiercely, even though it meant hugging the mess on Evanor's tunic as well as hugging Evanor himself. It felt too good to hold his twin, to know his closest sibling was still alive, to bother with such a petty complaint.

"*Dom, Dom,*" Ev whispered. He pulled back far enough to stare into Dominor's blue eyes. *"Are you all right? Did anyone hurt you? We talked to you just this morning! How did you get here so quickly? How long can you stay?"*

"I'm fine, no one hurt me, I can't tell you how I got here so fast, and I think I can stay for quite a while, before I'm needed overseas again," Dom reassured his brother. "With any luck, I can even persuade my wife to come here, in the interim."

"Wife?" Evanor repeated with a laugh, sounding rather odd, considering he could only breathe and hiss to make any sound. His gaze dipped to his twin's throat, where his brown eyes narrowed, staring at the glass torc encircling Dominor's throat. *"Married? You got . . . ?"*

"Yes, I got married," Dominor repeated firmly. "This afternoon, actually—Natallian time, that is. About an hour or two ago, if you need a reference."

"To that lovely lady we met, I trust?" a soft-spoken, familiar voice asked. Dominor stepped back from his brother's embrace, turning to meet Alys' gray gaze.

"No, to the nearest doorpost," Dom retorted sardonically, testing her to see just how annoyingly timid the girl still was. To his relief, she smiled at, rather than shrank from, his sarcasm. He grinned at her—and the torc encircling her own throat—before Wolfer could do more than bristle a little. "Little Alys of Devries. I always wondered if you'd be the one to snare our wild Wolf's heart. I trust you're doing *something* to civilize this big brute, now that you've leashed him properly?"

Wolfer growled, but Alys giggled. She hastily raised her hand, but it was a giggle nonetheless. Lowering her palm, she grinned at him. "You should be more worried whether or not he's *un*taming *me*."

"Oh, Gods forfend—of course, you *were* the first of us to jump into the Pawna River, when we were kids," Dominor remembered. "You just might have it in you. Speaking of wily women and boorish brothers, where is the rest of the family?"

"Rydan's sleeping, Trevan is tending the cattle that arrived with yesterday's trade ship," Wolfer stated, nodding at the meat they were processing, "we're preserving the remains of the one fool beast that fell off the dock during the unloading, breaking its leg, and Morganen and Koranen are on fruit-picking duty. The toska orchards are nearing the end of their peak ripeness, and the trade ship wants to take back a full load with tomorrow's tide."

"Saber and Kelly are supposed to be fruit-picking, too," Evanor agreed, making Dominor strain to hear his whispering, *"but I'd be surprised if they haven't snuck off to do other things while they're out in the forests. As soon as we're done with this, we'll be fruit-picking, too. Lunch is those 'sandwich' things Kelly showed us how to make. They're on a plate in the cold-room, on one of the shelves."*

"Wait a minute," Alys muttered, a frown pinching her brow. "If you just got married, why are you here? Why aren't you back there, wherever you were, with your bride?"

"She knows how concerned I've been over my twin's condition," Dominor answered, quelling his own concerns over how quickly he'd been dismissed from Serina's side. "I'll have a chat with her shortly through the mirrors, to let her know I arrived safely. My first priority was making sure Ev was all right."

"All right," Evanor snorted, turning away from his brother for a moment to slap his left hand on the nearest table. He whirled back, facing Dom. *"All right! How in the Gods' Names can I be 'all right' like this?!"*

The cleaver was still clenched in his right hand; Dominor flinched back as Evanor gestured with it in his increasing agitation.

"I've lost my voice, I've lost my magic, I've lost every Gods-Be-Damned thing that makes me who and what I am! How can I be all right with this?"

He whirled and chopped the cleaver into the meaty thigh he had been preparing. Yanking his hand free from the handle, he speared his fingers roughly through his hair, dislodging the cloth headband holding back the light blond locks from his face. A moment later, a strangled hiss that was a mockery of a yell escaped him. Thumping the meat with his fists, Evanor shoved it away from him and whirled, frustration eminently clear in the wire-taut muscles of his thin frame.

Dominor caught his twin before he could find some other way of expressing his rage. Crumpling, Evanor buried his face in his twin's neck, shaking with near-silent sobs. A glance over his brother's blond head allowed Dominor to meet Wolfer's gaze; a flick of his head toward the archway into the kitchen directed his older sibling to take Alys and himself out of the room. Preserving the meat could wait a little while longer, but his brother couldn't.

Holding his twin, Dominor firmed his resolve to get Evanor a Healer who could restore what he had lost. Mariel was doubtful of her rusty regeneration skills, so he would first ask his other brothers how far they'd gotten in their search for a more current practitioner. He still wasn't sure exactly how Evanor had lost his vocal cords, nor did he know the details of the battle with their unlamented uncle-in-law; Mariel might need to know the exact spell involved in order to repair the damage done. But right now, the most important thing was holding his twin, being there for him.

For whatever reason Serina had tossed him so quickly through the Fountainway, Dominor was grateful that he was here now, when Ev needed his strength.

Eventually, his twin sniffed hard and pulled back, raising his hands to his face. They were dirty, though, leaving him with nothing to wipe the tears from his cheeks. Dominor used his own fingers. Evanor sniffed again.

"Thanks. Jinga's Sacred Ass, I hate this," Evanor muttered. He looked down at his hands, at the stains on his own tunic, then his twin's, and released a sharp breath that might have been a humorless laugh, had he a voice. *"So much for your wedding day."*

"My wife is a very understanding woman," Dominor dismissed his concerns. "She knows I was fretting over you."

"Understanding enough to rob you of your wedding night?" Ev queried, lifting his brows. *"She must be a saint!"*

Cheeks warming a little, Dominor cleared his throat. "I didn't say *that* . . . and we didn't miss our wedding night. Even if it was technically a wedding afternoon . . ."

Evanor snorted, leaning back against the table. He folded his arms across his chest. *"And so another of us falls. The Threefold God of Fate must be laughing at me. My turn is next, yet I cannot even speak to a woman to woo her, let alone sing of the longings in my heart! Assuming there's a woman out there who would want me like this."*

Thinking of the petite Healer back at the Retreat, and her young son, Dominor smiled to himself. Morganen wasn't the only one who could match-make. "I think you sell yourself short, Brother. You still have plenty of good qualities that will make you an excellent husband and father. And there is hope for your voice."

That drew another snort from the blond man. *"We've tried every possible Healer we could think of contacting on the mainland, and the answer is always the same—no one is allowed to travel to Nightfall to aid us. We're lucky the traders are still willing to sail out and deal with us, especially since Kelly decreed we're not going to be giving away the salt and algae blocks anymore."*

Dominor had trouble hearing all of his brother's words, even as close as they were. He held up his hand, concentrated, and muttered. *"Desoullet, inconnuet, videm auridez! There, now I don't have to worry about hearing you."*

"Augmentation spell?" Evanor asked, arching a brow. His voice was still a whisper in Dom's ears, but it was a clearly hissed one, with no dropped sounds. His brow furrowed as he glanced at the archway leading to the rest of the kitchens. *"You'd think the others would think to do that. It's like I don't exist, half the time. Or rather, that, since I can't speak loudly, my input doesn't exist."*

"I find that hard to believe," Dom chided him.

Evanor shrugged, arms tightening across his chest. *"Well, Kelly goes out of her way to make sure I'm heard. And Morg, a little bit. The others try to keep me included, but not as much as they could."*

A bushy chestnut brown head peered around the corner. Seeing that his younger siblings weren't preoccupied, Wolfer came back into the prep room, a flush-faced Alys following. Both of them bore signs of having had a grope-and-kiss session during their time elsewhere. They quietly resumed cutting up the beef on the tables. Evanor followed suit, sighing.

Dominor joined his twin, picking up a knife and starting the same task as Alys, that of trimming off smaller portions from the larger pieces Evanor was carving and preserving them with a muttered spell. A few more stains on his tunic wouldn't ruin it that much more, and he did know the laundering charms for cleaning it, even if they were painstaking to apply. "So, tell me about this battle you had with our not-so-beloved uncle-in-law."

The other three looked at each other. Wolfer nudged Alys with his elbow, and she cleared her throat. She kept her gaze on her task as she spoke, visibly uncomfortable with her role. "Well . . . I was trapped into helping Uncle Broger tend his beasts . . . the ones he'd send here to torment you. I didn't want to, of course! I just had no choice."

"I believe you," Dominor reassured her, holding up his hand. "Why didn't you escape?"

"I was wrapped up in a lot of spells that would drain me of my magic and my life if I tried to escape, so it took a long time to come up with the counterspells. But when I did, I managed to fake my death, and that's when I came here. Uncle Broger sent Uncle Donnock to try and get a personal scrying of the island, since he couldn't send his menagerie here after you altered everything, and when your brothers kicked Uncle Donnock off the island, Uncle Broger, um . . . well, he killed Uncle Donnock and opened a Dark Gate onto the docks, which was where Donnock managed to get to before being cast off the island again."

Dominor blinked at that. "A *Dark Gate*? I pray to the Gods you got a priest to bless our dock by now!"

Wolfer grinned. "Better. We enacted a justice-death on Broger, and the Netherhells accepted the bastard with open, flaming arms."

"We had to enact a justice-death—" Evanor whispered.

Alys started to say something on top of him, making Ev frown at the interruption. Dominor held up his hand, stopping her. He gestured at his twin to continue; Ev did so with a curt nod of gratitude.

"Thanks. He had protective spells on him, that would backlash lethally against anyone who tried to harm him, whether physically or magically. We had these spell-reflecting mirrors made to cast his own magics back on him, in the hopes he'd try something lethal, but there were only a few mirrors made, and they were in the wrong place to be useful during the final moments of the confrontation. He was going to kill Alys with some sort of slicing hex . . . so I stepped between them, and Sang a reflection of it back at him," Evanor admitted. *"It was his own magic that killed him . . . but the protective spells disintegrated my vocal cords just for being a part of it."*

"I see," Dominor murmured. "Have you been checked for any lingering magic, perhaps some sort of Curse that would prevent your voice from being regrown?"

Evanor shook his head. *"There's no lingering Curse; Morganen checked thoroughly on that point. I just literally have no vocal cords. They should be regrowable . . . if we can get a Healer to come to the island to regrow them. Or smuggle me to the mainland, or something."*

"I don't think we'll have to do anything quite that drastic," Dominor mused, thinking of Mariel.

"*I don't need any platitudes!*" Evanor hissed, losing his temper and slamming his cleaver into the haunch of beef in front of him. "*I need solutions!*" He struggled visibly for a moment with his uncharacteristic outburst of temper, then let it go with a weary sigh. "*I don't want to talk about it right now. Not unless you can give me a guarantee that I'll be Healed. I'm not in the best mood for a discussion of it, right now.*"

"Not while you're wielding a knife, no," Dominor agreed dryly.

Evanor gave him a sardonic look at that, but said nothing more, returning to his butchering chore.

*G*ods Be DAMNED!"

Mariel jumped at the shout. So did Mikor. With the door leading out of the library closed and the workroom door undoubtedly closed as well, they shouldn't have been able to hear anything from the newlyweds. Mother and son exchanged wide-eyed looks. Another, wordless cry of feminine frustration made them blink.

A moment later, they heard a door bang open in the distance. A second door banged open, accompanied by a second frustrated yell. The third door that banged open belonged to the library. A red-faced, teary-eyed Serina stalked into the library, her gaze darting about the room, while her fists were clenched at her sides. With her pale blond hair rumpled into a half-knotted tangle, she looked horrible.

"Aunt Serina?" Mikor asked her daringly, if hesitantly. "What's wrong?"

She stopped in her tracks and blinked, focusing on him. "What's wrong? What's wrong is there's no Gods-be-damned vases for me to throw in this place! And I can't throw my slates, and I can't throw the *good* pottery, and I can't—"

Her breath caught on a sob. Abandoning her son, Mariel hurried over to her friend's side. Serina collapsed with a choked sob. Over the taller woman's shoulder, Mariel caught sight of her son slinking out of his chair and hurrying for the passage back to the solar. She didn't blame him for his quick escape. It wasn't often that his honorary aunt broke down like this, after all.

It did puzzle her, however, as to why Serina wasn't being comforted by her new husband. Guiding the mathemagician over to one of the padded reading couches set in front of the library hearths, she coaxed the younger woman into sitting down. Only when they were both settled and she had passed over a handkerchief did she ask, "Serina . . . where's Dominor? Why isn't he comforting you?"

Serina hiccupped, flinching at the name. Struggling to pull herself together, she sniffed hard and gestured vaguely toward the ceiling. "I sent him back home, through the Fontway. He needed to go back to his brother, and we were already there, so I just . . . sent him home."

That made Mariel arch her brow, wondering how the autocratic Dominor might have taken such a peremptory move on his brand-new wife's part.

"I should send his clothes after him," Serina mumbled, staring into the nearer of the two unlit fireplaces. She scrubbed at her face with the scrap of cloth wadded into her hand. "I mean, the rest of them . . ."

"Why don't you tell me why you haven't followed him? I mean, if you're so upset at his absence—" Mariel broke off as Serina shook her head.

"It's not him. It's my equations!" She paused to blow her nose, more tears leaking from her eyes. "I've calculated, and recalculated, and *everything's wrong*! I know what it *should* be, and it's *wrong*! There's something in my calculations that's Gods-be-damned *wrong*!"

She thumped the leather arm of the couch with each *wrong* before finding another clean spot on the kerchief to blow her nose on again. Mariel waited patiently, lending her silent support, even as she frowned in confusion. Serina gestured vaguely with her fistful of material.

"It's like there's a variable that I haven't accounted for. Something that's gone wildly off kilter. And it's reduced my probabilities of success by almost seventy percent in efficacy—and I *don't* have any damned vases to throw!" She started crying again, arms tight around her ribs, shoulders shaking in silent misery.

Or a husband to comfort you, Mariel thought, studying her friend. She shook her head. *She should've gone with her husband to Nightfall.* It was a really good idea, one worth repeating aloud. "I think you should've gone with Dominor back to his homeland.

It's not too late to join him, you know. And he's a smart fellow; I'm sure if you took your slates with you, the two of you could figure out what went wrong."

Jerking to her feet, Serina paced, ignoring the all-too-logical words of her friend. She couldn't bring herself to tell Mariel that she'd tossed Dominor out on his shapely rump because he loathed children, even if Mariel had been there when he'd sworn to never have any, thanks to Mikor's misguided blow. "I need to go buy some vases. I'll leave for the Potter's Guild in the morning—I'll take a cart through a mirror to Port Blueford, and back. I might stay overnight; I'm not sure. I'll have to tell Mother Naima I'll be leaving, so she can keep an eye on the Font for me—"

"Serina," Mariel interjected firmly, pushing to her feet, "why don't you just turn over the Guardianship of the Font to the Mother Superior? Right now, in fact."

That stopped the muttering mage in her tracks. She blinked at the petite Healer. "Be . . . because I'm the Guardian, and my work's not done! And . . . and she might not let me back into the Font Chamber to finish my work."

"Nonsense! The other nuns might not approve of what you're doing, if they knew what you were doing, but Mother Naima has always been a practical sort. And if you're not sure she'll let you back in to do your work, have her swear a mage-oath to do so, as a condition of handing over the Guardianship," Mariel suggested pragmatically. "It really is the best solution. She's certainly ready for the responsibility, and *you* are ready for a change of venue. In fact, I hear the western side of the world is quite lovely at this time of year . . ."

Serina bit back her retort that no, it wasn't going to be that lovely if she went west, after her husband. Who didn't know she was pregnant with his unwanted child. But her friend's suggestion about stepping down as the Guardian did have some small merit; she would have to run some calculations to see if constant exposure to the energies of the Font risked endangering her unborn child. "I'll consider it. In the meantime, I'm going to go pack for my trip back to Port Blueford and see if I can get a horse and cart harnessed and ready in the morning."

Blinking at her friend's rather cold dismissal of the idea, Mariel watched her leave. "Try packing for going off to join your husband! You'll be in a far better mood!"

EIGHTEEN

◆━━◆

The alarm jangled again, disturbing the slumbering mage. Anger boiling up within him, Rydan snatched up tunic and trousers as he rose from his rumpled bed. It took him a few minutes to reach the Fountain Hall. Rather than another visitor, however, a chest hung in midair, suspended by his net-spell. A scrap of cloth had been caught in the lid. Releasing the net, Rydan lowered the chest to the floor with a gesture. A second one opened the trunk, revealing clothes in the dark jewel tones his third-eldest sibling preferred.

Stalking over to the Fountain jetting its crimson copper mist in an east by northeast direction, he thrust his hand into the magic. *"Guardian Serina, could you not find some other way to deliver my brother's things, rather than disturbing my rest?"*

Silence met his words for a few moments, then he felt her touching the stream on her end. Her reply was tainted with something he hadn't expected. *"Just give them to him, please."*

A simple enough reply, but why had her breath caught mid-sentence ever so slightly? Why were the underlying resonances in her words so complex? Hesitating, damning himself for getting involved, Rydan asked, *"Will you be all right?"*

A short noise crossed through the aether between them. The

echoing effect of the mist distorted it, but it almost sounded like a mirthless laugh. *"I will be. I'll not disturb you again."*

He felt her withdraw her presence from the aether-stream and decided to not call her back. It wasn't his place to interfere in whatever was happening between his sibling and his fellow Guardian, after all. But it was with a thoughtful frown that Rydan withdrew his own hand from the magic, mulling over what he knew.

Saber watched as the fourthborn of his brothers exited the dining chamber, dishes balanced on a tray in his hands. He waited until Evanor was out of hearing range before speaking; the blond mage had lost his voice, not his ears, after all. Turning to Dominor, he addressed the dark-haired mage. "You've seen it for yourself now, haven't you? He's definitely not the man he used to be."

"Can you blame him for being upset?" Kelly challenged her husband. "I know if it were me, I'd have good reason to occasionally be surly!"

"I'd like to have our cheerful, happy brother back," Trevan muttered, glancing at his twin. "We already have one brooding soul in the family; we don't need another."

Rydan merely grunted, savoring the wine in his cup.

When he didn't rise to his brother's bait, Trevan shook his head and continued. "Anyway . . . we've tried all across Katan. The Council has banned travel to Nightfall, and the Healers who are powerful enough to restore Ev's voice are all afraid of losing their practices in the Empire."

"We *could* afford to pay a Healer to live among us under normal circumstances," Saber added, shrugging, "but not enough to coax them away from Katan; not with the current antagonism of the Council standing in our way."

"Without a Healer, he's not going to recover from his injury," Alys murmured. "Not to his way of thinking. He'll only get worse."

"There *is* a possibility," Dominor offered. The others glanced at him sharply. Having changed into clean clothes, he felt comfortable and confident enough to handle their stares calmly. "I met a Healer in Natallia who might be willing to come across, when I bring my wife over. Or even beforehand. But . . . she's out of practice, hasn't done any regeneration in over a decade. I haven't mentioned this to Evanor, because I don't want to raise any false hopes."

"How much practice do you think she'll need?" Kelly asked him. "And what would it entail?"

"It's common for Healers to practice regeneration techniques on animals," Morganen told her. "Usually food animals. Some people consider it a cruelty, but since they're food animals, they would normally be slaughtered and eaten anyway. I don't know what the customs of Natallia might be, but the priests of Kata and Jinga say that it is acceptable to practice upon a food animal if you take care to numb its pain throughout the process and treat it with respect for the gift of learning it is sharing with you, just as you must take care to give it a swift, painless death when slaughtering it for food."

"That's why I gave that cow a clean blow to the neck as soon as we levitated it out of the water, when I realized its leg had broken in the fall," Wolfer added. "The injury was too severe to heal quickly with our limited skills, and you cannot tell a cow to stay in bed for a couple weeks while its leg heals."

"I'd rather this Healer didn't practice on our cows," Trevan countered. "I confess I've been looking forward to fresh milk, myself. No matter how much you numb the pain, a dairy cow won't give milk for long if she's constantly injured."

Dom smirked. "Actually, I offered our citizen-chickens for her to practice upon. I certainly wouldn't take any great offense if they were used for such an experiment."

Kelly grimaced, wrinkling her freckled nose. "As much as the thought of animal experimentation is distasteful to some extent, however necessary it may be . . . I don't think I'd take offense over that idea, either. They've had their peck of blood from me, literally. I wouldn't mind seeing the favor returned."

Footsteps in the corridor alerted them to Evanor's return. Rydan spoke as the blond-haired brother came back into the dining chamber. "Tell us about your bride, Dominor. What is she like?"

Picking up his wineglass, Dominor considered the request. A smile curled his lips as he thought of his wife. "She is . . . perfect."

The others started to scoff at that, but Dominor's next words stilled their disbelief.

"She is a scatterbrained woman who forgets to eat half the

day, plays with her hair to the point where I'm honestly surprised she hasn't plucked herself bald, and smears chalk all over the bedsheets. And she is so stunningly brilliant, I am in awe of her intellect." At the skeptical look from his brothers—for Dominor rarely, if ever, admitted anyone was better than himself if he could help it—he elaborated. "She's figured out what's been keeping the aether so unsettled since the sundering of Aiar. Including a possible cure that will allow us to reestablish the great trade Portals that used to exist across Katan . . . and potentially the whole world."

The stunned looks on his siblings' faces pleased Dom. He hid his smile behind a sip of his wine. Evanor slanted him a curious, thoughtful look, but said—or rather, whispered—nothing.

It was Kelly, predictably, who had to ask, "And what does that mean?"

"Kelly, the great Portals of the old days allowed instantaneous transit of large objects—such as caravans of goods—across oceans and continents," Morganen explained to her. "In contrast, mirror-crafted Gates are limited in both size and distance. On a really good-aether day . . . a pair of spell-linked mirrors can allow a single person with a sack of belongings to cross half of Katan, a journey of a full turning of Brother Moon."

Koranen finished for his twin, shrugging. "On a really bad-aether day . . . linked mirrors can only span the distance a person can travel in two, maybe three days. On foot."

"The more magic used, of course, the more can be forced through a disturbed aether," Trevan enlightened her, "but you can only widen a mirror-Gate so far before you risk thinning the glass to the point where the slightest physical disturbance could shatter it . . . and the more magic you use, the more a mirror is likely to vibrate from it. It's a very nasty way to die, if you're still mid-transit."

"Using only one mirror halves the distance traveled and doubles the risk of disrupting the connection with whatever exit point is being scried," Saber added. "It's also a one-way trip, since without a second mirror, you cannot return."

"Wait—Morganen rescued me from my bed while I was burning in it," Kelly pointed out, confusion creasing her freckled brow, "yet there wasn't a magical mirror on my side of everything."

"Ah, but *I* was on the same side of the connection as the mirror,"

Morganen pointed out. "It was just like picking up those items we've taken from your universe; I used my powers on my side of the connection to bring you through to me. But it takes a very powerful mage to do that; it's far easier to send things from the mage and his mirror to a new location."

"The reason my uncle could send those beasts to Nightfall through just the one mirror with his more modest level of power," Alys told the others, "is because I think the place where he hid his menagerie was near the east coast of Katan. I think maybe in the Kathal mountains to the south, since the menagerie was kept in a place carved from solid stone. I do know that he couldn't try it on a bad-aether day. I also know he had special artifacts constructed that would allow him to tell when the aether was smooth enough for a try. As for crossing from Corvis to his menagerie, he used twinned mirrors, linked specifically to each other. That more than doubles the distance normally paired mirrors can span, but severely limits where those mirrors can be linked."

"With the shattering of the Aian Empire and the loss of the Portals, we lost most of our trade with other continents," Dominor added to Kelly. "However, with the twinned mirrors linking us with the Retreat in Natallia, I think we can open up at least a small amount of trade with that far-flung land. Or at least with the Nuns of Koral-tai. Ironically, they, too, have access to a cheap source of the *comsworg* oil that I traded the salt blocks to the Mandarites for, which resulted in my kidnapping. Plus spices and herbs, exotic foods, woods, minerals . . ."

"More than that," Morganen informed his thirdborn brother, "making twinned mirrors has turned out to be remarkably easy; I found a short-cut in the process while we were making the mirror we sent to you. We could make them at the rate of a pair every four days, if we wanted. They're very limited as to how big they can be, since they tolerate zero flaws in the glazing process, but they could become a very powerful artifact for trade."

"Powerful, but expensive," Koranen argued with his twin. "The *comsworg* oil will be more important as a trade item, because we'll be able to craft the lightglobes more cheaply, with a ready source of the most expensive ingredient. The lower price means more people will be able to afford them."

"*If* we can open up more trade," Saber warned his brothers. "I fear the Council of Mages might even consider banning the trade ships that come to visit."

Evanor snorted at that.

Dominor knew what his twin was thinking, for it was his own thought. "They'd be fools to try. We have too many customers eager for our wares. As things stand, with legal trade, they get their cut of the profits in sales taxes. If they force the sea merchants to smuggle goods in and out of the Island, they'll lose those taxes . . . and certain people are always drawn to the forbidden. Especially if it's profitable."

"Exactly," the blond mage hissed, nodding sharply. *"They'd be idiots."*

"Of course, they *are* idiots," Koranen derided, setting his empty goblet on the table. "So we should be prepared for just such an eventuality. I'll help you clear the table, Ev."

Nodding, Evanor leaned over and whispered in his brother's ear. *"I want to talk with you after this."*

Dominor nodded his agreement. As much as he wanted to try to contact Serina through the mirror after supper, since he hadn't had time beforehand with the need for the meat to be butchered and the fruit to be gathered, he didn't want to turn down his twin's request. Evanor's emotional stability was more important than his marriage, right now. It was why he hadn't gotten to the mirror earlier, choosing instead to stay by his twin's side.

He and Evanor were two very different men, but they were still very close.

Dominor closed the outer door to his suite. He and Evanor had spent three hours in a question-and-answer session about all that had happened to him since his kidnapping, and all that had happened to his twin. Most of it, however, had focused on Dominor's adventures, and on Dominor's absent bride, since Dom had heard about the island's little war earlier in the day.

To Evanor, he freely admitted the humiliation of being kidnapped, chained, and treated as a worthless, ignorable, sellable slave. He had revealed his disgust at being sold, the frustration of not being believed, and then of being ignored in spite of the Truth Stone verifying his claims. His twin had been very sympathetic, incensed on his behalf, though his invective had been confined to angry hisses and the thumping of his fist on the padded couch in Dominor's sitting room.

Retreating to his bedroom, Dominor stopped in the doorway

and looked back over his shoulder. His suite wasn't huge; it lacked a changing room, but it had the sitting room, and it had a refreshing room with a large bath. No rain-shower stall, though. And it might get a little small for two people, especially if his wife wanted to have a workroom nearby.

There are more than a hundred rooms in this place, he reminded himself. *And I'm competent enough to transform some of the amenities into something more suitable for our needs, given a bit of time and effort . . .* By tradition, each of the brothers had taken one of the ends of the Y-wings for their residence. They were free to pick whatever room or rooms they wanted to use, though they had all consented to confine their magical work to the eight outer-wall towers, just in case anything happened during an experiment that risked damaging their workrooms.

But Serina's work isn't potentially explosive . . . except for maybe her comment about throwing vases when she's frustrated. Which I have yet to actually see. So I suppose I could find a work-room for her here in this wing . . . and maybe a better suite. I definitely want one of those shower-things, one big enough for two . . .

The thought of what they had done in the Natallian rain-shower warmed his blood. He would have a cold bed, tonight; it was far too late an hour, Natallian-time, to try to contact his wife. Stripping off his clothes, Dominor made sure the dirtied set was still enchanted with a stain-treating charm that would work to loosen things until the garments could be washed, and then used the refreshing room.

Slipping under the sheets when he came back, he adjusted the pillows behind his back so that he could lie comfortably in bed and think of what he would do to his wife, if she were with him at that moment. He could almost picture her kneeling over him, astride his thighs. Her pale hair would look elegant, spilling down over the modest curves of her slender body.

Maybe she would touch her breasts, teasing him even as she showed him what she liked . . . while he would touch his own chest, mirroring her moves. Dominor lifted his hands to his pectoral muscles, copying his imagination. The bedding irritated him, getting in his way. Pushing the material down to his thighs, he stroked his fingers over his skin from nipples to hipbones and back.

The image of what they had done together in her Font Chamber came back to him. Closing his eyes, Dominor remembered the feel of her skin as he had caressed her limbs. The taste of her lips when he had claimed her mouth. The heat of her depths when he had pounded into her body. His hand feathered over his flesh, then gripped his shaft, stroking in time to the rhythm of his memory. Only, in this memory, he wasn't drowning in pure instinct. He could take his time to tilt her back, to catch one of her bared ankles and lift it to his mouth.

Bared ankles . . .

Something in that mental image disrupted his pleasure. It niggled at his brain, making him frown and open his eyes, hands stilling at groin and chest. Bared ankles. His memory flashed to the other day, when Mikor had struck him that blow. She had entered the salle in a footless set of hose, her feet and ankles bared partway up her calves as she moved across the sand-packed floor.

She was so graceful, like a willow tree swaying in the wind. Dominor closed his eyes, his hand moving once again. It was a poor substitute for actual lovemaking; he had grown used to having a real woman in his bed in their short time together, and this was paltry by comparison. There was no anticipation, no wondering where she might touch and caress him next. An image of her floating in the Fountain-bubble came back to him. With her hair unbound, her flesh bared, wearing nothing at all but a naked, lustful desire in her gaze, she had enthralled him.

His fingers stroked faster as he remembered the way her bare legs had wrapped around him . . . bare legs . . . bare . . .

She hadn't been wearing her amulet!

Eyes snapping open, Dominor stared unseeing at his ceiling. She hadn't been wearing her contraceptive amulet! She had *insisted* that he drink from a pool of fertility magic—she had *hedged* around confirming whether or not she would get pregnant in a piece of Tantric magic wherein the original casters had gotten *pregnant*—and she had cast him out of her life after reassuring him *he wouldn't have anything to worry about*?

She *was* pregnant, with *his* child, and she wasn't going to let him be a part of that child's life?

"SERINA!!" Scrambling out of his bed with that roar, Dominor lunged at the door. His feet tangled in the bedding, however, snaring his limbs and upsetting his balance. One of his flailing

arms could only cushion some of the blow, as his body twisted and his head cracked against the stones of his bedroom floor.

*B*ut, *you have to help me!"* Evanor stared at his youngest sibling in dismay.

Morganen smothered a yawn behind his hand. "No, I don't."

"Yes, you do!" the blonder of the two mages asserted. *"Your Destiny is to match-make us—so help me match-make my brother!"*

Morg ceased leaning against the doorway of his bedroom long enough to fold his arms across his nightshirt-clad chest. Blinking sleepily, he stared at his elder sibling. "I already have. Do you really think a Natallian warship would head straight for a port located so far inland that it's not even a viable target for the floating half of their little civil war? There were dozens of other places they could have offloaded their prisoners."

Evanor frowned at that revelation. *"How could you know where to send him? You're not a Seer. You said yourself you didn't know which woman would be right for him!"*

"I may not be a Seer myself, but I know some people who are, or at least were." Stifling another yawn, Morganen flicked his hand away from his mouth once he was finished. "Go see Rydan. He has what you'll need to help your brother, at this point."

Giving his sibling a chiding look, Evanor snorted. It came out almost normal sounding, despite his lack of vocal cords. His words were still whispered, though. *"One of these days, we're going to figure out how you pull off all of your little tricks, Morg."*

The younger mage said nothing in reply, though he smirked as he stepped back and closed his door.

*S*o *that's why I think it's totally unfair they're separated, just because of me,"* Ev explained to his younger brother. *"He wasn't completely clear on how he ended up here, but I know it has something to do with the Fountain she controls, because he said that's where he was when she sent him here . . . and that he ended up in your tower at the end of his journey."*

Rydan's black eyes narrowed at that, but he said nothing as Evanor held up his hand.

"You can keep your secrets all you like, Rydan," the blond mage promised his sibling. *"The thing is, Dominor is forbidden by his oaths to his wife to use her Fountain in any way, without her permission. He can't even suggest this to you . . . but I can. You sent that mirror to her somehow. That means you probably know how she managed the trick, and can duplicate it . . . which probably involves her Fountain and whatever secrets you're hiding in your work tower. So I'm going to order you, as your older brother, that I want you to figure out a way to bring her here. I don't want my twin growing as miserable as me, without his wife on hand. Not when he loves her as much as he clearly does. So you are going to help me bring her here. Got that?"*

Rydan snorted, arms folding across his black-clad chest. He drew in a breath, then paused, narrowing his eyes. Studying his older brother for a long, taut moment, he finally looked away. "You will *owe* me for this."

"More to the point, Dom will owe you, though I'll make the payment for him, if you like," Evanor returned in a triumphant whisper. *"He's in love with her, she's in love with him, and I want them to live happily ever after. What's not to like about helping the two of them be happy together?"*

Again, Rydan slanted him a sharp, dark-eyed look. He didn't explain what was going through his thoughts, however, just unfolded his arms. Gesturing for Evanor to follow, he headed for the door onto the ramparts, leaving behind the room with his summoning-gong. The panel opened before he came within a body-length of it, reacting to the black-haired mage's presence and intent. Evanor hurried to follow before the door could shut again.

It didn't take long to cross the ramparts in the dark, though it took a little longer to walk the long length of the northern palace wing. Inside, a few lightglobes had been softly rapped, emitting a faint glow that shed just enough light to not bump into any walls or doorways. Reaching the dining hall, Rydan snapped his fingers, making the globes hung in the chandelier overhead ignite and brighten. Normally they had to be rapped with a reaching-stick, but normality didn't always heed the rules around the sixth-born brother.

Tapping the edge of the mirror to activate it, Rydan spoke as soon as their reflection faded into a view of the dining hall at the other end of the connection, a hall that held only a dim light. "Ring-ring."

A chime rang on the other side of the connection; they waited for someone to respond. Nothing happened. Evanor nudged him, so he repeated the words sharply, louder than before. The mirror rang with greater intensity. Again, they waited. Right after Rydan made it ring a third time, a door just visible to the side of the mirror's view opened.

Evanor blushed, seeing the same petite, curly haired woman from before entering the dining hall. She was clutching a silky robe to her ripe curves, her hair mussed from sleep, and her face creased from wrinkles in her pillow. Her hazel eyes blinked owlishly at them as the crystaline objects recessed in the ceiling brightened at her presence. The blond mage couldn't help but wonder if this was what she looked like in the morning after a night of . . . thoughts he shouldn't be having.

Padding up to the mirror, Mariel blinked at them. "Yes? Can I help you?"

Nudging Rydan—since he couldn't be heard by the mirror— Evanor forced his younger brother to do the talking. He waited for Rydan to ask for Serina's presence, so that Ev could explain to her his plan to have her come across and live with her husband, rather than enduring an unnecessary separation. Dominor had explained, after all, that Serina had a sort of apprentice ready to step into place as the next Guardian, so there was no reason for her to not set aside her duties and come live with her new family.

Rydan had other ideas. "Why was Guardian Serina so unhappy about parting company with our brother?"

"Unhappy?" Mariel blinked at that. "She didn't say she was unhappy about that. Upset with some problem in her equations, but . . . wait, where's Lord Dominor?"

Elbowed by his brother, Rydan admitted, "Sleeping in his bed. Alone. Without his wife." *Nudge.* "An unnatural state for a newlywed. It is said that there is no reason for her to stay in Natallia. That she has a replacement awaiting a chance at her Guardianship. Why does she not come over?"

Mariel tightened her lips, compressing their normal pink fullness into a narrow line. Her hands went to her hips, allowing the light blue robe to gape just a little, showing a cream-colored sleeping tunic underneath. "Because she's stubborn? I don't know—if I didn't know it takes at least a handful of days for the hormones to kick in, I'd say she's already experiencing pregnancy-induced mood swings."

Evanor choked at that. *"Pregnant? But . . . she's not pregnant! She can't be! Dominor said that part of the ritual had been cut out somehow!"*

From the way she frowned and strained toward the mirror, she hadn't heard all of his exclamation. Rydan translated for him when Evanor whapped him in the arm with the back of his hand. His cheeks flushed as he said it, though.

"My brother claims that there was supposed to be no pregnancy as a result of their . . . whatever they did."

Hazel eyes widened. "Is *that* what she told him?!" Mariel gaped for a few moments, then whirled, hands on her hips as she glared in the direction of the door she had used. "I'm going to kill her! I thought they got all of this straightened out yesterday!" Spinning back to face the two men, she opened her mouth to say something, then snapped it shut. A calculating look crossed her face. Tugging her robe closed, she folded her arms across her chest, tapping the fingers of one hand on her opposite bicep. *"Someone* needs to teach that woman a *lesson* in *communication!"*

Rydan arched one of his black brows. "What did you have in mind?"

The short, plump woman mulled over the question for a few moments, then nodded her head. "She's leaving in the morning to go to the Potter's Guild, by mirror-Gate. I'll insist that she hands over the Guardianship to Mother Naima before she goes. *Then*, with the Mother Superior's collusion, when she comes *back* via mirror-Gate, we'll snare her, shove her through a second set of mirrors leading into our Font room here, pop her out at *your* Font—"

Evanor shot his brother a sharp look, in time to catch Rydan flinching a little at the revelation.

"—and you can bind her to a chair in her husband's bedroom until the two of them get this nonsense about her thinking he doesn't like nor want any children pounded out of her blond little head! Oh, and tell your brother that he has to keep a sharp hand on the reins where she's concerned, or she'll go wandering off into another little cloud of obliviousness at some point in the future. Just because she's a Gods-loving genius doesn't give her leave to be such an idiot!"

"I thought she was your dearest friend," Evanor hissed as loudly as he could, confused.

"Well, *yes*, she's my dearest friend," Mariel returned, blinking at him. "But that doesn't mean I don't occasionally feel the urge to turn her over my knee, like I would my son when *he* misbehaves!"

That stabbed a brief disappointment through him, before Evanor remembered she was a widow. Once married, but not bound to another man anymore. He found himself asking, *"And when she comes across, will you come, too?"*

"I'm sorry, I couldn't hear you—what did you say?" she asked him politely.

Evanor elbowed his brother. Rydan scowled but translated for him. "He wants to know if you'll come across, too."

She blushed at the suggestion and cleared her throat. "Well, I, ah . . . it *has* been suggested, I'll admit. And I'd be willing to come, if my son could come with me, of course."

Whapping his brother again, Ev gave Rydan a pointed look.

The black-haired mage let out an aggravated sigh. "You would be *most* welcome, son and all. By the others."

The implication stood that *he* wasn't too happy with the idea. Evanor leaned close enough to the mirror to fog it a little with his breath. *"Don't take offense at anything he says. He's just a surly bastard-by-inclination."*

It was Rydan's turn to whap him in the shoulder, giving the blond mage a black-eyed glare.

Evanor hardly noticed. *"So,"* he whispered, having to force the sounds out since his lungs were a little too taut with excitement at the idea to work right, *"how soon can you come across?"*

"Well, I'll have to spend some time packing up everything. We've lived here for several years, you know . . . um . . . unless there's not enough room?"

"There's a whole palace here," Rydan offered grudgingly. "Hundreds of rooms for you to get lost in . . . so long as you stay away from mine."

Mariel blinked at him, then nodded at Evanor. "Surly, yes. Well, I've been longing to move away from here for a little while, now, and my son could use a new location. And some male influences in his life, since he's getting close to that age. I would need to support myself, though; I've been paid up until now in coin, food, and shelter by the nuns, but once I leave, obviously those things would stop. Is there enough work for a Healer to ply her trade, on your island? Dominor admitted there weren't very many of you."

A Healer. Evanor felt his heart leap. He grabbed his brother's elbow. *"Yes! Yes, come, please! We'll pay you!"*

Rydan gritted his teeth. "In case you didn't hear him, my brother is overly ecstatic at the idea of a Healer being in residence. He lost his vocal cords in a mage-battle a while ago."

"Yes, I heard; I've been reading up on how to fix that. I'm afraid I'm very much out of practice," she apologized to Evanor, "but if you're willing to be patient, I think I can get myself back into top form for that."

"Yes, please come!" Evanor pressed his hand to the glass separating them. If the distance hadn't been so huge, he would've loved to reach through and pull her across right now. Even if she was "out of practice," a Healer who had the training and power to restore his lost voice, and with it, his lost powers, was the most precious thing to him right now. That she was comely and sweet and very feminine didn't hurt either . . . nor did the fact that, with his twin wed, it was *his* turn to have a Prophesied mate fall into his arms.

"Oh, do stop drooling," Rydan muttered. "And get your fingers off the glass before they smudge the scrying spell."

Evanor whirled to face him. *"Just because* you *don't want to fall in love and live happily ever after doesn't mean the rest of us want to live the life of a sour, emotionally eunuched bastard!"*

Leaning in close to his brother, Rydan snarled, "You know *nothing* of what drives me!"

"Boys! Stop that this instant!"

The motherly tone snapped them apart like the crack of a whip. They broke apart, facing the mirror, Rydan with a sullen glare, and Evanor with a chastised blush. Mariel had her hands on her hips once more.

"I don't care *what* your quarrel is with each other—you are both fully grown men, and you will act like such in my presence! The last thing I need is a couple of *bad* examples for my son to follow . . . unless you *don't* want me to come over there?"

Ice froze in Evanor's guts. He shook his head quickly, resolving to skewer his brother with a serious piece of his mind after this mirror conversation was through. *Nothing* was going to get in his way of getting his voice back. Not when it looked like this Natallian woman was his best hope for that.

"If you don't mind, I'd like to conclude this conversation as quickly as possible," Rydan asserted through gritted teeth. He rubbed at his temple with one hand, the other folded tightly across his chest. "This is giving me a headache."

"Fine," Mariel stated crisply. "You prepare things on your end. Be ready to have her come flying through the Fontway at any time after tomorrow midday, your time. I'll work things on my end so that she'll wind up in your laps. Or rather, in Dominor's. Make sure they clear up any and all misunderstandings between them, too."

Evanor nodded. *"And you? When will you come through?"*

"In a few weeks, depending on how long it takes to pack up everything. And presuming you'll both behave."

"Even if I have to bind and gag him," Evanor breathed, giving his younger sibling a hard look.

"What was that?" she asked, frowning in her inability to hear his barely audible words.

"Never mind," Rydan growled at Mariel. "Send her through. We'll be ready."

A slap of his hand on the frame ended the scrying link. Evanor faced him, glaring and ready to do battle—replete with clenched fists. Rydan's face twisted into a rictus of pain. Some of Evanor's rage drained, replaced with growing concern. "Rydan?"

The black-haired mage staggered back, one hand clutching the side of his head, the other raised to ward off his brother, his chest heaving as he struggled for air. He looked like he was about to be sick. Evanor took a step toward him, lifting his own hand.

"Stay away from me!" Rydan hissed, as if he, too, had lost his voice. In the next breath, he whirled and ran out of the dining chamber, the door banging open against the wall, then slamming shut in his wake.

Confused, Evanor stared at the door. *That* was unexpected.

NINETEEN

❖

Serina blinked at the Mother Superior. "What did you say?"

"I said," Mother Naima stated calmly, "that, since you are now married to a man who lives far from here, I am going to relieve you of the responsibility and burden of being our Guardian, so that you may go off and join your husband in his foreign land. With our deepest thanks, of course, for having served us for so long and so well."

The platinum-braided mage blinked at the veiled nun. "But . . . my work—"

"When you're ready to complete your Permanent Magic, you may certainly return through the Font to finish the deed," Mother Naima reassured her in a reasonable, even generous tone. "Already, I can feel the energies in the local aether beginning to shift back toward a feeling of balance between the genders. It is a subtle thing, and likely only noticeable here at the Retreat at the moment, but once you give birth and finish your task, we'll be able to truly begin healing the source of the strife causing this stupid civil war in our land."

"But . . ." She couldn't explain that she *couldn't* go to Nightfall, not without revealing her duplicity to her husband in regards to her pregnancy. Serina scrambled for a reasonable excuse. "It . . . it will take days to pack everything—weeks, possibly!"

"And you're welcome to stay here as long as is needed—even to come back and visit between now and the end of your task," Mother Naima agreed cheerfully. "Feel free to bring that fellow of yours back again, too. He's quite sensible, for a man."

Except for the fact that he hates children . . . Serina scrambled for a solution to this trapped-in-a-corner problem. By rights, the Mother Superior *could* dismiss her from the Guardianship, since there was a viable candidate to take over the job of protecting the Font. *If I delay "leaving" for a few weeks, I can figure out which direction to go. Maybe go to one of the other Guardians I've been working with—there's one up in Sundara, after all. I have considered going there, before* . . .

"All right. I'll hand over the Guardianship."

"Good! Let's get to it, so that you don't waste too much time before your trip down to the Potter's Guild. Oh, and if you can, I've a list of storage amphorae I'll need you to purchase while you're down there. We're having a rather bountiful harvest of *nutan* seeds this year."

Rising from the dining table, Mother Naima headed for the door. Serina glared at her best friend over her half-eaten breakfast. "This is *your* doing, isn't it?"

Mariel merely smiled with all the serenity and patience of a mother.

Aching agony woke Dominor from dreamless sleep. His body felt twisted like one of those strange, knotted bread-sticks his outworlder sister-in-law could make. Pushing himself onto his back, he felt his feet drop from their half-suspended position, thumping onto what he realized was a cold, unyielding floor. A groan informed him that he had a painfully hellacious headache. Gingerly sliding his hand up over his scalp, he found a very tender lump and winced. What had felt like a hangover seemed instead to be the lingering effects of a concussion.

Falling out of bed . . . bolting from his bed . . . remembering what his wife had *not* told him—Dominor's eyes snapped open, then winced shut against the bright morning light streaming in through his east-facing windows. From the angle of the patch of light illuminating the polished stone floor off to his right, he figured it was now close to noon in Natallia. Lunchtime. If he could get himself Healed and out to the dining hall, he could call her via the twinned scrying mirrors and give her a very vociferous piece of his mind.

If he could remember the spell his father had taught him for healing blows to the head.

Mumbling to himself, he managed to reduce enough of the pain and swelling to feel well enough to cautiously lever his body into a sitting position. That made his head throb, but at least it was bearable. A bit more of muttering, some improvisational enchanting, and he felt ready to stand.

Aware of his naked state—and grateful it was still late summer, otherwise he might have taken a bad chill, sleeping exposed on the floor of his bedchamber like that—Dominor crossed to his wardrobe to pull on something. He had two sisters-in-law now, with protective husbands capable of pounding his concussed head to a pulp, if he gave them an unexpected eyeful.

Not to mention his nakedness was now reserved for his wife's eyes alone . . . a wife whom he intended to somehow grab out of her sanctum, bind to his bed so she couldn't escape, and lecture until the Gods Themselves covered Their ears. She was *his wife*, the mother of *his child*, and he *would* have a huge say in where said wife and child lived, dammit.

Once his head stopped hurting.

Dominor winced as the mirror rang again, but the door in the wall opened and a curly haired figure scurried through. Grabbing a chair from the table, Mikor dragged it over to the wall with a bit of effort from his slender little body, climbed onto it, and grinned at him. "Hello, Uncle Dominor! I can call you that now, right? 'Cause you're married to my aunt Serina and all . . . How did you get all the way on the other side of the mirror? Aunt Serina said the mirror is connected to an island on the far side of the ocean!"

"That's what I wanted to talk to your aunt about. Could you please call her to the mirror?" Dominor asked, mustering patience to deal with the youth. His head still throbbed a little, but he didn't want to take out the pain of his foolish tumble on the boy.

"She's gone down to Port Blueford to go buy some vases. But I can get Mother in here!" Scrambling down from the chair, he raced out of the room before Dominor could ask him any questions.

Mariel came bustling into the room—alone—after a minute or so. She hurried up to the mirror, pulling the chair aside. "There you are. I wanted—wait, you look *terrible*," she stated, peering at him through the glass. "What happened to you?"

"Fell out of bed and hit my head. What's this about my *wife* being in Port Blueford?" Dominor growled.

The Healer gave him an apprising look. "I take it your brothers told you?"

He frowned at her, wincing as the act disturbed the reduced lump lingering on the side of his head. "Told me what?"

"Oh, dear. Then you don't know that your dear, idiotic wife didn't tell you about the, um . . . how should I put this tactfully?" she hedged.

"If you are talking about my wife *using* me to get pregnant, and *concealing that fact from me*," he half-snarled, half-winced, "I figured it out for myself. How the hell do my brothers know? And *which* of my brothers?"

"It was the black-haired one, what's-his-name, and the blond, Evanor. We had a little chat last night," Mariel informed him. She fluttered the fingers of one hand dismissively. "Don't worry; we figured it all out, and will be taking care of everything. You just get ready to yell at her when they deposit her on your doorstep, all right?"

He winced again, this time in confusion. "What?"

"We're *kidnapping* your wife, as soon as she's ready to Gate back from Port Blueford," Mariel enunciated carefully. "Trussing her up like a present, shunting her across through the Fontway, and dumping her in your lap. Now, I expect you to yell at her thoroughly, but I *also* expect you to dig out and straighten up any and all possible miscommunications the two of you might have," she ordered. "And for the Gods' Sake, stop *assuming* everything!"

"I'll *try*," Dominor agreed wryly.

"Good. Go take care of yourself," she ordered, flipping her hand at him again. "Go shave, and shower, and get your residence ready to hold your wife. The two of you clearly have a lot to talk about, so you might as well order a late supper and something to drink for when you're interrogating her, and yelling at each other. Oh—one last order. *Tell* her you love her *and* that you love and want children. That's your biggest communication error that I know of.

"Now, if you'll excuse me, I have to go back to packing up her belongings so that they can be sent through after her," Mariel continued briskly, reminding a blinking Dominor of how the plump, short woman had successfully managed Serina before he came along. It was rather like watching a normally calm creek turn into a sudden spring flood. "The Mother Superior managed to convince her to hand over the Guardianship this morning, so she'll have no ties to hold her here. You had better ready yourself to ensnare her into staying with you, if you want your wife and the mother of your future child to stay in your life. Which means you should be prepared to seduce and woo her, once you're done venting at her for being such an idiot over thinking you don't like children."

A flutter of her hand, and she left the dining hall, leaving Dominor staring at the mirror. After a long, thoughtful moment, he reached up and tapped it off, restoring the reflection of his dazed blue eyes. If *that* was the woman his twin was destined to marry . . . Kata help Evanor . . . and thank Jinga she wasn't *his* Destined wife.

Dominor paced in the southernmost courtyard, studying the enlarged mirror awaiting activation. He wasn't entirely alone; Trevan rested on the edge of one of the nearby stone troughs, waiting to help him in case there was trouble. The copper-haired mage kept glancing at his older brother's hair, which still shone with those odd, oil-on-water highlights, but Dominor didn't feel like explaining to his siblings why his hair looked so exotic.

After hunting down his twin earlier, he had managed to get Evanor to whisper a coherent explanation. It seemed his womb-mate had decided it was a crime for a newlywed husband and wife to be separated from each other so soon . . . and in the ensuing attempt to get Serina to come over to Nightfall, the proverbial cat had escaped the basket.

Now all of his brothers and sisters-in-law knew that he'd been duped by his bride . . . and he was definitely going to have words with his wife about *that*. Mere miscommunications, his aching head! His wife was going to have to learn that, when it came to mathemagics, yes, she was a genius. But when it came to managing her life, she was a village idiot.

He would manage her life, from now on . . . which included managing the stupid, idiotic, asinine idea that he didn't like children right out of her gorgeous mind! His initial fury had died down, but it had been replaced with an irritation that she hadn't *talked* to him, hadn't told him what was going on in that brilliant but utterly off-balanced brain of hers. *That* definitely had to be changed. It was probably a product of the same imbalanced, ultra-focused attitude that made her skip meals in favor of scribbling out her arithmancy spells. They were very important—he didn't deny that—but she clearly needed a keeper, someone to manage the rest of her life for her.

Lady Serina Avadan, soon to be of Nightfall, was going to get a thorough lesson in why *he* was called the Master.

Two hours, now, he had paced the courtyard, nerves strung tight with worry and outrage. As he turned to measure the distance between two widely spaced, age-worn stone troughs, he caught sight of the mirror's reflecting. It rippled, altered, and glowed with the familiar sphere of a Fountain. Facing the view, he braced himself for the impending confrontation, heart in his throat. A bulky object lurched into view, falling down through the mirror and landing with a clatter of hooves, a banging of iron-banded wheels, and an equine squeal.

Seated on the driver's bench, Serina winced from the impact, yanking on the reins. It was too late, however. No sooner had the back of her vehicle cleared the mirror than it shut down, reflecting the ceramic-laden cart. Before she could do more than draw breath and un-hunch her shoulders, opening her eyes to stare at her unexpected surroundings, Dominor's hand lashed out.

"Carrouavec! Kalsedec!"

She yelped as a golden stream of power zipped from his hand, winding itself around her body in the span of a single heartbeat. Shock from the lifting of his second spell made her drop the cart-mare's reins. She struggled, but the glowing bindings and the energies lifting her held her too securely to get free.

"What the—?" Craning her head, she peered down at Dominor. "You! What are you doing? Let me go!"

"Sulet." A flick of his hand, and a spangled web of silvery white magic slapped over her mouth, sealing it shut. Amber brown eyes narrowed into a glare as she struggled again. Dominor wasn't taking any chances, however. A gesture caused the golden bonds to secure her hands, pressing them palm-to-palm and sealing off the possibility of her using a gesture instead of a

verbal spell to counteract his enchantments. A slash of his other hand guided her away from the cart and the nervous equine. Her hair, he noticed, also bore iridescent highlights in its platinum strands. He wasn't the only one affected by their time in the Fountain together, then.

Trevan hurried forward, hauling himself quickly onto the wagon's bench. His shoulder had been injured by a bullet-thing from one of the Mandarites, but enough time had passed for him to heal and regain the full use of his arm. Picking up the reins, he urged the nervous but sturdy mare away from the mirror, intending to take her to the same stables that were being used for their new dairy herd. He did so with a curt nod to Dominor, who turned and guided his floating wife into the nearest door into the southern wing.

"Mmmf! *Mmmffmmmrrrr!*" Outraged amber eyes glared at him.

He met her stare for stare with a blue-eyed glare of his own, but said not a word as he floated her upstairs. All the way to his suite of rooms, she tried to struggle against her bonds, and failed. Guiding her into his bedchamber, he lowered her floating form onto his bed. A slash of his hand, a muttered spell, and her arms and legs shot out, splayed on the bed as the golden energies split into four pieces, binding her to the corners of his broad, velvet-draped bed. Clad in white riding leathers in some exotic, non-Natallian cut, her pale braid spilling at an angle, she stood out clearly on the rich, violet-hued coverlet.

A slash of his hand slammed shut the doors to his suite, warding them against anyone but himself opening them. Another curt gesture closed the windows, and a third flick of his wrist ensured that, warm though the late summer day was, the temperature inside the bedroom would stay comfortable. Neither of them was going to leave until they had certain things firmly settled, but that didn't mean they had to swelter while settling those matters.

Seating himself on the bed next to her, Dominor braced his right hand over her body, looming over her. "You. *Lied.* To me!"

She flinched a little at his carefully enunciated accusation, some of her outrage replaced by a hint of shame. Behind the edges of the webwork holding her silent, her cheeks had flushed with her distress. Dominor shook his head, his dark brown hair falling over his shoulders.

"You *lied* to me! You implied that there wouldn't be a

pregnancy—because you *assumed* that I wouldn't want any children! You *used* me to get yourself pregnant, and *didn't tell me I'm a father!*—Do you know how that makes me feel?" he demanded. "*Used*. Worse than that, because you didn't *ask me* outright if I didn't want to be a father! It makes me feel *ignored*—and I will *not* be ignored by my own wife!

"You may be the most intelligent mathemagician I have ever encountered, my Lady, but how could you be so *stupid*?"

"Mmm, fmm ffmmhn ffmm fmm-mmh, fmm-hmh!" she attempted to snarl back.

Passing his hand over the glittering strands covering the lower half of her face, Dominor released part of its grip—just enough for her to speak normally, though not to cast anything magical. He would free her when he was damned well ready, and only when he was ready. "What was that? Do you have an apology for me, wife?"

"I *said*—" She broke off, considered the fact that she could be heard under the webbing, and restarted her retort. "I said, well, you didn't talk to me, *either*! And it's not like you *cared* about having children!"

"I *do* care about having children! I *want* to be a husband and father!" Dom snapped back.

Her eyes widened in disbelief. "Then why was every other comment you made about children a derogatory one? What *else* was I supposed to think, when you kept talking about not wanting any kids, ever?"

He opened his mouth to argue the point, then shut it. She was right about that, dammit. Subsiding, Dominor leveled her with a firm look. "All you had to do was *ask me* if that was how I really felt. But you didn't. And you *should* have told me the truth, that the ritual required you to get pregnant, after all!"

"Well . . . you said at the very start that you didn't want to be a father right away, but the ritual itself demanded it! You were my best and soonest shot at getting it completed, and I had you in a position where I could extract a binding oath out of you to help me!"

"Yes, but you could have *told* me I needed to become a father!"

"I *told* you I'd take care of it, that you wouldn't be burdened by any lasting responsibility!"

"Having children isn't a *burden*!" he retorted. "It's a joy and a pleasure, even when it's a heavy responsibility—and it would be my *honor* to father and raise children with you! Jinga's Tits, for such a brilliant woman, you're as thick as chalk, sometimes!"

"Oh!" She glared at him in outrage, struggling to release her bonds. They held her fast, pinning her to the bed. "You . . . you . . . ! Let me go!"

"*No.* Not until I've explained a few facts of life to you," Dominor stated autocratically. "Fact number one: You are *my wife.* Your place is at my side, in my home, sharing my life. As my wife, it is your responsibility to *be* my wife. No gallivanting off to foreign lands without my permission and my presence.

"Fact number two: You are the mother of my child-to-be . . . and any other children we may choose to have. As such, you *will* take care of yourself and keep yourself healthy. I'll be watching over you and bullying you into eating meals, exercising, and taking breaks from your work when I deem you need to feed and rest yourself. Fact number three," he listed as she stopped struggling and stared at him, narrowing her eyes first in indignation, then in wary thought. "You will *talk* with me about any past or future concerns you may have regarding my feelings for you, instead of *assuming* you *think* you know what I'm feeling."

That arched one of her platinum brows. "And *what*, exactly, are your *feelings* for me?"

"That I love you—and our children-to-be—more than my own existence," Dom stated bluntly, ignoring her derisive, scoffing tone in favor of taking the question seriously. "That you are my Prophesied Lady, my equal and my mate . . . and that I am your Prophesied Master. Which means you will heed my every order from here on out, because I hold only your best interests in my heart."

She started to protest through the webbing half-obscuring her mouth, then stopped and frowned at him. "Prophecy? You still haven't told me what this other Prophecy is, you know! How can I figure out how to fix the problem with the Portals if you don't tell me what I need to know?"

"Because you don't know how to balance your research versus the rest of your life," Dominor told her, leaning down close enough to kiss the tip of her nose. He brushed his lips over her forehead next. "You *need* me, Serina . . . even if you don't love me, yet. But you will. You are my Lady, my Destined bride . . . and you clearly need me to master the details of your life."

She looked away from him and mumbled something.

Dom lifted his head, gazing down at her. "What was that?"

"I said, I never *said* that."

"You never said what?"

Giving him a brief, sharp look, she glanced away, avoiding his gaze again. "I never said I didn't love you . . . you arrogant beast."

Dominor shifted so that she was forced to look into his eyes, too close for her to avoid him. "Say it. Say you love me, that you will obey me, that you'll stay and be my wife, the mother of my child."

"That I'll *obey* you?" she scoffed. "What incentive do I have to agree to something that foolish? Why shouldn't I demand that *you* should obey *me*? Hmm?"

"Swear you'll obey me, and I'll devote my life to you," he coaxed her, kissing the skin just in front of her left ear. "To your health, to your comfort, to your pleasure . . ." He kissed his way down the side of her throat as he spoke. "Love me . . . heed me . . . be with me always . . . and I will enslave myself to you. Not just for nine months, either. Permanently."

Serina groaned, squeezing her eyes shut. "Dominor, you know I can't think when you do things like that!"

"Like what?" Dominor asked, licking his tongue in a figure-eight over the pulse beneath the soft skin of her neck.

"Seduce me!"

"If that's what you want, my Lady," he murmured, smirking and licking her again, "that's what you'll get. My word of honor."

"Do you really love me?" Serina asked almost wistfully when he finally lifted his head from her throat.

"Do you really think I'd be this upset with your little deception if I didn't?" he countered, nuzzling the vee neckline of her leather jacket. Though the foreign cut of her clothes were as exotic as Kelly's odd but attractive combination of skirts and trousers, it would be rather difficult to remove her garments while she was still bound to his bed. He contemplated the problem as he continued his reply. "Especially after you threw me out of your life. It wasn't just to send me to my twin, was it? *Was* it?"

"Well, no," she mumbled. "I didn't want you noticing I wasn't wearing my amulet and getting mad at me for conceiving what I *thought* would be an unwanted child, on your part."

"Wanted," Dominor stressed, rising up over her so that she

could see the fierce honesty in his gaze. "You have a *lot* to make up for, wife. Starting with the utter lack of a proper wedding night. *Sartorlagen!*"

Her clothing vanished from her body with a soft *pop*, reappearing about a body-length beyond the bed, off to the right. As did his own. The leather and cotton garments dropped to the floor in an untidy heap. Normally, he kept his chambers clean enough for his twin's housekeeping standards. Right now, he had other things on his mind. Such as suckling the nipples bared by his actions, and nuzzling the soft skin of her abdomen . . . pressing a kiss to the flesh just below her navel. Somewhere within her, right now, was the tiny, germinated seed that was their future child. Dominor kissed it again, and again, slow salutes of his lips that reinforced his statement that he wanted their child.

When he finally shifted lower on her body, he found the flesh below her pale curls wet. Ready for lovemaking. Arching a brow, he lifted his head far enough to look at her, amusement in his voice. "Is this because of my tenderness, or my binding you to my bed and staking my claim?"

"This, what?" Serina returned, lifting her head so that she could see him.

Lowering his mouth, Dominor licked her. *"This."*

"Oh . . . ohhh . . ."

She flexed her limbs against her bonds, then strained her loins into his tongue. He didn't stop tormenting her deliciously until she strained all the way to a shuddering, gasping climax. Smirking, Dominor soothed her with a few last flicks before crawling up the length of her body again.

Panting through the webbing still covering her mouth, she regained her breath. Brown eyes met blue, dazed to amused. "You are *seriously* detrimental to my higher brain functions. You do know that, don't you?"

"Of course. Does my Lady like the services of her slave?" Dom teased her.

Serina rolled her eyes. "Oh, please—you're about as convincing in the role of a slave as a cat trying to pretend it's a bird!"

A murmured command vanished the last of the magic covering the lower half of her face. He nuzzled her lips with his own, not quite kissing her. Teasing her. "True, but it's a pretense I'll only perform with you."

That made her laugh.

Dominor kissed her fully, once she caught her breath. The problem, Serina knew, was that he had taught her in just a sparse turning of Brother Moon how to be addicted to his kisses. And the knowledge that he *wanted* children with her and wanted her firmly in his life—that was a heady revelation. And an irritating one.

Serina knew he wanted to hear her profess her love for him; she just had a few things to say, first.

The moment he released her mouth, panting for breath, she asserted the first of them. *"Tuleroleru!"*

Their bodies spun, Dominor clutching at her with a yelp. It was no good; the spell literally reversed their positions. Now it was he who was trussed by the golden bonds of his own powers, while she knelt over him.

TWENTY

●━❧━●

Serina grinned down at her captive. "Didn't know I could do that, did you?"

"Not through magical bonds, no," Dominor forced himself to admit. He gingerly tested the golden bands lashing him to the bedposts, more disconcerted by the fact that this was ... exciting ... than by the fact that she had bound him at all. "How *did* you do this?"

"A spell I picked up at the Academy in Guchere, from a foreign mage. Well, a mage-priest," she amended. "They call them 'witches' in Darkhana."

Dominor frowned in thought. "Isn't that the land west of Fortuna?"

She smiled at him. "That's correct! But showing off your vast, worldly education isn't going to free you from these bonds."

One of his dark brown brows lifted at that. "So what is?"

"An apology. For all those 'jokes' you made, that *weren't* very funny."

"Apologize?" Dom spluttered. "I'm not the one who lied about getting herself pregnant!"

"Apologize, or I'll not let you go!—You know, you get awfully arrogant at times, and I'm *not* always going to put up with it!" Serina warned her husband.

That caught his attention. "Not *always* put up with it?"

Serina blushed. "Well, it's kind of sexy, when you get all bossy—when you're taking care of me, that is. It makes me feel . . . cherished."

His mouth curved into a smile that was too soft to be completely smug. "You're worth it."

Her blush deepened. Ducking her gaze briefly, Serina cleared her throat. When she met his eyes again, she gave him an arch look. "Well. Are you going to apologize, or am I going to have to have my wicked way with you and torture you into submission?"

Dominor snorted. *"Kallek."*

The bonds pinning his arms and legs in place vanished. Lunging up, he twisted to get her under him. She squirmed, twisted her limbs in something that wasn't quite resistance—and Dominor found himself pinned facedown in the pillows before he realized what she was doing to him. Or even *how* she was doing it to him. It was disconcertingly like the way his sister-in-law, Kelly, had once pinned him to the donjon floor at the heart of the castle, shortly after her arrival on the Isle.

Heat flushed through him as realization struck. *She really does know how to make me "eat dirt,"* Dominor discovered. He waited for a sense of outrage to sweep through him at the indignity, but found only an unexpected source of amusement. *Or should I say, "eat pillow"?*

"Now, apologize!"

Smiling into his bedding, Dominor twisted his face just enough so that he could be heard clearly by his wife. "I apologize profusely for being such an insensitive idiot. I apologize for any confusion or hurt feelings my poor attempts at humor may have caused. And I beg your forgiveness, and request the opportunity to make it up to you somehow."

"Apology accepted." She released the arm she had twisted and pinned, backing off from him.

Untangling his limb, Dominor flexed it as he sat up, making sure it worked. Eyeing her, he considered his options. He apologized of his own free will, and knew the apology was due, but she wasn't going to get away with doing that to him on a regular basis. "Now, are you going to apologize as well?"

She fingered her braid for a moment in thought, then nodded. "All right. I'm sorry I didn't tell you straight out at the beginning that you had to get me pregnant, as a part of the ritual. But . . . I didn't think most male mages would have gone for that willingly—the sex, yes, but the child, no—which is why I secured your cooperation before revealing it. And . . . I'm sorry I kept it to myself afterward. But, you *did* make a comment about not wanting to be a father, which only confirmed my fears, you know!"

"That is a *terrible* apology. *Lassoulu, lassumu, itreisa pathumu!*" Snapping his fingers, Dominor levitated his wife, lifting her from the bed with the same spell they had used to practice for the Fountain ritual. She gasped and twisted, trying to right herself, but there was no surface for her to push against. Catching her by the hips, Dominor drew her down into alignment with his gravity-bound body. Namely, with her hips aligned to his face, her thighs floating next to his ears. "And I'm going to torment you until you're *truly* repentant."

Serina drew in a breath to argue in protest. The air froze in her lungs, then escaped her in a moan when he lapped for the second time at her femininity. "Ohhh, Dominor . . . if you're thinking this will torture me into submission, you are *completely* out of your mind!"

"Am I?" he smirked, stopping for a moment. "Or am I smarter than *you*?"

With that as her only warning, he laved her, teased her, brought her up toward her release . . . and then stopped. Flicked just the tip of his tongue against her flesh, keeping her trembling until she groaned with frustration. Pausing, Dominor lowered her just enough to look up the length of her body.

"Tell me you love me, and all will be forgiven . . . and fully sated."

Craning her head toward him, she fixed him with a sardonic look. Her cheeks were flushed, and her amber eyes glittered with passion. "I'm your equal in magic, Dominor. I could counter this spell if I wanted to!"

Lifting her back to his mouth, holding her gaze with his own, Dominor slowly suckled on her flesh.

It wasn't enough to launch her into her pleasure. She groaned and thrashed in the air. "Dammit—yes, I love you! I'm sorry, and I love you!"

Her reward speared through her limbs as he sucked hard,

making her cry out in pleasure. She drifted down, literally and physically, until she lay on the bed, the levitation spell canceled. Covering her, pressing his erection into her flesh, Dominor rocked into her gently. His lips, warm and damp with her musk, nibbled at hers coaxing her into kissing him back. Not that she needed much coaxing; Serina wrapped her arms around his shoulders, returning each loving nip as she recovered.

Once again, it felt like coming home. Dominor soaked up her responsiveness as she reveled in their coupling. Urgency built between them, crested, and faded with shuddering gasps and soft cries. They kissed and touched afterward, until he slid out of her and shifted to one side. Snuggling close, Serina sighed. Then peered around the bedchamber, curiosity in her light brown gaze.

"Is this where you live, then?"

"This entire wing-end is mine to do with as I please. I picked this suite in specific for my quarters because it suited my needs," Dom confessed. "There are a few that are larger, with antechambers and dressing rooms . . . if you like, we can explore them. There are also reception rooms on the ground floor, which you can turn into a workroom for all of your slates."

"Which are all back at the Retreat," she reminded him, tucking her head more firmly onto his shoulder. "Are you going to come back with me while I fetch them?"

"Of course. We cannot let Mariel pack up everything on her own," he pointed out gallantly. "It wouldn't be fair to her."

"Hmm. Well, I owe her for her collusion in this little kidnapping plan of yours—and don't tell me she wasn't involved. She *pressed* for me to hand over the Guardianship to Mother Naima. You couldn't have interfered and Gated me through the Fontway without doing that, first."

"Actually, I didn't have anything to do with that," Dominor confessed. At her curious look, he elaborated. "I *would* have tried some way to get my hands on you . . . but I tripped and fell, knocking myself out. While I was unconscious, my twin colluded with Rydan. It was their idea to kidnap you, with Mariel's help."

"How did you do that?" Serina asked, amused. "Trip and knock yourself out, I mean."

"Well, I was lying in this bed, last night . . . touching myself as I thought of you," he added teasingly, "when I realized you hadn't been wearing your amulet. In my fury, I was a little too hasty in climbing out of bed, and . . . I fell. Didn't wake up until this morning, either. And I still have a sore spot on the side of my head, too."

"Oh, you poor thing." Scooting a little higher on the bed, she kissed the spot just in front of his ear when he pointed to it. "Next time, don't get so angry." She laughed softly, making him eye her. "Looks like I'm not the *only* person who needs looking after!"

That made him arch his brow in silent challenge of her statement.

"Falling out of bed!" Serina snickered. "Even I'm not that clumsy!"

"I am *not* clumsy—and if you don't behave, I'll tie you to my bed again until you apologize," Dominor mock-threatened her.

From the gleam in her eyes, she didn't take his warning seriously, either. "Promises, promises." A thought made her frown softly. "Dominor, what *was* the Prophecy you said concerns you, specifically? The one from your family?"

> *"Strong of will and strong of mind*
> *You seek she who is your kind*
> *Set your trap and be your fate*
> *When Lady is the Master's mate."*

She blinked at his dry recital. "What trap did you set?"

He'd given it some thought while waiting for her to arrive through the mirrors. "I tricked you into marrying me. I suspect you tricked *me* into marrying you, too, so that our child would be legitimate. Am I right?"

Her blush proved it. "Yes, well, it *was* also necessary for replicating the conditions of the original, botched ritual. Um . . . are you happy?"

Dominor considered the way she had made him "eat pillow," and nodded. "Yes. Very happy. You challenge me, and I need that. You're also more brilliant than I am—moments of thickheadedness set aside—and yet you need me. I find I like being needed."

"Good. I'm happy, too," she reassured him, snuggling close again. Then whapped his bare chest with her fingers. "But don't ever make stupid jokes like that again, got it?"

Catching her fingers, he lifted them to his lips. "So long as you promise to *ask* me what I'm thinking and not just assume that you know. Get *all* of the facts, before you make any more calculations."

"Deal. Now, let's get dressed so you can show me this island of yours. The nuns have more or less kicked me out of Koral-tai, you know," Serina added. "So I figure I might as well move in with you."

"I certainly wouldn't allow you to move anywhere else," Dominor agreed arrogantly . . . and had to catch her hand a second time as she tried to whap him with it.

They noticed the first shipment of shrunken chalkboards while they were exploring the possibilities of the rooms on the ground floor. The stacks had landed in front of the mirror still standing in the southernmost courtyard. Excited, Serina found the nearest door, rushing outside to get her hands on her precious slates. She rushed right past Kelly in doing so, completely ignoring the shorter, redheaded woman.

Kelly, summoned from one of the upper rooms in the castle by the sight of more objects in the southern courtyard than there should properly be, eyed Dominor, who had followed at a more leisurely pace.

"I take it that's your wife?" she asked her brother-in-law, glancing at the distracted, willowy woman again.

"Every last inch of her," Dominor agreed with a sigh. She hadn't even stopped to carry the slates inside, but instead was already expanding and placing them around the courtyard. It was a good thing it was a sunny, late-summer day; rain might have messed with her chalked spells. "I'd better stop her before she gets too involved in her work."

"Dominor, come here! I wanted to show you something. There's an anomaly in my calculations that I cannot track down," Serina told him, gesturing peremptorily for him to join her with one hand.

Her fingers were already smeared with chalk dust. She didn't wait for him to move closer, either; turning back to her boards, she expanded two more, and tapped them, showing the progression of her mathemagical spells. And did a double take, staring at the board. Blinking, she moved in front of the others, expanded another board, and stared at her calculations.

"That's odd . . . there *was* an anomaly in the figures—it reduced the success rate to a mere fraction of what it should have been—I *know* I saw it! But . . . it's gone! Everything's back to what it should be!"

Curious himself, Dominor joined her. "How do you mean?"

"This is exactly how all of the calculations should be playing out, as they monitor the situation. But, right after I cast you through the Fontway, everything changed!" Serina tugged on her braid, staring in confusion at the arithmancy covering the boards. "And now it's changed back. I don't get it . . ."

Reviewing what he knew of their task, Dominor offered the most logical conclusion. "Perhaps it was because you cast me out of your life . . . when the original couple did no such thing."

She blinked and turned to stare at him. "You think so?"

"I *know* so," he stated firmly, tugging her close to him. "Now that you've rejoined me, everything is right in the world." A cough from his sister-in-law made Dominor amend, "Well, aside from Evanor's injury, the fact that we're not only exiled from Katan, but that they're intent on blockading nearly all contact with the mainland, and that your best friend will need to torture the citizen-chickens before she can attempt to restore my twin's voice . . ."

"Which I have no problems with," Kelly quickly volunteered. "They're quite vicious, for poultry. Hi, I'm Kelly, Saber's wife, Dominor's sister-in-law, and Queen of Nightfall on weekends, holidays, and whenever we have visitors. Saber's in his forge, and the others are busy elsewhere, but you can meet them at supper in another hour or so."

Serina laughed and clasped the proffered hand. "Serina Avadan, former Guardian of Koral-tai, and currently unemployed mathemagician."

"Nice to meet you. How did you get your hair to do that?" Kelly asked, peering at the taller woman's hair.

"Do what?" Serina asked, confused by the off-the-wall question.

"It's sort of . . . iridescent," Kelly explained, gesturing at the mage's braid. "For that matter, so is Dominor's. It's a neat trick. How did you manage it?"

"It's from something we did while we were in the Font, I think," Dominor replied.

Serina blushed. "Um, actually, it's a property of the Sacred Fruit we used for our marriage ritual. It only lasts for about a week, but it's one of the signs that the couple actually drank the liqueur from the *myjii*, and not from some other fruit."

"Ah," Kelly returned. "Well. Interesting custom; you'll have to tell me all about it, sometime. In the meantime, I suppose we should be making room for you, here on Nightfall. Presuming, of course, that you'll be staying with us? We'd rather not give up Dominor again. He's arrogant and thus occasionally annoying," the redhead teased, glancing at her brother-in-law, "but we're fond of him all the same."

"We will be living here, yes," Dominor agreed. "Aside from at least one more trip back to Natallia to complete our task there, of course. Otherwise, this will be our home."

"Well, insofar as we're gainfully employed," Serina countered, eyeing her husband. "I don't like leaning on the charity of others, even if they're family." She turned back to the freckled woman. "I don't suppose you have a need for an arithmancer?"

"Does that mean you know accounting?" Kelly asked her, curious. "I've looked at the boys' books, and they're not bad, but they could be better. Unfortunately, a six-column system is as far as my business acumen can stretch, and not very comfortably at that—I used to own my own business, elsewhere, and it was a real headache."

"Six-column is easy for me; I could practically do it in my sleep," Serina dismissed. "If you want to show me your books, I can take a look at them. Do you have a system of banking established, yet? I gained the impression it's just the handful of you here on this island, but if you're going to turn it into a real kingdom, you're going to need a true Exchequery, eventually. I've studied half a dozen different systems; it'll be fairly easy to implement now and have it in place, should your kingdom continue to grow. And you don't have to worry about paying me, outside of food and shelter. I've my own source of wealth, otherwise."

The freckled outworlder grinned up at her. "You're hired, but we'll pay you anyway. My husband, Saber, oversees the trade with the sea merchants who visit us, but if you think you can get a better deal out of them, I'm all for it. And you can have a small percentage off the top for any trades you negotiate. If you can set up a taxation system for the future, arrange some sort of formal trade with Natallia, covering export and import fees, *and* increase our bottom line, I'm all for that, too."

"*First*, you need to pick out a workroom," Dominor chided his wife, recognizing the gleam of highly focused interest in her tawny eyes. "And a storeroom for all of these slates . . . *and* eat a decent supper, so you don't starve yourself in your zeal. Once that's settled, *then* you can look at our finances."

Serina eyed him, mouth twitching upward as she fiddled with the end of her braid. "You are bound and determined to manage my life for me, aren't you?"

"Of course. That's my Destiny." Pulling her close, Dominor kissed her, ignoring the amused look on the face of their grinning, freckled, outworlder Queen.

Song of the Sons of Destiny

The Eldest Son shall bear this
    weight:
If ever true love he should feel
Disaster shall come at her heel
And Katan will fail to aid
When Sword in sheath is
    claimed by Maid

The Second Son shall know
    this fate:
He who hunts is not alone
When claw would strike and
    cut to bone
A chain of Silk shall bind his
    hand
So Wolf is caught in marriage-
    band

The Third of Sons shall meet
    his match:
Strong of will and strong of
    mind
You seek she who is your kind
Set your trap and be your fate
When Lady is the Master's
    mate

The Fourth of Sons shall find
    his catch:
The purest note shall turn to
    sour
And weep in silence for the hour
But listen to the lonely Heart
And Song shall bind the two
    apart

The Fifth Son shall seek the
    sign:
Prowl the woods and through
    the trees
Before you in the woods she
    flees
Catch her quick and hold her
    fast
The Cat will find his Home at
    last

The Sixth Son shall draw the
    line:
Shun the day and rule the night
Your reign's end shall come at
    light
When Dawn steals into your
    hall
Bride of Storm shall be your
    fall

The Seventh Son shall he
    decree:
Burning bright and searing hot
You shall seek that which is not
Mastered by desire's name
Water shall control the Flame

The Eighth Son shall set them
    free:
Act in Hope and act in love
Draw down your powers from
    above
Set your Brothers to their call
When Mage has wed, you will
    be all

—THE SEER DRAGANNA

Keep reading for a look at the fifth book in
Jean Johnson's Sons of Destiny series,

The Cat

Coming in June 2008 from Berkley Sensation!

The Fifth Son shall seek the sign:
Prowl the woods and through the trees
Before you in the woods she flees
Catch her quick and hold her fast
The Cat will find his Home at last

Amara was so very tired. Tired to the point of feeling cranky, in fact. Tired of swimming. Tired of pulling. Tired of running . . . but there wasn't anything else either of them could do anymore. Resentful, too—and why shouldn't she be? Born to be a queen, but forced to be a refugee. Who wouldn't resent such a reversal of fortune? Oh, yes, she resented her situation, and was very, very tired of it.

But did she resent her sister? No . . . and yes. If it weren't for Arora, neither of them would be in this situation. Yet Amara didn't wish her sister to the bottom of the ocean; that fate she reserved for their pursuers, who were responsible for this mess. If they hadn't been so determined to capture her twin, Amara wouldn't be so tired, and not just physically. Tired of being strong, tired of putting someone else's needs before her own, tired of those needs being stripped from both of them, demanded of them, denied to each of them . . .

She was tired of swimming, tired of drinking seawater and eating raw fish, tired of being stuck in this sea-creature shape. Modified, of course; this kind of creature didn't naturally have a spiraling horn, but it was a necessary adaptation. The makeshift raft her sister rested upon was nothing more than several planks, part of a barrel, and a spar lashed together with a bit of sail-rope. That rope had a loop at one end, and into that loop Amara's horn went, allowing her to pull the raft forward. Southward, in the direction her sister insisted they go.

It wasn't as if she had a better idea of where to go. Except for north; Amara didn't dare let either of them return that way. Just because they had lost their most recent set of pursuers didn't mean others weren't still looking for them back on the continent. That left east, west, south . . . and Arora said south. Originally, their intent had been to try and reach Fortuna; surely the oldest Empire in the whole of the world had some sort of solution to Arora's problem. But Fate, Fortuna's Threefold God, had intervened by dashing their ship against the shallow coral reefs of the Sun's Belt.

So south it was. But how much farther? It felt like Amara never stopped swimming, save for a rare moment of rest. Even when she had to catch fish for the two of them, she *still* had to swim.

Amara blamed the storm for part of their predicament. It had swept up over them, driving their ship farther south than intended, into the treacherous, reef-filled waters of the Sun's Belt region. The other part of the problem existed simply because of what her sister was, an anomaly that—in the wrong hands—could cause an incredible amount of damage to their world.

Arora had learned through trial and error how to hide her uniqueness from mage-sight; only a direct touch from a mage could reveal what she was. Which meant avoiding mages, and avoiding crowds. They hadn't been able to find a ship without a mage, but they had picked a vessel with a relatively weak mage, and had done their best to avoid the woman until other ships had appeared on the horizon, pursuing them into the teeth of a storm too powerful for their on-board mage to avert.

Sheer luck had allowed the two of them to survive, where so many others on board had perished under the pounding power of the storm-whipped surf. Luck, and Amara's abilities. Few others of her kind could have managed to shift into a sea-adapted creature, coming from a landlocked kingdom as they did, never mind one capable of swimming her sister free of the disintegrating wreckage. But she couldn't swim and support her sister above the waves all of the time.

Providence had brought them close to a drifting scrap of hull and a floating chunk of barrel still bound by iron at one end. A spar torn from one of the masts had enough rope still clinging to it to allow Arora to bind everything together, giving herself a place to rest. When Amara needed to rest, she joined her twin on the planks in her smaller, human form, but that ran the risk of putting them at the mercy of the great oceanic currents, utterly unknown on this side of the Sun's Belt.

But that had been too many days ago, at least two weeks' worth. Tired and miserable, Amara now found herself having to dodge to the right around annoying patches of seaweed, something she hadn't seen since they had left the shallow waters of the Sun's Belt reefs . . . shallow waters . . . *shallow waters!*

That woke up her tired mind. Seaweed forests meant shallow waters and—she dodged to the left, avoiding an outcrop of rock that loomed unexpectedly through the darkness. Now she had to swim through the kelp-bed while trying not to deviate so much that she tangled the fronds in her tow-line from course corrections. It also meant a potential coastline, which her sister had been promising lay ahead of them, but it was difficult for Amara to gauge just how close they were to an actual shore. In this form her eyes were positioned for a broad field of view to either side, sacrificing most of her depth perception. Not all, but most of it.

She could also hear the faint rush of surf somewhere up ahead, the lapping of waves against rocks and other things. Surfacing, Amara twisted her body, peering into the fog that had risen while she was busy swimming underwater. Her sister called out to her, encouragement in her tone.

"I *knew* there was land in this direction. Keep swimming! Ahead and just to your right, if you can. I think I can see trees in that direction."

"I zzzee it!" The lips and tongue of this style of creature weren't designed for speaking clearly, but at least she didn't have the beak of a bird; the big tongue she currently had was bad enough, making her sound slow and stupid, but a bird's beak was even worse. "I sshall aim vor it!"

Ducking underwater again, Amara swam forward, surfacing from time to time to check her progress both below and above the surface. Her eyes were shaped for light-enhancement, making the most of the thin light from Sister Moon, a barely visible sliver rising on the horizon off to her left, to the east. Brother Moon was just now setting to her right, a larger, somewhat fatter crescent curled the opposite way, as He raced ahead of His Sister at roughly three times Her stately pace through the sky.

She was tired of the ocean, tired of water all around her. Amara was a worshipper of Mother Earth and Father Sky, not a follower of any water-based Gods. She wanted dry earth beneath her legs—for that matter, she wanted *legs*, rather than flippers, flukes, or fins. And fruit rather than fish, though it was doubtful any existed this far south. From the chill of the water, the rumor that the southern hemisphere had its winter opposite Aiar's summer was regrettably true. If it was indeed the start of winter down here, then fruit would be scarce, but Amara was so *tired* of catching and eating nothing but raw fish. She might be in the shape of a sea-swimmer, capable of digesting the necessary sea-based diet, but her taste buds were still quite human at the end of the day . . . and her sister was entirely human. Raw fish was taking its toll on Arora, too.

Putting more energy into her swimming, Amara thought longingly of sand between her restored toes, or maybe the lumpy clutter of a pebble beach, each rock rounded by centuries' worth of pummeling from the churning surf. She spotted sand down below, interspersed with clumps of seaweed, rocks, anemones, crabs—shore-dwelling creatures. Not far, now.

Not far at all; within minutes, the surface came so close, she had no choice but to shift her form, rising above the water with a gulp of air that was half salt water. She spat it out of a blowhole, shifting from gills to lungs, then shifted the rest of her body. Legs were now more useful than fins and flukes. And if she shifted legs, then she shifted some arms, too. Grabbing the rope as she did so, she let the horn phase back into her flesh. She didn't discard the scales or the thick layer of body fat, though; the air was just as cold and damp as the water, and her sister was wearing both sets of their clothes. Amara needed the extra insulation for the time being.

Literally, all the two women possessed were the raft, the broken half-barrel, the clothes on Arora's back, and the few things that had been on their belts. Well, that and the pair of boots laced to the half-barrel. Arora could only wear one set of footgear at a time. But both belts and their nearly empty money pouches were slung around her waist. They only had one knife between the two of them, but that was alright; Amara had never needed a knife once she had gained control of her powers.

Increasing her size, she hauled the raft well past the water mark. That half-barrel was important; it held their only fresh water supply, at least until they could find more. So were the planks, in their own way. Propped up by a tree limb or a rock, they could form a lean-to shelter. And one side was slathered in tar; if nothing else, once the boards dried out, they could be used to start a fire. If the sisters could *get* a fire going.

But being on land after the weightlessness of the sea was exhausting. Tugging the makeshift raft all the way to the tree line, she pulled it into a grassy patch between trunks and bushes, and collapsed onto the boards next to her sister.

"No farther," Amara panted, glad to have her own lips and tongue back in their normal working order. "I can't go any farther . . ."

Her twin planted a hand on her shoulder, pressing on it heavily in order to gain her own feet. "Rest. I'll look for something edible, *without* any fins."

"Mother Bless your quest," Amara groaned, leaning back on her elbows. She sat up a little, watching Arora stagger into the darkness, worrying. For over a year, she had guarded her sister. Exhaustion was no excuse to let down her guard. "Hey, don't go far—we don't know if this place is inhabited!"

A backward wave was all she got from her sister. Too tired to argue, no matter how much her paranoid nature demanded it, Amara lay back on the planks and rested. She wasn't concerned about her twin's ability to see in the dark. It wasn't the same as actually shifting the shape of her eyes, but Arora said she could *think* about seeing things in a different way, blink twice, and that was all she needed to do to *see* things in a different way.

What she saw, Arora couldn't always articulate. Amara didn't understand her sister's vague talk about "auras" and "half-images," whatever those might be. No, regular eyes were just fine, whether they were the eyes of a hawk or the eyes of a human. Right now she was enjoying the enhanced vision of a cat, sacrificing color in the quest to intensify overall perception, even if half-forms were considered sloppy shapeshifting.

Her sea-creature shape had been useful, but cobbled together.

As was her current form, plump and covered in scales, since scales were the easiest kind of hide to dry. Had she been back among her own people, Amara would have needed to don her own clothes at this point. A shifter could cobble together a covering of fur, scales, or feathers for casual use, but pure forms were what everyone strove to achieve. Modified forms were looked down upon as half-hearted, even undisciplined. Beneath someone of her status and ability.

There was a perfectionist side drummed into her that was irked by the whole being-chased ordeal they had undergone. Being chased required being stealthy and creative, which was good, yes . . . but it was a creativity fashioned of half-forms and pseudoness, and of running instead of standing and fighting like a proper Shifterai.

That was another resentment to try to shove aside. Once her twin's specialness had been grasped and understood, Amara had been given the task of protecting and guarding Arora, a task which had forced Amara to set aside her own ambitions. Here she lay, the best shifter in the two hundred years of her people's history . . . exiled by annoying circumstance from her rightful chance at the throne of her people.

She heard Arora coming back, and sat up. It wasn't her sister that annoyed her, but rather their circumstances. From the bulge swinging in her sister's gathered sleeve, Amara could tell Arora had met with success on her foraging quest. From her shiver, Amara gathered her twin was also chilled to the bone. Amara sighed under her breath and held out an arm. She was dry enough now to switch from scales to fur without the risk of trapping moisture beneath the guard-hair layer.

"Here, sit by me; I'll wrap myself in fur and warm both of us up."

Sighing with relief, Arora did as she was bid, curling up next to her sister. Amara extended pseudo-wings of furred flesh, wrapping them around her sister like a living cloak. The fur helped insulate her own flesh. Once she was settled, she let her twin feed her, since her own arms were wrapped around Arora's body.

"I should give back your clothes," Arora offered quietly after a few minutes.

"Keep them for the moment. At least until we can find a stream or something to wash them in, and a way of creating a fire to dry them out," Amara returned pragmatically. "Not to mention a fire to keep you warm."

Arora nodded, accepting her sister's offer, her green eyes drooping sleepily.

Summer-weight linens and leathers weren't enough to keep a person warm in this cold, damp place, not in just one layer. Two was barely sufficient as it was. True, they were now south of the Sun's Belt, but that meant going south was like going north; the farther away they went from the midline of their world, the colder the climate became.

If Amara's twin had been born a mage instead of . . . whatever she was, it wouldn't have been a problem. Even the weakest of mages could cast a simple cantrip-spell to keep themselves warm, or so she had heard. But her sister was something else, and the Gods hadn't exactly included a letter of instruction with Arora when she was born.

Whatever might happen to them, Amara couldn't stay awake much longer. It was with relief that Arora shifted in her reshaped arms, wanting to stretch out on the slowly drying planks of the raft. Settling down with her, Amara smothered a yawn. She thickened her fur, wanting both of them to stay warm against the damp pre-morning fog, and shaped her ears a little bigger, capable of swiveling and pricking up at any noise that sounded potentially dangerous. Tired or not, it was her responsibility to protect her twin.

Whether or not she wanted that particular responsibility.

Mara, her mother Ziella had once said when Amara was very young, *you have a great destiny ahead of you. You will be a Princess of our people, once you learn to control your powers. You will probably even become our Queen, one day . . . but being a Queen carries with it many responsibilities, and if you want to be Queen, you must prepare yourself in more ways than just shifting your shape . . .*

But when those outlander mages had first taken note of Arora, after literally bumping into her during a trading foray into an outlying kingdom, her parents' words had changed.

Mara, her father Fennon had warned her, *you must protect your sister against outsiders. The lust for magical power is what shattered Aiar hundreds of years ago. We of the Shifting Plains cannot use this power, so it is not a temptation for us . . . but others can, and they* will *use your sister if you do not protect her.*

They have proven they will harm anyone who gets in their way. You are the most powerful Shifterai that I have seen; you were also born as Rora's twin. It is clear the Gods wanted you to have the power to protect your twin, thus it is your responsibility, now.

Responsibility. Responsibility. Responsibility. Amara was tired of this responsibility, which had driven her far from her home, far from her people, far from her rightful place in the universe. Not her sister, who was already asleep, judging from the limp weight of her body and the soft steadiness of her breathing, but the responsibility of keeping her safe in a world that wanted to use and harm her.

They would be able to stay here for a while, as they had stayed in other places for a while, but eventually something would happen to drive them forth from this land. Someone would uncover what Arora was, or take too close an interest in what *Amara* was. This far from the Shifting Plains, a Shifterai was bound to be an attention-drawing novelty. But she would be better able to face that attention if she first got some real sleep, rather than the few hours snatched here and there, resting on the raft next to her sister while the southern ocean currents had swept them who-knew-where.

Ⓦakened by distant wardings, Morganen cleared most of the sleep from his mind with a deep inhale that ended in a stretch meant to tap some light into the room via the lightglobe attached to the corner post of his bed. Since breaking off officially from the Empire of Katan, he had started keeping a scrying mirror in his bed-chamber. The Katani were *supposed* to leave the Isle of Nightfall alone, giving the residents of Nightfall time to turn their incipient kingdom into a real one, but he didn't trust them to play entirely by the rules. Nor their other potential enemy, the Mandarites.

These were not the wardings tied into the recently erected crystal towers spread across the island. The alarm chiming in his mind was for ones set farther out. And something to the north, he realized, sinking onto the padded bench placed in front of the small table in the corner of his bedchamber. It looked like a vanity table, since it did have a mirror propped up against the back wall, but the rectangular surface wasn't meant to show his own face for long.

A mutter linked the ward-alert to the silvered glass. Like most of the mirrors in the palace, it was warded to prevent an outsider from tapping into it and scrying into the room, but that didn't prevent him from using it to scry outward. There were very few mirrors on Nightfall that weren't warded against outside scryings; two of them were in his workroom in another section of the compound, but then he wasn't being summoned to be engaged in a conversation.

The reflection of his own face, lean with almond-shaped aquamarine eyes, a straight nose, and plain, light brown hair mussed from sleep, faded like patchy fog. It was replaced with actual fog, dark from the fact it was still night. But the nature of the warding-spell highlighted the figures approaching the island, limning them and their makeshift vessel with a faint blue halo. Not that *they* could see the glow; it was just an enhancement of the spell, designed for his own viewing needs.

Squinting, and still a little tired, Morganen eyed the figure on the raft. Female, shivering, clinging to a scrap of hull. She looked young, but an adult. A bit plain, though; if Trevan was the next of his brothers to fall in love, as Seer Draganna's Prophecy proclaimed each of them would, the lady on the raft would need to be something special on the inside to make up for her average outside. That wasn't to say his fifthborn brother had only ever courted the prettiest of maidens back before their exile . . . but surely after knowing so many women, it would take someone extraordinary to capture Trev's elusive heart. Since it was Morg's job to ensure his brothers *did* meet their matches, he would have to study the approaching woman.

The . . . creature . . . towing the raft was his next target of interest. It was unlike anything Morganen had seen before. Something like a dolphin, something like a smallish whale, and something like a *yaskinna*, save that it only had the one extra long spiral horn on its snout, not the three shorter ones he was expecting. Tapping the edge of the mirror-frame so that it centered itself on the beast, Morg traced a rune directly on the glass. He would have to polish it later to remove the smudges, but it was important to know *what* the swimming-creature was.

It took a moment for the rune to sink through the scrying mirror and touch the nature of the beast with such a curious shape. For a moment, the image of the sea-swimmer glowed green. Katani letters swirled out of the glow, forming a brief, astonishing description in only five words, fading in and out as each gave way in succession to the next.

Human. Adult. Female. Aian. Shapeshifter.

Blinking, Morganen considered the second . . . female. If that creature was a shapeshifter, she was indeed extraordinary. Of course, there was no guarantee she was meant for Trevan; if there were two females coming to the Isle, not just one, then one of them would no doubt be meant for Rydan . . .

Rydan. Wincing, Morganen quickly reviewed in his mind the command-spells for the crystal towers. Any minute now, the pair on the raft would breach the range of the crystal towers, which had their own approach-sensitive wards. It was nighttime, which meant Rydan was awake and aware. Whatever it was that he did at night—not even Morg was completely sure—one of the sixth-born brother's tasks was to keep an eye on the island to protect it, including the newly enchanted towers and their scrying wards.

Rydan, unlike Trevan, didn't relish the thought of having a woman in his life, extraordinary *or* plain. He would object most strenuously to the presence of a second unattached female. He also controlled a Fountain, a wellspring of pure magical energy, through which he could toss said female to some other Fountain in some other, far-distant corner of their world, should any woman get close enough to bother him. There had to be a way to stop him from doing that. Prophecy was Prophecy, and Rydan's foretold Destiny had to be fulfilled, the same as the rest of them.

Serina's spell-equations finally came back to Morg; the Arithmancer had been quite thorough in her mathemagical calculations when creating the island's new communication system. There was a way to quell the wardings for a brief stretch of time. Stretching, he grabbed his cryslet from the nightstand behind him and flipped open the clasped lid of the communication bracelet. The spell-word to muffle the wardings, keeping them from alerting anyone for a short period of time, was *Pillulla-noh.*

That was it. The translucent, faceted, white cabochon mounted on the back of the lid glowed violet for a moment, then shifted to translucent, faceted, cream. Hopefully his elder brother wouldn't have seen the brief alteration. Morganen's Destiny was to match-make his brothers after all, to help ensure each ended up happily married. Whether or not some of them *wanted* to be happily married.

It was the only way *he* would get to have his own happily married Destiny, after all.

Thankfully, it wasn't necessary to hold the wardings in

abeyance for long. Turning his attention back to the mirror, Morganen watched as the pair of females managed to reach one of the northernmost beaches. The shapeshifter altered her swimming shape into something more humanoid; she pulled the raft up onto the shore, then the human-looking female went out foraging. They shared the small bounty that was available, and the shapeshifter grew fur, sheltering the two of them against the chilly winter air.

The worst they would have to deal with was a bit of cold, damp fog; the island wasn't placed far enough to the south to risk frost—not down on the beach, and not on a mild winter's day like today promised to be. The two women would be relatively safe, sleeping among the trees; there weren't any predators on the island large enough to risk disturbing two humans. Releasing the abeyance-charm on the cryslet, Morganen smothered a second yawn. Now that the outer wards had been passed, he could go back to sleep.

But not for too long. Morg had to come up with a way to get the fifth of his seven brothers to notice at least one of their visitors, and think up some way for the sixth of his seven brothers to *not* notice the other woman. At least, not until it was too late.

Glancing around his bedroom, sleepy from having been woken early, Morganen eyed the stacks of books on his dresser and nightstands. One of them caught his eye, the title embossed in gilt-leaf on the spine. *Dreaming of Love.*

He had found the original among the books in the library archives at Koral-tai, in Natallia. The opportunity had come while he was distance-scrying his thirdborn brother's adventures on the other continent, and had spotted the intriguing title on the archive shelves. A couple of spells, a blank book, and a keg of ink, and he had copied it for his personal collection a couple months ago, just as he had copied many other volumes through the years.

Getting up, he crossed to the dresser, extracted the copy from the others in the stack, and retired to his bed. A harder rap of his knuckle against the glowing, translucent sphere brightened the lightglobe's illumination. Propping up his pillows, Morg started idly flicking through the index, reviewing the spells, charms, amulets, and potions contained in the tome. It wasn't a weighty text by any means; most of these were simple enchantments, low-powered, low-key, and mostly designed to help encourage the divining and encountering of one's true love.

Since the Gods had wisely increased the odds of finding a true love by ensuring there was more than one person running around the world who might qualify, with even more who lurked unsuspectingly in other universes—ones who would qualify under the right circumstances, that was—such spells rarely showed the inquiring person who, exactly, their true love might be. But they often showed where to look, or under what circumstances they'd be most likely to meet, that sort of thing. Some even put the target into a more receptive frame of mind, which could be a useful thing for a mother suffering from a son or daughter reluctant to wed and provide her with grandchildren to spoil. Or so the compiler of the spells suggested in the side notes.

One of the potion titles caught his eye. Flipping through the book to the listed pages, Morganen read the description of its effects. As he did so, the last vestiges of sleepiness faded. This was interesting—this was *very* interesting . . . If he could administer *this* particular combination of herbs and energies, and did it *before* Rydan met one of those two women . . .

It didn't matter which one was the intended Destined bride; the Gods would provide the correct woman. It was They who had prompted Their greatest Seer to speak the verses of her Curse a thousand years ago. Marking the place in the book with a bit of ribbon, Morg abandoned his bed in favor of getting himself dressed and out to his workroom; he didn't have much time before breakfast.

The knock on his bedchamber door disturbed the tail end of another restless night's sleep. Scowling, Trevan sat up, shoved the covers aside, and padded across the scattered carpets lining the floor. His feet might have been protected from the temperature of the floor, but it was chilly in the room. At least it was helping to soothe his rampant, sleep-depriving problem.

It occurred to him at the second round of knocking, just before he reached the door, that it could be one of the island's four women on the other side of the wooden rectangle—one of the four *married* women. They probably wouldn't approve of such an unobstructed view of his current condition. Grunting under his breath, he padded over to his wardrobe, opened one of the doors, rummaged inside and pulled out a plain green dressing robe. Magic could have fetched the robe, but he was too tired to try at the moment.

Whoever it was knocked again, then spoke as well, impatient at the delay. "Trev? Are you awake yet? We really need to talk."

The voice belonged to Koranen, second-youngest of his siblings. Sighing roughly, guessing what it was about, Trevan shrugged into the robe, loosely tied it shut, and headed back to the door. Opening the door, he eyed his younger brother. Kor was like a leaner, darker-haired version of himself. They were both redheads, but his own chest-length tresses were more coppery-blond in hue, while Koranen boasted a rich auburn mane.

Kor's shadow-rimmed hazel eyes were just as bleary and bloodshot as his green ones felt. It wasn't likely one of their sisters-in-law would just barge in here without asking for permission, and Kor had shut the outer door of his suite before knocking on the inner one, but Trevan felt the urge to tighten the sash on his robe all the same. Mainly because he was just as uncomfortable about what he knew his younger sibling had come here to discuss. He waited for Kor to speak, giving him a sympathetic, tired look.

"It's not working, is it?" Koranen finally muttered, defeat slumping his normally straight shoulders. "I don't know what's wrong; we've tried everything we could think of over the last few weeks, but . . . it's just not *right*. At least the real ones giggled and squirmed and . . . and participated—that's the word for it, isn't it? They're not *participating*.

"Going through some of the motions, maybe." Running one hand through his locks, Kor gestured with the other, grimacing. "Jinga's Tits, the courtiers we made to impress the Mandarites were more realistic, and *they* were only designed for light conversation!"

Frustrated, Kor rumpled his dark red hair under both of his hands. Heat radiated from his half-naked body, clad as it was in light blue trousers stitched with anticonflagration runes. Trevan absently basked in that heat, even though it made him sleepy. As a Pyromancer, Koranen was much more popular to be around in the winter than in the summer. Frustration only lent itself even more to the younger man's radiant urges, and Kor was very frustrated by now.

Their mutual problem had begun with the somewhat recent visit of half the Council of Katan to Nightfall Isle, where the most powerful mages in the Empire had exiled the eight brothers over three and a half years ago. The brothers had activated the illusionary courtiers to fill out their ranks and make an impressive showing, since they were seceding from the mainland that had neglected them for so long. One of the Councilors had quipped that the brothers must be using the illusionary women as substitutes for real ones, since they had been exiled to the Isle without any female companionship.

If they hadn't been in desperate need of a show of imperturbable strength, Trevan would've whacked his head against the nearest wall at that comment. They *did* have enough magic to create tangible females, which meant they *could* have been interacting with said illusionary ladies for the last three and a half years, in the most tangible, interactive way a male and a female could interact . . . but which they stupidly hadn't thought up on their own. For all three-plus years, until now.

As soon as the Council had left, Koranen and Trevan had put their reddish heads together. Of the four remaining, unattached brothers, they were the two most desperate for female companionship. Trevan's younger twin, Rydan, loathed his Prophesied Destiny, while Koranen's younger twin, Morganen, was already enamored of an outworlder woman. The four older brothers had already snared their own Destined brides, so it was up to Trev and Kor alone to collaborate on creating adequate substitutes for feminine companionship.

Trevan didn't know what was wrong with their enchantments, but *something* was wrong. He *knew* how women responded; of the eight Corvis brothers, Trev had been the most licentious in their pre-exile days. Koranen was the one who had the least experience when it came to physical relationships; he literally burned with his passions, which was hazardous to any young lady wishing to dare the darker redhead's charms. Ironically, it was Koranen who had the most experience in creating illusionary people from enchanted glass beads.

Together, theirs was a case of the debauched and the desperate struggling to find a source of relief.

Koranen stared at him now, frustration giving his hazel eyes a plaintive glint. "*What* are we doing wrong, Trev? We can make a courtier who can bow or curtsy, who can laugh at a joke and carry on a reasonable length of conversation just like a real person . . . but *we*," and he gestured between them to emphasize that Trevan was equally, if inexplicably, at fault, "cannot make a woman who responds appropriately to her lover! Kata's Sweet

Sacred Ass—I can make an illusionary *man* who responds in all the right ways under my touch, but why not a woman?"

That quirked Trevan's brow and made him blink. While it wasn't forbidden, it wasn't exactly encouraged, either, in the Katani culture of their youth. "You made a *man* and tested it sexually?"

Blushing, Kor gestured in an awkward, explanatory way. "Well, as an experiment, and I only just, you know . . . what *we* do to ourselves. *Touched* him, a bit. It didn't really do anything for me—but at least *he* responded the right way! Why can't I make a *woman* who responds like that? For that matter, why can't *you* make a woman who responds like that? You know everything about what it's like to have a woman exploding in ecstasy in your arms, or . . . or whatever it is they do!"

Brain cells underneath his coppery locks finally woke up. Trevan blinked twice, then rubbed at his face, groaning. "Oh . . . it *can't* be that simple."

"*What* can't be that simple?" his younger brother demanded. "Brother, if you're holding out on me—"

Dragging both palms down, Trevan sighed wearily. The first few months of sexually frustrated exile had been bad, but he had eventually gotten used to being on his own when it came to those urges. Having the *hope* of feminine companionship—even if it was literally an illusion—had reawakened not only his sexual desires, but his sexual frustrations. But hope alone couldn't give them what they wanted.

"Kor, you managed to make a sexually responsive male because you *know* what it's like to be a sexually responsive male. We made interactive, joke-laughing, conversation-holding courtiers because *we* know how to interact by laughing at jokes and joining conversations. We can even curtsy like a woman, because it's something both men and women can do . . . But sex . . .

"Sex is *different*, between the genders. Women just don't respond at all like men do. We literally don't know enough reference points to *create* a truly, accurately, interactively functional female." This time it was his hand that flicked between the two of them. "*We're* not female! Even the few times I've tried enchanting myself into a female didn't help me simulate the right responses for a properly responsive female, and the Gods know I've tried."

It was Koranen's turn to groan in frustration and hide his face in his hands. More heat washed outward from his half-naked flesh, warming Trevan's equally half-clad skin, then it faded and died. Trevan wrapped the folds of his dressing robe tighter around his body, in the hopes of trapping the lingering heat from his brother against his skin, warding off the morning chill. Kor mumbled something, but his voice was muffled by his palms.

"What was that?" Trev prodded his sibling.

Kor lowered his hands, looking tired and drawn. "I said, I don't know if the others can help us. Kelly has no magic whatsoever. Alys does, but doesn't have much. I think Serina is still suffering bouts of morning sickness, and Mariel is just too . . . *nice*. If I asked her to let me record her sexual responses—even if it was indirectly, without actually being there at the time—she'd probably faint from the shock of it."

"Or Evanor would kill us," Trevan agreed wryly. The fourthborn of their siblings was the nicest and most polite of all the brothers, but when riled, Evanor could be just as formidable as any of them. Niceness didn't necessarily mean Ev would be willing to share, not even through something as indirect as remotely enchanting an illusion. "Serina *might* be willing to help us, since I've noticed she's rather open about those sorts of things, but Dominor wouldn't like it, and he is more powerful than either of us."

"Wolfer would rather beat the manure out of us than even suggest it around *his* precious, delicate Alys," Koranen agreed dryly, "who would be even more likely to faint from the shock of it than Mariel . . . And Saber would castrate us both if we looked sideways at Kelly. Or Kelly herself might do it."

Trevan laughed briefly. "Though she's weird enough, she might actually say yes to having her physical responses remotely recorded."

"Maybe . . . maybe, if we explained to *all* of them that we're not looking for *their* exact responses, but rather a general feminine-style physical response . . . maybe appealed to their sense of pity and compassion?" Koranen asked his elder brother, his tenor voice almost cracking, caught somewhere between wistfulness and burgeoning desperation. The vague gesture of his hands shifted once more into a rumpling of his auburn hair. "If I don't get some relief *soon*, I'm going to be seriously eyeing that male illusion I created, and I'm *not* actually interested in men!"

"*You're* desperate enough to look at men?" Trevan shot back.

He bit back the rest of his retort. At least *he* had known the pleasures of bedding a willing maid. Koranen hadn't ever gone past fondling. By himself, Kor could find relief in the usual solitary way, but with a female, he literally scorched the poor woman with his touch. "Alright . . . we'll raise the subject at breakfast."

Koranen's shoulders slumped with relief.

"Don't get your hopes up, Brother," Trevan warned his sibling. "You and I could be eunuchs before this particular type of conversation is at an end."

"Well, then at least I wouldn't have to suffer anymore," Kor muttered wryly, rubbing at his tired eyes with the heels of his hands.

"True. Go on and get dressed," Trev instructed his younger brother. "I'll meet you there. I get to help my twin make breakfast this morning."

Koranen snorted. "If only I could be more like *him*, and not give a damn about women—do you think he'd be interested in an illusionary courtesan-male?"

"Do you really want to ask him if he's switched his interests?" Trevan retorted dryly. "He *was* woman-oriented in his teens, you know."

"Sweet Kata, no." Koranen shuddered. "Morg may be more powerful, but at least my twin has a sense of humor. Rydan doesn't. See you at breakfast."

Nodding, Trevan shut the door between them. Once it was closed, he leaned his forehead against the solid wood. He was tired of being alone, tired of having to go without feminine company and companionship . . . Just plain tired.

It wasn't just the lovemaking he missed, though that was definitely part of it. He missed the *love*-making. The little things, like holding hands, prolonged glances, shared laughs, and just holding a woman in his arms . . . The kinds of aches that no amount of self-ministration could alleviate. The things that his elder brothers could now share at will with their delightful, loving wives. Things that made him flinch, because *he* couldn't have it, too. Not until his Destined bride arrived, whenever that might be.

Some days, Trevan wished he could just retreat from the others on the island, avoiding them all—save only for the most necessary of contact—like his twin had successfully done.

Enter the tantalizing world
of
paranormal romance

MaryJanice Davidson

Laurell K. Hamilton

Christine Feehan

Emma Holly

Angela Knight

Rebecca York

Eileen Wilks

Berkley authors
take you to a whole new realm

penguin.com